# COFFIN JACK

## A Western Duo

## TONY MASERO

**WOLFPACK**
**PUBLISHING**
— EST 2013 —

**WOLFPACK**
**PUBLISHING**
— EST 2013 —

Coffin Jack: A Western Duo

Paperback Edition
Copyright © 2020 (As Revised) Tony Masero

Wolfpack Publishing
6032 Wheat Penny Avenue
Las Vegas, NV 89122

Paperback ISBN: 978-1-64734-675-1
Ebook ISBN: 978-1-64734-674-4

# COFFIN JACK

A Western Duo

# COFFIN JACK

## Part 1: Deathdealer

# PROLOGUE

"Five across and two down."

Fat Boy Chen looked up mystified.

"What'd you say?"

"I said..." the ominous figure of Coffin Jack repeated patiently. "Five across and two down."

Fat Boy wrinkled his pudgy nose and glanced bemused at each of the no-neck and lookalike bodyguards who stood like bookends on either side of his chair. They were certainly big blocks of men, heavyset and tough but they were slovenly and way too sure of themselves. It was all too obvious that they had grown arrogant and overconfident across their years of service with the Chinaman. They stared back at Jack blankly, indifferent to the outcome, only waiting for the word from their boss.

"Five across, two down, what's that supposed to mean?" asked Fat Boy, pushing his unfinished meal away and turning his attention to the gloomy figure looming over his table. "You a crossword salesman or something?"

"Five across takes you out the door there, two steps down puts you in the street, and that's where I want you to be right now."

"Are you kidding me?"

"Hrmph!" answered Jack, who was a man of few words.

"Look, you cretin," rumbled Fat Boy dangerously. "You know who these two are?" He held up his chubby and well-manicured hands like a pair of scales as he indicated the two muscle bound shooters at his side. "These are the Destiny Twins, that's Dan," he raised his right hand slightly then the left as if he were weighing the balance, "And that's Deke. You heard of them? No? Then I should tell you they ain't boys to mess with. The 3D phenomenon that's what folks call them, Dan and Deke Destiny, might look like cutouts all rested and restrained as they are right now but you get them get them riled, well believe me, they can pop right out at you."

Fat Boy had long ago lost any of the Chinese accent he might have had and spoke and dressed like a true American businessman, in a neat Derby hat, wing-collared shirt, suit and tie with a diamond stick pin and a gold pocket-watch chain stretched across his broad girth.

Jack said nothing, the two guards looked about as interesting to him as stone monoliths, so he nodded only a slow recognition without taking his eyes from Fat Boy.

"You expect me to leave off my lunch and go out into the street?" Fat Boy went on in angry complaint. "Is this some kind of call-out? I don't do that, mister.

Why would I do that?"

Jack waited patiently, not moving from his station before Fat Boy's personal dining table.

The rest of the Humble Pie Eatery had gone deathly quiet; there was a nervous shuffling of feet and the occasional scrape of a chair as the curious looked around but mostly the lunchtime crowd had frozen in place.

"Go on, get along out of here!" dismissed Fat Boy irritably as he pulled his dinner plate back before him. "You lousy deadbeats coming in here interrupting a man at his meal. I get sick of it, what're you complaining about this time? There's always something; can't pay the dues on your miserable loan, is that it? One of the girls upset you in some way? Maybe you caught a dose, eh? You're pathetic, the whole bunch of you." He curled a lip in distain, rolling the fat on his cheeks and lifting the shoelace thin mustache that hung down each side of his heavy jowls like rat-tails.

"Take the walk," rumbled Jack.

Fat Boy shook his head in dismay and in tired exasperation flicked a sidelong glance at Dan Destiny. The bodyguard got the message and solemnly raised a restraining hand to Jack, holding it out before him as if he were a lawman stopping traffic on Main Street or a road agent bringing down the mail coach. It was a beefy paw, thick and horny and the eyes behind it were pale and glazed but full of meaningful intent.

It was fast!

In a blur, Jack's Colt was out and he loosed off

a shot that blew a hole clean through the palm of Dan's upraised hand as if it were tissue paper. The lead didn't stop there though, before Dan could even holler, the bullet went on to pop his eyeball, drill on through the socket and mess up the jelly of his brain before it exited with a pressure wave that blew a hole in the back of his skull the size of a bunched fist.

Jack spun around to face the man's brother, but Deke was also quick on the draw and the two men fired their pistols simultaneously. Jack was accurate and his aim true and the bullet went home, trouble was, brother Deke was also on target. Only thing is, as explained earlier, he was a mite slovenly and the black powder paper cartridge had not been rammed home sufficiently in the chamber of the elderly Navy Colt he favored.

The firing cap of fulminate of mercury went off okay and that ignited the powder in the cartridge all right but the misplaced ball at the head shot off at a weird angle as a result. The ball missed Jack completely, but the flaring explosion of gas did not and that caught Jack square in the left eye. He howled in pain and dropped to his knees as red-hot particles of powder embedded themselves in his eyeball and the heat burned away the liquid covering.

Deke Destiny didn't have much to say about it though, he was already lying flat on his back, dead as a post and stretched out next to his twin brother on the dining room floor with any symptom of the third dimension having left them both permanently.

Jack fell to his knees and scrabbled in agony on the floorboards under the table whilst Fat Boy pushed back his chair in terror. He was well named though and was truly as fat as a barrel of baked fish so getting out of the chair was not an easy matter. As he struggled with the chair and the table before him, Fat Boy was also trying to reach the .44 pistol he carried in a shoulder holster in his armpit.

Jack heard the chair scraping and did not hesitate; he still held his Colt and despite the searing pain in his face he raised the gun and fired three fast shots directly up through the bottom of the dining table.

All the bullets, blasting away at four hundred and sixty feet a second, rocked and splintered the tabletop, they ended up slamming into Fat Boy's fat gut and throwing him back into the chair he had just managed to extricate himself from. He slumped there, wedged between the chair arms with the .44 forgotten and the holes in his waistcoat leaking rivulets of blood down the front of the neat material.

Jack rose from below, one hand over his destroyed left eye and the other holding the smoking Colt. His ugly face was twisted in agony and he glared at Fat Boy with vengeful menace, his good eye glowing with a kind of malevolent light.

Fat Boy was panting hard, his blubbering lips hanging loose and dribbling strings of spittle down his double chin as he stared back up at Jack.

"Why?" he managed to gasp. "Why'd you do that?"

Jack lined up the pistol on Fat Boy's hairline; he shrugged enigmatically, cocked the hammer, pulled the trigger and with his last bullet sent Fat Boy Chen on to his eternal rest.

Jack could have explained that it was a man called Fu Wen who had sent him on this murderous mission. But, as already remarked, Jack was short on words.

Fu Wen had been a hard-working immigrant Chinese, toiling tirelessly as a laborer on the railroads. Treated more as a slave and earning half the pay of his white co-workers, Fu Wen labored for only one purpose and that was to make enough money so that his thirteen-year-old daughter could have a future. Unusual for a Chinese to treasure a female member of the family in this way but Fu Wen's wife and two sons had died of typhus on the journey over and his daughter was all that he had left.

Fat Boy Chen had been the pimp who bought up the unwanted daughters of the Chinese workers for a pittance and then forced them to prostitute themselves in his brothels at the gold diggings. They were all young girls and Fu Wen's daughter had been swept up in one of Fat Boy's raids on the railroad work camp; his men could not care less who they took just as long as they made their quota.

The girl was brutalized and abused for a year by a train of rough miners, became an opium addict and was made pregnant, miscarried and was dead inside of eighteen months.

That left Fu Wen with a pocket full of cash but no child to leave it to.

He spent it all on Coffin Jack instead.

And that's the true story of how Jack lost his eye.

# CHAPTER ONE

But all that had been years before and since then Jack had seen and experienced a whole heck of a lot more. Not so much that he had changed in himself but more that he had become set in his lonely assassin ways. Now though he travelled with a known name and a whole set of other unearthly attributes that marked him out from the rest.

So it was, that whenever Coffin Jack rode into town there wasn't a soul that did not shake nor a tender body that did not tremble.

His coming was often forewarned by a looming storm cloud. The horizon would darken, and the sun would turn a pale sickly yellow under the clouds. Buzzards would whirlpool way up high, like blow-flies circling over rancid meat. Amidst the towering mass of turbulent sky, those birds would wheel and scream in high-pitched calls, an awful sound like the crying of unwanted babies left out to die on the cold windswept prairie.

Dry lightning might flash in the distance, illuminating the interior of the oncoming storm, and the muted rumble of thunder would vibrate in the overheated air, air so dense it was difficult to breathe. Some said it was not thunder at all but in reality, the hoof beats of the Deathdealer's dark pony as he rode nearer.

A blanket of shadow came with him, spreading out with a flow of darkness not dissimilar to a great wave of water in flood. Fingers of this shade teased out across the land, filling and encompassing every hollow and structure it touched before passing over to run on again unchecked. There was no up or down for the shadow, it bore itself between heaven and earth as a shade cast by a light unknown and was ignorant of gravity or purpose. It just was.

They say that in the cemeteries the ground heaved, and the bones of the dead rattled underground as Coffin Jack passed. The dirge they sang in their hollow tombs was a pantheon of respect for the dark rider, as he had slain so many of them and the path of his journey was marked by the stones of that passage, smooth white tombstones with the writing of his tally dug deep into the surface.

He was a tall man of a lean frame, so tall that his shoulders were bowed by the weight of his height. Or maybe it was his humorless gauntness that bent him over as if trapped in the throes of an intractable sorrow. His scarred face, barely seen under the drooping brim of a large span hat with a creased crown folded in front, held only one aspect of particular interest. A single eye that glowed with an eerie and unnatural light, so weird and full of hell's promise that one might pray that it never looked you over. The other eye, no more than an empty socket, was hidden beneath a black patch fashioned from padded cloth and leather that ran by a strap around his head under the greasy tendrils of long hair that reached down over his collar, hair as black and reflective as a raven's wing.

He wore a dark green coat with a shoulder cloak in the old military style, tattered now by the years and hanging flapping around his limbs. The movement of his passage or the accompanying fetid breath of ruined air that travelled with him carried aloft the frayed ends. The worn coattails flapped wing-like as he moved and added to the gloomy air of omnipresent danger that surrounded him, as if the Angel of Death sat upon his shoulder and had moved into the vicinity.

Which, if truth was told, it surely had.

For there was one thing that was certain, if you ever saw Coffin Jack coming you could count on it that someone or something was heading for the grave.

Only one thing shone from this figure dressed in a sorrow as forbidding as the interior of his own soul and that was the weapon. At his side hung a great silver-plated Colt revolver. He wore it in a leather holster and ammunition belt, much oiled and used, slick to the touch and as coldly repellent as a serpent's skin strapped down with a leather tie spanning his thigh. Even his spurs were blackened steel and they clinked and rattled under his booted tread, the sound foretelling his approach with as much promise as a jailhouse door closing on a condemned prisoner.

Coffin Jack lived, if one can call it that, in a lone shack set on a perfectly rounded mound of a hill surrounded by the bleak mountains of the Four-Point Range. There were domestic cats gone to the wild that dwelt there with him. Creatures, he for the most part ignored, for he was often away in both mind and spirit as well as body and they were left to their own devices. Feral beasts, grown sleek on their hunting, as they were a group of ferocious animals not above cannibalism on their own kind if it so suited and the hunting were poor. They moved silently about his property adding to the shadows that were as much a part of Coffin Jack's existence as the air of gloom and despondency that was his constant companion. They hissed at one another on meeting and mated with bloodcurdling screams when the urge was upon them, producing offspring that were as crazed and dangerous as the parents. That is if the young ones survived.

When he was there, Coffin Jack sat. He did nothing else; he did not read or think or divert himself in any way. It was a solemn mode of waiting he occupied and so he sat and if he did anything at all it was only to look out with his one good eye at the mountain range visible through the window. But this was a vacant gaze not composed of any intake of information and with no consideration of the twisted shapes of the distorted stones that surrounded him for they were empty of life and fulfilling no other purpose than to prop up the four corners of the world.

He never saw the messenger.

Nor did he hear his coming or departure, all he knew was the sense that something had happened, and some shift had imposed itself on his mind and awoken him from his torpor. With reluctance, Coffin Jack rose from the seat he had occupied without moving for an entire seven days and went to the door.

The envelope had been rolled tightly and wedged into the neck of an empty whisky bottle left on his doorstep.

*"Hero,"* it said. *"For that is what you surely are and I have need of such a man. Come to my home if you will accept the challenge. For a fee in gold there is blood to be spilt and more accolades to be gained if you do so.*

*I sign this with much respect, yours in sincerity, John Fellows Carne.*

*You will find me at the Homely Crossing Spread just outside of Doomesville on the Longspree Pike."*

Coffin Jack nodded understanding and prepared himself.

Firstly, he peed copiously, for a week of full bladder can take some time to empty. Then he did the same with his other bodily functions but on those we shall not dwell overlong as the immensity of dealing with such a task can only be treated with a tactful indifference. He stripped his pale and scarred body naked and walked downhill and washed himself in the bitter stream that ran below the property. He shaved the beard from his chin with a razor-sharp knife and barely noticed the cold mountain water that still carried ice melt in its flow as it passed around him. And then he fetched his horse from where it grazed.

After this was done, he sat at his table with the letter propped before him and cleaned his weapons.

It was a task that soothed him, the shine and sheen of the bullets each one slotting so neatly into the chamber, the machined fit so exact it pleased his passion for perfection. It held a completeness for him, an almost magical delight that each leaden slug cast from the home of its cartridge casing by the simple pressure of his long finger could rip through sinew and tear out lifeblood all gave him a momentary sensation of pleasure.

He did not pause to wonder at the possibilities of the upcoming challenge for in truth he had no capacity for imagination. He dwelt in a nether world that left him free of distraction and allowed him an overriding ability to focus with an acuteness that was terrifying. Which was a factor all too satisfying for one such as he and in his particular line of work.

When he was done, he went outside, closed the door behind him, and mounted the blue-black stallion that he called Nameless and left.

# CHAPTER TWO

It was the young thirteen-year-old town's gofer that ran excitedly into The Forbidden Fruit Saloon with news.

Breathless he stood at the entrance, the swing doors already flapping behind him in the approaching wind.

"He's coming," the boy panted. "It's the Death-dealer."

The wind rose to a howl outside and the sky darkened at his words, almost as if he had spoken a necromancer's spell and opened up a portal to another darker existence.

There was a hush at his words. The men playing cards froze at their green felt-covered table, their hopeful poker hands forgotten. The bartender almost dropped the shot glass he was drying ,and Molly Daws, the young prostitute he had brought in from Lyons City to service the cowhands, allowed her painted mouth to open wide and her powdered jaw to drop.

"You sure?" husked the bartender. He was a tub-by man in a striped waistcoat, pomaded hair and a curling mustache and known as Brewster Droop. Usually a bluff, rosy-cheeked fellow, but now his skin had paled and the chubby flesh at his cheeks sagged.

They all heard the heavy sound of footsteps and the rattle of spurs on the boardwalk outside.

In the time it takes to draw a breath the place had cleared and was suddenly empty.

As Coffin Jack pushed open the swing doors, he stood there a moment, a dark outline against the looming sky outside, he noted that there was only one person left sitting in the saloon. A stranger, whom it might be surmised, knew no better.

Jack looked around, his glittering eye taking in the last remaining sign of any custom in the place. That being a solitary playing card fluttering gently to the floor over by the deserted card table. His gaze swept back to encompass the stranger, who had not moved but watched his entrance with some interest.

Jack clumped across to the bar.

Without further ado he leaned over and hiked up a bottle and a glass, poured himself a shot and drank it down as a man with a long dry throat might, in a long single glugging pull.

"Sir, may I ask, do you always have this effect on people?" the stranger called across the deserted room.

Jack raised his eyebrow to cast a look at the stranger. He drew back his lips and sucked on the last taste of the whiskey through his big white tombstone teeth. Taking up the glass and lifting the bottle by the neck in the fingers of his left hand he moved across the room to stand before the stranger.

Coffin Jack towered silently over the sitting man never taking his eye from him as he set the bottle and glass down heavily on the table.

The stranger offered his hand, "I'm Lowell Devereux, sir. Pleased to meet you."

Jack ignored the hand and drew up a chair and seated himself across from Lowell.

"Down here doing some research for my newspaper," said Lowell in way of explanation. "Looking particularly for articles of uplifting interest."

Jack poured himself another glass.

"The Holy Roller is my magazine, perhaps you have heard of it?" Lowell eyed Jack doubtfully. "Or perhaps not. No, well, I'm not surprised, it is little known. A small publication, you understand. But I was a journalist for the Chicago Tribunal before that, I'm sure you know them…"

The slight negative inclination of the head indicated that Jack had no knowledge of either.

"Well," Lowell continued. "It was Miss Beatrice that took me on. A lovely person, quite lovely. Indeed, an inspiration to all the ladies of society as to how a respectable young woman should be."

For a moment Lowell paused his babble, drew a breath, and looked away in dreamy memory of his "quite lovely" employer.

"Miss Beatrice Hicks, she inherited the paper from her father, Pastor Abner Hicks, now deceased. He was a most respected leader of the church, a devout man and his passing was noted across the country but, em…perhaps you missed that particular obituary. Quite honestly, I have little interest in such religious publications myself, but Miss Beatrice impressed me so with her determination to make it a success that I just could not resist her. I had to come on board, as it were. She is a most remarkable young woman. Anyway, that is why I am here doing what I can to discover genuine acts of spiritual favor and charitable kindness. Perhaps you may know of something of that nature, sir?"

Lowell waited expectantly.

Jack cleared his throat and made to answer.

"K…lar. G…g…gop!"

"Oh, dear," said Lowell. "A speech impediment. I am so sorry, sir. I did not mean to press you."

Jack tried again, "Yi…don…Noo…"

"Please, sir. Do not test yourself."

"Iy…Down… Know…"

It was not that Jack had real difficulty with his tongue, it was just that he had not spoken more than a word or two to a living soul for eighteen months and before that for six, and before that twenty-four. He was just not used to speaking to people and had to take a moment to recover the skill.

"I…don't know nothing…'bout nothing," he finally growled with satisfaction.

Lowell sat back, a little bemused by the way things were going with this rather strange character. As can be seen, Lowell was something of an innocent. A short, round-faced young man, with gold-rimmed spectacles and a bookish style about him. He wore a small-brimmed bowler on his fair head of short-cut hair, a celluloid collar with a knotted bowtie and a neatly turned out three-piece gray suit.

As a rather hopeful and adventurous investigative reporter he had imitated his journalistic betters and purchased a pair of explorer's sturdy gaiters that laced up to the knee and he carried a canvas portfolio to hold all his writing equipment. Originally a stringer for the Chicago Tribunal on the Homes and Garden section, a job he had received through his father's Freemasonry connections, he had been swept off his feet at sight of the fetching Miss Beatrice Hicks and fallen instantly in love. Within a fortnight he had left the Tribunal and presented himself at The Holy Roller in search of desperate employment at the feet of his beloved.

The fair Miss Beatrice was indeed a lovely creature. Tiny in stature but full bodied, with curling locks of bright golden hair as winsome and shining as spun filaments of gold. Simple too in her own sweet way but with a strain of determination that had brought her, out of love for her father whom she doted on, into the world of publishing where she determined to make a success of her late father's edifying missive.

"Well," said Lowell, not deterred by the big man's reticence. "May I enquire your name, sir?"

"They call me Coffin Jack."

The voice was steady, Lowell noted, even and flat, almost lifeless as if were some mechanical device that was speaking.

"A privilege, Mister Jack," smiled Lowell. "Might

I offer some refreshment. A meal perhaps?"

"All right, I could go that, I ain't eaten in a while."

"Then allow me, it would be my pleasure to treat you to an evening meal. I'll go and find the landlord, it seems the place has suddenly emptied. I suppose it is that storm brewing outside, doubtless these good folk must go and protect their homes and livestock against the approaching deluge. Excuse me, sir."

"There won't be no rain," Coffin Jack promised. "But go get some vittles. You seem a regular fellow, Mister Devereux, maybe I won't have to kill you."

"*You what?*" gasped Lowell and then his face broke into a smile. "Oh, you jest," he chuckled. "Really Mister Jack, that is too much. Rough Frontier humor, I suppose. Now sit you there, I will fetch the owner of this establishment and arrange everything. Oh, Mister Droop! Where are you, sir? We have custom here."

Leaving his seat, Lowell made his way over to the bar and searched behind it to no avail.

"Where is that wretched fellow?"

He made his way behind the bar and poked his head through the dividing curtain hanging there to find Brewer Droop crouched in terror behind some stacked barrels of beer in the storeroom beyond.

"Ah! There you are. Stocktaking, are you? A supper, Mister Droop, if you will be so kind. My friend and I would be most grateful for some service if you please."

"You know him?" whispered the fearful Droop in a low voice.

"The gentleman outside? A brief meeting no

more, a new acquaintance you understand? Now, what kind of fare can you offer us?"

"You don't know who he is?"

"As I say, just met."

"*That is Coffin Jack*," hissed Droop.

"Surely, as I am aware, we are introduced. Now if you will, a meal for us would be most welcome and you will place the cost to my account. Tell me, sir, why do you hover here when you have customers?"

"I ain't going in there, Coffin Jack's a killing man."

Lowell snorted, "Don't be ridiculous, my good fellow. He is a man like any other, there's no need for any fear."

"He ain't like any man unless you include the Devil himself. Get out of there, save yourself, sir, I beg of you."

"That's enough," snapped Lowell. "I don't know what's going on here but I want a supper set on our table immediately or I'll want to know why."

"*GET IT!*" came the loud roar from the barroom beyond the curtain.

"Oh, shucks!" wailed Droop. "Now you've done it." And then louder, "Coming right away, Mister Jack. We're on it here, have no fear, be with you tout-de-sweet." Droop had spent some time in New Orleans and fancied himself as something of a Francophile. "Go on, sir. I'll have Molly bring it through."

"I should hope so too," frowned Lowell.

The journalist left the bartender mumbling excitedly to himself and frenetically tugging at his waxed mustache as he turned this way and that in his panic.

"I don't know what's the matter with the fellow,"

said Lowell, seating himself again. "He seems frightened out of his wits."

Coffin Jack sniffed and poured another glass for himself.

He sat and stared at Lowell through his single glowing eye and then suddenly stabbed a bony finger in Lowell's direction. "You an educated man?" he growled.

"Well," said Lowell, fumbling with his bowtie in a show of humble embarrassment. "I certainly hope so."

"You can read your letters and write words?"

"I can, sir. That is my mode of employment."

"I see," nodded Jack. He reached inside his ragged cloak and brought out the letter that had been left at his door. "What do you make of this?"

Lowell scanned the letter, "It appears to be an offer of employment. This Mister Carne mentions gold but aligns it with blood and some sort of praise."

"Is that what "accolade" means, "praise" is it?"

"Yes indeed, a tribute or honor of some kind. But why he should place that alongside mention of blood I have no idea."

"It will be wet work that's why," rumbled Jack, throwing back his glass of whisky.

"Wet work? Perhaps some kind of cleaning task. Never turn down a job of work for decent pay, Mister Jack, no matter how menial. However lowly it appears there is nothing that can be considered bad in an honest day's labor for honest pay."

"Hrmph!" grunted Jack, indifferently pouring himself another glass.

"And this is where you are bound, to go see Mister Carnes, is it?"

"That's what I do," agreed Jack. "I sit, I wait, and the call comes."

"You are much in demand then?"

Jack sighed, a long drawn out deadly sound, as if a draught had just blown in from under Hell's door. "You ask a lot of questions."

Lowell smiled depreciatingly. "I do, for my sins. I know it; my mother always said I was a curious child. But then, if I am to discover acts of generosity and kindness, I must ask questions."

The advance of Miss Molly Daws bearing a tray with their supper interrupted them. She was not so much coming under her own steam as being propelled by a long-handled switch broom that Mister Droop manipulated from behind, pushing her steadily into the room.

"Y… Your supper, s…sirs," Molly stuttered, barely daring to take a step any nearer.

"Well, then," said Lowell. "Set it down on the table, girl. We cannot partake when you stand over there."

Jack swiveled his head and eyed Molly up and down. A low rumble began, that seemed to emanate from his nether regions and work its way up eventually to his throat where it lodged.

Molly's hands shook so much that the plates and cutlery on the tray began a jig that rattled noisily.

"Here, girl," said Lowell snatching the tray from her shivering hands. "Are you sick of palsy or something?"

"N…no, sir. It's just…it's just…HIM!"

Lowell looked across at Jack to see what about him was upsetting the girl so. All he saw was his companion's ugly face set in a grim mold of unmoving stone as if carved from raw granite. The lips hooked downwards at the corner, the sharp chin jutted forward, and the head tilted up so that he might study Molly better from his available eye.

"How so, miss? Why do you tarry?" asked Lowell. "Are you vying for custom of a carnal nature here? I don't think either of us would fit into that bracket; we are both upstanding gentlemen, I assure you. Are we not, Mister Jack?"

The growl rumbled again from deep in Jack's throat, like that of a hungry mountain lion.

A tight grin of total terror was fixed on Molly's face. She was not one to usually demonstrate such abject fear, she had after all met all kinds of bedfellows carrying out her chosen profession, but somehow Jack's awesome presence evoked a more earthmoving experience than any supplied by her customers. She stood frozen, transfixed by his glowing eye, her ample bosom swelling as her heart palpitated wildly beneath the stays of her corset.

Molly was not too unpleasant to look at in a battered bar girl kind of way and to many of her customers, who saw the female kind only too infrequently on the wild Frontier, she appeared the most beautiful creature they had ever seen. Offers of marriage abounded, yet Molly had found that a different husband every night proved a much more refreshing pastime than some regular dummy that she would have to cook and clean for on a daily basis. Who? She reasoned, could want such a lifestyle, and why? With a new stud each night she had more than enough lustful pleasure for her young body and into the bargain she was paid for it as well. Only a fool would want otherwise.

"Is there anything else b…before I g…go?" she stuttered in a wan voice.

Lowell was already tucking into his supper with relish, dicing steak and spiking potatoes into his mouth with regularity, for he was also indeed most hungry.

"Then I'll…*whooohoooo!*" wailed Molly, her last comment breaking off into a long wail as Jack leapt to his feet and swept her up. The growl he offered was one of a deep vibrating lustful nature as he lifted Molly from her feet and enclosed her until she totally disappeared from sight within the folds of his cloak.

"Oh, Mister Jack! Surely not," cried a reproving Lowell. "Why you have not finished your supper yet."

Jack was making excited glagging noises as he swept across the room, whilst the muffled mewing of Molly came from somewhere deep inside his enfolding arms.

Lowell shook his head in dismay. "The sins of the flesh," he muttered and offered a silent prayer of thanks that his own love for Miss Beatrice was of a pure and untarnished variety and above such disdainful acts. "Like beasts of the field, these Frontier types," thought Lowell as he cut deeper into his steak and considered the possibility on the evils of covetousness and fornication as an article for his magazine.

Where Jack had taken the girl was not clear but his presence somewhere in the house surely was. For the thumps and screams, the groans and moans, crashing and banging that accompanied the distant act of sexual congress seemed to shake the very foundations of The Forbidden Fruit Saloon.

Lowell, who was a forbearing kind of fellow, ignored such carrying on and completed his repast with some satisfaction. Sitting back when finished and picking contentedly at his teeth with a match from the pot of Lucifers set on the table.

"Most amenable, Mister Droop," he called to the invisible bartender, who was keeping his head down behind the bar and listening with upraised eyes to the sturdy acts of fornication going on over his head. The floorboards creaked above, and the ceiling bowed under the determined ministrations that Coffin Jack was obviously offering to the comely young Miss Daws.

"It appears," Lowell continued, with one arched eyebrow at the rifts of dust falling from the tortured ceiling, "that our friend certainly finds himself in dire need of some caring attention."

Brewster Droop did no more than utter a mournful sounding moan.

It was then that the swing doors of the saloon opened with a crash and three rowdy cowhands strode in.

"Hell's Teeth!" cried the first, a young buckaroo

with a flamboyant air about him. "Seems like there's a rare storm a-brewing out there. Hot damn! Where is everybody? Droop! Where are you, fellow? It's Colby Toll and two of his friends. I come to see my sweetheart; where is she now?"

The three men strode to the bar with only a casual glance in Lowell's direction.

"Good evening," called Lowell as they ambled across before him.

"Evening," the three mumbled in a disinterested fashion.

Colby Toll peered over the bar and saw the owner crouching there. He leaned across and caught Droop by the collar hoisting him up. "Come on, Brewster," he said with irritation. "A drink for me and the boys. Now, where is she? Where is the sweetest gal this side of Perdition? I come to pay court."

Droop, with a shaking hand, lay a bottle and clinking glasses on the counter and said nothing, only raised his eyes heavenwards in answer.

The three men looked up at the trembling ceiling as Droop sunk down in the other direction and returned to his hiding place beneath the bar.

"She got custom, has she?" asked Colby with a nose wrinkled in displeasure.

"I fear, sir," called Lowell, "my friend Mister Jack has first call on the young lady. A sad thing, I'm sure you will agree but as I have come to understand on my visit to the Frontier, it seems the needs of the fertile are strong in this part of the nation."

"Sure sounds like it," agreed one of Colby's companions, another bold young cowboy known as

Teets Bowrinkle.

The tallest of the three, a fellow with a long neck, large head and high domed forehead, that they called Ostrich, agreed, "Like to break up Heaven's Door he's knocking at it so strong."

Colby turned to Lowell to question him more closely on this unwelcome intrusion into his expectations of a pleasant evening spent with his beloved, for it was true to say that he was one of the many admirers who were much enamored of Miss Daws' charms.

"Who…" He began but was interrupted by a sudden deathly silence from the rooms above.

The pause was long enough for all to take heed and it lasted as long as a drawn-out breath and then was followed by an ominously sounding and loudly rising volcanic rumble. A long, crescendo-ing roar, so potent that it rattled the glasses on the shelves and shook the pane in the large plate glass window that fronted the saloon.

"It appears," Lowell concluded in the silence that followed, a little unnecessarily under the circumstances one might observe, "that Mister Jack has reached conclusion."

"Goldarn it!" growled Colby with an annoyed grimace. "I don't like that."

"Sure beats all," agreed Teets soberly.

"'Pears there's some kinda animal up there with your Molly," frowned Ostrich.

"If he's done her harm…" snarled Colby.

"I'm sure not," reassured Lowell in an attempt to calm the obvious ill feeling and then, attempting to take their minds from such thoughts, he continued. "Tell me, gentlemen, are you from a local ranching establishment?"

"What're you?" snapped Colby, turning a malevolent gaze on Lowell. "You acquainted with the asshole up there with my gal?"

"I…" mumbled Lowell. "No more than a brief meeting."

"Then why don't you shut your mouth and mind your own affairs?"

Lowell's reply was uttered in a hurt tone, "My apologies, sir. I assure you I mean no harm or offence, I'm most positive your lady friend is quite alright. Mister Jack will be a friendly and gentlemanly soul, I'm sure of it."

"I guess this sucker rides along with the so-and-so upstairs," observed Teets, frowning at the journalist.

"Looks like a goddamned grocery clerk to me," said Ostrich. "If his partner's the same I reckon they may need a lesson or two on how things are handled around here."

"You're right there, amigo," Colby agreed with a leering grin.

The three started across the room, heading for Lowell with heads lowered and mean intent in their eyes.

It was then that Coffin Jack, still fastening his trouser buttons, made his entrance.

What happened next occurred with such startling brevity, Lowell was later unsure if it had happened at all it was all over so quickly. He could barely believe his eyes as the three cowboys turned at the sound of Jack's heavy tread, and all simultaneously drew on the pistols at their belts.

Then it was as if a whirlwind had entered the room.

Jack moved with such speed and determination it seemed he flowed through the air. The first he met was the one called Ostrich and with a swift twisting motion he caught the long neck and domed head in his big hands and twisted once as if strangling a chicken or game bird. There was a crack not unlike a carrot snapping and the tall man's legs went instantly limp under him and he dropped to the floor with his fingers still barely brushing the grip of his gun.

Spinning, with tornado velocity, Jack knocked aside Colby's drawn revolver and at the same time and with a blur of motion drew his own silver Colt.

Teets managed a shortly barked, "Hah!" before he found Jack's Colt pressed into his stomach and with a tight-lipped grin, Jack let loose with a single shot. The cowboy folded in half like an old newspaper and went shooting across the room to slam up against the bar room counter before sliding down silently to sit, rather like a meditating baby on his potty, on a big brass cuspidor set beside the foot rail.

Colby uttered a terrified gasp of recognition, "*Coffin Jack!*" before he too met the Deathdealer's bullet. A .45 slug took home in his chest and catapulted the wild young fellow over, to crash into the card table behind him. He lay amongst the upturned table and chairs and glanced across accusingly at Lowell, "Why didn't you tell me?" he wheezed. With aplomb, Jack loomed over and placed a final bullet between the already glazing eyes.

"Oh, my God!" uttered a shocked Lowell. "Mister Jack, I fear you have killed these men."

Jack sniffed. "Looks that way," he assured. "Seems a body can't even get his ashes hauled without some interruption these days."

Obliquely, Lowell was suddenly concerned for the cause of all the distress. "Did you leave Miss Daws in a fair state?" he asked, staring in awe at Jack.

"Been a long time since I indulged but she ain't complaining none," Jack confessed, plunking down on his chair and pouring himself a glass of liquor. "I'm out of practice some but I think I done her fair well. Leastways, it sure feels like I got some relief out of it or so I believe." He was vague on the subject and quickly putting it out of his mind. "I been thinking," he went on after draining his glass. "I reckon I'll take you along with me. Could be you'll be of some use, I like them long words you use, and I reckon I could do with some educated assistance in my dealings with this Carne fellow. 'Pears he's as learned as you."

Lowell glanced through the still hovering mist of gun smoke at the scene of death and destruction around him in the bar room. "I... I don't know about that," he managed.

"Sure you do," Jack urged. "Seems like this Carne fellow is fond of them long words, might be I'll need your translation services again when we meet."

"But surely there will be some delay now. The law will need to be apprised of all that went on here. But don't worry, I will assure the sheriff it was self-defense, I'm afraid these gentlemen meant you harm; it was most obvious in their demeanor. It seems that one of them was engaged in some kind of relationship with Miss Daws."

Jack chuckled rustily, a dry sound from deep in his chest. "Along with half the male bodies in the whole State of Texas I reckon and don't worry about the law. If they come calling at all it will only be for a brief visit and shortly terminated, I promise, but I fully doubt that will happen. The law around here is somewhat disconnected and better given to discretion rather than valor."

"Oh dear, oh dear," mumbled Lowell in a fluster of momentary distress until he recalled Miss Beatrice's last constraints to him.

*"Go forth, Lowell,"* she had said. *"Seek out and explore the new frontier, boldly go forth where no reporter has gone before. Discover for us unknown wonders in undiscovered places, bring us tales of marvel and majesty. I know you can do it, Lowell. I have the utmost faith in you."*

Lowell preened at the memory.

He would do it, for love of Miss Beatrice he would risk all, he would go and journey with this strange man called Coffin Jack and see where the path led.

# CHAPTER THREE

So it was on the next day early they set out together.

With Jack mounted on his dark stallion and Lowell following behind on a mule they left town, and with the rumbling storm clouds accompanying overhead, made their way towards the eastern horizon.

For Lowell it was a mysterious start. The shadow that swept across before them held what was at first a bright sunlit skyline chained to an ever-present shade of gloom that seemed locked to their passage. He could not for the life of him understand how the storm continued to be a part of their sky and how lightning and booming thunder did not break into rainfall. He turned his collar against the expected downpour that never came and shook at the reverberating thunder that troubled the heavy air and yet never cast any streaking lightning in their path.

Lowell gave up wondering and set to study the back of his companion riding solemnly in front. The tattered fringes of Coffin Jack's cloak fluttered like the fronds of a large carrion bird and his back was set as straight and unmoving as a tent pole.

Jack looked neither to left or right, his attention did not stray as most other curious traveler's would. The surrounding countryside held no interest for him and neither did it hold any fear of danger. Lowell had to marvel at the confidence that showed all the assuredness of a man capable of holding his own in any circumstance that might arise.

Neither of them spoke, although Lowell was keen to find out something about this odd fellow called Coffin Jack but he intuited that it was inadvisable and for some reason understood the mood was inauspicious for any probing.

However, as has been seen, Lowell was prone to verbosity and could not contain himself for long.

"Oh, Mister Jack?" he called out tentatively.

"What?" grumbled Jack, his thoughts rather set on reviewing his pleasurable assault on the lush fields of Miss Molly Daws the evening before.

"I see dust raised before us; do you see?"

"I seen it."

"What is that, do you know? We have this storm constantly with us already, surely it is not another one ahead."

"Nope, it ain't no storm."

"Then what, pray tell?"

"Indians."

"*Oh, Lord!* Savages, you say?"

"Yep."

"But we must avoid them at all costs. Where shall we run to?"

"Don't fret so, I ain't moving aside for any man,

red or white."

"But, Mister Jack," Lowell insisted, "there may be too many of them, we might be overrun. I have heard that they are prone to taking the hair from your head with sharp objects. That and using white males in an unseemly manner as a catamite might in performing unnatural acts."

Jack was a little puzzled by the latter turn of phrase. "The first is a fact, the second I ain't too sure about."

"They do! Oh, my word! Might we not take a small detour, do you think?"

"Hold your water," Jack advised. "It'll be okay."

They rode on without changing pace as the dust cloud advanced nearer and Lowell clung onto his mule with a terrified grip as the gap closed.

The dust cloud grew in volume until it filled the path before them and finally Lowell saw the charging band of red men advancing towards them and churning up the dust as they came. The painted riders were stripped bare to the waist, their coppery skin glinting in the sunlight as if oiled. Some wore animal heads and others feathered war bonnets that streamed out behind them, and in their hands they carried spears and rifles that glinted dangerously.

The sound of their charge and the screams of their war cries sent an answering shiver down Lowell's spine as the party neared.

"Oh, Mister Jack, I fear we are undone," he wailed.

"That'll be the day," rumbled Jack, sliding his Henry rifle from its scabbard.

The leader appeared to be a man with a body

painted one half in black and the other in white giving him the appearance of a divided creature spliced down the middle. He was sitting high on his pony's back and shouting bragging challenges as he came.

"See me! I am Man-of-Night-and-Day, a great warrior. Come to me, feel the blow of my war axe. Be touched by my mortal hand and die gloriously."

"Sure says a lot, don't he?" growled Jack. Then pulling his stallion to a halt so suddenly that Lowell almost ran into him, Jack drew himself up in the saddle, then hollered back loudly, "And I'm Coffin Jack, you punk-assed redskin! Prepare to meet your Maker."

At his words, the war chief did a double take it seemed. His brow furrowed, the black part twisting over the white in consternation. Then a unified cry rose from the oncoming warriors around him, "*Deathdealer!*" they wailed in chorus.

Man-of-Night-and-Day pulled on his reins sharply and his pony slid to a long sliding halt so fiercely that it almost threw him over the neck of the animal. The rest of the war band were travelling too fast to manage the same and they sheared off on either side, racing past a bemused Lowell who noted the frightened looks beneath the war paint on all their faces.

Man-of-Night-and-Day threw a shaky hand in the air, "Ho! Great Annihilator, I give you greeting."

"Best give me the road, you dung heap, or get ploughed under it," growled Jack in response.

He held his rifle across his waist but made no move to bring it higher and the Indian eyed the weapon cautiously.

"It is a good day," he managed, a slight tremble marking his lip.

"A good day to die, d'you mean?" finished Jack with a sneer.

"For some," Man-of-Night-and-Day said. "But not for you, respected Chief-of-the-Body-Levelers."

"Like to see you try," said Jack. "You and the rest of your miserable flea-peckers."

Lowell's gaze followed the war band but they had not stopped their racing ponies and were still pounding on and fast disappearing from sight behind them.

"Move on, shit-for-brains and make a wide path," ordered Jack, his good eye glowering with a strange ethereal light.

With a cowed expression of resentment, the Indian did as he was told and moved his pony to one side, stepping slowly in a broad curve around them.

"I am a powerful chief," Man-of-Night-and-Day barked suddenly as if to reassure himself. "I have no fear of the white men, but your medicine is known to be great, Deathdealer."

"You want a pill then I'm your doctor," promised Jack, following the Indian's passage with a steely gaze.

Man-of-Night-and-Day shook his war axe, which was a great wooden, curve-shaped weapon covered in magic emblems and fixed with a hooked tip of sharpened steel. It was obvious he was circling in an attempt to come up on Jack's patched-eye side, at an angle he thought he would not be seen so readily.

Coffin Jack grinned evilly; he raised one hand and gently lifted the edge of the eye patch exposing the raw meat of the empty black hole underneath.

"I see you," he snorted. "I'll cut out your eyes just like this, red man. You want to go to the Spirit World blinded, Mister Half-and-Half? You won't find your way home to your family lodge when I take out your eyes. See here, I'm looking at you real close." Jack leaned threateningly across the saddle, looming towards the Indian with his empty eye socket, and the Chief plainly shivered at the threat.

"*Aiyee!*" wailed Man-of-Night-and-Day and he began a chant that sounded to Lowell ominously like some kind of death song. The Indian dithered, obviously undecided as he walked his pony in small circles.

"Either piss or get off the pot!" bawled Jack crudely whilst cocking the Henry.

With a cry of shame and humiliation, Man-of-Night-and-Day dug in his heels and jerked his pony away and ran off up the road following after his war band.

As he disappeared in a cloud of dust, Lowell allowed a long breath of relief to escape from his lips.

"That was amazing, Mister Jack," he gabbled. "Do you realize you have just seen off a whole army of wild natives without a single shot being fired? Truly outstanding, I must say. Such downright stern heartedness and unbelievable courage."

"'T'weren't no big thing," Jack answered, turning away and casually raising the Henry and resting it over his shoulder, the muzzle pointing towards

Lowell. "Feller weren't nothing but a poke of wind and hot air."

Lowell eyed the black hole of the rifle nervously, "I wonder, Mister Jack, if you might point that rifle in another direction?"

"Not just yet awhile," promised Jack.

Lowell started bolt upright as the rifle went off with a loud bang, his eyes widening as the whip of the bullet snapped close by his cheek, so near that he felt the wash of its heat.

"*Mister Jack!*" he screamed. "What are you doing?"

"Fool wouldn't desist," answered Jack in easy justification.

Lowell turned in the saddle to see the figure of Man-of-Night-and-Day as he fell from his returning pony. The Indian chief tumbled head over heels in the dust at the feet of his charging horse, the rifle slug having punched a neat hole where the black and white bisected on his forehead. Man-of-Night-and-Day's war axe flew from his hand and cartwheeled away to embed itself harmlessly in the ground.

"But you didn't even look to aim," sighed Lowell.

"Didn't need to," sniffed Jack. "Can read those suckers like an open book."

Jack levered the empty shell from the Henry and holstered the still smoking rifle before geeing on Nameless. "Come on," he said. "Wasted enough time on this foolishness already."

# CHAPTER FOUR

It was not until they reached the forest on the Buzzard Fork wetlands in north Texas that Lowell really saw the effect that Coffin Jack's passing had.

It was a dense and dark wood, full of wild and interlocking trees that had grown rampantly in the fertile soil. No one had cleared the land in hundreds, possibly thousands of years and the forest had avoided any debilitating forest fires and so it had grown thickly wooded in tangled and distorted convolutions of wild abandon.

As they entered the forest their accompanying shadowy cloud moved before them, seeping out through the trees, and filling the undergrowth, darkening the already gloomy forest. It appeared to Lowell as they moved amongst the trees that the leaves themselves seemed to cringe back at their approach. There was a distinct impression that the branches themselves shrunk away at their passage and it was definitely true, he observed, that all the wildlife had vanished. There was no birdcall or sight of any creature and all around them was silence except for the sound of the storm wind lashing against the high branches that screeched and wailed in complaint as the wind rubbed them mercilessly one against the other.

The few dwellings that they came across amongst the trees were isolated places settled by lonesome types and those prone to find solace in separation from the rest of humanity. But their windows were empty, and the doors left wide open to the elements, in fact every decaying building demonstrated clear evidence of being hurriedly deserted.

There was a bleak air of loneliness hanging amongst the shadows that surrounded them as they moved deeper.

"How do you bear it?" Lowell finally asked.

"What?" rumbled Jack, without turning.

"This setting apart, the way everybody avoids you?"

For a moment Jack was puzzled. "Do they?" he asked in a bemused fashion.

"Of course, look they've all left their houses as you come near."

Jack pouted, his already grim features taking on an even more sunken appearance, "You sure it ain't you that upsets them?"

"*Me!* Good Lord, no. Why could they possibly want to avoid me?"

"Well, you're the one with the words, you tell me."

Lowell had no answer for that, so they travelled on in silence.

Maybe the old man was a little deaf as well as blind and that was why he had no sense of their approach.

He was a short man so grubby with filth that he appeared a yellowish-brown in color. Big shoul-dered and hunched yet limber enough, he found his way about with a long wooden staff to guide him. Bald headed on top with wings of white hair that sprouted wildly from over his ears and ran unchecked down his back except for a tail that he kept tied with a leather thong. Pot-bellied and wear-ing a stained buckskin vest over dirty Long Johns with improvised pants that were unevenly sewn from some ancient broadcloth, he stood in a forest clearing, his head tilted up at an angle, the milky eyes staring sightlessly skywards as he sensed their approach. A lone, fat black crow sat on his shoulder and it was to this that he spoke.

"Strangers coming," he observed.

The bird cawed once with a sound like an un-oiled door shutting, and promptly took off to dis-appear amongst the upper branches.

"Don't like them, huh?" muttered the old man.

As they entered the clearing, Lowell spotted the man standing before his home, a hovel built of logs and saplings, its roof a turf covered slope. So close to the forest edge that surrounded it and with the deep undergrowth of high grass and weeds around the walls the cabin appeared to be a part of the foliage itself.

"Howdy there," called the blind man.

"How do you do, sir?" Lowell answered.

"Name's Calumny Hermit, least that's what they call me. It ain't my given name but that's the one I'm labeled by. Get on down, I ain't got much but what there is you're welcome to. Sure been a long time since I had travelers passing through. Where you bound? Say, you ain't got a piece of taffy about you, have you? I ain't had a taste of taffy in a ten-year. Got a craving, seems to be all I think about these days. Last time I seen a chaw of taffy…"

The blind man rattled on loquaciously, obviously so unused to having company that at the first meeting he tended to pile on all the bottled conversation he had kept stored away.

"We'll rest the horses," said Jack, cutting the old man off and dismounting. "You got any coffee?"

The blind man rubbed at the wispy hairs on his chin, "Not your regular sort; ain't seen none of that in many a year, but I got a brew I make up from the tree bark. Fine chippings, you know? You soak 'em long enough and they make a passable stew. It's healthy too, being all natural products, keeps your wits fresh and alert and your bowels moving."

"So I see," mumbled Jack dismissively.

"Most kind," Lowell said, getting down from his mount. "How long have you been out here, Mister Hermit?"

Calumny Hermit scratched his bald head. "Now there's a question. Let's see, I was not much more than a younger when me and my folks passed through, we was wagoning it back in them days. Had us a prairie schooner and was headed for better lands but we had a run-in with the savages. Nasty vicious people they was, burnt us out, roasted my old man over a slow fire and what they done to my old lady ain't worth mentioning. Anyway, I was left all on my lonesome then and I run wild for a while, living on berries and roots, anything I could find, even ate tree rats when I could catch 'em..."

"You getting that coffee?" Jack cut in.

"Oh, yeah, sure, sure. Come on, come along in," he scampered off, tapping the way with his staff into the gloomy interior of his cabin.

"An impressive escape, sir. How was it the Indians let you be?" asked Lowell, ducking his head as he entered through the low door.

"Oh, it weren't no Indians," said Calumny, already working on a battered pan, filling it with water from a bucket.

It was a low-ceilinged single room inside with all the fittings made from tree branches; rickety chairs and a table of sorts bound together with strips of leather. The floor was beaten earth and a variety of oddities dangled from the roof, animal bones in chains and sacks fashioned from animal bladders. A pallet bed lay in one corner, a simple thing of timber and leather straps covered with pelts.

"Not Indians, then pray who?"

"Them, the Black Ones."

"*The Black Ones?*"

Calumny clattered about, his hands ranging over a shelf where a few ancient preserving jars stood, misty and dirt encrusted and holding dark earthen colored mixtures.

"Managed to save a few things from our wagon," Calumny explained. "Not much but enough to keep me comfortable."

Lowell looked around the grimy hovel. Seeing nothing but poverty and desolate destitution and wondered how the old man could consider this poor home "comfortable".

"The Black Ones?" Lowell persisted.

"Yes, them," muttered Calumny, concentrating on pouring a fine gray powder into the saucepan. "They lives here, been here a long, long time. Way back before us white folks ever came to the country."

Coffin Jack stood patiently still and said nothing, his looming body crooked forward with his head almost reaching the roof. Lowell had noted before how he could at times descend into a kind of waiting mode, during which he made no movement or seemed to register anything that happened around him. It was almost as he were in some sort of a trance state, Lowell surmised.

"If they are not Indians, then what sort of folks are they?" he asked.

"Skinny beggars, move around like stick people in the woods. Always paint themselves all over with black soot mixed with grease. Smelly too, you know full well when they're coming, as the air gets real ripe. But they are mean, sir, I tell you that. They eat anything, cannibal folk, prone to chewing on human parts if they can get them."

"So how did you manage to avoid them for so long?"

"I didn't," Calumny confessed. "They catched me soon enough, made me a blind man as you see me now."

"That is terrible."

"How come they let you live?" growled Jack, suddenly coming to life.

"I reckon they thought they'd done me enough harm. They let me alone now, don't trouble me no more. Strange folk, no understanding them." Calumny handed them each a mug made from animal horn and full of his hot dark brew. "There y'are, enjoy."

"Most obliged," said Lowell, taking a careful sip.

Jack drunk his straight down and smacked his lips. "Passable," was his only comment as he handed back his mug.

Lowell thought it tasted like pig's bile and smelt like damp moss. He wrinkled his nose and pretended to drink more. "Most satisfactory," he said politely.

"Like another?" asked Calumny with a vacant-eyed grin.

"Not for me," answered Lowell quickly.

Then both watched as Jack, stiff as a board, suddenly fell forward and dropped as straight as a fallen pine tree to smack helplessly face down on the floor in a cloud of dust.

"What th…" Lowell started to say but then wooziness overcame him. He stumbled sideways as if the ground had suddenly tilted.

"Oh, Lordy," he heard Calumny mutter. "Hope I didn't overdo it."

Lowell found the dizziness overtaking him and his legs went numb and gave out from under him and he slumped semi-conscious to the ground.

"Waar hev yoo dun?" he tried to ask, but his mouth seemed frozen and the words were slurred and barely recognizable.

"See here, you boys," said the blind man, feeling around for them with shaky fingers. "'Fraid I wasn't quite straight with y'all. The Black Ones, well they let me live on one condition only. I has to do them the favor of any passing traffic, that's the way they leaves me alone. Sorry 'bout that, hope you understand. Nothing personal."

Dreamily, Lowell saw him move over to the door and hoist down a long buffalo horn from over the doorway. Then placing it to his lips, Calumny let out a blast that boomed off eerily into the forest.

"They be here directly," Calumny promised. "Be over soon enough."

Lowell was struggling to retain consciousness; he realized that he was only remaining with some of his faculties because he had taken so little of the potion. Jack had supped the lot and taken the full force of the drug. Helplessly, Lowell sat propped against the wall, feeling limp and helpless as he stared at Jack, desperately willing the Deathdealer to recover.

But Jack slept on, his face pressed into the dirt and his body stretched out straight and stiff as a board.

Calumny raised his head and sniffed the air, "There y'are. You catch it? That's them sure enough."

Even in his present state, Lowell smelt the pervading stink. It was as if a skunk with dysentery had made its way into the clearing, a penetrating invasive odor that clagged the back of the nostrils and hung repulsively heavily in the air.

He tried to turn his head and it moved sluggishly

so that he was able to see the creature that appeared in the doorway.

A tall, bone thin skeletal thing, its round head shaved clean and the body painted entirely black. Slender fish bones pierced its cheeks and ears and it moved slowly and cautiously in insect fashion as it peered around the doorjamb. It was man-shaped and stark naked, and every part of the skin was covered in the sooty grease and pins of bone. From one hand dangled a long club with the sharpened jawbone of a wild pig fastened to the head.

The creature stepped inside, tip-toeing cautiously; its eyes glinting white in the painted face as it searched the room.

"There y'are," said Calumny, his head rotating as his blind eyes sought direction for the visitor. "See, I brung you two fat ones."

The creature ignored him, moving slowly and with a high-stepping spider-like grace as it made its way inside. It stared down at Jack and Lowell, the lips parting and emitting a purring growl of satisfaction. Lowell watched with horror as he noted that within the open mouth the rows of even teeth were stacked one row behind the other and each serried rank was as needle sharp as a shark's teeth. Suddenly, there were two more of them at the door. They were so tall that they towered over everything, seemingly filling the room, and barging the blind man aside as they entered.

"Yeah, yeah," muttered Calumny. "Get a good look, you ignorant assholes. Come on, get on with it and take them away. I don't want to breathe your pokey stink longer than I have to."

The lead creature bent low over Lowell studying him from his head to his feet and as he stuck his head closer Lowell caught a wave of the dreadful smell. It jolted him and was so sharp with an ammoniac tang not unlike stale urine that he found his head suddenly clear as if a dose of smelling salts had been offered.

With long bony fingers the creature reached out and plucked at Lowell's shirt trying to feel the plump skin underneath. He chuckled then, a low rolling noise that rose from deep inside and came out between his lips with a popping sound.

Revolted, Lowell moved his head aside in a sudden move and the black one leapt back, his club raised high. He uttered a gargling sound and was about to bring down the club when Calumny said, "It's all right, they ain't going nowhere. You fellas is as touchy as startled deer, I got 'em well dosed you don't has to fear nothing."

The creature backed off a delicate step, his club still raised and never taking his glinting eyes from Lowell's face. Then, with a clucking note he ordered his companions to concentrate on Jack. They tried to lift the heavy form, each of them encircling the limbs with their thin arms and heaving. They jabbered at one another, straining, and hauling but unable to make much headway as Jack was such a heavy load. One of them tentatively lifted Jack's eye patch and peered curiously into the empty socket. He poked an investigative forefinger into the hole until the leader barked at him and they returned to their struggle.

Lowell noted that Jack's good eye had suddenly blinked open.

The eye rolled around a moment, taking in its surroundings and the bony creatures intent on lifting him up. Lowell could swear that the eye changed tint, it appeared to roll through a shade of yellow to a glowing orange.

With a momentous roar, Jack rose to his feet, throwing the three creatures aside. It was as if an explosion had occurred in the cabin. The Black Ones tumbled aside and then as if on wire springs they jumped back up, each of them brandishing their weapons.

A long slender barbed spear made its way towards Jack, who caught it two-handed and snapped it in two as if a stick of firewood. With the barbed end held in one hand, he rammed it into the nose of the creature on his right-hand side, the other hand slashing out with the broken end at his remaining attackers.

The recipient of the barbed tip went cross-eyed as he tried to figure out what had transfixed his nasal passages so neatly from side to side. Then, Jack kicked him solidly in the chest with a blow so hard that the creature was sent sailing across the cabin and Lowell clearly heard the rib cage crack open under the boot.

The swinging jawbone club was coming Jack's way and he knocked it aside it with an arm as he whip-slapped the spear end across the black leader's bone-pierced cheek, raising a painful scream from the man. Wrenching the club away, Jack whirled it down with such awesome power that it cracked the eggshell dome of the round bald head open in a center parting and the leader fell soundlessly in a crumpled heap like a pile of broken twigs.

The remaining black warrior was jabbering loudly and lifting what looked like two daggers fashioned from sharpened tusks, one in each hand as he advanced on Jack. With a tired shrug, Jack looked at him questioningly, "You really think so?" he asked blandly.

The creature hissed spitefully and crouched, preparing to leap forward.

Fast as a flash, Jack drew his Colt and panned off three shots that sent the skinny creature spinning back as the bullets slapped through his bony frame and nailed him to the wall of the cabin.

Thankfully, feeling was returning to Lowell's lower limbs and he turned to see Calumny fumbling to find the doorway and make his escape. Lowell stuck out a rigid leg and the blind man tripped and fell forward over the extended limb.

Jack lunged forward and caught the old man by the long mane of white hair hanging down his back. Swinging the squealing figure loosely by the tail of hair, Jack rumbled an irritated growl and continued the swerving loop until the old fellow slammed headfirst against the doorjamb with a blow so hard it shook the entire structure.

Jack sniffed and then, breathing heavily he stood over the prone figure and cocked the Colt, pointing it down at the dazed blind man.

"No!" gasped Lowell. "He's only an old man."

"*Old man!*" spat Jack. "Damned asswipe is bait, that's all. He feeds these critters any traveler passing through."

"But still," Lowell insisted. "He's just a sight-impaired elderly and infirm person, one should have some pity, I do insist."

"You wouldn't be saying that if those three had you roasting over a fire right now," grumbled Jack.

"Mister Jack," Lowell said firmly. "Show some mercy, I beg of you."

"Hrmph!" grunted Jack. "Go get the horses."

Lowell dragged himself upright and weaved away, his body still recovering from the drug as he staggered across to their steeds.

"You know," he said over his shoulder. "It does not hurt for one to show a little charity, some understanding goes…"

The single shot was loud and reverberated through the forest, cutting off anything more of the morally upright tone that Lowell could utter.

"Oh, my!" breathed Lowell in defeat.

"Let's go," said Jack, swinging into the saddle and riding off without a backward glance.

Lowell looked back once and shuddered as he saw that the black crow had descended and with its broad beak was delicately picking at the facial remains of his one-time blind companion.

# CHAPTER FIVE

Lowell was writing in his large leather-bound notebook by the light of their campfire that same evening when Jack prompted him.

"What're you scribbling in there?"

"Just a record, Mister Jack. A daily account that I might form into an article later."

"Account of what?"

"Whatever has been happening. The events and things we encounter."

Jack frowned, the shadow under his hat brim darkening and his eye taking on a reflective gleam from the fire. "Like what?"

Lowell shrugged, "Today for instance, how you boldly saved us from an attack by those dreadful indigenous people."

"Is that what they were? Never heard of no "Digenous" folk before."

"And your amazing stand against the redskins. Truly an act of supreme daring."

"What about them in that saloon back there?"

"Yes, that too. One man against overwhelming odds."

"Sounds like someone else you're putting down there."

"No, sir. I assure you, it is all you."

Jack shuffled uneasily. "You wouldn't be making me out to be some kind of hero figure, would you?"

"But I think you are, Mister Jack. An absolutely unique character, I'm sure my words will bring your superbly original personality as a bold man of action to the attention of many readers. Perhaps not in any reverential and proselytizing manner, as Miss Beatrice might prefer, but certainly in a dashing heroic mold. She even may bend a little if I throw in some Biblical context in reference to the great warriors of the Old Testament, mighty men such as King David for instance. I see you as a moral man at heart and serving as a great example of forthrightness and determination in the face of uncertain chance. Certainly, as a role model for many of our younger readers."

"Don't be so dumb," Jack sneered. "I ain't no jackanape figure of up-righteousness," he paused doubtfully, a curious frown crossing his brow. "Am I?"

"Of course, you are."

"Bullshit!" rumbled Coffin Jack, lifting his eye patch and scratching at his socket. "I'm a killer, they don't call me "Deathdealer" for nothing."

"Pooh!" said Lowell dismissively. "*Words*, Mister Jack. That's all that is, just "words" and believe me, I well know the value of those. One can manipulate the use of such things to say anything one desires."

"Hrmph!" grunted Jack. "Almost like the way you're making me out to be some sort of upstanding character, you mean?"

"Well, no," frowned Lowell, a little surprised by the perceptive comment. "Em - not quite, no. This is a true representation of how I, as a verified and objective scribe, observe you."

"You don't think you're a tad biased, do you? Seeing as how I saved your butt a time or two?"

"Certainly not," stressed the offended Lowell. "It is a totally impartial opinion, I assure you."

Jack froze suddenly, going as still as a statue and leaning forward with ears pricked attentively.

"What is it?" asked a bemused Lowell and Jack held up one finger sharply for silence.

Lowell looked around suspiciously. It was a moonless night and pitch black outside the glow cast by the fire and all he could hear was the soft hush of the breeze blowing across the buffalo grass.

"There's noth..." he began and then he saw Jack slowly draw his pistol.

"There's somebody out there," Jack warned in a hushed voice.

"Hello the camp!"

The cry came suddenly. The high-pitched wailing sound of a woman's voice and not that far away from them.

"What you want?" called Jack, loudly cocking the hammer on his pistol.

"Help, please, we need help."

"Come out where I can see you," ordered Jack.

The woman who stepped into the firelight was young and quite pretty under her poke bonnet. She held her hands nervously high and moved forward one cautious step at a time.

"Don't shoot, I am not armed," she said, with a nervous tremble in her voice.

"You alone?" barked Jack, eyeing the surrounding darkness.

"Good Lord, miss!" cried Lowell, jumping up despite Jack's suspicions. "What on earth are you doing out here at this time of night?"

"I'm alone but desperate," she promised. "I pray you will help us, good sirs?"

"Come on in," said Jack.

As she came closer, Lowell could see that her hair was ruffled under the bonnet and hanging down in dark curls alongside an angelic-looking face of sweet proportions with long-lashed eyes of a striking blue. She wore an ankle length gingham dress and her neat pinafore nipped it in to a narrow waist. White stockings, stained with dirt, showed below the dress and a pair of simple, button-down black patent leather shoes covered her feet.

"My dear girl," gushed Lowell, putting a protective arm around her shoulder. "Come, warm yourself at the fire."

"Thank you, thank you," she breathed, coming forward hands outstretched to the flames.

"Now tell us, pray do, what are your difficulties?" asked Lowell.

"Our wagon," she began in a rush. "My family, so

much has happened. The wagon train…" she stuttered in a flustered tone.

"Now, calm yourself," advised Lowell, taking her small hand in his and patting it gently. "Please take a moment, steady and slow, that's it. Deep breaths."

Jack watched him nonplussed, his eye still roving away occasionally to study the surrounding blackness.

"Tell it, girl," he grunted abruptly and she looked at him wide-eyed for a moment, studying his tall, dark figure, his torn cape and low-slung hat that hid the patch in shadow yet showed the glowing eye as a single bleak orb.

"Be still, Mister Jack. The poor child is terrified, give her time."

Jack raised an eyebrow at the panting chest and swelling bosom over a more than fulsome figure, "Ain't so much of a child to my way of thinking," he mumbled.

"Oh, bless you," she gasped. "Bless you both. It is so good to find such God-fearing and blessed folk out here in the wilderness."

"You are in safe hands now I assure you," promised Lowell. "But do tell us what is it that ails you?"

"I am Mistress Gwendolyn Fairfax and we, that's to say, I and my family are part of a wagon train out yonder," she waved vaguely into the night. "We have fallen on bad times, I fear. The wagon master, Mister Boomster, a truly terrible man, has gone completely insane."

"What has he done?" asked Lowell.

"Why, all of a sudden, he has become a ranting

lunatic. The poor man has taken to accusing us all of the most terrible crimes, he has taken up an axe and has already slain one of our number. Young Robert Stains who tried to remonstrate with him," she bowed her head, her lower lip trembling and tears filling her eyes. "Mister Boomster cut off Robert's head. It was awful."

"Oh! Oh!" gasped Lowell. "How shocking, you poor little thing, that is ghastly. That one such as you should see such a thing."

Jack raised a critically judgmental eyebrow as he watched Lowell fussing over the girl. "He a drinking man, this Boomster?" he asked.

"Sir, he is a fallen soul," said Gwendolyn. "So bereft of fellow feeling that he has raided our medicinal cabinet and consumed all kinds of medicaments and drank every small barrel of liquor and liniment we carry. He grovels in the prairie grass and prowls like a wild beast amongst us; nobody knows what to do. We are all trapped in our wagons and hide away fearing the worst."

"So how'd you get away, if he's so darned awful?" asked Jack.

"He began to call my name, hailing me as his intended. Promising me he would... He would..." She drew a deep breath, "He promised the most awful things of a deeply private nature," she managed.

"The scoundrel!" blurted Lowell.

"Father said I should flee, at least into the prairie and there I would be safe and free of Mister Boomster's advances."

"Jack," Lowell burst out. "We must do something

about this fellow. This is absolutely outrageous."

"What you got in mind?" asked Jack blandly.

"Well, we must bring him to book, there's no doubt of it."

Jack sniffed and looked away at the fire. "Off you go then."

"What? You will not come?"

"Nope, I reckon I'll stay in the camp and protect the young miss here."

"Well, I – er – um," fumbled Lowell. "Right, yes, I will do it then."

"Oh, so brave," gasped Gwendolyn, clutching both hands prayer-like before her ample bosom.

Lowell dithered; unsure of what to do now the onus had been placed squarely on his shoulders.

"You got a pistol, ain't you?" asked Jack. "Reckon you might need it if this fellow's so all-fired crazy and him waving a wood ax about."

"Oh, dear! Do you think so? No, I have nothing like that."

"Then best take my Henry rifle; you can borrow it. Mind you bring it back in good shape though. Don't let that nasty fella go chopping at it or anything."

Lowell pulled a distressed face and then spun around to grab the rifle from Jack's saddle, "Are you sure you'd rather not come along, Mister Jack?"

"No, sirree," said Jack, leisurely stretching his legs out to the fire. "I reckon someone's got to stay here and guard things, wouldn't you say so, missy?"

Gwendolyn looked at him a little coquettishly. "It will be a blessing," she said. "To have someone so big and strong to watch over me, why, I feel safer already."

Jack nodded at Lowell. "Get on it then, we'll keep the fire going for you."

With many a backward glance, Lowell stumbled off into the darkness. At his leaving, Jack gave Gwendolyn an appreciative glare from his eye and said, "Why don't you sit alongside me here on this blanket, girl? Mite warmer and more comfortable than standing up there shivering."

With an upright waggle of her delectable hips, Gwendolyn arranged her skirts and sat down primly on the blanket edge as if she were a pert participant in a society picnic.

"Are you of a religious persuasion, sir?" she asked, with a tilt of her head and a flutter of eyelids.

Jack pouted, his lower lips jutting out over his unshaven chin. "Couldn't say. You?"

"Oh, yes," she said brightly. "We are of the Church of Heavenly Obfuscation. All my family belongs to it and it is a truly desirable congregation brought to us in a wondrous vision by our leader, Pater Cyrus Bowes. We go now to begin a new settlement according to the instructions handed down to Pater Bowes from Above."

"That being what exactly?"

"Ah," she sighed, her open face shining with innocence in the firelight. "It is a long and ponderous testament to explain; perhaps it might take a while to enumerate all the finer points. Broadly speaking, ours is of a more liberal experience and unfortunately much persecuted by those of a narrow perception and limited interpretation of the enlightenment offered by Pater Bowes. We have been forced from our homes and farms by those who could not understand that the fertility of the seed and the procreative act is the righteous harvest propounded by a correct understanding of the prophet's words."

Jack arched one dark eyebrow. "Cutting to the chase then. As I understand it, this is how you people feel about sexual congress?"

"We have no objections at all," she said airily. "Except with those outside the faith that is. I believe that was the problem with Mister Boomster, he could not quite grasp our laws and thought such acts were gratuitous and being frustrated he was driven beyond constraint."

"I believe I just got religion," breathed Jack throatily.

She cast him a sidelong glance, her eyes lidded seductively.

"*Really?*" she said, a quirky smile tilting her sweet lips.

"Oh, yeah. I hear them heavenly choirs of cherubim singing already," Jack promised fervently.

"My, that is the fastest conversion I have ever heard of."

Jack licked his lips. "Well, now we're all of a party, what say we indulge in a little prayer meeting?"

"Of course, that would raise my spirits and bring me no end of joy. Let us lie down together and offer our thanks for another soul saved. Pater Bowes will be so grateful that I have managed to bring such a bold supplicant to our Church."

Gwendolyn rested down gently on her back and lay out straight, her soft blue eyes fixed on the heavens and hands crossed and folded expectantly over her heaving breast.

"Okay, girl," rumbled Jack, getting to his knees and unbuckling his belt. "Time to open those Pearly Gates and let another sinner come marching in."

Lowell, meanwhile, was stumbling around in the dark.

He had fallen numerous times over tussocks and was quite tired of bumping his knee and crashing into unseen stands of thorny vegetation.

Almost near exhaustion, at last he saw in a valley below the glow of oil lamps and made out a collection of five covered wagons standing in a loose circle inside some stands of cottonwood. As he watched he made out the figure of a man weaving between the wagons and roaring drunkenly into the night.

Wrinkling his nose in distaste, Lowell saw the long-handled ax that draped from the man's hand and dragged in the dirt behind him. Carrying the rifle across his body, Lowell rose with determination and made his way down the slope towards the wagons.

"Come on out!" he heard the fellow bellow in a slurred voice as he neared. "I gotta need of poontang, you dirty beggars. Why you hiding so? I seen you all at it. Like rabbits you is, allus jumping each other. What's to stop a body like me having a taste?"

Curling his lip Lowell boldly marched forward.

"Where is you, Gwendolyn Fairfax? I'm right hot

and ready for you," cried the man.

At mention of the name, Lowell felt a sudden flood of anger course through his body. It was in his mind that his own beloved Beatrice had taken on the role of the young maiden in danger and supplanted that of Gwendolyn and he was so full of chivalric outrage that he was now intent on protecting her. The sudden welling of indignation in his chest overcame any trepidation he might be feeling, and he barged forward.

"You there!" he shouted as he broke through the surrounding trees. "Stand aside and desist your foul intervention against these good people."

Boomster, for it was indeed he, swung around blinking shortsightedly at the figure that came towards him out of the darkness.

"Wha' you want?" he blurted.

He was a short set, blocky man, with a densely muscled torso without any visible neck showing to support his glowering square head. The man was marked most remarkably by a bar of dark eyebrows, so thick, that they appeared to band his forehead from side to side in a continuous line.

"Put down that axe!" Lowell barked.

The weaving Boomster looked at the bloodied ax in his hand curiously as if unsure as to how it got there.

"You are intoxicated, sir," Lowell continued. "I suggest you leave off this act of riot immediately."

Lowell noticed flaps on some of the wagons moving back as a few curious faces peered out.

"Get off and leave me be," sneered Boomster.

"'T'ain't none of your affair. I got me some noodle coming and I aim to get it."

"You are a foul and detestable creature," snapped Lowell. "I tell you now drop that ax, or I shall be forced to act."

"That right?" said Boomster, raising his heavy eyebrows questioningly. "Listen stranger, you don't know what we got here," he tilted forward precariously and confided in a loud stage whisper. "It's a bed of damned preeverts, I tell you. They gets into it every opportunity, why the whole pesky lot of them hump regular come day or night. It's more than a human body can stand, I never seen the like."

"Bah!" snorted Lowell. "The intoxicants have confused you and twisted your tongue. Leave off, I say."

They were interrupted by a wailing voice from the wagons, "Save us from murder, sir. I beg of you."

Reinforced by the cry for help, Lowell replied, "Have no fear this fellow will receive short shrift from me if he does not surrender forthwith."

"That so?" sneered Boomster lunging forward. As he moved, the dragging ax handle became entangled between his legs and he tumbled, looming dangerously close to a startled Lowell. Fearfully, Lowell leapt backwards, tripped on an exposed root and with his nervous finger on the rifle trigger, the jolt fired off the Henry.

The boom of rifle fire echoed around the camp and raised a cry of concern from all the watchers in the wagons.

The poor drunken Boomster, not inches away

from the barrel, took full collection of the rifle bullet neatly between his heavy eyebrows and it completely excised his brain pan through the back of his square head. He fell in a heap flat on his stomach, his broken head held upwards by the chin in the fashion of a tiger rug.

Lowell stared in horror at the accusing grimace that the dead Boomster offered him.

"Bless my soul!" he gasped and then a little stupidly he added, "I do beg your pardon, sir."

People tumbled noisily from the wagon beds. "We are saved," they cried. "Bless you, stranger. You have rescued us from this bloody murderer."

"I must apologize," gasped the shocked Lowell, still staring agape at the ruined figure of Boomster.

But the travelers were crowding noisily around him, slapping his back and shouting their thanks and his words were not heard.

"Bless you, friend," cried one large, broad shouldered man with a goatee beard and the look of a farmer about him. "You have surely saved us from bloody murder. Tell me, have you seen my daughter as you approached? I have sent her out into the wilderness to be safe from this wretch." He came close and enclosed Lowell in an energetic hug, "She is a fair-haired girl, not more than eighteen year."

"Miss Gwendolyn Fairfax?" Lowell answered limply.

"Indeed!" cried the man excitedly. "You have seen her then?"

"My travelling companion has her in his company and he takes good care of her. She is quite safe, have no fear."

"The Lord be praised," roared the fellow. "You are twice Salvation's Angel, sir. May I ask your name?"

"I am Lowell Devereux, at your service."

"Thank you, Mister Devereux," said the farmer, taking Lowell's hand and shaking it fervently. "I am the girl's father, Jonathan Fairfax. I would ask you to stay and celebrate our rescue from that toad Boomster but her mother and I am most anxious to have our precious returned to us. Would you be kind enough to lead me to your camp that I might collect her?"

"Of course," said Lowell. He was still stunned by his luckless slaying of the wagon master and the excuse to escape from the scene only filled him with relief.

As they left the rest of the wagon train, members were cavorting joyfully and to Lowell's frame of mind strangely enthusiastically after such an act of slaughter but he put it down to relief at their escape from the ravages of the insane Boomster.

Dawn was beginning to break the skyline as they marched up the hillside and Lowell was pleased to find that he could see his way more easily in the dim light.

Fairfax strode out alongside, humming happily. He appeared a strong and forthright character and Lowell considered that the wagon train appeared to be full of equally upright folk who were only too keen to settle in new lands and enjoy a happy and productive life.

"An unfortunate scene you saw below," said Lowell as they crested the hill.

"No more than the sinner deserved, Mister Devereux," smiled Fairfax.

"Indeed so, I dare say. Still, one takes no joy in such a killing."

Fairfax nodded. "I see you are a proper man, sir. I am most glad my daughter fell into such trustworthy hands."

"She is surely a tender child," Lowell agreed.

"Ah, yes, our Gwendolyn is most certainly a fair thing brimming with promise."

"Just so, she puts me in mind of my own dear sweetheart," answered Lowell, his mind wandering off into visions of Beatrice. "A sweeter girl you could never hope to meet."

"Is that so? And is your lady a fecund creature, may I ask?"

Lowell frowned at the strange question. "Fecund! I really could not say."

"It is just that we of our wagon train travel on to find our promised land of milk and honey and are always glad to accept fellow travelers of a higher nature and those most keen to populate the earth."

Lowell pondered on the obscure query and wondered just what Fairfax was getting at. "Well – um – I really don't know. I'm sure Miss Beatrice will fully fulfill her feminine role should the occasion arise."

"Good, good," said Fairfax placing an arm around Lowell's shoulder in an affectionate manner. "You must know, Mister Devereux, we would be only too happy to have such a man as yourself with us.

Feel free to join and bring your good woman with you. As our leader the blessed Pater Cyrus Bowes promises, "A woman shared is a joy forever and a pleasure multiplied"."

Lowell did not like the way this strange conversation was going, and he gently slid out from under Fairfax's arm.

He struggled on to try and discover the whereabouts of their camp and get the man his daughter and relieve himself of this strange behavior. But it had been full dark when he had left and was not at all sure in which direction the campsite lay. So it was with some relief that he saw their hobbled horses standing patiently on a nearby rise.

"Ah!" he cried. "We are here at last. The camp lies yonder."

"God be praised," smiled Fairfax. "It will be a true joy to see our dear Gwendolyn again."

"Of course," Lowell agreed.

As they approached the rise Lowell was dismayed to see a sight that made his blood run cold.

A great naked pair of hairy buttocks were rising and falling with regularity on the horizon.

"Oh, no!" moaned Lowell faintly. "Mister Jack, you didn't."

As they came even closer, Fairfax stopped suddenly and leaned forward to peer at the awesome scene of copulation being performed.

"Bless me!" he cried. "Is that my Gwendolyn in an act of worship with your partner, Mister Devereux?"

Lowell's face fell, "I fear there is no worship involved here, sir," he said in a low voice, only wishing he could crawl away and hide somewhere. "Mister Jack I'm afraid is not one prone to respecting the formalities. I am truly sorry, sir, it is a most unseemly thing for a father to witness."

"Why!" cried Fairfax. "Bless you no; it does my heart good to see Gwendolyn so engaged. This conjunction is a wondrous thing and Gwendolyn serves the strictures of the Pastor well, she is mighty in prayer and great in the ways of the Church, there is no doubt of it. Why, look at them go? I believe a true fervor is upon them."

Lowell gaped at Fairfax, his mouth opening and shutting wordlessly like a fresh-caught fish thrown on the riverbank. Can this man be in his right mind, he wondered? His young daughter, the virginal Gwendolyn was being pounded on by the great and lumbering mass-murderer Coffin Jack and he thought this was a righteous act of reverence?

"Oh, Mister Devereux, I am much moved by such devotion," Fairfax sang out in a booming joyful voice. "Shall we join the moment and fornicate together?"

"No, we shall not!" bleated Lowell, staring in horror at the deranged man.

"Come!" cried Fairfax, hopping about enthusiastically. "This is a divine moment and we should partake in it by singing our praises."

Speechless, Lowell backed away before turning and running off in wild panic.

"Come back, Mister Devereux," he heard Fairfax call after him. "Do not miss out on such a jubilant congregation."

"Not on your life," panted Lowell, stepping up the pace and stumbling on.

His mind raced as fast as his feet and as he ran, he began to wonder at just how lawful his shooting of the wagon master had been under the circumstances. Could the man, in fact, been driven over the edge by the licentious behavior of those occupying his train? Had they all been involved in such barbaric acts of bestiality that he had slain an innocent man pushed too far by such behavior? It made his heart sink even deeper and when he stopped, at last out of breath and far away from the campsite, he crouched down despondently.

How could he face Miss Beatrice again? How could he possibly write anything uplifting for The Holy Roller with impunity? He'd taken a life and was now a killer, a plain murderer for the basest of reasons but his own arrogance. No matter it had been an accident, he bore the blame and he no longer had a right to instruct others through his words, nor was he any longer a suitable companion for Miss Beatrice Hicks, the love of his life.

Lowell wept bitter tears. He felt cast out and adrift and in such a numbed and tearful state, he fell into a black sleep.

# CHAPTER SIX

"Come on, fellow, get your ass in gear."

Lowell awoke to feel Jack's boot nudging him in the ribs. He rubbed his eyes and looked at the ragged figure looming over him holding both their ponies by the reins.

"Time to be moving on," grunted Jack.

"I fear I cannot," said Lowell sadly.

"Can't what?"

"I cannot go on. I am a beaten man, Mister Jack. I have sinned grievously and taken a life."

"Well, I done plenty of that," said Jack offhandedly. "Both the sinning and life taking but now I got me religion this night past."

"Born again? You cannot think that," sighed Lowell, looking away. "Surely not that."

"I done it," said Jack. "I took on the holy word and prayed with that young gal all night long. My, but she was an earnest one. I'm near tuckered out with all that praying. I reckon I could take on board this religion thing right well, all said and done."

"No, no, Mister Jack that was no proper religion, it is a most unseemly faith and not according to Holy Scripture. Do not be fooled by the prospect of such improper readings of Divine Word."

"Don't know nothing about that, I just know I seen the Light and I'm a confirmed religious now."

"Oh, Mister Jack," wailed Lowell. "Would that I could educate you properly, but I am sorely unfit for the task. I am as lost as you are now, cast out and thrown down."

"Hellfire! Will you stop moaning and get up. Mount that pony and ride a-ways, it'll clear your head and give you a brighter prospect."

Slowly, Lowell sat up. He looked around in surprise, the sun was shining, and the day was indeed bright. The long accompanying storm clouds that had always been with them on their journey had disappeared and there was no longer any distant ominous rumble of thunder. Even the shadow that had constantly darkened the land before them was not there.

"Where has that storm gone?" he asked.

Jack looked around indifferently and shrugged. "Told you, I seen the Light."

At a loss, Lowell accepted the reins from Jack and pulled himself up into the saddle. "Well then," he sighed hopelessly. "Let us ride, I no longer care where we go or what we do."

"Sounds like a healthy attitude," grunted Jack, digging in his heels and taking the lead.

The fort at Mohsap Draw was a regular wooden palisade type of structure named Fort Bendix. It was a long rectangular site and the walls enclosed a series of buildings with everything necessary for a military post, from stables to administration.

Colonel Bertran Bendix had been commissioned to oversee building the fort as a protective base on the trade road that ran clear through to Albuquerque. In reality it had merely been an attempt by the War Department to rid themselves of the troublesome colonel, who was an important politician's son much addicted to strong liquors and often in trouble over his alcoholism. An only child and late born to doting parents, his indulgence had been great, and due to his father's official position any unpleasant scrapes during his growing years had been safely swept under the carpet. With such an errant officer, frequently appearing drunk in the halls of Washington with his tunic undone and a blousy woman on each arm, it had been deemed that the young Bendix might better serve his country somewhere far away and preferably on the wild Frontier where he might be nicely forgotten.

A handsome-looking and dashing figure of a man, slender and fair-haired. Bertran stood a good six feet tall and his parents had made sure that a protective minder, a man named Gray Denton, constantly accompanied him. Denton had been made up to Master Sergeant and was always at Bertran's elbow, forever seeing that his back was covered when he was in his cups and that any vomit cleaned from his uniform when he overindulged.

Sergeant Gray Denton had been raised a miner in

the gold diggings of California and as a result was a rough-hewn, squat, chunk of a man with hands as large as dinner plates and being of a glowering disposition was generally feared and avoided by the rest of the complement at the fort. He was a no-nonsense hard head whose only aim in life was to loyally serve and defend the colonel to whom he was wholly devoted and in a silent and often extremely protective manner he saw that nothing ever stood in the colonel's way.

The fort itself was of no particular strategic value, as Bertran had constructed it when he was seven-sheets-to-the-wind, as they say. In a grand argument with the engineering officer seconded to the task, Bertran had ordered the engineer be placed in irons and then drunkenly misunderstood the placement of the site and had it built in the wrong position due to studying the map upside down. So the fort stood miles distant from its proper situation, away from the trade road and set amongst dust-dry land that needed a regular water wagon supply from the river seven miles distant. To add to the improbabilities of the position it stood vulnerably in the depths of a valley overlooked by high hills on each side providing prime cover for renegade Indian snipers or any passing vandal who fancied a potshot at sentries patrolling the walls and they often took full advantage of the situation.

As Coffin Jack and Lowell approached the double gates of the fort a voice barked from a peephole alongside.

"What you want here?"

"Just passing through, need to rest up a mite and ask directions," answered Jack, wondering why there were no guards evident on the walls.

Slowly the gate creaked open and they rode in to be immediately confronted by a sentry with a Springfield rifle held high.

"How'd you boys get here unharmed?" he asked suspiciously.

Jack shrugged. "Just rode in, why?"

"So what d'you want here?"

"You're mighty curious for a gate guard, soldier," growled Jack. "What's your problem?"

"Look here, Private," Lowell interrupted quickly before Jack's temper became aroused. "We only want to rest our ponies and purchase some supplies. Be most grateful if you could direct us to the sutler's store."

The guard sniffed, somewhat mollified by Lowell's politer tone. "Over there," he said, nudging direction with the rifle.

They looked across the pure white and deserted parade ground that was bordered by a perfectly rectangular square of white painted stones and with a flagpole stationed at the center bravely flying the Union flag.

The sutler's store was one of the wooden huts opposite across the parade ground marked out with a hand painted sign standing on its porch roof. In front of the porch steps a lone man weaved his way. His tunic was dusty and torn and fixed to one ankle was a long chain with a heavy log cleated to one end.

The captain, for that was what he obviously was, as the marks of his rank were evident on his shoulders, dragged the heavy log and at the same time carried two slopping buckets, one in each hand.

"What the hell did he do?" asked Jack.

"Some engineer that upset the colonel, he got the post stockade as residence and a course of the ball and chain," the soldier grinned impishly. "Sucker never knew what hit him."

"Seems a mite harsh for an officer."

The soldier's brow darkened. "Listen, be advised, you don't want to go upsetting the colonel."

"Why's that?" asked Jack.

"You just don't," stressed the sentry.

"Obviously a stickler for discipline, what is this colonel's name?" asked Lowell.

"That would be Bendix, Colonel Bertran Bendix."

"Where is everybody?" asked Jack, staring around at the deserted courtyard.

"We tend to keep out of sight during the daylight hours," said the soldier. "You'd best do the same."

They were interrupted as a woman approached from the shadows under the fort walls. She was tall and willowy and elegantly clothed in a fine dress and carried a small parasol that kept her face from view.

The sentry promptly snapped to attention. "Mrs. Bendix," he said in way of greeting.

"Good morning, Private."

The voice was hushed and well-modulated and as she neared the two riders, she raised the edge of the parasol and Lowell looked into the face of the most beautiful woman he had ever seen. Their eyes met for a moment and the deep tranquility that Lowell experienced at sight of two wide and bright sea-green eyes made him feel as if he had just been immersed in the warm waters and soft caress of a welcoming ocean.

He gaped momentarily and the woman started in surprise as if some unspoken message passed between them.

"G…gentlemen," she faltered, before quickly lowering her parasol and hurrying on.

Belatedly, Lowell raised his hat and called after her, "Good morning, ma'am."

"Come on," grunted Jack, guiding his pony on over the parade ground.

"Did you see that?" breathed Lowell, following on behind. "Wasn't that the most beautifully refined creature you did ever see?"

Their ponies puffed alkali dust in a trail behind them as they angled over the white square towards the store and Jack looked over his shoulder after the disappearing woman.

"Fair piece of tail," he agreed solemnly.

They were midway across and approaching the flagpole when a loud vibrant scream penetrated the fort and echoed across to them.

"*What are you doing?*" came the bellow.

Both riders pulled up sharply and looked around to see where the call came from. They finally spotted the originator lounging amongst the shadows under the porch of the administration building. The lanky figure sat sprawled in an armchair, one booted foot up on a small table where a large empty decanter lay next to a full glass.

The man's face was suffused with rage and he waved limply in their direction, the shirt he wore falling open to expose his bare chest as he did so.

"Sergeant Denton!" he roared. "Get those infidels off my parade ground this instant!"

Lowell looked around to see the cause of their distress and noted that the pure, flat and white alkali dust covered floor of the parade ground had been tracked up by their passage and now a trail of exposed dirt marked the pristine surface.

"Oops!" he muttered. "Looks like we just stepped in it."

The squat sergeant and a few armed infantrymen ran out, then stopped dead at the stone marked boundary and trained their guns on the two isolated riders. The sergeant leaned across the stone barrier his battered face twisted into an ugly growl.

"Get off there right now!" he ordered, fixing them with an evil grimace.

"What's the matter with them?" Jack asked innocently.

Colonel Bendix had swayed to his feet on the porch as the two were brought before him.

"You blasted civilians," he snarled. "Coming in here unannounced and tracking your filth all over my post. Who do you think you are? Wretched trouble-makers."

"We just…" Lowell began in explanation.

"*Don't talk when I'm speaking,*" spat the Colonel. "Don't think I didn't see you, you cur. Insulting my lady wife with your licentious looks, I was watching. Mean-eyed, that's what you are, leery mean-eyed perverts."

Mrs. Bendix who had sidled up nervously onto the porch folded parasol in hand, mumbled softly. "We were just passing the time of day, dear."

"Be quiet, Ariadne. When I want your opinion I'll ask for it, in the meantime pray keep your pretty mouth closed!"

The embarrassed woman mewed quietly and visibly shrank at the tirade whilst Lowell fumed in anger. The sense of offense rose in his chest as he drank in the vision of the fragile and stunningly beautiful woman being browbeaten by her intoxicated husband.

"You, sir!" Lowell barked, the words tumbling unbidden from his mouth, "are indefensible. Have you no sense of propriety? One does not treat a lady in such a manner. As an officer and one would hope, a gentleman, by now I would have thought you could have learnt to control your tongue. A disgusting display of ill manners."

Colonel Bendix stared at him bug-eyed for a long, silent moment. His body twitching and contorting, as Lowell's critical words coursed through him.

"*Chains!*" he suddenly bellowed. "Sergeant Denton, I want to see them in chains, this instant."

There was a cry from the ramparts and they all spun around to see a sentry, his body stiff and rigid as he tumbled in a gentle arc from the firing step at the top of the walls and fell heavily, an arrow transfixing his neck.

"Another one," muttered Sergeant Denton tiredly as the body bounced in a cloud of dust and lay still.

"That's the third this month," snapped Bendix. "Haven't I told them often enough to keep out of sight? Blasted fools."

"Never should have built this darned place here under the hills," observed Jack. "What idiot decided on that?"

"Get them from my sight," snarled Bendix in response before turning his back and plunking down in his armchair. "Ariadne," he muttered, "can't you see my decanter is empty? Fetch me another this instant."

"Yes, dear," his wife whispered meekly and quickly hurried away inside the building to comply.

"What an absolute beast," observed Lowell as they were marched away. "How can such a man be permitted to command?"

"You shut your gab," snarled Sergeant Denton. "You don't speak of the colonel that way or you'll have me to answer to."

"And what might you be that's so special?" asked Jack indifferently. "I don't see any label on the jar."

"I'm your worst nightmare," promised Denton viciously. "That's who I am. You tangle with me and you'll regret it the rest of your lives."

"Sergeant, just thank your lucky stars I got religion recent," growled Jack.

"Is that right?" sneered Denton. "Well, don't worry, I'll forgive you your sins any time you want to make a go of it. We'll step right in and I'll take you on bare-handed whenever you want."

"Don't tempt me," rumbled Jack imperiously.

"You men," said Denton turning to the surrounding guards. "Get them to the stockade pronto and the blacksmith's to fit them with leg irons right away."

The men mumbled in reply and Denton bellowed at them, "*What?* I didn't hear you."

"Yes, Sergeant!" they promptly all echoed obediently louder. It was obvious that they all went in terrified fear of the man.

"Goddamned sissies," snarled Jack.

They found they had one companion in the stockade's cell house.

It was a simple log-walled room with little dressing, only a bare earth floor, latrine buckets and four bunk beds set one over the other against two of the walls, there was one barred and glass-less window allowing a thin stream of light to enter.

The other occupier was the chained captain they had seen earlier and he could be smelt clear across the room. He sat morosely on one of the lower bunks and watched dumbly as they were fitted with leg irons that left a three-foot length of chain between each ankle.

"What's the scene here?" asked Jack, once they were alone.

The captain shrugged, motes of dust rising from his dirty and ragged tunic as he did so. "The man's mad, pretty obvious isn't it?" He tugged his chain and the worn log at the end over nearer to him and played with the links as he looked at them.

Lowell leaned across and offered his hand. "Lowell Devereux, a pleasure, sir."

The captain looked at the offered hand a moment and then with a slight smile took it. "Captain James Audebourn, recently serving with the Corps of Engineers. You must excuse my state, I fear I am not allowed to bathe and must clear out slop buckets all day long."

"You designed this fort?" Jack asked in surprise.

"Certainly not," snapped Audebourn. "I was commissioned to do so but that crazy idiot overrode me and put me in here."

"But what did you do? Surely there is a charge?" frowned Lowell.

"Oh, yes. Apart from arguing with him about the geographic placement of the fort he did not like the way I looked at his fair wife. The man's extremely jealous of Ariadne, he treats her like dirt yet cannot abide the thought of anyone approaching her with a modicum of respect."

"She is a work of art," mused Lowell, suddenly going dreamy at thought of the vision. "What on earth is she doing with such an ogre?"

"Family fell on hard times during the war," Audebourn supplied. "I believe it was some sort of arranged convenience to save their fortunes. Poor dear woman suffers for it every day."

"Despicable!" hissed Lowell.

"I thought you was promised to your Miss Beatrice," Jack cut in a tad critically.

"That was before," said Lowell dismissively. "Before I made myself unworthy."

"Hrmph!" Jack snorted.

"So, what are you fellows up to?" asked Audebourn. "How came you here?"

Jack studied him a moment with his good eye. "On our way to Doomesville on the Longspree Pike, you know it?"

"Mm, yes. Doomesville, it's about a hundred and twenty-miles due north of here, I believe."

Jack rumbled contentedly, "Least we know where we're headed," he said, tugging his hat brim over his eyes and laying back down on the bunk.

"Are you going to sleep, Mister Jack?" asked Lowell. "Surely we must make plans?"

"Later," sniffed Jack.

"But we must get out of here," Lowell insisted.

"Hrmph!" was all he got in reply. And within minutes, the low rumbling buzz-saw sound of Coffin Jack's snoring filled the cell.

"Who is this gentleman?" asked Audebourn in a hushed voice when he was sure the dark figure was fast asleep.

"Coffin Jack?" asked Lowell.

Audebourn nodded assent. "And he is whom exactly?"

Lowell pondered on it a moment. He had started his acquaintance with Coffin Jack in a simplicity of innocence, expecting little more than an engaging tale that he might offer to his employer. But now, since all that had happened and in his new despondent frame of mind, his assessment was shifting. Not only had he witnessed the amazing dexterity by which the Deathdealer laid his enemies low but he himself now suffered a crisis of conscience that he had not expected to come his way. A crisis that he surely would not have confronted unless he had been in the company of Coffin Jack.

"I'm not quite sure," he finally admitted. "Sometimes I have to say I think perhaps he is the very personification of Death itself. For if ever you might imagine the Grim Reaper in human form then Coffin Jack surely fits the bill."

"That bad, huh?" nodded Audebourn, finding the description a little exaggerated and not quite believing what Lowell was telling him but politely accommodating his new companion.

Lowell looked down numbly at his feet and the chains that bound him. "He carries sorrow around with him it seems. I am beginning to wonder why on earth I am accompanying him."

Audebourn frowned seeing Lowell's obvious despair. "Seems like you'd better take a parting of the ways, sir."

"I cannot, I fear. By some strange means he binds me to him, and I feel compelled to continue until some resolution in our association is reached."

"Well," sighed Audebourn, "unless you can get out of this pretty pickle here there will be not be a resolution of anything."

"You have been imprisoned long?"

"Six very long and hard months, ever since I first cast my eyes on Ariadne."

Lowell tilted his head curiously as he saw the captain's obvious romantic attraction. "And are your affections favored, Captain?"

"I believe so. But it is most trying, for I find myself

destitute with desire for the woman. To see her in such a dire condition breaks my heart. I believe she cares for me but is unable to demonstrate it in any fashion as long as her despotic brute of a husband oversees her every action. But there is something in her eyes that tells me each time we meet that we are meant to be together."

Lowell wondered at that for it was the same experience he had suffered himself. One glance from the perfect Ariadne and he had felt himself swept away on an aching tide of passion. How could that simple and retiring woman hold overwhelming temptation in only a single glance and yet be so innocent of any apparent seduction? Did Ariadne, he wondered, hold the secret capacity of inspiring this deep desire, unknown even to herself, like the mythical Sirens of old. Those enchanting temptresses that would draw unsuspecting travelers to their shores and those who did not resist their magical song would surely end their days in death and corruption.

His thoughts were interrupted by the sound of a light tapping on the bars of the window.

"Who is it?" Audebourn whispered.

"It is I," came the soft reply.

"Ariadne!" gasped Audebourn, hurrying towards the window. Lowell made it faster, hopping and skipping with his chains whilst Audebourn had to drag the heavy log after him and that slowed his progress somewhat.

Lowell pulled himself up and peered out to see the placid face of the colonel's wife staring up at him. Her pale features glowing in the coming evening light and lighting the perfect lines within a gentle haze that softened and molded her into an agonizing picture of desirability. The enchanting eyes swam before him and Lowell felt himself instantly engaged despite all his earlier troublesome considerations.

"Dear lady," he said, "how are you here?"

Audebourn struggled to push his way up beside him. "Ariadne," he breathed, "it is so good to see you."

"I do beg pardon, I am so sorry that it has come to this," she whispered, looking around nervously. "This is my entire fault. Forgive me, I cannot stay long but I just had to come and see how you all fared."

"No, no," both men insisted. "Please do not blame yourself."

"If I could change things for the better, I would," she promised.

Audebourn and Lowell juggled for position at the window, each of them elbowing to take prime place before the bewitching creature.

"You are such brave men and so roughly treated," she whispered, her blue eyes seeming to magnify to engaging wells of promise as she swept her gaze across them both. "Oh, if things were different."

"Can you help us, do you think?" asked Lowell.

"I fear to," she pleaded. "My husband has such a temper."

"I'm sorry to ask," said Lowell. "But does he treat you so sorely?"

She dropped her elegant head in a shameful pose. "As husband he has the right to use me how he may. I must not complain, but sometimes the things I am charged to do… I admit they are offensively base."

It was as if a dagger had struck through both men's hearts at the prospect of such a thing. The thought of any kind of violence or abuse against this sweet and chaste creature was an anathema to both men.

"My God!" swore Audebourn. "If ever the opportunity comes my way, I swear he will never harm you again."

"But what can we do?" she asked, raising tear-filled eyes towards them.

There was a distant scream and the hefty sound of a body hitting the ground somewhere out in the compound.

"What was that?" asked Lowell.

Ariadne half turned her head with a wistful look. "Another poor sentry has been struck down on the parapet, I fear."

"Dear Lord!" frowned Lowell. "*Again?*"

"It is a regular occurrence," Audebourn assured him with a shrug.

"We must get out of here," urged Lowell.

"Indeed," agreed Audebourn. "But how?"

"I must go," said Ariadne. "Someone is coming. Please, be brave and stay well the both of you. Do not forget me." And then she was gone.

It was as if a taste of something sweet had been torn from both men at her departure and Lowell almost sighed aloud at the loss.

"She is unbelievable," sighed Audebourn.

"What a creature," Lowell agreed.

Both men were mesmerized by the sight of Ariadne, she represented to the pair of them a desirable vision of their ideal of womanhood. She seemed a bold and courageous figure, yet at the same time so weak and vulnerable and in dire need of their protection. Her presence brought out every inherited protective gene that had lived in man since the earliest days.

The sound of the key turning in the lock sent both men tumbling to the floor and returned them to the present as if they had both been lost in a dream for a while.

Sergeant Denton swung the door wide.

"You!" he said, pointing at Lowell. "Outside."

"What? Where are you taking me?"

"We're short on guard duty, you'll take a place on the wall."

"Me! But I am no soldier."

"You can keep watch can't you?" growled Denton. "That's all that's needed. Can't keep losing men like we do; you'll have to spend a term up there. Just holler out if you see anything. Now come on, get up."

Resentfully, Lowell climbed to his feet. "I don't see why I have to fulfill this task, I am a civilian after all."

"You're a prisoner on army property," sneered Denton. "And here you'll do what I tell you." Roughly he caught hold of Lowell's arm and cuffed him about the head. "Now get up the ladder and stand your watch or I'll beat the living daylights out of you."

"Leave him be, Sergeant," said Audebourn. "Take me; I'm a serving soldier. It's proper I take a place."

"You shut your mouth, Captain. The colonel sees

you up there on his pretty fort, smelling like shit and looking like a beggar and he won't like it one bit. No, you sit here with that other asshole snoring in the bed and share your stink with him."

# CHAPTER SEVEN

Lowell shivered on the fire step.

It was cold and he huddled in the shadow of the rough-hewn timbers that marked the parapet walkway. The jagged teeth of the wooden palisade ran away from him and the dark night was doubled in gloom by the ascending walls of the valley that surrounded the fort on all sides.

Lowell burrowed down against the chill wind that blew along the valley and crested the high walls to sweep down into the courtyard below. It was too cold to sleep and restlessly Lowell patrolled up and down hopping with difficulty thanks to the chains still linking his feet by the heavy manacles around each ankle.

He felt sorely alone; the rest of the fort was asleep and not a light showed anywhere. At every sound he cringed, expecting some arrow or bullet to wing out of the darkness from the overhanging cliffs and strike him.

But he was not alone.

A shadow flitted and Lowell spun around, his heart beating fast in his chest.

"Who goes there?" he asked, considering that under the circumstances, the military charge was to be the right course of action.

"Nobody, soldier," slurred a voice. "Nobody but the night."

"Colonel!" gasped Lowell, recognizing the swaying figure of Bendix.

"How loyal you are, stalwart sentry," announced Bendix. "Bravely keeping the watch and all the rest of us safe. I bow to you in respect."

He attempted drunkenly to do just that and almost tumbled into the courtyard far below but for Lowell's saving arm.

"Thank you, thank you," blurred Bendix. "A little under the weather. A touch heavy on the after-dinner liqueur."

Lowell could smell the distillery stink coming off the man every time he opened his mouth.

"A beautiful fort, don't you think?" asked Bendix, drawing a deep breath, and recovering his balance. "I built it myself, you know? I love this fort, it's mine, all mine. You see?" he swayed forward holding a wagging finger in Lowell's face. "My father is rich. Did you know that? Rich as Croesus and everything he owns is his and he continually reminds me of it. *This is mine, that is mine,* that is what he says always reminding me that I would have nothing without his damned generosity. But this..." Bendix reached out a wavering hand and patted one of the timbers. "This, this is mine alone. Built it with my own hands, y'know?"

"Very impressive," Lowell said, thinking diplomacy the best way to handle things. "A staggering achievement."

" *'Staggering achievement',* I like that. Yes, it is, isn't it? Not many people could build such an edifice out here in the wild, not many at all. You're a perceptive fellow," he leaned nearer to Lowell until their noses were almost touching. "Don't know you, do I? What's your name, fellow?"

Lowell started back as the rank blast of hundred-proof liquor blew in his face.

"Lowell Devereux, sir."

"Ah, yes, Debbabow. I'll remember that, perceptive fellow like you deserves some rank. Not enough people here quite grasp the difficulties of command. Nice to meet a kindred spirit. Well done, Debbabow."

Bendix started to slide sideways, and Lowell had to reach out and steady him again.

"Oops!" said Bendix. "Suppose I should head for my bunk now. But it's lonely, you know? She won't let me share my own bed; have to sleep on the couch. Blasted woman. Looks like an angel but acts like the devil, wouldn't believe it would you?"

"*No, I wouldn't,*" replied Lowell in an offended tone.

"But she is," stressed Bendix. "A harridan, a regular witch, I assure you."

"I find that hard to believe, sir."

"Most folks do, Bennadone. Most folks do."

"It's Devereux, sir."

"Of course, of course it is. Look, I wonder if you

could give me a hand?" Bendix burped softly. "Don't know if I can manage that ladder again."

"I'll do my best, Colonel. But these chains, you see…"

"*Chains!* Chains? What on earth are you doing in chains? Bright fellow like you keeping the watch should have freedom of movement. What would you do if a horde of savages came down on us? For heaven's sake, take those things off, Debennoh."

"I would if I could, sir. But I'm afraid it is under your order that I wear them."

"Ahh! Been a naughty boy, have you?"

"It was considered so."

"Well, have no fear, we'll have them off you soonest, don't you worry. Need men like you. It was probably that Sergeant Denton, wasn't it? You know, he spies on me. I'm sure my father set him up to it. Silly beggar thinks I don't know, but I know," Bendix rubbed the inside of his nose. "Not as stupid as they think, I know what goes on."

They were staggering a path to the end of the walkway where the ladder rested, with Lowell taking one of the colonel's arms over his shoulder. It was not easy in the dark what with Bendix swaying unsteadily and Lowell struggling with the officer's weight and the strictures of the short chain between his feet.

"There we are," said Bendix, reaching out shaking fingers for the head of the ladder. "Not to worry, I can make it myself now. Goodnight and bless you, Hexadrome."

With that, Bendix drew himself up straight to a

shaky pose of attention and gave a wavering salute. Then the colonel, promptly and straight as a rod, fell over backwards and sailed away out of sight into the darkness.

Lowell heard the colonel utter a soft, "Oops!" on the way down before a resounding thump followed and then silence.

"Colonel!" Lowell called after him. "Are you all right?"

There was no sound from below.

"Colonel Bendix?" Lowell repeated loudly. "Sir, is everything okay?"

There was only the rushing sound of the wind in the valley in response.

"Oh dear," muttered Lowell. "*Help!*" he called. "The colonel has fallen. Is anyone there? *Help!*"

It was Sergeant Denton who eventually answered the call of alarm. He came onto the courtyard carrying a lantern and dressed untidily in his shirt and uniform pants with his suspenders hanging down behind.

"What's going on?" he bawled up at Lowell.

"Look there below," said Lowell, leaning over the edge of the parapet. "It's the colonel, he took a tumble."

"He did what..." said Denton, a distressed look crossing his face.

The yard was filling with other soldiers now, many of them armed and carrying lanterns.

"Can you see him?" Lowell asked. "He fell straight off the edge."

Denton had dropped to his knees over the

spread-eagled body of the colonel who lay awkwardly in the pool of light from the lanterns.

"Oh no!" he cried. "Colonel dear, what have you done?"

"He's finished," one of the soldiers said. "Looks like he broke his danged neck."

"No, no!" wailed Denton, taking the colonel's body up in his arms as tears dripped from his face. "My precious, my dear boy."

All the men were looking awkwardly at each other over the normally hard-nosed sergeant's weeping so affectedly.

Tearfully, Denton looked up at Lowell's pale face staring down at him, "You did this, didn't you?" he roared accusingly. "You killed my colonel. Pushed him over the edge, you little bastard. Some of you men get up there and bring that swine down here. *Murder!* That's what this is, bloody murder. I'll have you hung for this, you little pox-ridden coward."

Plaintively, Lowell tried to explain but men were already noisily mounting the ladder.

"Tomorrow early," Denton cried in an apoplexy of vengeful anger and loss. "I want the entire command on parade, everybody here will witness this dog hung by his scrawny neck. You hear me? All of you, out here dressed in your best and bring a length of rope with you." He looked down at the sad bundle in his arms. "Now, some of you help me carry my dear colonel. But handle him gently, tenderly, you hear, or I'll rip your damned heads off!"

When Jack was rousted from his bed next morning, he had no notion of what was happening. His sleep had been deep and profound, in fact it was the best sleep he had in his entire life. Jack put it down to his newly found religion and the clarity of soul he felt as a result.

So it was that in something of a haze that he was hustled out onto the parade ground with the rest of the fort's company.

"What's going on?" he blurrily asked Audebourn, who stood still chained alongside him.

"They're about to hang your partner."

That woke Jack up with a start.

The complete company of the fort stood stiffly on parade, all the forty infantrymen and twenty-five cavalry that made up the complete roll call were present. They stood at silent attention on the parade ground before the flag with only the peripheral service attendants, the cooks, farriers, blacksmith and sutler's personnel watching from the side.

Denton strutted impatiently in front of the administration building waiting for the troops to form up. Whilst behind him, barely visible in the porch shadow cast by the early sun sat Ariadne. She sat quietly with obvious poise, dressed completely in black, her silken hair hanging down and a veil covering her face whilst her hands rested passively cupped on her lap.

She was the picture of a grieving widow and yet somehow managed to look attractively elegant in her simple dress and there was not a man on the parade ground that did not wonder in passing at the splendid form that lay under that dress. It was not any overt display of sexuality on her part but somehow the woman just could not be anywhere without naturally drawing men's eyes to her.

Jack's one good eye roved over the congregation until he spotted Lowell being held in the firm grasp of two sturdy soldiers. They had obviously been mistreating Lowell as one of his eyes was blacked and his lower lips split.

"You all know why we're here," Denton bellowed, his voice echoing around the parade ground. "Last night, this foul wretch here, Lowell Devereux, did to death our beloved colonel. I served with Bertran Bendix for many a-year and never found a better man, his poor widow who you see sitting there, never had a better and more attentive husband. Colonel Bendix liked a drink, we all know that, but it never impaired his judgment or gave cause for complaint."

"That a fact?" mumbled Jack wryly.

"It is our finding," Denton continued, "that late last night in the early hours…"

He was interrupted by a cry of pain and all heads turned to see a cloud of dust rise over by the main gate as the gate lookout stationed there received a feathered spear in the chest and tumbled down dead from his post.

"Attention! Face front!" roared Denton. "No more interruptions! It's unfortunate the renegades keep nailing us as we stand watch but that's life in the army. No point complaining, we all got to do our duty. Now, where was I? Yes, late last night this dastardly fellow crept up on the commander as he patrolled the parapet seeing that all was well with those in his care. The coward took brave Colonel Bendix from the rear and cast him down from the walls," Denton's voice broke as he imagined this fantasy as some kind of reality. "Killed him," he sobbed. "Killed him stone dead and left a grieving wife without a loving husband."

All eyes turned to look at Ariadne who made no move but continued to gaze downwards at her hands.

"Now we come to punishment!" bawled Denton.

The company's heads rotated to look upon the sorry Lowell, who hung beaten but with a gleam of anger in his eyes.

"I did nothing," Lowell called out in a cracked voice. "He was drunk, and he fell."

"The prisoner will be silent!" Denton roared over Lowell's plea. "Sentence will be carried out; the charge is murder and the punishment death by garrote."

A glow was beginning to form in Jack's eye as a large and heavy, flat board was trundled out into the compound. The board was fashioned at a man's height with a hole bored through approximately where the neck would be, a loose loop of rope hung through the opening, both ends of the rope tied off at the back with wooden handles. With the victim's head passed through the loop, the rope would be placed about his neck and twisted from behind until the sufferer was slowly strangled to death.

"Bring the prisoner forward," Denton ordered.

The rolling sound of thunder rumbled distantly over the mountains as Audebourn whispered to

Jack, "This is obscene, that ass has no right to do this without due legal process."

"Guess he thinks he's law unto himself," Jack replied. "'Bout to find out he ain't the only one that thinks like that."

The sky was darkening as gloomy clouds came out of nowhere and swept across the blue sky with an ominous darkness that blanketed the parade ground.

Lowell made a fight of it, struggling hard as he was carried towards the standing board, but he was not able to free himself from the two strong servicemen that dragged him. Binding Lowell's frail body with his back against the board, Denton placed the loop of rope over his head and around his neck.

"There y'are, sucker," he breathed spitefully into Lowell's face. "This one is for the colonel."

Denton nodded at one of the big men behind and the fellow stripped off his jacket and rolled up his sleeves showing the bulging muscles and rippling sinew underneath.

"*Say, snot-nose!*" interrupted Jack in a loud voice. "Those stripes on your arm where you wipe it?"

There was a stunned silence in the parade ground as all eyes turned to look at the tall figure of Coffin Jack. Lightning cracked in a jagged flash above the heights overlooking the fort and the resounding boom of following thunder filled the courtyard with an electric stench not unlike that of brimstone smoldering.

"What you say?" growled Denton.

"You still up for it? Your offer still stand?"

"What offer?"

"To take me on man-to-man or has your girly love affair with your colonel got the better of you?"

Denton fumed, "Anytime, anywhere."

"Okay, right now, right here," Jack answered, his good eye glowing a deeper orange color. "You got the advantage. I got these chains on and it should be easy for you."

"Later," said Denton. "When we've seen to this yellow dog of yours."

"No! Now, sissy boy. I beat you he walks. You beat me you get to do your worst. That won't happen but I have to offer a fool like you something."

Denton studied him a long moment as the skies darkened and the clouds rolled lower.

"You're on," said Denton, unbuttoning his jacket. "Company will form a square."

The ranked soldiers dutifully shuffled into position their eyes gleaming with the prospect of a good fight.

"Just a minute!" shouted Audebourn. "This is all most unethical."

"Be quiet, Captain," snapped Denton. "You'll get yours soon enough."

Jack tossed off his hat and ragged cloak and the two men squared off in the tight square of watching soldiery.

Denton hunched his shoulders and bunched his fist, taking up the pose of a barrack room brawler and he sloped around Jack in a slow sideways moving circle. With chin lowered, Denton peered up from under his heavy brows, his face locked into a grimace of meanness as he stared at his opponent.

"Going to make you crawl the rest of your days," he promised. "You won't never walk right again. Gonna break your back and crack your skull so hard you won't think straight never no more."

"Oh, please," said Jack off-handedly. "Spare me."

Denton waltzed in, gliding easily on his feet as he delivered a testing jab. The blow ended a few inches from Jack's nose as Jack swiftly moved his head back out of range.

"Best you can do, pussy willow?" Jack said, a slight grin creasing his weathered lips.

Angrily, Denton moved in fast, his arms flying in a whirling panoply of blows. Jack took them all, seemingly unmoved by the impact as he sought for a moment of exposure. He found it finally under Denton's raised arm and delivered a tremendous punch from a fist as hard as iron that sunk into the sergeant's ribs. Denton gasped and folded to one side, a momentary look of surprise in his eyes.

"Yeah, didn't think it could happen, did you?" grinned Jack evilly.

Denton lumbered in again only this time Jack popped him straight-armed neatly on the forehead and the sergeant's head rocked back. Jack came on relentlessly now as Denton blinked back the stars filling his stunned eyes.

Jack picked his blows, delivering solid repetitive punches from bone-hard fists. A cross to the jaw, a hefty uppercut to the gut followed by a swinging roundhouse that sent a spill of blood streaming from Denton's mouth. Jack did not let up and the dazed Denton could see the one eye staring wide at him as it changed color from deep orange to bright yellow light whilst the angry fuel that lay within Jack was fed. He was rising fast into a killing mode.

Jack smacked a resounding hit that raised a welt and split the skin over Denton's eyebrow; blood poured down and Jack continued without pause. Heavy hits one after the other turned the sergeant into a rag doll, his knees buckled but Jack held him upright with one hand as he continued to rain blows into the beaten man's face.

In desperation, Denton, his ruined features a mass of blood and cut flesh, dived forward and clutched onto Jack's waist dragging at him with his full weight. Jack let him come, rolling to the ground and over onto his back and then bringing up his legs and crossing them over so that the chains between his ankles locked around Denton's throat.

Jack tightened the grip and Denton gagged, clutching at the strangling chains with both hands.

"Let's see how you like a spot of garroting now, mister," growled Jack.

Denton's lips parted and his eyes rolled up, his bloody face beginning to turn a pale shade of blue.

"*Enough!*" roared Audebourn sharply. "You men, pull them apart before we have a murder here."

There was a moment of indecision amongst the troops before authority took hold and the soldiers bounded forward to separate the struggling men.

Jack shook them off easily and stood up by himself. He towered over Denton a moment and watched the beaten man begin to crawl off unsteadily, leaving a trail of blood in the dust behind him.

"As senior officer remaining here," Audebourn called out, "I now take command of this fort. Some of you men see to the sergeant. Blacksmith, over here! Strike off these chains and somebody release that man from the board there. We will have order in this command from now on, is that understood?"

Obediently, almost gladly it seemed, the men moved to obey and Audebourn drew himself up to his full height. "The command will be departing this post forthwith and the remaining fittings will be razed to the ground," he called out loudly. "The entire situation will be moved to a more secure location. Original plans placed it some miles distant with good visibility, nearer to water and the main trade road, that will now be accomplished under my command."

There was a ragged cheer from the gathered men and a general lifting of heart as not only the escape from the death trap of a fort was promised but also a true officer once again took command and the false rule of Bendix and Denton was overthrown.

Ariadne finally raised her head from her silent vigil as she heard Audebourn's proud call and she studied him for a long assessing moment.

As Jack had the chains knocked from his feet by the blacksmith, men came up and slapped him on the back and shook his hand. Most of them grateful and only too glad that Bendix was gone, and Denton had received his just desserts.

Lowell sidled up to him. "Once again you have

saved me, Mister Jack. I must thank you."

Jack eyed him ruefully. "Getting to be a regular habit, ain't it?"

Lowell looked up at the gray bed of overhanging cloud and wondered if it signified a shift in Jack's religious persuasion.

"I shall purchase our supplies from the store," he said.

"You do that," said Jack, a slow frown creasing his brow as he watched the journalist walk away.

"How will you book this down, Captain?" asked Jack, as he leaned over from the saddle and took the officer's hand in farewell.

The captain, now resplendent in clean uniform, freshly shaved and bathed and looking every bit the part of a genuine officer again, smiled. "I think it probably went exactly as Mister Devereux said it did, the colonel fell whilst intoxicated," Audebourn replied. "I shall make report of it so."

"And what about that pesky sergeant?"

"He has fled, I fear. Deserted with a few of his cronies, doubtless he saw how the wind was blowing and took off before he could face charges. But I expect he will be found and brought to justice before too long."

The fort was already packing up and men were busily moving about around them as belongings and equipment were packed into a series of wagons ready for departure. Bales of firewood were being stacked ready for the final demolition of the ill-favored place and a general atmosphere of relief filled the air.

"Well, luck to you," said Jack, looking over his shoulder at the sad figure of Lowell sitting his mule dolefully behind him. "Come on, scribbler. Let's be on our way."

Lowell made his farewells with the captain, and with a subdued air of defeat that he could not quite throw off; he took station behind Jack as they headed for the gateway out of the fort.

They were almost through when a strange event took place.

Ariadne still in her black widow's weeds came running up and hurried alongside them, her face a picture of concerned desperation.

She took hold of Jack's stirrup and clung on. "Mister Jack," she begged, "a moment please."

Jack pulled to a halt and leaned over the saddle horn, his head tilted a mite imperiously as he looked down at the woman.

"Will you take me with you, sir?" she pleaded, her beautiful face full of yearning. "There is nothing for me here any longer and I would leave this place. I beg of you, will you carry me off?"

For any other man it would have been an irresistible request, but Jack only stared back at her coolly.

"You think I don't know what you is?" he asked her.

She stepped back a pace, her luscious lips parted in a surprised gasp as if she had just received a slap.

"What can you mean?" she asked.

"You're one of those creatures that cling to a body like a poison vine," Jack went on. "You suck the sap from a man, girl. I see you for what you are, there ain't no good in you. You move on, as insidious as a snake worming from man to man, taking what you can, feeding off of them until you've had your fill and they can't give you no more. Then you make out with another."

Lowell gaped open mouthed at Jack's cold assessment of the angelic woman and then he noted that Ariadne's features were altering. There was a hardness coming into her features, the soft eyes that always held so much soft promise had bulged and turned a more brittle ice-cold shade of blue. The jaw had tightened, and the taut muscles turned the mellow lines of her features into a square rock-hard semblance of its former self.

"You think so?" she snapped spitefully. The gentle softness of the tone that Lowell remembered so fondly becoming a rasping husk more reminiscent of stone grating on stone.

"I know so," said Jack harshly. "Don't you come begging your way with me; you ain't no more than a leech on all menfolk, lady. It's a nice disguise you hide under there, real pretty. But you're a right witch really, ain't you?"

Ariadne's lip trembled and her limbs quivered, shocking Lowell as he watched the transfiguration take place. Her body straightened rigidly, the head rising from an extended neck and as if by magic the once magnificently fetching features distorted into an angry and malicious parody of its former self.

"Then you should know," she whispered intently. "That there is little left of love in this world for you anymore, Coffin Jack. And I shall now take from you all that there is."

She held one hand out towards him, the palm cupped and from a distance anyone observing would think that she was merely pleading with him. Lowell watched in awe as Jack suddenly bent forward from the waist as if he had been sharply jabbed in the side. Then with an audible sigh, Jack dug in his spurs hard and Nameless squealed at the stab and leapt forward as they rode away fast.

Ariadne stood a moment watching Jack depart, her arm still outstretched, hanging in the air as if in either a gesture of supplication or as if she held the bud of a small flower in her palm and then she closed a tight fist over it before sobbing with a sudden show of tears and collapsing to her knees in the dust of the gateway.

In one swift motion her real self was hidden, and she returned to the former vulnerable image she more commonly projected.

"Oh, my Lord!" breathed Lowell as he took in the transfiguration and rode past her following Jack. He glanced back over his shoulder as he left and saw Captain Audebourn come running up to kneel beside the saddened woman and place a comforting arm around her heaving shoulders.

Lowell wanted to call out and warn the captain, but he knew it would be to no avail, he would not be believed. He knew from his own experience how Ariadne's power over men was totally bewitching and he thought how sad it was that whatever might be said, the captain, poor fellow, was already doomed.

# CHAPTER EIGHT

Things were not going well between Lowell and Coffin Jack.

With the storm clouds following them full of the rumbling thunder that rode with it, Lowell knew that something had altered in his travelling companion. Darkness encompassed him and his dour presence seemed to be beset by the same miserable gloom that had surrounded Jack when they had first met.

He spoke little to Lowell other than monosyllabic grunts and the sourness was evident between them.

When they camped that night, Lowell determined to have it out with him.

"May I ask what distresses you so, Mister Jack?" he asked across the campfire, where Jack sat glowering at him from under his hat brim.

"It's you," growled Jack abruptly.

"How so?"

"I'm getting kinda tired of hauling your ass out of trouble."

"Well, I freely admit that I in no way match your expertise as a man of action, Mister Jack, but I thought my purpose was merely to serve as some kind of verbal interpreter if you should need."

"It's bugging me, is all."

"I'm sorry," said Lowell, somewhat at a loss for words.

"Think it's time to split the blanket and part ways," added Jack, his face turning way, the firelight flickering on the downturned lips and rigid jaw.

"If that's what you want, of course then we shall. But may I ask what has brought this on, apart from my failure as a steadfast companion. Does it have something to with what happened at the fort?"

Lowell was thinking of the strange actions of Ariadne and the almost supernatural effect of her parting shot on Coffin Jack.

Jack sniffed indifferently. "It's going to be different now," was all he said. "I got work to do and it ain't something you're up to, that's all."

"I only wish to observe."

"Look, boy. I can't do what I have to and be always considering you. There'll be some killing involved, you understand? Might be it gets tricky, it's better I handle it alone."

"I see. Well, I shall be mighty sorry to leave but if that's what you wish."

With that, Lowell turned away and pulled his blanket over him. He was disappointed but he could see that there was no use in pursuing the matter. Something had happened between Jack and the woman Ariadne, something he did not quite understand but it was obvious that the previous sense of new found gladness that Jack had engaged in had been taken from him and he was fast returning to the cold and heartless self he had once occupied.

When he awoke next morning, Lowell found the fire gone out and Jack nowhere to be seen. He had left silently in the early hours, and looking across the smoldering ashes of the campfire at the empty space his companion had occupied, Lowell felt a wave of emptiness at the loss of Jack's company.

He stood up with the blanket wrapped around his shoulders and wondered what he should do now. The prospect of returning to his former tasks and of even thinking about Miss Beatrice, whom he could no longer consider in any sort of relationship due to all that he had been through, left him with a serious blank space in his future.

Lowell went to recover his notebook from his saddlebags and with some surprise he noted that Jack had left him a revolver. A spare gun and obviously left as one final act of generosity as Jack departed, to leave Lowell with some means of protection now he himself was gone. Lowell took his notebook and crouched down beside the dying embers, determined to try and rediscover some of his earlier purpose. As he thumbed through the pages of the notebook and recounted his adventures since starting up with Jack, slowly a new resolve formed in him. He saw no reason he should leave off. Just because Jack wanted it otherwise, he could still follow at a distance and log the events of Jack's passing. There was no reason for them to meet up again, but he could see that his record would not be complete as it was. Some kind of resolution was necessary, not only for himself but also for the story he was reporting.

If he could have admitted it to himself openly, somewhere deep inside there was another reason for continuing. Despite the awful things he had seen and experienced and the fact that he had killed a man in the process, Lowell knew a new kind of excitement and it was that thrill that secretly lured him into making a rational excuse for taking up Jack's trail.

They had camped that previous night on a high rocky outcrop situated at the side of a mountain slope and the ledge gave a decent view off into the distance. Lowell peered at the land below his vantage point that stretched away across an open plain to a further range of hills. Distantly, making their way towards those hills Lowell could see the rolling storm clouds that now marked Jack's passage again and he knew his erstwhile companion would be easy to track.

With a new determination, Lowell packed up the camp, mounted his mule and set off down the slope to the plain below.

It took him three hours to catch up and when he did it was to arrive in the middle of a disturbing situation.

It was the whickering of horses, the smell of wood smoke and the sounds of unruly laughter that warned him somebody was ahead. Having learnt some caution whilst in his dealings with Jack and not wanting to run into the Deathdealer again unannounced, Lowell dismounted and made his way forward cautiously on foot.

He came over a rise that overlooked a shallow valley and there below him on a boulder-strewn floor he saw three men crouched around a blazing fire. They were passing a bottle around and obviously enjoying themselves. One of the men looked the worse for wear, his face a mass of yellow bruises and scabbed cuts and with a sinking heart Lowell recognized the beaten features of the deserter Sergeant Denton.

Beyond the three stood their ponies tied off to a line set between some scrub bushes and there between the fire and the ponies and stretched out on a open patch of ground lay a half-naked figure spread-eagled and staked out.

It was Coffin Jack that lay with his wrists and ankles bound tightly to wooden stakes. He had been laid out star shaped, and the clothes ripped from his body leaving his modesty intact only by the ragged pair of Long John pants he wore.

Denton was standing over Jack and nudging him in the side with his boot.

"Come on, sucker," he snarled. "Get ready to play? It's time for you to wake up." He turned to the others who were sharing their almost empty bottle of whisky, both of them still dressed in the jackets and pale blue pants of their army uniform. "Hey!" called Denton. "Bring some water over, slap it on this fool.

I want him wide awake when we go to work."

Jack was groaning and rolling his head from side to side and Lowell could see a streak of blood coursing down one side of his face where he had been cracked on the head. It was apparent that he had been ambushed and a vengeful Denton was about to have some payback for the mistreatment he had received at Jack's hands.

One of the deserters lumbered to his feet with a canteen in his hand and strolled over to the sprawled body of Coffin Jack.

"Why waste good water?" he asked tossing aside the canteen and unbuttoning his fly. "I'm going to piss him awake."

"Murphy," chuckled Denton, watching his partner unbutton. "That is one damned good idea,"

"Come on over here, Smithy. Get your pecker out and join the flood."

The other trooper cackled a rusty laugh of agreement, stood up a little unsteadily and weaved his way over to join the others. Together they all released a stream of steaming urine over the supine figure that twisted uncomfortably under the impact as it was sprayed.

"Yeah, there, and there too," laughed Denton, working his way up Jack's chest. "Boy, that liquor sure gives you a bladder full, don't it?"

Lowell smelt the rank odor clear across to where he lay hidden and he wrinkled his nose in distaste. It rankled him even after their falling out that they should treat Jack so disrespectfully, and he wondered how they had managed to take the usually careful Jack so successfully by surprise. With a determined twist to his lips Lowell worked his way back to the pony and eased out the revolver Jack had left with him.

"You with us now?" sneered Denton, leaning over Jack who was blinking himself awake.

"You bastards pissing on me?" growled Jack.

"Yeah, hotshot. About all you're worth. Latrine placement, that's what we call it in the army," sneered the man named Murphy.

Jack was struggling with his bonds, wrenching, and twisting against the ropes that bound him. But they were good and strong and despite his mighty strength the bindings would not shift.

"You ever seen a branding, Jack?" asked Denton. "No? Well you're going to see one right now. Smithy, go fetch it from the fire."

Still staggering, the drunken Smithy made his way to the blazing fire and by the use of two stout sticks worked a glowing horseshoe from out of the midst of the embers and looped it over the end of one of the sticks. Lowell smelt the wooden staff smoldering under the red-hot metal, the hook of the horseshoe running with golden sparks along its scarlet rim as it charred the stick.

"Bring it quick," said Denton, his battered face creasing into a spiteful smile. "I want to see this. Oh boy, Jack! You just don't know how bad I been wanting to do something like this to you since the fort. You just don't know."

"Come on," urged Murphy excitedly. "Drop the damned thing on him."

With concentrated perversity, Smithy, almost tenderly, slid the smoldering bright red horseshoe along the length of stick.

"Here we go, you ready, big boy?" he chuckled.

Lowell saw Jack grit his teeth, his good eye going as red as the color of the glowing horseshoe.

"I'll spit on your graves, you sonsabitches," he cursed.

"There you are," said Smithy, allowing the burning metal to slide free and drop onto Jack's bare chest.

There was a hiss and rising steam as Jack bucked under the impact. He howled in pain and twisted his body violently until the shoe slid free leaving a blackened ridge of burnt flesh in its passage.

"Oh, wow!" cried Denton. "That sure hit the spot, didn't it Jack? I think you need a matching one on the other side. Fetch it up Smithy, let's go again."

They were drunkenly chasing the horseshoe around with sticks trying to pick it up again and avoid burning themselves when Lowell got the first one in his sights. With lips tightly compressed, he held the pistol that Jack had left him in both hands and fired.

The great jarring spray of blood that flew out in a cloud from Murphy's head sent the trooper spinning away sideways and brought the other two around in shocked surprise.

"What the devil?" cried Smithy a second before Lowell's next shot hit him full in the upper chest and sent him cartwheeling over to fall across the fire in a blaze of sparks and roll to the other side and lie still with his clothes ablaze.

Denton raised pleading hands as his partners fell, "Don't shoot, I surrender! Whoever the hell you are, don't shoot," he begged.

Without pause and almost lost in a mesmerizing dream of the shooting, as if he could not stop even if he had wanted to, Lowell fired again and then again.

Denton bucked under the impact of the shells, each one slamming him around at an awkward angle. He staggered and walked a few steps in a lopsided fashion trying to move away but Lowell climbed to his feet and stood in full view aiming down the barrel with care.

"Don't!" begged Denton, his swollen and bruised face turning pitifully towards Lowell.

Then, almost of its own accord it seemed, the gun bucked in Lowell's hand and the front of Denton's forehead disappeared under an explosive eruption of blood and brains. The sergeant dropped instantly; one hand raised in a final twitching appeal for pity.

With a shuddering breath, Lowell lowered the smoking gun. His throat was dry, and his head swam with the battering sound of the gun still ringing around in his ears.

"Goddamn it!" snorted Jack in awe. "*Goddamn it!*"

In tottering steps, Lowell made his way down to where Jack was stretched, and plunked down beside him, the smoking pistol still held forgotten in his hand.

"Where'd you learn to shoot like that, boy?" asked Jack.

"I used to hunt bird with my daddy," mumbled Lowell numbly. "I always used a shotgun, but I guess it's not too different."

"Not if you hit what you aim at."

"I had to do it," said Lowell. "I could not abide what they were doing."

"I'm sure glad you did. Hellfire! I don't know how much more of that damned hot shoe I could take."

"Oh, Mister Jack," wailed Lowell, sinking his chin onto his chest. "I do fear what's happening to me."

"You saved my hide, young man. Look here, I reckon I misjudged you a whole lot, why you got more sand than most other men I met in my time. You just took on three men and laid them all low, that ain't no mean feat."

"It doesn't feel like that," said the woeful Lowell.

Jack arched a curious eyebrow in disbelief and shook his head in despair. "Say, I'm sorry to impose on you a little further at this touching moment but I got a question." He twisted his head to the side to look more closely at Lowell. "You reckon you could hoist a knife from one of those men there and cut me free?"

It seemed that harmony had been restored between them and although Jack continued with his same rueful attitude and Lowell followed in his own confused state, they later made their way on together again.

Finally, Lowell broke the silence.

"Oh, Mister Jack?"

"Hrmph!"

"How is that unpleasant burn on your chest?"

"Sore."

"Don't you think we'd best get it doctored? Some salve or something before it festers."

Jack grunted, "Makes sense."

"How far are we from this Doomesville? Maybe they have a doctor there."

"I reckon, we'll wait, it ain't far now."

Their approach to the town was marked at first sight by an extensive cemetery with a sign at the pine-pole gate advising that the occupants therein numbered three hundred and sixty-five. This number had been amended a number of times as was evident by the crossings out and multiple additions.

The graveyard was a bleak, flat, open field with wooden grave markers scattered around in a collective jumble that followed no pattern. A few bare trees stood around the perimeter, their leafless black branches occupied by an army of crows that fluttered unpleasantly and cawed noisily as they approached.

"Nice place," Lowell observed cynically.

"Dunno," said Jack, "I quite like it; good to see a burying ground with some character."

Lowell could not swear to it, but he was sure that ground amongst the tomb markers moved and rippled of its own accord as Jack passed by. But he then thought it must have been an illusion probably caused by the fading light.

They rode on until another rough sign introduced them to the town of Doomesville.

This one counted the population and started at six hundred and forty-three and went down from there before it became apparent by simple subtraction that all the alterations had ended up back at the cemetery.

The town where the remaining two hundred and seventy-eight lived was a collection of shacks laid out on the flat plain and beset in lonely isolation on the forlorn landscape.

The sky was lowering towards a crimson evening as they came in and a cold wind blew across the level land causing Lowell to raise the collar on his jacket. Dust and tumbleweed scurried along the empty streets and only the light from lamps in few windows showed that there was any life in the place at all.

"What a destitute place," observed Lowell.

"Yeah, it's real good ain't it? Makes me feel right at home."

"Mister Jack, how can you possibly find delight in such a bare and grim township?"

Jack shrugged. "My kind of style, I guess."

"Where might we find some information about a doctor, do you think? I see no shingles hanging."

"They ain't got many signs at all. Best try a drinking house if we can find it, bound to be one of them somewhere."

They did in fact soon find the saloon, a porch fronted plank-wood building where the dry timbers had turned gray and were cracked and curled from the sun. A dim light shone through the glass panel in the door proving someone was in residence and

Lowell looked up and read the panel sign above the door with some trepidation.

"The Abandoned Hope Saloon," it read, in hand scrawled paint.

Without hesitation, Jack dismounted and pushed open the rattling door and stepped inside.

It was a long and large single room, mostly lost in shadow. The floor was made from heavy wood boards that looked like railroad ties, and the bar along one side was a dark addition in black ebony. As also was the Negro bartender, a burly, big-shouldered man with a shiny bald head and suspicious eyes.

"What y'all want?" he asked brusquely.

Jack looked around and found only one other single customer in the place, an old man in ragged clothes sitting alone at one of the tables with a half-finished schooner of beer before him.

"Can see why you ain't got much custom in here," growled Jack, casting a beady eye at the bartender's abrupt greeting. "Sorry to disturb you."

"Now look," boomed the Negro bartender. "We don' want no trouble in h'yah."

"My dear sir," piped up Lowell. "Is this the way to treat regular custom? We have just travelled far and are in search of some respite and information, that is all. There is no need at all to take that tone with us."

The bartender rubbed his chin with a large hand. "You ain't with *him* then?" he asked.

"Depends on who *him* is," replied Jack.

"I guess you ain't," said the Negro in a somewhat

mollified tone. "You just passing through?"

"Can a body get a drink in here without a grilling?" asked Jack stomping up to the bar.

The barman apparently decided by a slow process of deduction that they meant no harm and his demeanor gradually changed. A broad smile cracked his black face and his eyes shone, "Sho' thing; name yo' pleasure."

"You *do* sell liquor apart from attitude, don't you?" asked Jack.

"Certainly, suh," grinned the Negro. "We got all kinds. We got red whisky and we got white whiskey and we got brown whiskey. Yo' take your pick. We also got supplies at back, if you need 'em. Running a special on a three-pack of chicken claws this week, best not miss it."

"Guess I'll just take a whiskey," said Jack in defeat.

"That the red, white, or brown variety, suh?"

"Just pour the damned stuff," snapped Jack.

"And yo' friend?"

"I'll take a small aperitif," said Lowell. "Have you such a thing as a sherry? Manzanilla preferably but Oloroso at a pinch."

"No, suh," replied the bartender with a dumbfounded look. "Don' have none of that, whatever it might be."

"Very well," sighed Lowell. "A glass of water then."

"Water's off."

"Dear Lord! What *do* you have then? No, don't tell me, I can guess. I'll just have a tipple the same as my companion here."

"You're Coffin Jack, ain't you?"

The voice came from behind them in a cracked rustle and Jack turned to study the old man with the beer.

"It speaks," Jack said. "And who wants to know?"

"They call me Ebenezer Bucket," creaked the old man. "I seen you take out sixteen Mexicans one time. Six of them with a Arkansas toothpick, most amazing damned thing I ever did see."

"That so?" mused Jack. "Can't say I recall that one."

"Yeah, it was down just outside of El Paso."

"Sorry," Jack shook his head, having forgotten the matter entirely.

"Tell me, Mister Bucket," asked Lowell. "Do you know of a place in this locality…"

"Been living here the best part of thirty years and some, son," the old man interrupted. "I guess I know most places around here."

"Yes, the n…"

"Why, I can remember when there weren't nothing around here but buffalo," the old fellow continued, his rheumy eyes taking on a faraway look. "Far as the eye could see, you could nail lunch with a slingshot they was that profuse."

"What we want…"

"And the air was cleaner, you know? Why, you could drink from any creek you found, pure fresh water. Ain't like that now, folks coming in spreading their muck around, despoiling things so bad you can't drink it no more. See here, everything around here is tainted, been that way even before *he* turned up."

"Ol' Mister Bucket do go on like this an awful lot once yo' get him started," confided the bartender as Ebenezer babbled on. "Now I reckon yo' gonna wish yo' din' wind him up an' get him goin'."

Whilst he waited for the ancient to draw breath, Lowell took a draught of the whiskey in his glass. He wished he had not. The liquor was a truly potent mix and it left Lowell gasping and speechless, so he considered it quite handy the decrepit old man was dribbling on, as it gave him time to recover his voice.

"Sky was clearer too," Ebenezer continued. "None of this miserable looking gray cloud like you see today. It's weird, I tell you. Used to be crystal clear, so bright you could see way off, all the way up to Anchorage in faraway Alaska, I swear it. I was up there one time; right nice it is too, clean. White snow, real pretty."

"You've been around an awful lot, sir," Lowell managed to get out, working around the raw effects of the alcohol. "But we only want to know where…"

Meanwhile, as Lowell struggled with communication of one sort or the other, Jack was paying little attention and solidly working his way through the bottle on the bar top.

"I'm Ahab Barnes," the bartender introduced, holding out a hand.

Jack glanced at the hand, then lifted the bottle and poured himself another glass, "Right," he said by way of greeting.

"Mister Barnes?" asked Lowell, giving up on the old man and leaning across the bar was at last relieved to find someone who actually drew breath between words. "Perhaps you can tell us where the Homely Crossing Spread is? We believe it is somewhere nearby off the Longspree Pike."

Ebenezer droned on in the background glad to hear the sound of his own voice and totally oblivious to the fact that no one else was paying him any attention.

"Sho' thing," said the Negro. "That would be up the road some, 'bout five mile outside of town. Y'all lookin' to go see Mister Carne?"

Jack wrinkled his nose and frowned. "Maybe we is and maybe we ain't. You got a sawbones around here?"

"Doc Lester," supplied Ahab. "Couple or two doors down, yo' can't miss it. It's the wooden house."

So are the other two hundred and seventy-seven, thought Lowell.

They paid up and left, Ebenezer still rambling and Ahab Barnes staring dreamily at nothing in particular. It was to Lowell as if they had drifted momentarily into a local reverie outside of time. Barely noticed, they came and left and the fugue state inside the saloon returned to its normal condition again.

Jack wiped his mouth on the back of his hand and eased himself up into the saddle. "Not a bad bottle they got there," he said. "Really cuts the stuff."

"You think so?" asked Lowell, still feeling the burning aftereffects of the firewater. "I believe I've known better."

"Yeah, but you're educated. For us poor folks, that is the cream-de-la-cream, you know?"

"It's nothing to do with education, Mister Jack. It's a matter of refinement and acquired tastes that's all."

They both rode the few yards to the doctor's door and dismounted.

"You suppose at least this sucker is in the land of the living?" asked Jack doubtfully as he rapped on the door.

Lowell looked up and down the deserted street and wondered himself if anything at all in the town was still conscious.

"Who is it?" snapped a voice from inside. "Ain't handling nothing but toothache and childbearing today."

"How about burns?" Jack called back.

Bolts slid and chains rattled behind the door. "Okay, burns we can do."

The door swung back to reveal a long pointy, red-tipped nose attached to sharp features on a small center-parted head of thin hair. Gold-rimmed spectacles hung from the nose that also supported a dewdrop hanging from the very end.

"Where you burnt?" asked the head with a voice like hard chalk scratching on a board.

Jack looked down and pointed a thumb at his chest, and then he observed "You got a drip on your nose."

The doctor's spectacles slowly travelled up Jack's full height. "And you are too big for your britches."

"You going to let us in?"

"Come on, come on," scratched the pinch-backed man. "I'm the local medical practitioner, you may address me as Doctor Herbert. M. Lester, follow me."

They followed the small hunchbacked man down a narrow corridor, and he ushered them into his surgery. It was a cluttered room, full of medical books and journals stacked to the ceiling and various physician's instruments; a stethoscope, listening trumpet, surgical shears and so on lying amongst the dusty piles. A rotating office chair sat before a knee-hole desk that was barely visible under the piles of paper that lay across its surface.

"Now then," said the doctor sitting down on the chair that squeaked in loud protest as he did so. "What seems to be the problem?"

Jack undid his shirt and pulled it back to reveal the nasty horseshoe shaped burn scarring his chest.

"Perhaps you have some ointment for this?" suggested Lowell politely.

"*You a doctor?*" snapped Lester, spinning around so fast on his chair to face Lowell that the drip from his nose flew across the room as he did so.

"No, sir, I am not."

"Then I would be glad if you would let a professional assess the ailment, make a diagnosis, and recommend the cure," sniffed the doctor pompously whilst running a shirt cuff under his weeping nose.

"Of course," said the admonished Lowell. "My apologies."

"No need for "sorry", can't abide dithering, speak your mind. Say it straight. I'm so used to people coming in here and avoiding the issue, it pains me." He began mincing a voice in imitation of a visiting client. "Doctor, I believe I have an ache in my foot, I don't think it can be anything serious... You wish, says I. One look and I can tell its gangrenous multiple fractures, have to come off, I tell them. Oh, no, they say, not the toe. No, damn it, says I, the whole blasted leg." He broke into a series of choking gasps that Lowell finally identified as laughter.

"Most reassuring," muttered Lowell under his breath.

Doc Lester peered down his nose at the burn, squeezing and pinching the skin around it. "Yes," he said finally. "Not bad, you'll need some ointment on it, that's all. Shoeing a horse, were you?"

"More like it was me getting shoed," answered Jack.

"Well, get yourself some bear or goose fat and slap that on, be right as rain in a couple of days. That'll be ten dollars."

"*Ten dollars!*" gasped Lowell. "Why, I could have made that kind of diagnosis myself for nothing."

"Then why didn't you?" replied Doc Lester sharply.

"I already did, and you told me I should let a professional take charge."

"Well, there you are," said Lester smugly. "Now you have my professional opinion. That'll be ten dollars."

"Doctor!" spat Lowell, slamming the door as they left. "More snot than sense."

# CHAPTER NINE

The long gray sheet of lowering sky followed them from town and through rolling fields of bleak scrubland that had all the inviting prospect of a never-ending windless ocean. The doldrums seemed to hover in the air itself and Lowell felt the uncomfortable weight of the oppressive atmosphere pressing in around him. Jack, meanwhile, rode on as jauntily as if he were looking forward to a festival hayride.

They came on the spread from the top of a long ridge that swept down to the ranch from a height that gave them clear view of the buildings and herds of cattle spread below.

The ranch house itself was a large, single-story property with wide corrals, open barns and bunkhouses. There was no hint of green anywhere, not a single tree or bush showed anywhere on the horizon and whatever it was that the cattle grazed on it was mean and there was little enough of it.

There was some activity in the corral fronting the ranch house and Coffin Jack and Lowell made their way down towards it.

The girl who was seated sidesaddle on the top bar of the corral fence was dressed in men's work denims rolled at the heel of her boots and a checkered woolen shirt open at the neck. Her shirt sleeves were rolled up to show bronzed arms that although slight looked strong and sinewy. A trim figure and there was no doubt she was well endowed as the cleft at her open necked shirt proved, but her honey-colored hair was thick and unruly and cut short at the nape. The girl's attention was firmly fixed on the corral where a group of Mexican vaqueros were breaking in a fiery mustang.

"Come on, boys!" she yelled. "Get that pony saddled and let's ride. Goddamn! I have to come in there and do it myself."

There was nothing raucous or masculine in her voice it was merely an urging for action from the rather poor-looking raggedy bunch of Mexicans scurrying around the bucking pony in the dusty yard.

"Ma'am," rumbled Jack, as they rode up.

The girl turned her attention away from the corral and studied them steadily.

"Good day, gentlemen," she said evenly.

"Coffin Jack and Lowell Devereux," Jack introduced, and Lowell raised his hat politely.

"Well, hi there. I'm Rita Bodey, how can I help?"

Her eyes glittered with a bright sparkle of interest, Lowell noticed, and her smile was broad and open, showing a row of even white teeth. Although there a touch of tomboy about her, she had pleasantly open features and was healthily put together. Not a tall person but compact and personable.

"Looking for a Mister Carne, I got business with him."

"Indeed," she said, dropping down lightly from the rail. "That will be my uncle, he's up at the main house just now," she inclined her head in the direction of the building. "You want to get on down and I'll have a boy care for your horses and take you up there myself."

Both men climbed down, and she had a young sombrero-hatted Mexican take the horses away as she led them up towards the house.

"You fellows come far?" she asked as they walked over.

"Some," grunted Jack evasively.

"Only ask as you might fancy refreshment," she explained not wanting them to think her too curious.

"That's most kind," said Lowell. "You have any tea, Miss Bodey?"

"Tea!" she smiled. "We don't have much call for that around here I'm afraid."

"No," said Lowell. "Well, just thought I'd ask."

"You a city boy?" Rita frowned.

"Does it show?" smiled Lowell in reply. "I started out as a newsman although I'm not quite sure what I am now."

Rita looked him over curiously at his statement of dilemma and then her brow cleared. "I guess this country can do that," she said.

"It certainly can," Lowell agreed.

She was not a stunningly beautiful woman but there was a reassuring freshness about her plain features and simple dress that Lowell admired.

"Old Lowell's got hidden depths," Jack rumbled enigmatically.

"I see," said Rita, a cheeky grin lighting her lips as she studied Lowell's dusty and stained bowler and his once pristine but no longer gray suit.

"I am afraid I appear somewhat in disrepair, Miss Bodey. A trying trip, I fear."

"No sweat, sir. This is rough country and well I know it. Come on up, it's through here." She opened the front door and ushered them inside.

They were confronted by a large living room, with hide-backed chairs and the walls hung with wide longhorn cattle horns and elk antlers and a dark-haired stuffed buffalo head at one end. Apart from the hunting trophies it was a pleasantly light and well-appointed room with tall glass-paned windows and a carpet covering the polished wood floor, with framed tin-type photographs stationed on side tables and book-laden shelves.

"Wait here if you will. I'll go get Uncle John."

As Jack went into his apparently vacant waiting mode in the middle of the room, Lowell took his time studying the books on the shelves.

"Hmm," he said, taking out his spectacles and reading the titles. "It does seem our Mister Carne is quite a well-read man."

A roll of thunder interrupted him as it came racing across the plains outside and shook the window-glass rattling the panes in the frames. Lowell looked around to see the darkening sky ripped by cloud and a peculiar rosy tint lighting the far horizon, he turned to comment on it but saw that Jack was already paying close attention. His single eye bugging and staring out of the window and Lowell noted the peculiar orange glow that emanated from within.

"What is it?" Lowell asked.

"Something's coming," Jack warned gloomily. "Something bad."

"Mister Coffin Jack! What an honor, sir."

They turned to see a strongly featured thickset man bounding energetically across the room, his hand outstretched in greeting. He took Jack's hand in his and bounced it up and down shaking it firmly.

"I am so glad you came. I have followed your impressive career for many a year and can only say my admiration is most high."

"That right?" mumbled Jack.

"'Deed it is, now, anything we can get you? Was it a long journey? My, but it's good to see you finally; there is so much to discuss." He was a man between fifty and sixty years but obviously still full of an energy that seemed to fill the room with eagerness.

"Uncle," advised Rita calmly from the door where she leaned casually with arms folded. "Won't you offer our guests a seat?"

"Of course, of course, how remiss. And you are?" he asked swiftly turning to Lowell.

"Lowell Devereux, at your service," said Lowell, removing his hat and offering a short tip of the head in recognition.

"Well, howdy-doo Mister Devereux; any friend of

Coffin Jack is most welcome here. Please, gentlemen, won't you be seated?"

Whilst Lowell was only too pleased to enjoy the civilized pleasure of polite company and relaxed easily, Jack sat perched on the edge of his chair, his head cocked to one side as he kept his eye fixed on the window.

"Don't concern yourself about the coming storm, Mister Jack," beamed Carne, patting Jack on the knee. "It is frequently with us and one of the problems I intend to discuss with you."

Jack dragged his attention away from the window. "You got something mean out there," he offered it as a statement rather than a question.

"We have indeed, sir," said Carne, suddenly serious. "Have you heard tell of a low creature going by the name of Ska Venger?"

Jack pouted, his brow furrowed in thought. "Rings a bell but I just can't hang a brand on it."

"Well, *he* is the problem."

"Can you elucidate further, Mister Carne?" Lowell asked.

Carne sat back and dropped his chin on his chest and steepled his fingers before his face.

"Ska Venger is the very hell of a man, and when I say *hell*, I mean just that. He came into this vicinity about four months ago. Some say he was a mountain man at one time and he certainly is big enough to have been just that. A great, ugly, hirsute fellow, broad in the body and mighty tall. Strong as an ox, well over six feet in height, more like seven I would say. Still wears buckskin and favors a long blade and an Indian tomahawk; never seen without them and I have to say he knows how to use them."

"This man been bugging you?" asked Jack.

Carne nodded. "Most sorely. He's either murdered, beaten or driven off my hands, I cannot get local men to work the ranch anymore and have to go below the border for staff. Don't get me wrong, the vaqueros are fine workers and cheap too, but I would like to have our own people here. However, Ska Venger has put paid to that with his murderous ways."

"He's a rustler then?"

"He is but he will kill more for the pure pleasure of it. I mean the cattle as well as the ranch hands. When he comes through here it's like a tornado just past, dead beef litter the fields. And cruelly taken, heads and limbs ripped off, by his bare hands I would not be surprised to discover. Murdered men lie with their chests cut open, hearts taken along with the liver. What he does with those I dread to think. The man is worse than any pestilence, it's like the very devil himself prowls the land."

"Can't you just posse up and hunt him down?"

"That is the strange thing," Rita interrupted. "He has some strange power of intuition and avoids capture all too easily."

"Strange power!" frowned Lowell. "What can you mean?"

"It is said," Carne went on, "that when a child he was stolen from his folks by Indians and taken under the wing of the tribe. They were Indians of a peculiar sect of the Aquackanok clan, some distant branch of the Delaware and Algonquin who claim descent from the original ancient cave dwellers in this country. A dark brood indeed, their own people call them "The Forbidden Ones" and avoid them at all costs. Suffice to say that the Indians purportedly raised Ska Venger as the child of the tribe's shaman who taught him their old secrets and many say their black arts as well. The story goes that the whole tribe were wiped out by the smallpox and he was saved by a Baptist missionary, who attempted to bring him up in the faith. Venger went a touch mad after that it seems. Being torn apart by the two cultures and not really wanting to be separated from the Aquackanok, finally it became too much and he broke away and made off on his own finding a solitary existence in the wilds where he practiced the weird rituals of his adopted parent until he was adept in their black arts."

"Sounds quite a charming soul," observed Lowell cynically.

"Oh, he's a weird one all right."

"So he travels alone?"

"Unfortunately, not any longer. There are four others that follow his evil ways. All of them wanted outcasts and renegades, just as murderous and low natured as their leader."

"You got a name for these fellows?"

"Not all men, I hasten to add. One is Venger's personal consort, a particularly venomous piece of work. A woman known as Vile Spider, who at one time used to be a tattooed lady in a burlesque show until she cut off her employer's vital parts when he made an unwelcome pass at her. They ride with a cunning half-breed Indian tracker called Phantom Dog and two others. Both men of a particularly despicable variety, Casper Lee Krome, a wanted villain and a Mexican fellow known only as Malodor."

"And you reckon he's heading your way right now?" asked Jack.

"That tainted color on the horizon indicates his presence nearby, but you will know full well when he is even closer. He makes no secret of his coming such is his arrogance. He rides a hand-built chariot of sorts, a cut down version of a buckboard with only two wheels remaining and a long tongue with four black horses harnessed to pull it. It is a truly terrible sight to see. This great beast of a man with his paramour alongside charging across the prairie, roaring like a lion, and waving his weapons overhead, it is a thing to freeze the heart, believe me."

"Somewhat excessively dramatic perhaps," advised Lowell.

"Scare you boys, does it?" asked a smiling Rita.

Jack shrugged noncommittally and Lowell quirked an unknowing lip.

"Well, gentlemen, there you have it. That is our problem, a testing challenge I assure you but one I believe you are up to given all I have heard," said Carne. "Are you prepared to help us out?"

"You tried the law, I take it?" asked Jack.

Carne harrumphed a dismissive laugh. "Didn't last a day. We called in the county marshal and the poor man was stripped naked and run through a thorn bush before they ran him off, fellow was lucky to get out alive."

"Sounds like a fitting contest, wouldn't you say, Jack?" asked Lowell.

"Hrmph!" was Jack's only reply.

"What say you fellows settle down here for the night and you can come back to us when you've made up your minds?" suggested Rita. "The bunkhouse suit you okay?"

The bunkhouse turned out to be a long and low-ceilinged log cabin with plain frame beds set up along each side. The eight Mexican ranch hands were grouped together at the far end around a pot-bellied stove and they all went silent as Jack and Lowell entered with their bedrolls.

"Who's the head honcho here?" growled Jack, sniffing the air and crinkling his nose in distaste.

The five men looked at Jack sullenly, one of them laid aside the guitar he had been strumming and the twang of the settled instrument reverberated loudly in the silence.

"Comprendez?" asked Jack irritably. "The big boy? The one who runs the shop?"

A slender, wiry figure unwound itself from one of the bunks. "That would be me, senor."

He was a sharp-faced fellow, the skin tanned a chocolate brown and creased and drawn tight on his features with deeply sunken eyes set in a gaunt face. Even so you could see the flakes of dirt on his neck, and a following ripe odor of unwashed socks and bodies permeated the room.

"And you are?" asked Jack.

"My name is Tomas, senor," the Mexican answered respectfully.

Jack turned slowly and looked up and down the hall, he could see that the Mexicans stuck together at the far end, their belongings scattered around their rumpled unmade beds.

"Well," said Jack. "Seeing as you and your buddies consider it unnecessary to commit yourselves to any ablutions and you all stink to high heaven, me and my partner will take the other end here to bunk down. If that's okay?"

"Excuse us, senor," said Tomas with an offhand shrug. "We are simple people. If we offend you, I am sorry, please take whatever empty place you prefer."

"You all speak English?"

"Only me, the others they do not speak so good."

"So what do you know about this Ska Venger guy?"

There was a hurried murmur of whispering at the name amongst the rest of the crew and it was apparent that they all understood that part of any English.

"This one is bad, senor," frowned Tomas, a touch of awe in his voice. "They say he comes from amongst the dead and carries death with him like a plague."

Jack looked a tad affronted at that and he turned to Lowell with a raised eyebrow, "Seems like I got competition," he observed.

"Please, senor," Tomas continued. "If Mister Carne has hired you to hunt down this man you would be better advised to leave now. Ska Venger is not a party to involve yourself with."

"You boys run into him, have you?"

Tomas shook his head, a faint shiver running down his thin body, "Thank God, we have not as yet. It is something I would not wish on my worst enemy. But I have seen his work, terrible things, senor. Cattle with their heads torn off by the roots and their intestines scattered like snake trails in rivers of blood. Not done for the meat, you understand, but only for the pleasure of the destruction."

"Pray tell me?" asked Lowell. "If you are all so terrified of this man, how is it you continue to work here?"

Tomas shrugged again. "We are poor people, senor. There is no work for us across the border and our families starve so we must come here and work the cattle for Mister Carne."

Jack sniffed the air with a show of distaste. "Well, Tomas, like it or not, you're a dirty little son-of-a-bitch so you and your buddies keep downwind of me and we'll get along just fine."

"They do say," Lowell added, not unaware of the fetid atmosphere that was as dense as a soggy bottom fog, "that cleanliness is next to godliness."

"It is strange, what you say," answered Tomas, his head cocked innocently to one side. "But neither I, nor my companions, can smell this thing you speak of. Are you sure you did not step in something on your way in and are bringing this unpleasant odor with you?"

"No, sir," rumbled Jack, striding off down the bunkhouse. "I know which way my nose points and rough though I am I don't carry no dead skunk stink around with me. This one is all yours."

Tomas shrugged again and turned to his companions and explained in rapid Spanish. The Mexicans sniggered and whispered to each other.

"My friends would like to know how you are called?" Tomas asked the rapidly disappearing two.

"That's Coffin Jack and I am Lowell Devereux," Lowell tossed over his shoulder.

This information evoked another bout of whispering amongst the Mexicans.

"We have heard of this man called Coffin Jack," Tomas called after them. "A man to fear, they say. So you have come for the one called Ska Venger?"

"You just go stick your head in a bucket," was all Jack would say. "And wash your feet while you're at it."

Throwing his bedroll down, Lowell turned to Jack and asked him quietly, "Well, what do you think?"

Jack peered at him. "About what? Them smelly critters up there?" he gave a nod in the direction of the Mexicans, who were watching them sourly from the far end.

"No, of course not. I mean this Ska Venger and party; they do sound a trifle worrying."

""Sounds" is a long way from "Being"."

"You think maybe there has been some exaggeration of their volatility from Mister Carne?"

Jack shrugged. "It don't make a heap of difference to me, they is what they is. Just a mark to go out and nail far as I'm concerned, that's all."

"So do you have a plan?"

"I just got here, Lowell. Get real, will you? So far I ain't seen hair nor hide of this fellow, maybe I'll get a "plan" when I know what we got here."

But Lowell's concerned brain was already racing with possibilities.

"Perhaps we should map out the surrounding terrain in preparation, don't you think? I believe that's what any military commander would do in such circumstances."

Jack settled himself on his bunk, crossed his boots one over the other and with a sigh tugged down the hat brim. "That's a real neat idea. Why don't you get that pretty farm gal to show you the sights? She seems right keen for your company."

"You think so?" asked Lowell, surprised to find he was quite pleased at the notion. "Maybe I will, perhaps tomorrow."

"Hrmph!" rumbled Jack.

Lowell looked off dreamily at nothing in particular. "Yes, Miss Rita does appear to be a pleasant young woman, doesn't she?"

Jack's only answer was a long rasping snore. He was already asleep.

# CHAPTER TEN

Lowell looked out over the pale sea of bleached bones that stretched out across the plain below them like the crests of frozen waves on a dead ocean.

"Two thousand head of cattle," Rita informed him. "That's all Ska Venger's work."

They sat side by side on their ponies on a small hillock and stared out at the miserable scene of wanton destruction.

"Seems most impractical," Lowell observed. "Surely theft is more profitable that plain murder."

Rita drew a long breath. "I wonder about that," she admitted. "I have a theory that Venger has some other motive than the simple enjoyment of massacre."

"Oh, yes?"

"I believe he's attempting to drive out the homesteaders and ranchers. Maybe he is mad but there's some kind of method in his madness. By culling the herds so viciously he will drive us all out of business, forcing us to quit the land."

"But why?" asked Lowell, looking around at the barren plain and dry and desolate countryside. "What is there here that he could possibly want?"

"I don't know," she confessed. "Wanton destruction just seems too shallow a reason for all this slaughter. There has to be another reason."

"You believe that he is perhaps in the pay of other forces?"

She shrugged. "It's a possibility."

"Have you studied on the inherent value of the land, mineral deposits and that kind of thing?"

"Not really," said Rita, her eyes reaching out over the skyline with blankness. "What could be of value out there? There's little enough even to keep the cattle alive as it is."

"I admit it does look something of a wasteland, yet who knows what might lie underneath."

Rita grinned. "You're thinking perhaps of a rich gold strike maybe?"

Lowell raised his eyebrows. "Who knows? Perhaps you had better check."

"A good thought, Mister Devereux. Doubtful but I shall look into it."

"Please, Miss Rita," Lowell faltered shyly. "I wish you would call me by my given name."

Rita cocked an eyebrow and looked at him speculatively then she smiled. "Of course, Lowell, and if you would do the same."

"My honor," gasped Lowell, his breast swelling with pleasure. "Rita."

"You really are a gentle soul, aren't you?" said Rita, still grinning.

"Oh, I don't know," replied the flustered Lowell.

"Now don't be offended, I like it," Rita went on. "Most of the cowhands around here can't cross a T and don't know how to dot their I's and have no idea how to talk to a lady. It's mighty refreshing to meet someone with a touch of refinement."

"Y… you really are m… most kind," stuttered an embarrassed Lowell. "I never would… I mean, I could never have hoped…"

"What? Spit it out, Lowell. I ain't some tender Lily with one hand on the teapot, speak plain."

"Y… you are just so beautiful!" burst out Lowell in an explosive gasp.

"Me!" she shrieked a laugh. "Lord! I'm a rancher's daughter, Lowell. We don't have much that's pretty around here."

"Oh, Rita, believe me, you take my breath away."

Rita's face changed, and she studied Lowell closely. "You're not kidding around, are you?"

"No, my dear lady. I am lost, there I confess it. If you could consider it, I would much appreciate the kindness of your attentions, in any way you would care to offer them."

Rita was taken aback and did not rightly know how to reply, as she had never heard such a tender declaration of affection before in her life.

"I don't quite know what you're saying, Lowell, but it sounds real sweet."

"You have won my heart, dear lady."

They sat on the horses across from each other and Lowell took off his battered bowler and held it pressed to his chest.

"Does that mean you intend to kiss me?" she asked nervously.

Rita's experiences in the areas of lovemaking up to that time had not extended beyond a quick fumble and stolen kiss at a local barn dance or the occasional chaste scrabble at the back of her daddy's barn with the better looking of the cowhands. Whilst she was inexperienced she knew how it went, she had seen enough of the livestock mating to get the basic principles, but in her heart she knew little beyond the inexplicable overheated desire that ran through her young body now and then when alone in her bed on dark nights.

"That would be more than I could ever expect," breathed Lowell, leaning forward across the gap, his lips puckered.

"Sure," she said. "We can try that."

Their kiss when they met was soft and full-mouthed and Rita felt the tingle of a thrill that coursed through her with a strangely calming influence. When they eventually parted, she felt stunned and dizzy.

"Lord Almighty! Lowell, you sure are a fine kisser."

"You think so?" he asked, his heart pounding in his breast. "Might we try again, do you think?"

"Might be better if we got on down from these mounts."

"Of course," said Lowell, quickly throwing himself from his pony and offering his hand to help her down.

Rita ignored the hand, not knowing what it was meant for anyway, and slid herself easily from the saddle. She fought against the first natural stiffness she felt as Lowell took her in his arms and then as their lips met again, she relaxed and folded into his enfolding embrace.

"Oh, Lowell," she breathed. "I don't know what you're doing but don't stop it."

"Rita," he whispered.

The two of them were lost in the moment and Lowell had forgotten all thoughts of Beatrice or Coffin Jack and his mind instead was full of a whirlwind of excitement and pleasure. Rita too was forgetting all other thoughts and as Lowell kissed her again and again, she felt herself vibrating with the inexplicable nighttime urge that made her blood run hot on lonely nights.

"I never done it before," she confessed in a whisper.

"You've never kissed a man before?" asked a puzzled Lowell.

"No, I mean the other thing, you know…"

"Oh! You mean that. Well, no, I would not dare, it would not be proper."

Rita frowned. "You don't think so?"

"Rita, we have only just met. I have this minute confessed my love; there is a protocol, a way of going about these things. Although," he added hastily, "the mere thought is a heavenly prospect."

She stared into his eyes a long moment and then caught him by the arms in a strong grip and kissing him hungrily, she pulled him over until they both fell to the ground and lay tangled in each other's arms.

"You can, you know," she breathed hard. "I don't mind."

"Rita, Rita, I care for you too much," said Lowell, barely able to contain himself. "I want to, I will, but we must behave with consideration. There is your position, your status in society, I would not destroy that for the world."

Rita looked up at him suspiciously through lidded eyes. "What's the matter, Lowell? You never done this before?"

Lowell swallowed. "Well, I have touched, if you know what I mean. But never, really, you know? Gone the whole way."

"Me either, about time we did, don't you think?"

Lowell's conservative mind was crumbling, the restrictions of his upbringing and the social mores that had governed his life for so long were tumbling as he thought of the free way Coffin Jack entered into such adventures.

"It's true, life is indeed all too short," he panted, struggling with his jacket, and tearing at his shirt buttons. Rita complied with equal haste, fighting with the belt in her jeans and loosening the shirt she wore. In minutes they were both bare assed naked and fell on each other in a fire of all-consuming desire. Lowell marveled at the softness of Rita's body, the swell and line of her limbs and she explored him just as easily, tightening her grip on him as they came together.

It was a hurried, amateurish, rumpty-dumpty union on a bare hillside with the horses standing dumbly alongside and only the pale bleached bones of dead cattle surrounding them to take note.

Afterwards, they lay dusty and pleasantly full of

post-coital lassitude, staring up at the sky.

"Well," said Lowell, "I never thought…"

"Me neither," agreed Rita. "It was good wasn't it?"

"Oh, yes."

"What do we do now?"

Biting his lip, Lowell turned his head to look at her. He said nothing but his notion was as clear to her as daylight.

"Again?" she breathed. "Really? Can we do that?"

Lowell only answer was a long, lingering kiss as he rolled over to cover her.

"Well, well, well, what we got here?"

The voice was a harsh awakening and Lowell looked over his shoulder to see two silhouettes hiding in the bright light of the sun and looking down at them.

"Who?" he gasped. "What do you want? Please, gentlemen, have some propriety, there is a lady here."

"Looks like you got the matter well covered, son," came the amused reply.

Quickly, Lowell snatched up his discarded shirt and threw it over Rita, hiding her nakedness.

"Aw! Don't do that," complained the voice. "Me and old Malodor was enjoying view of them fine attributes the young lady wears so well."

Lowell scrabbled for his trousers and squinted up at the two, one of them wore a wide brimmed sombrero and the other, the one who had spoken, stood with one hand resting casually on his hip. Not far, Lowell noted, from the worn holster and six-shooter that hung there.

"What you say, Malodor?" he said. "You think we could share this young fella's good fortune with him."

"Si, senor Krone. It would be a pleasure to taste such a meal."

"Don't know if I can go for sloppy seconds though," Krone complained.

"Well, I don't mind," leered the Mexican huskily.

"Really!" spat Lowell. "Have you no shame? You men might show some decorum."

"I will if you tell me what it is."

"Turn away, sir," said Lowell. "Let the lady attire herself."

"He speaks very strange, does he not, senor Krone?" said Malodor.

Krone stepped forward and brusquely pushed his boot into Lowell's chest, shoving him down onto the ground.

"You from the Carne ranch, young buck?" he asked.

"I am, indeed, I am Lowell Devereux and this is Miss Rita Bodey. I warn you men, you had best mind your manners."

"That a fact," chuckled Krone. "Well, I'm right concerned about that, I truly am."

Rita, clutching the shirt about her sat up, "Leave him alone," she cried. "This is Carne land you're on. You fellas get any crazy ideas and you'll surely pay for it."

Both men laughed. "Looking like you do right now, missy. I reckon we have a whole lot to fear. What you going to do, beat me to death with them two fine titties of yours?"

"She is pretty," purred Malodor. "Maybe she will pleasure me."

"Not now, Mex," said Krone, relieving Lowell of his boot's pressure. "Listen to me you pair of love-birds. I come with a message for Carne. You tell him he's got three days to quit his land. He don't go, then the wrath of hell is going to fall on his head. We ain't playing here, folks, this message comes from Ska Venger himself, so best pay heed."

Lowell looked at Rita cautiously, it was obvious the pair saw them as no more than casual young lovers and not any close associates of the rancher.

"One other thing," Krone continued. "We hear tell that Carne's hired some paid guns to watch his back. Well, they will be the first to go, you can let them know they'll be top of the list they interfere. And that's a personal promise from Casper Lee Krone. You got it?"

Both Lowell and Rita nodded emphatically.

"Well, let's make sure you do. Malodor, you pick up them duds of theirs. Take the horses too," he grinned evilly. "Like to be a fly on the wall when you suckers explain this one away when you get back."

Malodor wheezed with laughter as he picked up their clothes. "You will give me your pants, senor?" He smiled at Lowell.

"Certainly not!" snapped Lowell, clutching his waistband.

The Mexican pulled a wry face, turned as if to leave, then whirled around and delivered a kick that threw Lowell's head back and sent him sprawling.

"Now you give me your pants, *por favor.*"

Ruefully, Lowell unbuttoned and slid out, covering his crown jewels with one hand, and wiping the blood from his split lip with the other.

"This is outrageous," he complained. "Most unseemly. You scoundrels have no right to do this."

"Sonny," said Krone. "You don't know how lucky you are. I let Malodor here loose on your gal and you'd only have pieces left to take down the aisle."

Strangely, it was the first time the idea of marriage had entered Lowell's mind and even if it had been presented in a rather unpleasant manner and despite the situation, he realized he quite liked the idea.

"You as well, little girl," pressed Krone. "I want you two going back naked as Jaybirds. We're making a point here and it's got to go home." With that he snatched away the shirt from Rita and flung it at the heap in the Mexican's arms.

"Okay, folks, adios," said Krone, swinging into the saddle. "Let's ride, Mex."

It was a long, hot, and dusty walk back and their feet were blistered from the sun-heated sand as they stumbled onto the rise overlooking the ranch.

"What do we do, Lowell?" croaked a dry-lipped Rita, attempting to cover her vulnerable parts with her hands. "If my uncle figures out what we've been up to he'll take a shotgun to you."

"Don't worry," said Lowell. "You stay here, I'll go on down and come back with a blanket. Leave it to me, we'll just say we were surprised by the two villains and they forced us to disrobe."

She held out a hand to stop him as Lowell started

off down the hill. "One thing," she said softly, looking into his face. "You know? Before they came it was fine, Lowell. I liked it real fine."

"There is only one thing for us to do now, you realize that, don't you, Rita?"

"What is it?"

"We must become man and wife, it's the only proper way to go."

She frowned and chewed her lips, "Well…"

"You don't like the idea?"

"Kind of a surprise, I guess. You think we could do that? I mean, you're a city gent, educated and such. I'm just a regular down-home farm girl, could we make out, being that different?"

Lowell turned to face her, and he took both her hands in his, the pair of them as naked as Adam and Eve in the Garden and standing alone on the bleak hillside composed an innocent picture of almost primitive simplicity.

"You see me as I am, Rita. I have nothing to hide… Literally. I promise I will care for you as no other," Lowell swore it to her with all of his fervent desire.

Rita lowered her eyes then looked up to meet his. Her former tomboy brashness had melted completely away, and she responded to his obvious ardor with an almost childlike ease. "Well, alright then," she whispered. "I guess that will be alright."

With that, Lowell turned away and started striding purposefully towards the ranch house, he felt enervated by his proposal and as free and liberated as his total nakedness allowed in the great expanse of the wide-open prairie.

# CHAPTER ELEVEN

"Three days?" rumbled Jack.

"That's what he said," Lowell concurred.

Carne sat in his chair, a deep frown creasing his brow. He had still to get over seeing Rita brought in dusty and footsore with only a blanket wrapped around her.

"Unspeakable renegades!" he muttered. "I'll see every one of them in their graves."

Jack was sitting staring out the window at the distant rosy pink skyline. "We'd best get ourselves ready then."

"Surely," agreed Carne readily. "I'll get the vaqueros fortifying the property. We'll build ditches and lay barbed wire across the approaches."

"Yeah," mumbled Jack noncommittally.

"You don't think it's a good idea?" asked Lowell.

"No, it's fine," Jack answered. "But I don't figure on waiting no three days. I reckon on taking out some of Ska Venger's support well in advance."

"Can we do that?"

Jack's lips compressed into a downward curve. "Why the hell not? We cut off his legs first and then take his head."

"I would certainly like a go at those two scoundrels, Krone and the Mexican, Malodor," said Lowell bitterly.

"Speak with Tomas," advised Carne. "I believe he heard tell something about those two."

"We shall indeed," promised Lowell eagerly. "Come along, Jack. Let us go speak to the vaquero. The sooner we get to grips with these animals the better."

Jack hooked an eyebrow. "Look at you," he smiled thinly. "All fire and vinegar all of a sudden. Who put a burr under your blanket?"

"Well," sniffed Lowell evasively. "It's the insult and offense suffered by Miss Bodey that stirs my blood."

"Well said, young man," piped up Carne. "If I were a few years younger I'd be right alongside you."

"No, sir," said Lowell hastily. "Best you stay here and organize our defenses and make sure Miss Bodey is safe."

Jack chuckled softly but said nothing.

"What?" snapped Lowell irritably.

Jack widened his good eye innocently, "Nothing, nothing at all. Come on, let's go visit with Tomas."

"Where is he?" asked Lowell.

"We'll find him easy," Jack growled. "Just follow your nose, pickled goat cheese don't smell no riper."

"*There is something else!*"

The voice came from behind them and it was Rita

standing in the doorway. She looked fresh as a summer rose, having washed and brushed her hair and put on clean clothes, and Lowell's heart fluttered, she appeared a picture of loveliness and he gaped in appreciation.

"Best close your trap, Lowell," Jack whispered from the corner of his mouth. "A bug might take residence you got it open so wide."

"What is it, dear?" asked Carne. "Are you feeling better after your ordeal?"

"I'm fine uncle," she replied firmly. "I'd like you to send for your brother."

"Uncle Carmody?" asked Carne in surprise. "Why on earth would you want to do that?"

"Lowell made a suggestion whilst we were out on the range and I think it is a good notion that we should follow up."

"My younger brother Carmody," Carne explained. "He is something of a wild card. A little strange in the head, he's chosen a rather solitary lifestyle and we barely see him. How can he help us?" he asked Rita.

"He knows the geology of this country and spent years prospecting out west in California, it may be that there is something of value in the soil here. If there is, as Lowell suggests, then we'll know why Ska Venger is so intent on driving us out."

Carne pooh-poohed the idea. "There's nothing around here but space, Rita. Nothing of value except space for cattle."

"Humor me, will you, uncle? Call in Carmody, he may know something we don't."

Carne shrugged. "If you think it will help, of course I will. I'll send out one of the men to fetch him in but for the life of me I can't see any value in it. Poor Carmody is given to fancies and not really one to be given much credence."

"He's a learned man and you know it, uncle. Why, most of those books on your shelves here are his."

"What's this about?" Jack asked, turning to Lowell.

"Well, it came to me. Why would they expend such effort to wipe out the livestock, for what logical purpose? Everybody thinks that Ska Venger is just plain crazy, but supposing he is in the employ of others of a more sane frame of mind, others intent on clearing the land for their own devices."

Jack raised a doubtful eyebrow. "What kind of devices?"

"I don't know but it's best to question, don't you think?"

Jack shrugged indifferently. "Don't matter the reason, whatever it is, that son-of-a-bitch has still got to go down."

As they strolled across to the bunkhouse, Jack cast a rueful glance at Lowell.

"Been playing fast and loose with the rancher's niece, have you?"

"Nothing of the sort," said Lowell haughtily.

"Can't say I blame you," Jack gave him a teasing look. "Wouldn't mind a dally with that little lady myself."

"*Don't you dare even consider it!*" snapped Lowell.

"Rita is a fine young woman, I'll have no one speak ill of her."

"Oh, it's *Rita* now, is it? But don't worry; I'm only joshing you, Lowell. You're right, she's a swell gal and if you two make it out okay, I'll be glad to dance at your wedding."

Lowell was mollified somewhat by Jack's words, although the idea of the gaunt and ragged figure of Coffin Jack doing a two-step around a dance floor was a picture he could not quite envisage.

They found Tomas in the barn working on some harness, the rest of the Mexicans being out riding the herd.

"Holy snakes!" muttered Jack as they approached the ramrod. "Can smell that hombre from half a mile out."

"Really, Jack," frowned Lowell. "There's no need to be so forthright all the time. Some people just cannot help their personal state of hygiene. It may well be a personal problem of some kind."

"A stink is a stink," grumbled Jack. "Hey, Stinky! You got a minute?"

"Si, senor?" said Tomas, turning to them as they entered the barn. "How can I help?"

"The boss says you got some word on this guy Krone and his buddy?"

"What is it you wish to know?"

"Whereabouts the two rats hang out, you got any idea?"

Tomas shrugged and scratched at his fetid armpit. "I am told they visit town sometimes. You know, the saloon there."

"We do indeed know the establishment," supplied Lowell. "Why exactly do they go there? I can't imagine the ambience is of importance."

"They like the liquor, I think."

"See," Jack was smug. "I told you it was good stuff."

"I think also it is the woman they go for," added Tomas.

"*The woman?* We didn't see no woman when we was in there."

"No, the owner he keeps her out in the back room."

"This some kind of whore he has there?" asked Jack.

"Well, she is kept chained up for that purpose."

"*Chained!*" started Lowell. "What can you mean?"

"The lady is a little simple in the head and the owner; he does that to stop her running off. She is kept on a long chain fixed to the bed in a back room. It is said the one called Malodor favors such visits. These are bad men, senors, they enjoy the lowliest of pleasures."

"You ain't kidding," growled Jack. "Poking some poor hogtied halfwit, they really is of an inferior order."

"That is so distasteful," Lowell agreed.

"Well, I guess we'd better mosey along and check it out," mused Jack. "Reckon I could do with a taste anyway."

Nothing much had changed in The Abandon Hope Saloon when the two entered but at least they were saved the presence of the garrulous old timer

Ebenezer Bucket who was thankfully not present. The place was deserted except for the Negro bartender, Ahab Barnes, who looked up casually from his pastime of toying with a train of soldier ants that were making their busy way across his bar-top in a long single file.

He yawned widely and looked at them with sleepy eyes, "He'p you?"

"Sure hope so," said Jack.

"What can I do for you?" asked Ahab dreamily.

"Take a stab in the dark," advised Jack.

Slowly it penetrated and the bartender got the picture and eased a bottle and two glasses up from below the bar.

"Y'all been having a fun day?" Ahab asked dutifully.

"Endless excitement," said Jack, looking around the darkened room. "You ever get any custom in here apart from that leery old soul we saw in here last time?"

"Yessir, why some nights it's right jumping in here. Especially when we have the Bingo."

"That a fact? That is surely something I'd like to see."

"Yo' hold on a mite and you'll see something. That'll be when *his* boys get into town."

"*His* boys?"

"Yessir. *His* boys."

Jack poured himself a liberal glass and pushed the bottle along to Lowell who looked at it disdainfully and nudged the bottle away with his forefinger.

"Who's *his*?" asked Jack.

Ahab looked cautiously around the empty saloon and leaned forward over the bar as if about to impart a secret that nobody else should overhear. "*Him!*" he whispered.

Jack studied the Negro angrily. "You talking about *SKA VENGER*?" he said loudly.

"Shh!" hissed Ahab, his eyes rolling wildly, and restraining fingers raised to his lips. "Don' be saying that name out loud. It be bad luck to mention *him* in company. Yo' better to call up the devil hisself before you say that name."

Jack swallowed his glassful and, smacking his lips, rapidly poured another, "You really think I care?" he asked. "Damn! But this is fine liquor. Go on, Lowell, have a shot."

"I'll pass if you don't mind, I'm just fine."

Ahab was jittery now, his eyes glancing around the room as if the presence of Ska Venger was indeed waiting in the shadows at the far end.

"Yo' fellas about done?" he asked nervously. "I gots to clear up now, be near closing time."

"That so?" said Jack. "Well, I hear tell you got some special female entertainment here. Now, maybe I'm interested and I know my friend Lowell here will be, ain't that a fact, Lowell?"

"Can't wait," said Lowell wryly.

"Oh, you be talking about Maybelline, well she's a mite indisposed at the moment."

"Aw! Come on, fella. It won't take us long, been a while, ain't it Lowell?" he cast a doubtful sidelong glance in his companion's direction. "Well, it has for me anyway. Come on now, show us your wares, that is if *SKA VENGER* ain't got in there first."

Jack deliberately stressed the name loudly and Ahab literally jumped a few inches off the ground in fear. "Please, mister."

"What's wrong?" asked Jack. "You don't like the name *SKA VENGER*?"

"N... no, sir, you really shouldn't... Okay, okay, I'll go see if Maybelline is fit. Yo' hold still there a moment."

"If you're sure it won't upset Mister *SKA VENGER*," chuckled Jack as the bartender hurriedly scurried off to the recesses of the saloon and disappeared into a room at the far end.

"Oh, Jack," Lowell said, smiling at the Negro's distress, "you really are a wicked man."

Jack sniffed his liquor before sipping a mouthful. "You only just noticed."

"Alright, gentlemen," Ahab called from the door of the room. "The lady be ready to receive you now."

"Let's go see," said Jack, setting down his glass and leading the way.

The sight that greeted them brought both men up sharp.

It was dark in the room and lit only by a stub of candle but even by that poor light it was possible to see that the place was filthy. Unwashed plates of half eaten food lay on the floor and ragged items of clothing were strewn around. In the center of the bare wood floor stood a large iron-frame double bed and in the middle of the grubby and wrinkled sheet that barely covered the tick mattress underneath, lay the woman.

She was striking a bizarre pose of supposed

provocation, but one eye roamed uncontrollably skywards, and the great head of frizzy unkempt hair nodded in time to a beat no one else could hear. She was dressed only in a stained shift that covered her obviously thin frame and from her bony and man-acled ankle stretched a long thick-linked chain that shifted with a snake-like rattle when she moved.

"Now don' yo' mind that there chain," said Ahab ushering them in. "That be just to stop her running off; she can be a mite wild sometime."

Lowell fumed at the sight. "This is inhuman," he growled.

Jack looked at the woman and then at Ahab. "Un-lock that manacle," he ordered quietly.

"But I tell yo', she be gone I do that."

Jack turned to the bed. "You want to stay here, Miss Maybelline?"

The woman mewed a pitiful indeterminate sound.

"See, she don't want to stay. Now go get the key," ordered Jack.

"She don' know what she want," pressed Ahab. "She be simple in the head, she got a good life here. I feeds her an' she have a place to stay..."

His justification was choked off as Jack clamped one large hand around the Negro's throat and lifted him up on tiptoe.

"*Get the key!*" he snarled.

When Maybelline was free of her chain, Lowell wrapped her in the sheet and with an arm around her shoulder he led the nervous creature from the room.

"You should be ashamed," he snapped at Ahab as they passed.

"What I do?" pleaded the bartender.

"If you don't know then I cannot explain."

"Well..." he began but Jack jerked him off his feet and upended the bartender, dangling him by the leg and quickly snapping the manacle and chain around his ankle.

"What yo' doin'?" begged Ahab.

"There, now you give it a go," said Jack, throwing him into the dim room and slamming the door shut.

Maybelline suddenly began making a distressed wailing sound and the two quickly looked around to see the Mexican, Malodor standing at the doorway to the saloon.

"*Oho!* Senors, where you going with this woman?" he asked down the length of the long room.

Jack stepped forward. "Somewheres better than here," he snarled, his brow lowering and good eye flickering with a demon light.

"I don't think so," said the Mexican.

He was alone but obviously not perturbed by the fact that he was outnumbered two to one.

"You are the white boys hired by the rancher?" he asked, a slow smile spreading across his face. "Yes, I think you are. Now you are come to take my woman from me, this is most foolish."

Confidently, he tossed aside his sombrero and drew the long blade of a sharp machete from the belt at his back. The blade gleamed in the dim light, its sharp edge glistening with a ripple of malevolent light.

"You hombres don't know what you have walked into here," said Malodor. "It is best you leave, I think. You will leave your guns and the woman behind and go, that would be most wise. This way I will let you live."

"You got it all wrong," growled Jack, moving towards him. "You got any last words other than that bullshit, hombre. Now's the time."

"Hah! A confident man," said Malodor, dropping into a crouch, the machete held before him. "I like that. For you it will be quick, maybe I leave your head on your shoulders and just take your insides out."

"And maybe I make you eat that butcher knife you got there."

They circled each other warily in the center of the room in a clockwise rotation, moving in a space clear of tables and chairs. Behind, Lowell could hear Ahab rolling around inside the closed room cursing and trying to free his leg of the chain. Beside him, Maybelline was moaning and jerking spasmodically, and Lowell held her tight and tried to console her.

"Don't concern yourself," he whispered. "Jack will sort this out, I'm sure. Then we'll take you to a nice place where you'll be taken care of. Please, don't worry, ma'am, it will be fine."

Malodor slashed a ream of light as fast as a lightning flash as he swung the blade. Jack moved easily out of the way and the machete tip passed his nose by no more than an inch or two.

Malodor chuckled. "You like that one eye you still got?" he asked, darting a jab at Jack's face.

"You like the shape your face is now?" Jack replied. "Enjoy it while you can."

He snapped out a straight left and his big fist rapped against the Mexican's forehead, jerking Malodor back a step. Malodor quirked an eyebrow in surprise. "So you have a bite, eh? Americano."

Whirling his blade arm in a convoluted pattern of swings, Malodor rushed forward, and Jack ducked and swung his body to left and right as the machete whistled past on either side of his body. It was all a tornado of spinning movement, fast and hard to follow and Lowell was dazzled by the dexterity with which Jack read the attack and avoided each blow.

Jack slugged out once, catching Malodor in the pit of the stomach and sending the Mexican staggering back. But Malodor was soon on the attack again, jabbing now and using the length of his reach to keep Jack backing away.

Jack was forced into one of the group of chairs and tables behind him and became tangled in the chair leg. His balance went and he fell over backwards to lie on the floor. Lowell gasped as Malodor leapt forward swinging up the machete ready for a final deadly blow. Quicker than the eye could follow, Jack grabbed the leg of the card table next to him and swung it over himself as the blade descended.

The machete sunk deep into the tabletop with a heavy *thunk* and Jack wrenched the table aside dragging the stuck blade with Malodor still hanging on. In an instant, Jack's long frame bounded up and as Malodor attempted to free his trapped machete Jack thumped him hard in the ribs. Malodor groaned and bent over in time to collect the heavy uppercut sailing up to meet his chin. His head rocked back, the neck stretched out by the force of the blow. A swinging roundhouse caught him full in the chest and drove the air from his body with an explosive gasp of air.

Dazed and surprised, the Mexican was teetering on his feet and he wobbled away as Jack followed, unrelenting in his attack.

Jack's face was fixed in a bitter and stony mask of determination as he pounded into the staggering body. Left and right short punches buried themselves in the undefended frame and the Mexican tottered back on shaky legs. Jack followed, slamming punch after punch into the stunned torso.

Barely conscious, Malodor was hardly able to stand on his feet as Jack took hold of the greasy head of hair and lifted the battered face up. Jack drew back his arm and delivered a final sharp sounding smack that flattened the nose and brought a cross-eyed response from the Mexican, who waivered a moment and then fell over stiffly to crash down onto the floorboards in a cloud of dust.

Jack sniffed in satisfaction as he looked down at his fallen foe.

"Bravo!" gasped Lowell. "That was certainly a bold show of fisticuffs, Jack."

Jack tuned to face him, a slight smile curling his lip. "Why waste a bullet on a dumb sucker like that?"

Lowell's eyes widened, "Look out!" he cried.

Behind Jack, the bloody-nosed and puff-eyed Mexican was dragging himself up onto his feet, a six-shooter already pulled from his waistband.

"Now, gringo, it will be I who will waste the bullet," grinning inanely, he cocked the pistol.

In one swooping and continuous motion, Jack spun around, grabbed the handle of the embedded machete, lifted it from the table as if it were held by no more than a block of butter and threw it full force.

Two feet of sharpened steel smashed its way between the grinning teeth, snapping off two on the way and ramming with fluid ease into the Mexican's throat. Malodor's eyes rounded and he glugged for air as the blade dug deep, its sharp edge widening his smile and bringing a fountain of blood from between his lips. He stood a moment, eyes popping and body shaking in a wild jitter as his lungs filled with liquid.

Jack stepped up, snatched the pistol from the nerveless fingers and with a casual two-fingered push sent the rigid Mexican falling back over.

"I told you I'd make you eat it," Jack said, glaring down at the Mexican as Malodor's eyes glazed over and he went on to a better place, or maybe, in his case, it was a worse one.

# CHAPTER TWELVE

When Casper Lee Krone arrived at The Abandon Hope he was expecting to find his buddy Malodor busy with Maybelline and a bottle ready and waiting for him on the bar. Instead it was Ahab Barnes who was in chains and Malodor stretched out on the barroom floor with a mouthful of machete.

He was not amused.

"What the hell happened?" he asked after he had kicked open the backroom door and found the squirming bartender still manacled.

Ahab noted the angry gleam in Krone's eye and the gun in his hand and was quick to form an answer.

"Two men," he blurted. "They been in hyah before, just the one time. Ask the way to the Carne place. They done took my Maybelline and did this to me."

"Two men?"

"Yeah, one was a big fella, mighty ugly looking in raggedy clothes. The other one littler, fancy dresser in go-to-church duds."

Krone breathed heavily through his nose, staring down at the chained barman. "They killed the Mexican?"

"I guess, I couldn't see bein' in hyah and kinda tied up at the time but I sure heard all the crashing about. Did they bust up my place bad, Mister Krone?"

Krone scratched his chin thoughtfully. "Ska is going to want to hear about this."

"Say, Mister Krone, yo' think yo' can he'p me out here?" he lifted the chain plaintively.

But Krone's thoughts were elsewhere, and he turned on his heel and strode away without a word.

"Say, Mister Krone!" Ahab called after him. "Won't take a minute to get these chains off'n me. Key's on the bar."

Krone ignored the bartender and brusquely brushed past the old man Ebenezer Bucket as he left the saloon.

"Hey! What's going on here?" snorted Ebenezer.

"Thank God!" called Ahab, seeing the old man entering the saloon. "Ebenezer, yo' going to he'p me? I'm kinda in a fix hyah."

"Well, look at that," said the old man, squinting along to the open door of the back room where Ahab lay wresting with the long chain. "What you playing at, Ahab? Done got yourself locked up?"

"Yessir, come on now, he'p a fellow out."

Bucket started to walk down the barroom but his eye caught the glint of a bottle behind the bar and he paused in mid-stride.

"Can't you get yourself out of there, Ahab?" he

called, looking from bartender to bottle.

"No, I cain't. Obvious, ain't it," replied the Negro lifting the chain in his hand and waggling the links.

Ebenezer's toothless lips formed a tight little smile as a notion entered his calculating brain.

"Well, well," he hummed to himself. "A captive audience, now ain't that something," and he moved off behind the bar.

"Wait! Where yo' going, old timer?" called Ahab desperately.

"Just going to get me a little restorative drink, Ahab. It's a cold night out there and my old bones need a warm, I reckon."

Ahab heard the steady glug of a bottle being emptied and it went on for a long time so he reasoned it must be a very large drink.

"Yo' going to pay for that ain't yo', Ebenezer?" he called.

"That a fact?" Ebenezer smacked his lips. "You never would give me no strong liquor, would you, Ahab? Always stuck me with that lousy beer you serve. Well, here I am all alone in here and I have a whole array of bottles waiting. But don't you worry, I'll take care of business if we get any."

"*No, no, no!*" shouted the enraged Ahab. "Yo' can't do this to me. Come on, let me out of hyah."

Bottle in one hand and a full schooner glass in the other, Ebenezer made his way over to the back room.

"That's it," cried Ahab. "That's it, old man. Yo' going to set me free, ain't yo'?"

"Maybe I will," mused Ebenezer. "And maybe I

won't."

He toed the door of the room shut in Ahab's face. "I'll have to think on it some."

Ebenezer turned away from the howling sounds of complaint that came from behind the closed door and made his way back to the bar.

"Never ran no proper drinking parlor before," he mused, taking a long pleasurable sip from his glass. "Think I might get to like it. Say, Ahab!" he called. "What say we go into business together? You can be the sleeping partner, you just rest up in there and I'll take care of things out here, how's that sound?"

Muffled screams came from the back room.

"Well okay then, glad to hear you approve," chuckled Ebenezer, pouring himself another liberal glass full. "Now, you just settle down and I'll tell you about the time I was running with a trapping crew back before this place got all run down. I remember it well, that would be back in the days when the sun shone around here and there was trees growing and such. You listening, Ahab? Good. Happened to be about the year of '46 when I started out from back east…"

And he droned on for hours and hours until the liquor took effect and he finally fell asleep on the bar top. So engrossed in his drinking and tale-telling was Ebenezer that he barely noticed the frustrated sounds of sobbing and wailing that came with weakening decline from the back room.

Krone found Ska Venger in the line shack he and Vile Spider had taken over for the duration.

It was a lonely, single-room wooden shack

stuck out on the extremities of the Carne land and stood alone and isolated below the rugged set of a low mountain range that stretched from horizon to horizon on the flat plain. The sky above was lowering and filled with an unearthly pink light that appeared to roll in broken skeins within the clouds as if they were staining the vapor with threads of blood.

Burning with low rage over his partner's death, Krone rode up at speed and dismounted fast, entering the shack without introduction.

The small room inside was rich with the stench of testosterone as Krone slammed inside and he knew the two had been engaged in some kind of wild act of copulation. The couple looked up at him from their bed with mild disinterest, unmoved by his sudden appearance.

Ska was a huge beast of a man whose presence seemed to fill the shack, almost a giant in size with a distorted body pumped up with muscle and covered with thick veins straining under the skin like writhing worms. His face was lantern-jawed, meaty, and pockmarked, and the ratty unwashed hair that hung down each side of his grossly featured face reached to his bulging and hair covered shoulders. By some strange feat of nature his long-nailed fingers had blackened and each broad hand looked like it had been dipped in black paint at the tips.

He sat on the edge of the bunk bed clothed in only a dirty singlet with Vile Spider draped across one massive thigh. She naked lay on her belly, one arm hooked over and her chin resting on her hand as she eyed Krone through long lashed and lidded eyes. She was a slender long-limbed dark beauty, with sleek black hair and an entire body covered with a series of blue/black ink tattoos. Fanged pythons with skulls for heads climbed each arm and coiled across an array of spider-covered webs, centering on one big red-eyed, and spindle-legged monster spider crouching evilly between her small breasts. Each breast was marked with a web that centered on her nipples and her back was covered with an image of demonically spread membranous wings, their tips fashioned into curving spiked talons. She stretched her bare body lethargically as Krone entered and her entire skin surface moved as if the limbs were alive with a myriad of small creatures. Spiders scuttled as horned centipedes moved a trillion legs across the backs of her legs and a viper slid into the cleft of her buttocks as if it were truly alive and seeking sanctuary there.

"Look who's back," she whispered, her voice a husky and barely audible sound.

Ska grunted. His expression unchanging as he looked at Krone from under a low, Neolithic brow with eyes that were solid black and held no symptom of any color or reflection of light. They were dead eyes, deep pools that held no pity and registered no symptom of humanity only the ability to draw in life and succumb it to his will. His breath came heavy as if a man with a chest complaint and it rasped loud and sonorous in the small shack.

"Speak!" he growled.

"They done for Malodor, forced his own knife

down his throat."

"Oh, dear," breathed Vile Spider, raising one cynical eyebrow. "How careless."

"Who?" asked Ska. He rarely spoke in more than a few monosyllables, expecting to be understood in the briefest of terms.

"Two men, I guess it was the hired guns that Carne brought in."

Ska released a long sigh and said nothing, only staring blankly at the gunman.

"So, what do we do?" asked Krone. "They killed Malodor, we can't let that pass."

"What do you think we do, sweetie?" asked Vile Spider, scratching a long fingernail slowly along the inside of Ska's monstrous thigh.

"Bring them to me," growled Ska.

"You want me to go do it alone?"

"Can't you do it all on your lonesome?" teased Vile Spider, lifting her middle finger, and placing it between her puckered lips with a slow sucking motion. It was an overtly sexual gesture and it irritated Krone; somehow she always managed to get under his skin with her obscene implications. He had never liked the woman and felt they would be better off without her, but Ska favored her attentions and there was no debate when the giant ordered it so.

"We don't know what we're up against," Krone reasoned.

"Then fetch someone we can find out from," said Vile Spider as if she were speaking to a small child.

"They have three days," grunted Ska distantly, almost as if he had not been listening to the ongoing conversation. "Then I come for them all. No one gets out alive; I will kill everything on that ranch. Every dog, chicken, woman and child, every living thing."

"Sure, I know that, Ska," said Krone. "Just that maybe we ought to know what we're heading into."

"You scared, big boy?" asked Vile Spider with a slow smile that showed an array of perfect teeth.

"I ain't scared, bitch. Why don't you leave off riling me?"

Vile Spider smiled at him and waggled her behind on the bed, setting off a chaotic display of movement on her skin.

"She is *my* bitch," rumbled Ska. "Watch your mouth, Krone."

Smugly, Vile Spider allowed the tip of her tongue to ease from between her lips and then she poked it full out and curled the end at Krone as if she were a rattlesnake tasting the air.

"No offense," said Krone hurriedly. "Just that she's always on my back. I can do without it, Ska."

Ska lowered his massive head ponderously, his great hand caught hold of Vile Spider by the hair at the nape of her neck, jerking her head up.

"You," he grunted. "Can put that tongue to better use."

She stared back up at him with a look of total devotion. "Whatever you say, lover."

"Krone," Ska ordered, "bring a prisoner we can question."

"Sure thing, boss," said Krone, looking down at Vile Spider with obvious distaste and mimicking her response. "Whatever you say."

"Go now, take Phantom Dog and do it," rumbled Ska, a pinpoint of light gleaming in his dark eyes as he stared at the woman held in his grip. "Vile Spider needs some attention."

She hummed happily and spread herself expectantly, murmuring approval.

Suddenly, Ska raised a brawny arm and brought his hand down hard on Vile Spider's bare behind with a sharp smack that sent her body fat shaking.

"*Ahh!* Good," she sighed, squirming in perverse pleasure. "It's that kind of attention."

Feeling slightly nauseous, Krone hurried from the shack.

Outside he looked around for the tracker, wondering where the half-breed could be. He was about to give up and go on his own when a hand descended on his shoulder and frightened the life out of him.

"Goddamn it, Phantom Dog!" he gasped. "Where the hell did you come from?"

Krone had heard nothing. The tracker had the ability to appear and disappear as if by magic, no one ever heard or saw him arrive or leave as he could move it seemed indeed like a ghost.

A big, broad chested buckskin-clad fellow with a stone face that never showed expression, and Krone was always surprised that one so large could slip so silently through shadows as if he were one himself.

"We go," said the half-breed.

"You know what Ska wants?"

"I know."

How the hell he knew, Krone had no idea, but the half-breed was a mysterious and secretive entity whose life was one of silence and observation and all he did for the gunman was give him the creeps.

When Krone and Phantom Dog arrived at the Carne ranch it was full dark, and they looked down on the collection of buildings to see the main house ablaze with lights. It caused them a moment of caution and Krone lay out on the overlooking ridge and stared at the lighted windows through his telescope.

They had company below, Krone realized, and he wondered just who the hell had come calling. It occurred to him that maybe Carne had called on even more gunfighters with the expected raid they had been forewarned about. Krone needed to know, if Ska was determined to head in whatever awaited them, Krone was not so sure he wanted to be a part. Running into a small army might appeal to the kill-crazy Ska Venger but Krone was a somewhat more careful soul.

He signaled the half-breed and they began to work their way down towards the ranch, hoping to find out more or collect one of the ranch hands and take him back for questioning.

Inside, the main house, Carne and his niece had seated everybody in the living room after they had enjoyed a full supper. Carne's brother Carmody had been fetched from his retreat and sprawled in a leisurely manner in Carne's favorite chair. He was a fit looking man for his age, with handsome features and a shock of gray hair and although tanned from an outdoor life he wore a serious demeanor and a certain studious quality about himself.

"I take it, brother," he smiled as Carne offered him a tumbler of whisky, "that I wouldn't get this treatment unless there was something you needed from me."

"Now, don't be like that, Uncle Carmody," piped up Rita. "You know you are welcome here at any time; we'd be glad to see you."

"My brother is determined that I would keep him from my door," Carne explained to Jack and Lowell. "But, of course, it is far from true. He just prefers his own company and a separate life, free to go his own way."

"True enough," grinned Carmody. "I must admit I'm not a social animal. I like the wild and open spaces and pleasing myself. Selfish, I know, but it was the way I was made."

"Admirable that a man should recognize his own limitations," chipped in Lowell.

"Thank you, sir," said Carmody. "But I prefer to think of them as expectations rather than limitations."

"Of course, I do beg your pardon," said Lowell, slightly cowed by Carmody's forthrightness.

"Not at all. You are a journalist, I believe, Mister Devereux?"

"Lowell, please and yes I nominally serve The Holy Roller magazine."

"*Nominally*, Lowell?"

"Well, yes, I am commissioned so but lately I have been experiencing some life changes that are effecting my thinking in relation to my career," Lowell could not help himself from glancing across at Rita, who answered his look with a secretive smile.

"And you, Mister Jack," Carmody asked. "You are also in the newspaper business?"

"Hardly," answered Jack gruffly.

"Coffin Jack has certain other abilities," Carne put in quickly, his brother as yet had no idea of their problems with Ska Venger. "But let me ask you, Carmody. You have explored this region for many years can you tell us anything about the substance of the soil around here?"

"Well, it's dying, I can tell you that."

"Dying! How so?"

"Why, the copper beds, of course."

"Copper? And how does that affect things so?"

"This area is unusual for the region, dear brother. Rich in a bed of high-grade copper that is leeching into the water table. That's the reason everything is dying off, the toxic capabilities of the dissolved mineral are well known. Usually the larger copper deposits are found further south across the Pecos and there has only been a small production in this region, no more than eighteen tons at last count I believe. But I reckon in this little corner we have an extensive and very rich seam underground."

"That a fact," frowned Carne.

"You were right, Lowell," chipped in Rita. "There *is* something of value here after all."

"You thought that, did you?" Carmody asked Lowell. "Most astute of you, sir. I've been ranting on about it for years but nobody would credit me as there was so little found elsewhere around here."

"Who'd you tell about this?" Jack asked bluntly.

"Well, I approached several companies. With the advent of the telegraph service nationwide there's been a high call for good grade copper to use in the wire."

"They use copper wire?" asked Rita.

"Indeed, many miles of it in fact," confirmed Carmody, taking on a schoolmasterly air. "Electricity, you see. The wire is an excellent transporter of current and by breaking the supply using a key they can evoke a signal similar to the Morse code type of messaging."

"Who are these companies?" Jack insisted.

"I went to see Western Union first, they're the biggest at the moment holding almost ninety percent of the market but they were not interested, preferring to take up all the cheaper imports from Mexico. There are other companies in competition now but none of them showed any interest at all, so it appeared I was getting nowhere and dropped the whole thing. You see, without an excessive amount of funding, mining and processing would not be possible."

"Well, it would appear one of them is interested now," cut in Carne. "Why didn't you tell me about this, Carmody?"

"Come now, brother. Your interest has always been the cattle, there seemed little point in advising you of something that was going nowhere."

"Who else d'you go see?" asked Jack.

"The only other real competitor to Western Union was a newly rising business, The Electric

Telegraph and Post Company, run by a man called J. J. Jameson. He made a fortune in the gold diggings and has set about buying up all the smaller telegraph companies, those going bankrupt or just too small to compete. The man is building up a network and I thought he would be ideal for the source, but no, he turned me away as well."

"J. J. Jameson," muttered Jack. "Guess that's maybe our man."

"You think he will have hired Ska Venger?" asked Lowell.

"Seems likely," Jack agreed.

"Ska Venger?" asked Carmody. "Who is this?"

"A troublesome fellow," said Carne. "He has been causing us a great deal of distress at the ranch and Coffin Jack is here to help us sort it out."

"Ah!" sighed Carmody. "I see, a Regulator of sorts, is that right, Mister Jack?"

"If you like," sniffed Jack, not particularly bothered one way or the other by what label they used.

Carmody nodded and studied Jack closely. "I do now indeed recognize your skills, sir."

There was a silence as each digested all the information they had received. It was finally broken by Rita rising from her seat.

"I think I'd best see how our guest is doing," she said.

"Yes, a good idea, do that, dear, go see how the poor thing is faring," said her uncle.

Maybelline had been brought back to the ranch and the bemused creature had been washed and fed and dressed in some of Rita's clothes. Being insufficient spare room in the ranch house they had cleared a small storeroom in the barn and set up a bed there for the distressed woman. It turned out her real name was Jane Margaret Fray and "Maybelline" had been a name foisted on her by the bartender as he considered it "mo' fetching fo' a ho'". Jane had been the only surviving daughter of a family of settlers who had all been struck down by the mysterious illness that was decimating the town and once alone had been taken in as pot washer by the barman and eventually forced to act as his sex slave.

She had little notion of what was happening but at least recognized the kindness being shown her and Rita was determined to get Doc Lester to examine her come the morrow. In the meantime, one of the vaqueros was outside the storeroom keeping watch over her.

"Perhaps you would like to accompany me, Lowell?" Rita asked.

"It would be an honor, Miss Rita," said Lowell, leaping from his seat barely able to conceal his eagerness. "A breath of air would do me the power of good."

"And that ain't all I'll bet," rumbled Jack quietly.

# CHAPTER THIRTEEN

Krone had made his way down unseen to the corral and from there worked his way towards the barn where a light was showing. Phantom Dog had drifted off on his own and Krone had not seen or heard him go. The half-breed was a law unto himself and Krone instantly forgot about him. He had spotted the vaquero watching over Maybelline and was determining to rap the fellow on the head and take the Mexican back to Ska when Rita and Lowell made their way out of the ranch house.

He watched from the shadows as the two hurried over towards the barn and Rita pulled Lowell inside to one of the stalls where they could not be seen by either the vaquero or by those in the house. She kissed him hurriedly and Lowell forgot all else as he held Rita in his arms.

"I thought we would never escape," she chuckled.

"It is so good to be close to you again, dear Rita," said Lowell, kissing her fervently.

"What are we going to do now, Lowell?" she asked.

"I must see your uncle, of course. I shall speak to him first thing, I cannot wait, my dear. I must marry you the soonest it can be arranged."

"Oh, Lowell," she sighed, kissing him again.

It was an opportunity too good to miss and Krone worked his way nearer through the darkness. His tread was soft through the straw lying on the ground and the snuffling of the stabled ponies made it easy for him to approach unheard.

The first Rita and Lowell knew of it was when a dark shape rose suddenly out of the shadows and a raised pistol butt descended on the back of Lowell's skull. She gasped as he fell silently in a crumpled heap to the ground, not quite understanding what had happened.

Krone did not hesitate. He quickly grasped hold of Rita and trapped her cries in a tight grip across nose and mouth.

"Make one sound," he whispered in her ear. "And I'll gut you from crotch to chin."

She did not give in easily though and wrestled hard in his grip.

"Goddamn it, girl," cursed Krone, whirling her around and socking her hard on the chin.

He laid the unconscious woman across one of the stable ponies and quietly led it from the barn, making his way past the corral and heading back to where they had left their horses.

Suddenly the half-breed appeared beside him.

"Where the hell you been?" hissed Krone.

Phantom Dog said nothing only holding up a bloody hank of hair.

"That vaquero on guard?" Krone asked.

Phantom Dog smiled thinly.

It was some minutes before Lowell began to recover consciousness. When he did, he was disorientated, and it took him some time to realize what had happened.

"Rita?" he called, rubbing the painful lump on the back of his head. "Rita, what happened?"

Staggering, Lowell made his way out from the barn.

"Rita! Where are you?" he called desperately. "*Help! They've taken Rita!*"

His cries brought not only the bunkhouse vaqueros but also those from the house.

"What's going on?" asked Carne as they gathered around the stumbling man.

"I don't know, I was attacked. Somebody struck me and Rita is gone... I think they have taken her."

"Who, boy?" barked Carmody. "Who took her?"

"I don't know... I was struck from behind... It was dark..."

They were interrupted by the clatter of hoofs as Jack raced by on horseback.

"Where's he going?" asked Carne.

"He will be after them," said Tomas with grim certainty as he came running up, a rifle in his hand.

"You had a guard out here, didn't you, Tomas?" asked Carne.

"We did," Tomas agreed solemnly. "He is dead, they have taken his hair."

"You mean as in *scalping*?" gasped Carne.

"There is an Indian with them," Tomas advised somberly.

"Yes," sadly Carne agreed. "The half-breed tracker. Oh my God! That my dear Rita should end up amongst such villains."

There was a rumble of thunder over the mountaintops and a great crack of lightning that lit up the yard for an instant as if bright day had come. The shock of sudden thunder hit the air and reverberated through the atmosphere around them with the bow-wave pressure of a canon blast. Muted rolls followed the first and the air crackled with the ozone scent of electricity and with the mounting ominous sense of dark clouds boiling overhead.

"*Mount up!*" roared Carne to the vaqueros. "We must be after them."

There were hurried movements in the thrashing darkness as the men obediently dashed to fetch their ponies and saddle up.

"You think it was this Ska Venger character?" asked Carmody.

"I'd bet on it," agreed Carne.

"Do you know where he's holed up?"

"No, but wherever he is strange red clouds seems to hover."

"*Red clouds?*" Carmody repeated in disbelief.

"Yes, believe me, brother. This man is one of the ungodly."

As if in answer to his words the sky opened up with a heavy downpour that soaked them all in seconds.

"Damn it!" snarled Carne, squinting into the

sheeting rain. "It'll be hard to pick up any sign in this."

"We must try," said Lowell, heading for the barn.

Hours later, wet, and disconsolate the party of riders returned unsuccessful. Soaking wet and shivering it was a downcast group that made their way into the ranch house and Carne ordered up hot coffee and a change of clothes.

Lowell slumped defeated into a chair, his boots squelching as he did so.

"Get changed, Lowell," Carmody advised. "It will do no good if you sicken."

"It's all my fault," Lowell mumbled.

"Don't be silly, man. You were taken unawares, there was nothing you could do."

Despite Carmody's reassurance, Lowell suffered deep pangs of despair.

"I love her, you see," he confessed. "She means more to me than I can express."

Carmody looked around to see if his brother was in earshot, but Carne had already gone, overseeing the hot coffee in the kitchen.

"Yes, I could see that from the way you looked at each other over supper," Carmody said quietly. "But we are not beaten yet. Your friend is still out there and if I am not much mistaken, Mister Coffin Jack is a man who does not give up at all easily."

"True," said Lowell, perking up. "If anyone can find her, he will."

Just then the front door slammed open and the dripping wet figure of Jack stood in the doorway.

Lightning flashed behind him and by its light the continuing steady fall of rain could clearly be seen as a shining curtain.

"Any luck?" cried Lowell, leaping up from his seat.

But Jack's grim face told it all. "They headed east, three horses, but I lost them in the rain."

"That will be towards the mountains," interjected Carmody.

"You know the country?"

"I do, there is little out there. The plains run right up to the mountain range."

"If he's in the mountains," said Carne, coming in from the kitchen, coffee pot in hand, "then it'll be cursed hard to find them."

"We must try," said Lowell desperately.

"Oh, we shall," Carne promised. "First light we shall be out there."

Lowell was impressed by Carne's calmness, after his initial surprise at losing his niece he now had settled into a more steady and pragmatic approach.

"Mister Jack, some hot coffee?" he asked.

"That'd be welcome," said Jack, removing his hat and releasing a stream of water onto Carne's fine carpet.

"You think they mean to harm her?" asked Lowell, his face a picture of sad concern.

Jack shook his head. "They'll use her to bargain with. It has to be that."

"I most assuredly hope that's all it is. I could not bear to think of anything bad happening to Rita."

"*Wait!*" cried Carmody suddenly. "I remember now, there is nothing but an old line shack out that way, is there not, brother?"

Carne paused a moment, his lips pouting as he tried to recall, "There is, by heavens. You're right, Carmody. We have not used it for years, and certainly not since the herd was been reduced so radically but it must still be there."

"A good place to start," Jack allowed.

"If they have harmed her in any way," promised Lowell grimly, "I will see to their hanging by my own hand."

Jack eyed him ruefully. "Now you're talking, boy."

"Don't worry, I think we would all be prepared to help on that score," added Carmody.

Jack stood at the window watching the dark flashes of rainfall; his hand clutched the hot coffee mug in a tight grip. He knew, in truth, that someone like Ska Venger would care little for the girl's life even though he had told Lowell differently. He was surprised to discover that he should care that much to form such a lie and it needled at his dark soul. Jack had cared little for anything or anybody else up until now and the new sensation left him troubled with the uncomfortable fear that it might temper the task that lay ahead.

"Get some rest," he grunted, without turning from the window. "We got an early start."

Rita waivered slowly into consciousness.

She was lying on her back on a dirt floor, her vision was blurred, and her chin ached appallingly. Dark shapes loomed and moved in a dimly lit room and she blinked to bring things into focus.

"This one's back with us," said a female voice.

And Rita looked into the face of Vile Spider; the dark hair framing her bizarrely tattooed face as she stared into Rita's eyes. Behind her a bigger shape loomed and a large ugly face came into her vision.

She smelt him then, an animal smell, thick and heavy with dense overtones of feral male scent. He was a huge man, she saw, his bunched shoulders covered with a mat of hair that bristled from the sleeveless singlet he wore. The deeply overhanging brow was furrowed, and the eyes lost in the shadows below glittered with an evil light.

He leant nearer, his breath rasping loudly as he appeared to sniff at her, tasting her smell as a wild animal scents its prey.

"Who are you?" he breathed, his voice a deep sound as if it came from the bottom of a barrel.

Instinctively, Rita lifted herself up onto her elbows and backed away.

"Better speak up, girl," advised the woman. "Ska don't like to be ignored."

"Rita Bodey," Rita said, with an attempt at boldness in her voice.

"I remember you" said Krone, from somewhere behind the couple. "You were making out with that fella on the hillside that time, wasn't you?"

"What do you want with me?" asked Rita nervously.

The woman chuckled and moved sinuously nearer, her ink marked arm reached out and Rita saw a venomous looking python as its skull head came near. Long fingers touched her face lightly, tracing a line across her cheek and into her hair.

"That's to be seen," said Vile Spider slowly.

Rita jerked her head back. "My uncle will make it go hard for you, if you harm me."

"Your uncle!" rumbled Ska Venger. "So, you are related to Carne."

"Hey! That's interesting, ain't it Ska?" perked up Krone.

"It is," Ska agreed.

"Can I have her?" purred Vile Spider, her head tilted to one side as he eyes ran over Rita.

"Wait a minute," cut in an offended Krone. "Who was it went and fetched her in the pissing rain? Should be me who has first call."

"And what about Phantom Dog?" teased Vile Spider. "He was there, wasn't he?"

"All he done was nail some pesky Mex and now I guess he's off dressing his new scalp. Damned fellow creeps me out."

"Ahh!" sighed Vile Spider softly. "*So* sensitive."

"They will come for her," said Ska, his big head weaving thoughtfully. "They will come soon."

Vile Spider continued to stroke at Rita, who cringed under the distasteful feel of the fingers whispering on her skin.

"Don't be like that," said the smiling Vile Spider. "I walk with a soft touch."

"Leave me alone," spat Rita.

"That's right, leave her alone," growled Krone. "This one's mine."

Vile Spider turned on him with a sharp hiss, "You'd best watch your mouth, Krone," she snarled.

"I might just gobble you up."

"Oh, yeah," answered Krone. "Who would that be? You and the rest of that army of tats. Woman, you ain't nothing but a walking picture gallery and that don't frighten me."

"*Quiet!*" barked Ska.

He lifted himself up away from his study of Rita and she saw his true height as he filled the room with his bulk.

"Nobody touches her just yet. We need the bait and she will do right well. Krone, put her with the other one."

Vile Spider moved over and kneeling before him she clutched at Ska's leg, her fingers spread on the great muscles of his thigh.

"Oh, Ska," she pleaded. "Can't I have her to play with? I won't hurt her, well, not much. Please, pretty please, Ska."

Ska husked a rasping chuckle deep in his chest. "Later, Vile Spider. Maybe later."

"What about me?" asked the offended Krone. "I ain't had any for weeks."

"Just put her with the other one and stop whining," ordered Ska. "Do it *now!*"

With a snort of anger, Krone took Rita by the arm and roughly dragged her to her feet.

"Don't see why I should be left out all the time," he grumbled to himself as he pulled Rita from the shed and into the night air fresh from the recent rainfall. "You and me, girl," he breathed in Rita's ear as his hands roamed feverishly over her body, probing and prying her wet dress. "We're going to play some, you'll see."

"Get off me!" she spat.

"Heh, heh," he laughed, pulling her to the rear of the shack. "I like that, a woman with a bit of fire. You and me are going to get along just fine."

Lifting the lid of what appeared to be a store cellar, he pushed Rita into the darkness below. "There y'are, you get along with that other one in there for a while. I'll be back real soon."

With that promise he slammed the door shut and Rita heard a bolt slide across.

Rita shivered and stared around but could make out nothing in the pitch darkness. She was wet through and the damp dress was chilling her body. She sat crouched on the dirt floor; conscious there was limited headroom in the underground cellar.

"Hello," she said tentatively, rubbing her arms to encourage some heat. "Is there someone else here?"

There was silence in answer and then Rita heard a faint shuffle from somewhere off in the blackness.

"Who are you?" asked a female voice.

"Rita Bodey; are you held prisoner also?"

"You might call it that," came the bitter reply.

"How did you get here?" asked Rita, turning towards the voice.

"Through my own stupidity," said the voice. "I'm Ariadne Bendix. Was married to the colonel at Fort Bendix."

"An army wife?"

"Until the colonel broke his foolish neck."

"So how did you get here?"

"It's a long story."

"We have time, but first, have they hurt you in any way?"

"I have to fight with that wretched creature covered in snake tattoos; she is an unnatural animal. And despite all my skills, that beast of a giant, Ska Venger, is outside my influence and that I cannot understand. Most men I can control but that one has powers beyond even mine."

Rita did not quite understand what Ariadne was telling her, but she let it slide. Her eyes were adjusting to the dark and she could dimly see the outline of the woman crouching across from her. Her clothes, that had once been fine, were torn and dirty and her hair hung in sad disarray. Her face was invisible under the fallen locks, but it looked to Rita as if she had suffered some form of beating.

"This whole gang is unnatural, I think," said Rita.

"Miss Bodey, I fear we are in a hell of a mix."

"Don't worry, my uncle will come. He has men, they will find us and rescue us, I'm sure."

"Let us hope so and soon."

"So how did an army wife get to be taken by these people?"

Ariadne drew a deep breath, "After my husband died, I took up with the captain at the fort. He determined to close the place down and move its situation. About time, I thought. My late husband was a foolish drunk and had built it in an unworthy and dangerous place," she paused, and it seemed to Rita that she was controlling herself with difficulty. "I chose to take up with the captain who remained in charge of the post; he was the malleable sort, you know, easily led and simple to control."

Rita detected the tone; the darkness gave her the ability to hear behind the words without any visible distraction. She understood that Ariadne was a conniving woman, the sort who appeared simple and unaffected and yet had the ability to manipulate men to do her wishes. She found she was beginning to dislike the woman who shared her imprisonment despite their common predicament.

"We were on the march when it happened," Ariadne continued. "Moving to the new site. I like to ride, you see. The captain ordered me to stay with the column, to keep in the van. It irritated me, him thinking like that, as if he could control me. Impossible man! So, I took off, I gave my horse its head just to feel some freedom from all the military constrictions. That's when they caught me. This dreadful giant and his pack of cronies were lying in wait. I thought I could win him over, seduce him with my abilities but he is stronger. I must say, the first man I've ever met with the ability to do that."

"You admire him, this Ska Venger?" Rita asked in disbelief.

"I must say there's something of an attraction. He is after all also immensely strong in the bedroom department."

"You've slept with him, with that great ugly creature?"

"I've had little choice in the matter, my dear." There was haughtiness in her tone as if she were dealing with a child. "He comes and takes me whenever he feels like it. I have after all been with many men and usually I'm able to handle the business quite ably but he… Well, he is something quite different. Strangely hypnotic in a way and very fertile if you take my meaning."

"Good Lord!" breathed Rita.

"It's all about survival, you understand? Best just to go along with events and let them unfold if you want to live. I'm sure my time will come, I'll win out in the end."

Rita was shocked by the confession and determined that in no way was she about to surrender herself so easily.

"I don't think I can do that," she admitted.

"Really, it's quite easy. Although his tattooed companion is another matter."

"Yes, she is rather unpleasant."

"I wouldn't mind too much, I've known others in that way but unfortunately this one likes to cause pain in the process."

Rita was beginning to wonder if her companion was little better than the people who had captured them.

The door to the cellar was suddenly swung back with a crash and light from the starlit night sky bloomed in. By its light, Rita saw that the woman she had been talking to was a slender and beautifully elegant creature despite her ragged garments and battered appearance.

"Come on up here, soldier's wife."

It was the voice of Krone.

"Oh, dear," sighed Ariadne, slowly getting to her feet. "It's the other one, still at least he's easier to handle."

"Come on, lady," ordered Krone, hurrying her up. "We ain't got all night and the boss is impatient."

"Is it Ska Venger who calls for me?" asked Ariadne in a subservient voice. Somehow, she managed to inflect some eagerness in her tone as if she were only too willing to concur.

"Maybe, honey. Although I ain't too sure on that score, maybe that bitch Spider has first call."

"You don't have to go," urged Rita. "Come, we'll stand together."

"Shut up!" shouted Krone, overhearing her. "You want me to come down there? You won't like it if I do."

"It's alright," Ariadne assured her in a confident whisper. "I can handle these idiots."

"I pray you can," answered Rita in a low voice.

The cellar door slammed shut and once again Rita was enclosed in silent darkness.

It was a full fifteen minutes before the screaming started.

They were dreadful sounds, hiccups and strangled wails rent from the depths of an anguished being and they echoed dully around the cellar. Rita had to press her hands to her ears to try and stop out such awful cries so full of lingering agony.

She began to shake then, her whole body quivering with terrible fear.

# CHAPTER FOURTEEN

They saw the figure from a half-mile out.

Lonely and propped up on its knees in the middle of the open plain before the shack, the ripped clothes about the body were stained dark red and the head hung down limply. The loneliness of the pitiful form was enhanced by the rising chain of bleak mountains behind that rose like a shivering curtain in the heat haze.

"Is it Rita?" gasped Lowell desperately.

"Impossible to say," Carmody answered, squinting against the rising sun, and peering into the distance. "I cannot tell."

They were grouped as a posse, Carne and Tomas leading the remaining complement of seven Mexican ranch hands and Lowell riding up front with Jack and Carmody.

"Spread out," Carne ordered the Mexicans. "Ride each flank."

Obediently, the band of vaqueros split and rode out in an arc on either side of them with rifles drawn.

"What do we do?" asked Lowell. He was biting his lower lip and desperate to know if it was his loved one that sat exposed on the plain before them.

"That the line shack yonder?" asked Jack, indicating the structure just beyond the lone figure.

"That's it," Carmody confirmed.

"If they're in there, they got us cold," said Jack, viewing the open plain bare of cover that surrounded them clear to the horizon.

"At least we're out of range just now," said Carmody.

"There's no choice, if we want to see if that's Rita we have to go in," pressed Carne, his brow furrowed deep with concern.

It was all too much for Lowell. "Well, I'm not waiting," he cried and drove his heels into his animal's side sending it charging forward.

"Aw, hell!" groaned Jack, slapping his pony's reins and taking off after Lowell.

"Bring those men in on either side of the shack," Carmody called to his brother as he followed.

"Yes, indeed," Carne answered, and the band set out, riding fast in a curving run towards the sagging figure and the suspiciously quiet shack. The ground underfoot was flat and dry, and dust rose in a cloud behind them as they raced across the cracked plain.

As Lowell sped along on his bobbing pony, breathlessly he promised repeatedly, "Rita, oh Rita, I'm coming, sweetheart."

He pulled up the pony before the woman, who sat on her heels; her hands tied behind her and head and hair hanging down so that the face was hidden.

The hair color was indistinct it was so dirty and bloodstained and yet to Lowell's dismay he made out a hint of yellow amongst the filth.

"Rita!" breathed Lowell desperately as he stumbled from his mount.

Carefully, he lifted the pummeled face and started back in surprise.

"Good Lord!" he gasped, barely able to believe his eyes.

Jack swung from the saddle and brought his pony around to shield them from the shack.

"That her?" he asked.

"No, by God, it's Ariadne Bendix."

"*What?* That witch from the fort?"

"The same," Lowell answered, staring at the blood-soaked figure. There was not a stitch of clothing that was not marked by bloodstain, and the clothes hung in ripped strips of material that exposed bruised and slashed skin.

Carmody was beside them, without a word he too dismounted and approached the woman. Lifting her chin carefully he studied the battered features.

Ariadne moaned weakly through cracked lips.

"She still lives," Carmody said, kneeling and swiftly cutting Ariadne's bonds with his knife.

"How did she get here?" asked a bemused Lowell.

"Don't matter none," said Jack, looking off towards the shack. "This here is a warning."

He looked up at the sky and noted it was clear of clouds either pink or black. "They already gone, I reckon."

"This woman needs immediate attention," said

Carmody. "She is in a terrible state. What have those people done to her?"

"A knife, nails and teeth by the look of it," observed Jack with a twist of disdain.

"I have to get her back for medical attention," said Carmody, lifting the limp figure in his arms. "I shall take her to the doctor this minute; there is not a moment to spare."

Swiftly, he threw the limp form across his saddle and mounted up behind.

"Tell my brother where I am," he called, digging in spurs, and racing off.

Jack and Lowell watched his dust trail rise in a straight channel as he sped away across the flat desert.

"Most surprising," breathed Lowell, pondering over Ariadne's presence.

They turned to watch Carne and the vaqueros advancing on foot from each side with rifles drawn and ready to overrun the shack.

"Ain't nothing in there," said Jack with certainty.

With his head hanging low in despair, Lowell started towards the shack leading his pony by the rein.

"Where can she be?" he groaned.

It was then Jack heard a rumble as of distant thunder.

"What's that?" asked Lowell, spinning around towards to the sound.

"Get your gun," advised Jack grimly. He slid his Henry from its scabbard and thwacked the pony on the rump with the barrel driving it away.

A rolling cloud of red tinted dust was approaching from across the plain, and coming from amidst the cloud could be heard a loud drumming sound. Above them the sky was altering into a haze spread with a strange greenish light that tinted the ground below with an ugly pallid color that held all the unpleasant hue of desiccated bone.

Carne and the Mexicans were almost at the shack and they all turned to see the advancing dust cloud.

"What is it?" called Carne.

"It ain't good," replied Jack curtly.

Tomas raced for the shack door, his rifle held ready. He booted the door in and followed by four of the Mexicans, rushed inside.

Lowell was torn between the two events; he stood out in the open between the shack and the oncoming cloud and was unsure of which way to go.

"Stay put," grunted Jack, dropping to one knee and cranking a shell into the chamber of his rifle.

Dutifully, Lowell followed suit and knelt alongside Jack.

"There is no one in here," they heard Tomas call from the shack door.

The clouds before them parted and out of the midst of the dust came an awesome sight.

With Vile Spider at the reins and the gigantic figure of Ska Venger stationed beside her, the chopped-down chariot fashioned from a split buckboard came roaring across the plain. Four horses pulled the vehicle and their necks were bent forward with the strain as the lithe figure of Vile Spider leaned over and lashed the beasts to even greater speed.

Ska Venger began a terrible roaring sound, his bellowing voice rising above the sound of his galloping team, so loud it seemed to echo back from the mountain range behind. He held a rifle in one hand and a tomahawk in the other and began firing as soon as he came in range, spinning the rifle in one hand to lever each shell into the chamber. Two of the exposed vaqueros bucked and spun away, slammed down by Ska's shooting.

Jack raised his Henry and took careful aim, but Vile Spider instinctively swerved the chariot, sheering up a cloud of dust that momentarily hid them from view. She was screaming wildly, her eyes wide and fierce as she dragged the charging horses back around and headed straight towards the shack.

Jack fired and Lowell noted the splinters that flew from the chariot's front but Vile Spider's evasive move had kept them safe.

Jack compressed his lips and levered another shell in.

"Don't watch, shoot!" he growled at Lowell.

"Oh, good Lord, yes," said Lowell, momentarily having forgotten the rifle in his hands he was so shocked by the terrible apparition nearing them.

Carne and the remaining vaqueros were all firing but by some miracle their wild shots left the couple in the chariot unharmed.

Swerving in skidding curves and coming in at speed, Vile Spider brought the chariot in a charge straight towards one flank of the crew standing outside the shack. She sped in and Ska Venger leaned from the side swinging his now empty rifle by the barrel as he swung left and right with both gun and tomahawk, smashing at the vaqueros.

Jack and Lowell trained their rifles following the run and firing fast, bullets smashed into the side of the adulterated buckboard, holing it, and ripping great strips of splinters away in clouds of exploding woodwork.

As they moved away, Jack pivoted around on his knee; at last having a clear shot of their departing backs he drew a bead on the spread shoulders of the giant.

"Now, you sucker," he growled.

His finger was easing the trigger back when there was a tremendous explosion and the entire shack erupted into a gigantic ball of fire, the blast blew Jack and Lowell from their feet and sent them flat onto the ground. A great expanding flame-filled dust cloud covered them, billowing out away from the destroyed building. Debris fell all around, flaming planks of shattered timber and shredded roof; even body parts began flopping down in bloody heaps. As the component parts of the shack fell all around, so did the more everyday contents come raining down; a battered coffee mug, dented tin plates and distorted cutlery fell, a hefty cast-iron fry pan large enough to hold twenty eggs dropped from the sky and embedded itself in the dust next to Jack with a resounding *thump*.

Lowell shook his stunned head, trying to clear the ringing sound from his ears.

"What was that?" he managed.

Jack was already on his feet. "They mined the

damned shed, some of them hiding yonder in the mountains fired it off."

Jack was searching the dust cloud, looking for the expected return of the chariot. He stood spread-legged, rifle at the ready, ragged cloak flapping about him as he heard the oncoming rumble of the chariot.

"Your girl will be with the ones who set it off, go find her, Lowell. I got to settle these two."

Lowell needed no second urging. He ran to find himself a pony and left Jack standing alone amidst the drifting smoke and dust.

The loose ponies were milling about, confused, and disorientated by the settling fog of dust and smoke and Lowell grabbed at the hanging reins of one. He threw himself into the saddle and lurched off, riding around the smoldering remains of the shack and heading fast in the direction of the mountain foothills.

Jack waited.

He could hear the cries and sobs of the wounded vaqueros behind, but he paid them no heed.

Then he heard the rumble of the oncoming chariot. Ska Venger was laughing with hysterical victory, his roaring cackle loud above the sound of the chariot wheels.

They burst through the skimming clouds of smoke and Jack picked his target and fired.

The front horse took the bullet on the chest and dropped instantly, the others in the team colliding with the body and tumbling over, dragging the wagon's shaft down in sharp contact with the ground. Such was the speed and weight of the vehicle that it was pivoted up into the air and catapulted over. Both passengers were lifted from their feet and thrown high in a sailing arc.

The ground shook beneath Jack's feet as the massive body of Ska Venger landed. He hit the ground solidly and bounced up again to fall and roll on like a tumbling boulder. Vile Spider had an easier time of it, her lighter athletic body was able to drop into a roll as she landed, and she was up on her feet in an instant. With flaring eyes and lips drawn back she launched herself at Jack, curved daggers like twin needles held in her hands. Jack stood his ground the rifle leveled at her charging figure.

He fired and cranked continually, levering shell after shell into the chamber of the Henry with amazing speed. The running Vile Spider collided with the fusillade, her body twisted and leapt in mid-air as if she had run into an invisible wall. Blood flew in splayed ribbons as the bullets peppered her midsection. Her run slowed to a stop and she tottered on her feet, her angry gaze fixed determinedly on Jack. She sagged in place her mouth wide open and an insistent raging scream pouring from between her blood-stained lips as she realized her inability to continue the attack.

Jack's rifle was empty and with a face fixed in stone he drew his Colt, walking directly at the staggering tattooed figure his gun arm held straight out before him. He cocked and fired three shots, blowing parts of the screaming head away.

The disintegrated body tumbled sideways and dropped in a heap.

There was a bellow from behind and Jack felt as if he had been suddenly struck by a charging herd of crazed buffalo as Ska Venger barreled into him. Jack spun away, both guns flying from his hand.

Ska roared his anger at Vile Spider's loss and tore dementedly at his singlet, his grotesque face a ravaged picture of hate as he ripped at the cloth in his anguish.

Dizzily, Jack rolled onto his back and looked skywards. Above him the sky was alive with rolling clouds, oily black and red tinted billows that boiled and sped with unnatural speed as they clashed in a monstrous imitation of the battle below. An unearthly net of electrically charged ribbons was building up above their heads, it rippled and glowed with strange luminosity as if it were the uncanny event known as St. Elmo's Fire and the air below took on the pungent super-charged ozone scent of all the electrical power locked in the heavens overhead. There was a sparkling clash of lightning fed thunder and Jack felt himself plucked from the ground as Ska lifted up his large frame as if it were a feather weight and twirled it in the air before slamming Jack down again onto the hard ground.

"I will rip you apart," Ska promised, pushing his face close to Jack so that he smelt the foul body odor of the man as he leaned near. It was a nauseous stink reminiscent of long dead corpses decaying in dank places underground.

Grimly, Jack swooped his arm up and speared his bunched fingers into one of Ska's leering eyes. The giant backed his head away with a howl, and Jack, still on his back, kicked out with both feet landing his boots successfully in Ska's exposed crotch.

The giant doubled over, screaming, and cursing whilst a string of white spittle flew from between his gritted teeth. He threw out a brawny arm that caught Jack across the chest and sent him rolling away. Jack felt as if a ten-by-ten fence post had struck him and he winced with the pain as he hit the ground yet again.

Ska was coming at him remorselessly, crouched over with his wild head poking out from the massive shoulders. One eye was blinking where Jack had hit, and a stream of weeping liquid ran over his cheek from the wounded eye. The muscles in his outstretched arms were alive with snakelike ribbons of bulging veins that pumped and rolled across the surface of his swollen body with a life of their own.

He grabbed at Jack, one huge hand clutching at the thin layer of fat that covered Jack's stomach and Jack howled in pain as he was swung up and held high with his feet free of the ground. Ska hit him with his free hand, the bunched fist as solid as a granite rock and it split the skin on Jack's cheek and knocked him semi-conscious.

Ska drew back his massive arm, cocked his fist and struck again sending Jack's head snapping back from the pile-driver force. Jack hung there, held up by Ska's grip on his stomach as the giant roared laughter in his face.

"You puny wretch," Ska howled, his clawing fingers reaching for Jack's throat. "I will tear out your spine through your mouth."

Then his expression changed slightly, a curious expression crossing his face and his lips twisted in a show of momentary concern.

Through his dizziness, Jack heard the firing.

He looked past Ska's hunched shoulders to see the remaining survivors of the explosion. Carne and Tomas and one other of the vaqueros were advancing, the three men firing steadily as they came. Bruised and burnt by the blast with their clothes shredded and hanging in rags, the battered band were relentless, they marched forward shooting continually as they came. Gun smoke and flares of flame spat from their rifles as they kept up the continuous barrage.

The giant was a hard target to miss and as each shot hammered into him, he shook and juddered. His staring face fixed on Jack as he wrinkled his brow and tried to understand the insistent beating of the bullets that rocked his monstrous body.

"What d'you make of that, you sorry piece of shit?" husked Jack into Ska's face.

Ska's lips curled and he frenziedly tore away the remainder of his singlet. "I cannot be stopped," he leered.

His muscle-bound back was bare now and the great curving slabs of hairy tendon were studded with random patterns of silver from the lead that had struck him. So powerful was the evil inherent in him that the bullets had not entered more than a fingernail deep into his tough skin's surface. He laughed confidently. "I serve a darker force than you know," he promised, throwing Jack aside easily.

Jack tumbled down onto his back and worked his way on heel and hand backwards away from the advancing giant.

Plumes of the enraged ethereal electricity crackled and danced in the charged air above and the looming clouds seemed to pulse with an expectant air as black and red vapors mixed luridly in streamers across the sky.

Jack's hand behind him brushed against the large fry pan's handle and as Ska neared he swung up the skillet, curving a heavy blow that struck the giant resoundingly on the side of the knee. The pan bounced back as if it had met a solid brick wall and Ska came on barely pausing in his stride.

Jack struggled to his feet and swung again, two-handed like a batter at the base he brought the iron pan around. There was a metallic *bong* as it struck the side of Ska's head and the giant frowned in a mute show of displeasure. Reaching up, Ska grasped the fry pan in one large hand and lifted it and Jack from the ground. Before he could pull the metal free of Jack's grasp, Jack reached up to the coiling net of electrical plasma stitched through the air above his head. He plunged his free hand into the sparkling blanket of hovering power and instantly became a conduit. The current shot through his arms and body and along the pan and into the grip of Ska Venger who stood with both feet firmly planted on the ground.

There was a hissing crackle, a spark, and a vital bloom of azure blue light as an arcing sheet of voltage buried itself into the giant. He vibrated and shook where he stood, his whole body cavorting with the massive flow of electricity streaming into him from the charged atmosphere. Smoke came from his hair and for once his usually dim eyes burned with an inner glow that was not of the evil nature that occupied his soul; he was burning from the inside out.

Jack released the pan and fell away, watching as the giant's exterior crisped all over and black lines tracked in an advancing rush through the pattern of veins running across his body. Ska opened wide his howling mouth and a great plume of putrid blue flame gushed out in a pillar. Ska Venger seemed to implode, his great body collapsing in on itself, folding and shrinking, curling as it began to dissolve.

"I will come back for you," Ska Venger promised determinedly as he faded. Jack heard the words whispered on the wind and he stepped back as the giant crumbled into a great heap of smoldering ash and the rising wind tugged and swept the remnants away.

Jack stood staring down expressionless at the disappearing pile of dust, his torn cloak flapping loosely in the wind. He felt nothing but the pain of his beaten body, no sense of victory or vengeance only a vague knowledge of completeness, of a bleak job well done.

"In the wind, sucker," he mumbled. "Ain't nothing you can do about it now."

That's when he heard the distant scream.

# CHAPTER FIFTEEN

Lowell found Rita's pale and bloody corpse lying wedged between two boulders at the foot of the mountains.

Her throat had been savagely slashed, and a section of hair and scalp torn from her forehead.

Vaguely, he heard the clatter of stones and looked up to see two distant figures fleeing up the mountain slope above. The two of them, leaping and hopping over the rocks high above and quickly disappearing from view. The shock was absolute and with disbelieving and glazed eyes Lowell stared stunned at the mutilated body of his beloved.

"No, no, this cannot be," he muttered, stumbling forward as if sleepwalking.

She lay hemmed in by the rocks, her arms pressed close in beside her breasts. There was nothing pretty left, the gaping wound in her throat had shed a fountain of blood that had soaked her front. The slash of the scalping knife had bared the bone and spattered her face and left her resting in a corona of blood pooled in a ghastly halo around her head.

Lowell fell to his knees, his eyes locked on the body but not daring to touch it.

He was screaming in anguish, he knew it, but it was a distant sound as if it belonged to someone else. Lowell was set apart, alone and inside himself looking out, he felt detached and apart from this physical self that cried out with so much grief and agony of loss.

He was still wailing when Jack arrived with the other survivors and they found him, a catatonic creature, doubled over and kneeling pitifully before the feet of Rita.

With something rivaling pity, which was an unknown emotion for Coffin Jack before now, he put his arms around Lowell and lifted him to his feet.

"Cover her up," he grunted to Tomas, standing alongside. "Then see to your boss."

Carne also stood frozen and speechless, staring at his niece with one trembling hand resting on a boulder to prop himself up.

Jack began to lead Lowell away. "Come on, pard," he rumbled in a low voice. "Ain't nothing here for you no more."

"I don't understand…" mumbled Lowell wretchedly. "I don't see the purpose."

"Ain't no point to it, boy. It's just plain meanness; don't try working it out."

"But she was here a minute ago. We had everything…"

"See your feet, Lowell? Look down at your feet. That's it, one step at a time, going forward. We need to get to our horses. You looking now? Go on, watch where you tread."

In such a manner, Jack guided him to the ponies and helped Lowell mount up.

Jack led the pony back to the ranch by the rein as Lowell was a rigid figure slumped in the saddle helpless and unable to move by himself.

The ranch was deserted when they arrived, with no sign of either the crazy woman Maybelline or of Carmody or Ariadne, and Jack reasoned that maybe Maybelline had run off and the other two had travelled directly on to see Doc Lester in Doomesville. He looked across at Lowell and tried to think of what was best. He recognized that there was little point on staying around the ranch; it would only bring fresh memories of Rita constantly to Lowell's mind.

Jack was not one to ponder overlong.

"Goddamn it!" he cursed, taking Lowell's reins in his hand and dragging the pony behind him, he set off at the gallop into the southwest.

Why the hell he cared at all about this tinhorn, he could not figure. It did not make much sense to a man who had lived his whole life alone without concern for another living soul. And here he was considering on what to do with this dumb kid so full of grief he could barely function. It was a first, he reasoned, that was for sure.

As they made the ride back to Jack's place in the Four-Points Range he had plenty of time to consider what had gone on. Lowell was silent and numb the whole journey and responded little to Jack's advances. He sat at their nightly campsites without saying a word, he would nibble the food Jack placed in front of him but it was all a mechanical reaction and no more.

"Come on, buddy," Jack urged, finding himself at first taking on an encouraging tone. "Let's get ourselves together, shall we?"

Later, this devolved into impatience as he gained no success and his tone changed to one of irritation.

"Listen, you useless asshole, buck up or I'll leave you out here to fend for your stupid self!"

But neither way proved fruitful and instead Jack took to pondering on what they knew about the events at the Homely Crossing Spread. He mentally listed the facts as they rode.

To him it seemed likely from what they had ascertained that Ska Venger and his crew had taken on the job of evicting John Carne from his land most likely under orders from the telegraphy tycoon, J. J. Jameson. There was no doubt that Casper Lee Krone and the half-breed Phantom Dog had murdered Rita Bodey, and Jack also held some suspicions about the disappeared Carmody Carne. Where had he gone to so rapidly under the guise of helping Ariadne Bendix just when they were about to be attacked? He had also known an awful lot about the copper beds under the ranchland and on the surface done little about it. Why would such a man pass up the opportunity so easily and without even telling his own brother that he sat on a virtual goldmine? It appeared mighty suspicious to Jack.

They were all matters that needed to be resolved but as they neared the bleak hillside that housed Jack's lonely shack he left it aside and felt a mood of gratification come over him at the prospect of being there.

But there was something about the place that felt different.

At first, he could not figure it out and thought that maybe it was the presence of another human being in his treasured isolation that was throwing him off.

The cats were still there, hissing and spitting as soon as he showed his face although, bizarrely, they seemed to take a liking to Lowell and were constantly winding themselves around his boot heels as if he were their best friend. A thing that made no sense to Jack.

The mountains out back were the same miserably bleak and faceless gray and the same ice-cold water continued to flow in the creek below the hill. It was home as he knew it and he should feel content to be there, yet something had changed, some imperceptible shift had occurred that rubbed at his nature.

He saw that the sky was clear overhead, no promised storm clouds gathered and there was no sound of distant thunder at his presence.

The absence disturbed Coffin Jack and made him feel even more restless.

He set Lowell on his one chair outside the front of the shack and went down to the creek to clean up. There was only the waiting, he reckoned. The waiting for the next task to arrive, maybe by then Lowell would have woken up from his comatose state and he could shuck himself of the young man. Send him back to where he came from and get back to normal.

But still the unresolved affair needled him like an unreachable itch.

As he stepped his aching body into the freezing stream and bathed the fading bruises and scabbed cuts that Ska Venger had left him with, his anger returned over the injustice of Krone and the half-breed's escape and J. J. Jameson's dirty little plan. He strode naked from the water and still wet, dressed and went back up the hill to see to the horses.

He found Lowell standing waiting for him.

There was a hard light shining in Lowell's eyes, the vagueness and lack of presence was gone.

"Jack," he said firmly. "We've got some unfinished business to attend to."

# COFFIN JACK

## Part 2: Gravedigger

# PROLOGUE

It was a cold night and the full moon was bright over the Eternally Laid-Low Cemetery.

The twisted trees inside the ancient bone yard hung down like silhouettes cut from black drapes and a pale mist crawled with long slow fingers through the tombstones. There was humidity in the air, a wet cloying drift that clung to the skin with a creeping, otherworldly touch and even the damp shadows seemed to have a life of their own. Only a half-life though, for surely nothing here was left living.

Not a thing felt right in the place, it was somewhere out on the edge of normal perception and the two men making their way between the gravestones sensed the jaded paranormal shift and felt distinctly uncomfortable. It was as if the open prairie they had just crossed to get here existed in another time altogether and this was a dimension occupying a unique space all of its own.

"You sure he's here?" asked the gunman, Casper

Lee Krone, in a worried whisper to his companion. "He's got to be here, ain't he? Ain't nothing else could make this flakey place home."

Krone waited for answer.

But silence followed and curiously he turned sharply to find that he was alone. Krone looked around frantically.

"*Hell!*" he burst out. "Where the heck are you, Dog? *Phantom Dog!*"

The big half-breed Indian tracker, that had a second ago been alongside, was now nowhere to be seen. But that was typical of Dog, one minute here and the next gone. The silent tracker had the ability to vanish as quietly as a summer breeze and reappear as easily as a shadow on the wall.

"Goddamn it!" cursed Krone, stumbling on alone through the high weeds and long grass that clung like fronds of wet seaweed to his boots. "Why I put up with that sonofabitch, I don't know. Sucker never says nothing worth hearing and ain't ever there when you need him."

Krone crested a rise and looked down into an uneven tumble of rough ground covering a hollow that was populated with crazed and cracked headstones resembling ranks of rotten teeth in a skull's head. They leaned in odd directions haphazardly, the slender markers appearing as lazy and tired as the whole process of death itself.

Amidst them, in the center of the sad bowl crouched a dwarfish figure.

No more than a hunched silhouette, a black unmoving shape resting on the handle of a spade.

Round backed, a domed head with short spikey hair lit to a cresting silver sheen by the moonlight.

Krone froze on the spot at sight of the dwarf, his hand tentatively reaching for the pistol in the worn holster at his side.

The creature below, as if sensing his presence, turned his head slowly in Krone's direction and the gunman saw a yellowish glitter in the eyes.

"You *him?*" called Krone.

The thing below tilted to one side, the eyes now taking on a definite yellow glow in the shaded face as they studied Krone. It issued a sound, a nasal sound from the back of the throat, a low humming growl and Krone felt the hair on the back of his neck rise.

"I'm looking for the one they call Gravedigger; that you?"

Up until that moment there had barely been any movement from the figure below but now it shifted, an almost mechanical stirring as if the gears of its makeup had suddenly come into play and with a stuttering gesture it raised a hand and beckoned Krone to come down.

Krone swallowed and sniffed in an attempt to recover his failing courage, then with a show of bravado he braced his shoulders and started down the slope.

"Been looking all over for you, fella," he said loudly. "First, they tell us you're in some hole-in-the-wall in the western mountains, way beyond the Pecos. Then it's down south across the border in a Mexican abattoir; even had one fool say you was in a retirement home in Pennsylvania. If half of it was true, you sure get around."

"Tell your friend to come out now."

The voice was low, no more than a whisper running through the bleak trees and grave markers, yet it carried plainly to Krone.

"That'd be the Indian breed, Phantom Dog," admitted Krone. "He'll be along directly, I reckon."

"Tell him… *now*!" said the voice in a bolder and harsher tone.

Krone saw the hunched figure raise his shovel to shoulder height and by the moonlight gleaming along the curved edge he could tell that it was in reality a blade as sharp as an axe.

"Whoa!" said Krone. "Don't take on so, we don't mean no harm. *Breed!*" he called. "Get the hell out here where we can see you, will ya?"

Then as if a page had been flicked over in a book, the half-breed was standing beside him.

"I, Phantom Dog," he said in sonorous introduction.

"And I am the one you seek," the black outline admitted.

"Casper Lee Krone, pleased to meet you."

The two continued to approach the crouched figure cautiously and it followed their movements slowly, the bladed shovel swinging down to a position across its middle. It became apparent the nearer they came that the dwarf was in fact a powerfully built creature, with his body muscles hunched into a wire sprung coil ready to leap at any given moment. The pale features, barely visible in the dim light, were chalky white with flaked skin cracked with fissures like the surface of a dried-out riverbed.

"What you want?" asked Gravedigger suspiciously.

"We'd like a word," said Krone, pulling up a few steps away. "We heard tell you don't just put them *in* the ground, that you're one of them resurrectionist fellas as well."

The yellow eyes glimmered and dimmed, flickering as a candle might when fluttering in the wind.

"Maybe," the hunched shoulders twitched in a shrug. "Depends."

"On what? You got some kind of fixed price, or do it work on a sliding scale? Like how long they been under and that sort of thing?"

"Something like that."

"Well, we got one for you, a big guy, he met his end a while back and ended up a heap of dust up there in north Texas. We was wondering if maybe you could fetch him for us."

"He have a name?"

"Sure, he was called Ska Venger. He had this tattooed bitch used to run with him but we ain't so interested in her."

"Ahh!" the sigh was long and drawn out. "I know of this one, I felt the passing. Met his end at the hands of the Deathdealer, did he not?"

Krone nodded energetically. "You got it, that's it, Coffin Jack done for him."

Gravedigger rubbed the blunt fingers of his broad hand across his chin thoughtfully. Something fell away as he did so and there was a patter on the ground as if crumbs of grave dirt had dropped.

"And you want this Ska Venger returned from the

Beyond, is that it?"

"Sure do, he was our boss and a mighty good man when it come to the mayhem and destruction side of things."

"Didn't fare so well against Coffin Jack though, did he?" There was a moment of pause, "But that ain't all, is it?" asked Gravedigger with a sly tilt of the head. "You got more to tell, ain't you?"

Krone sniffed indifferently and both he and the somnolent Phantom Dog remained silent.

"You killed a girl, didn't you?" asked Gravedigger.

Krone shrugged dismissively. "Ah, well, she weren't of no account."

"But she was, wasn't she? She was the consort of Coffin Jack's partner and now the two seek you out. This is why you come here, to find sanctuary in Ska Venger. You think he will protect you."

"Well, true to say we got a mite of trouble with Coffin Jack but if you can just reunite us with our old boss, I reckon it'll all be hunky-dory again. Old Ska would love a second go around with Jack, I'm sure of it. He was mighty pissed when his tattooed lady, Vile Spider got hers, although I can't say the same. Personally, I was right glad to see that inked-up slut get her just desserts."

"It don't work as easy as that," said Gravedigger.

"No? Why not?"

"I need substance to do my work and I need payment too."

"*Substance!* What do that mean exactly?"

"Something; his dried heart, a ring, a thread of hair or a strip of flayed skin. Some personal item to make contact with the departed one."

"But he was blowed away as dust, there weren't nothing left of him."

Gravedigger turned away in disinterest. "Then there is nothing left of him to bring back."

"Now hold on," said Krone hurriedly. "We'll find something, I'm sure. Just tell us how much you want to do it."

"It cannot be done."

"You telling me we come all this way for nothing?"

The crouching shape paused bowing its head in thought. "Perhaps not nothing. There was gold to be made was there not? A substantial amount, I believe."

"Sure," said Krone, with an offhand wave. "But that was mostly going to the prime mover; the boss of the telegraph company, J. J. Jameson, he had the finance to make it happen."

"Tell me exactly what was involved."

"Copper ore," Krone confessed. "An almighty big bed of it and this fellow who runs the telegraph company needs the stuff for his wires. We was to move out John Carne, the body owning the land, so Jameson could go in and dig it out."

"He still waits?"

"Sure, he does but that scene's over now, Coffin Jack put paid to that. We been running a six-month with that bastard and his sidekick on our tail. It's getting right tiresome so that's when *I* decided..."

Phantom Dog gave a low aggrieved snarl of annoyance.

"Well, okay," Krone continued, giving the half-breed a dirty sidelong glance. "*He* came up with the idea of coming to you."

Gravedigger was silent a long time, lost in consideration as the other two fidgeted impatiently.

"I like gold," Gravedigger said finally, his voice rising in an almost Messianic tone as he began a slow rant. "Gold never dies, it holds its color and no matter what you do it, it survives. And in my world that is beyond value. The days of ordinary men are numbered, I see them come and I see them go, sleeping, sighing, and screaming. It makes no difference the manner of their passing, when the time is come, they move beyond this place whether they like it or not. But gold now, that is a substance that rises above mortality. It lives forever."

Krone looked across at Phantom Dog speculatively wrinkling a downturned lip and crooking a curious eyebrow. He had no idea what the ghoulish dwarf was talking about.

"This got some point?" he asked tentatively.

Gravedigger growled nastily, "Of course, you fool! You know nothing do you? Ska Venger might be vaporized and gone forever but did you ever think he might have somebody who may be inclined to take such news badly?"

"Never thought of that, somehow old Ska never seemed the sort to have any loving kin."

"Well, he did, his foster-home brother, Ka Daver. He still lives and I'm sure would be most interested to hear of his brother's demise. Both of them were orphans raised by the same church minister. Ska Venger went off to live in the wild but his brother

Ka stayed behind and became a churchman full of zeal and determined that those on the edge of righteousness should be brought to salvation by his hand alone."

Krone scratched his unshaven chin thoughtfully. "I still don't get it."

"Here is how it will be. I shall oversee this, we shall drive this man Carne from his land, you will get the gold for the copper that lies below and you will pay me a handsome share for the privilege."

"Oh, wait up! Hold on now," Krone's voice quavered. "That's not what we had in mind, not at all. I don't want to go back there, besides we got Coffin Jack to consider."

"Do not worry about Coffin Jack, he is nothing. I shall bring an army of my own to take care of him."

"An army?" asked Krone dubiously. "Where you going to get an army?"

Gravedigger chuckled, an awful dry and rusty sound. He raised his spade high and brought it down hard so that the sharp tip stuck quivering in the ground.

"From here!" he growled.

The soil shook under their feet and the rippling sensation spread away from them as if the minor rumblings of an earthquake were beginning. The entire graveyard hollow began to shiver, the grassy topsoil rolling away from them in waves as if a stone had been cast in a pond.

"Wh… What're you doing?" wailed Krone nervously.

"It is time a count was made," cackled Gravedigger dementedly. "Let them come in their ranks and stand in order."

With a groaning creak a nearby pale wooden marker rose from its bed and fell over, the loose earth below boiling up as if the ground were too full to contain it. It seeped and spilled in liquid form, the earth bubbling dark and mobile under the harsh moonlight. All around them the grave markers were leaving their place, some flying away in spinning skims and others dropping noiselessly to lie flat on the shifting earth.

Krone felt himself going faint and even the stony-faced Phantom Dog took a step back as the earth split open and Gravedigger's army slowly rose from their beds and moved towards them.

# CHAPTER ONE

"What's that on the end of your nose?"

The telegraph clerk's eyes crossed as they focused on his squashed nostrils under the green eyeshade covering his brow.

"Looks like a tube of some kind."

"Sure is," affirmed Coffin Jack. "That's the barrel of Mister Samuel Colt's .45 caliber pistol you're staring down."

"Is this nonsense supposed to impress me?" said the clerk. He was a rather foolish and belligerent upstart of a man, whose time in office had given him all the arrogance of a civil servant with a sense of power over individuals that far outweighed his actual intelligence or common sense. "If you are thieves then take what you will. Personally, I could not give a rat damn about it, none of it belongs to me anyway."

Jack sighed in exasperation. "We ain't no robbers or road agents. Just that my friend here," he explained with a nod towards Lowell Devereux standing behind him, "has asked you six times for attention. We knocked the desk, rang the bell, even sang your goddamned praises but you persist in showing us your back."

"I got urgent business to attend to, I can't be dealing with everybody's little problems all at once."

Jack screwed the barrel of the Colt in harder. "It don't take a minute to leave off your tippy-tapping on that telegraph key and give us a *"good day and how can I help"*, do it?"

"Sir," complained the clerk, "I will ask you to remove your weapon and take note of the sign on the wall there." He twitched his eyes sideways to indicate the notice tacked on the office wall, then rotated them back to stare at Jack's one good eye, the other one being an empty socket covered by an ominous black patch.

"What's it say, Lowell? I ain't taking my eye off this fellow."

The clerk noted that the eye that bored into him was a strange shade of orange as if an inner fire burned behind the ball. He was so bumptious and full of self-importance that he rather foolishly did not feel intimidated by the ugly and scarred face confronting him, nor by the looming frame that carried it and was wearing a dirt-stained raggedy military style coat with cloaked shoulders.

Lowell drew a breath and sighed. He was well used to the vagaries of his irate companion, knowing full well that Jack was impatient with petty officialdom and could never stand it at the best of times.

"Jack," he said, "is this really necessary? I'm sure

the gentleman will get around to dealing with us in good time."

"No, Lowell. There ain't nothing good about this numbskull, he just have a high opinion of himself, that's all. Now, read out that sign."

"Very well, it says: *Our staff will suffer no abusive or violent treatment. They are here to serve you with good will and any impolite or vile language will not be tolerated. Cases will be treated with utmost severity by the law and caution is given that the company will take all legal action necessary to ensure the safety of our staff. Signed The Electric Telegraph and Post Company.*"

"There, you see," said the clerk smugly. "So, you had best remove that firearm from my person this instant or I shall have to call on the sheriff's services immediately."

"That a fact?" growled Jack. "How about I pull the trigger this instant and we put a full stop in that sign? Right above where your brains scatter along the way."

"Jack, Jack," pressed Lowell, taking hold of the Deathdealer's sleeve. "Please, ease up a little."

"Don't touch me," snarled Jack and he bored the Colt in a little deeper. "You paying attention now?" he asked the clerk.

The clerk weakened as he saw that his pompous stand as an official was not quite working out. "Very well then, what's your problem?" he asked with an irritated sigh.

"There, that wasn't so hard, was it?" said Jack, removing the gun barrel and leaving a neat circle of red on the end of the clerk's button nose. "Tell him, Lowell."

"We are on the road, sir," Lowell explained. "Travelling for some time now and I am having forwarded any telegraphs or mail that may come my way from my employer, Miss Beatrice Hicks of The Holy Roller Magazine. I wonder if you have received any in my name?"

The clerk eyed Jack ruefully and rubbed the end of his nose. "That will take a while," he said. "I shall have to refer to our incoming ledger for any outstanding receipt slips and then go through the store boxes for held mail, after which I shall have need of a verification of identity and a witnessed signature." He glanced at the rack of recesses behind him that were stuffed with waiting mail. "Come back in an hour."

"*An hour!*" snarled Jack. "Look for the damned thing now, will you?"

"Sir, that is not proper procedure; the correct protocol must be followed. It is more than my job is worth not to complete everything according to the exacting methods laid down by the company."

"Why, you stuck-up little dumbwit. I'll…"

"Jack!" cried Lowell. "Will you leave off. The fellow is only doing his job."

"Well, he ain't doing it right well, is he? Look at this place, it's empty of custom 'cept for us. He ain't got pressing business. Fellow's just being awkward."

"I assure you," said the clerk primly, baring his

teeth in a fake approximation of a polite smile. "I shall attend the matter as soon as possible. As you can see, I am alone here and only have the one pair of hands, so please, come back in an hour."

Lowell tugged at Jack's sleeve and worked him towards the door. "We shall attend in an hour," said Lowell apologetically. "Come, Jack, perhaps some liquid refreshment whilst we wait."

Mollified at the notion of alcohol, Jack subsided and grumbling he followed Lowell from the office.

"Damn jerk-off, what the hell difference does it make to him?"

"No matter," said Lowell patiently. "Look there, across the street, a homely looking drinking house, wouldn't you say?"

They were edgy, tired, and hungry after the months of travelling.

Their appearance in the small cross-roads township of Simpering Blessing had meant to be no more than a short stopover to check the mail, rest the horses and get some supplies.

Since Lowell had lost the love of his life, Rita Bodey at the hands of deceased Ska Venger and his gang, they had searched across the land to find the surviving culprits and exact some justice. It had been an exhausting time for the one-time journalist, his emotions had been battered by the shift from naïve young man in search of goodly and uplifting events to record for his magazine, The Holy Roller, to the darker associations found in the company of the assassin-for-hire, Coffin Jack.

An odd couple to strike up an association and with the already disturbing introduction to the wild and weird uncertainties of the Frontier it had been an additional culture shock to the young eastern writer. Bravely he had tried to accommodate himself to the company of the lonely and cold heart of the gloomy personage of Coffin Jack, who led an isolated life beset by the darker forces that walked a forbidding land full of anarchy, murder and disorder.

The Crown and Hound Emporium opened its doors to them, and they walked into a high-ceilinged room with a surrounding balustrade gallery and apartments, a small stage with a discrete pianist at play and a few groups of midday drinkers in place. The bar itself was a nicely presented piece of polished dark-wood carpentry, with sculpted and decorously clad female figures supporting well stocked shelves and beveled mirrors.

"Quite nice, wouldn't you say, Jack?" asked Lowell, leading the way across to the bar.

"Hrmph!" grunted Jack, the man of few words.

"And what will we be having, gentlemen?" grinned the barman, a slender, somewhat effeminate looking fellow with a large spotted bowtie and a small round head occupied mostly by a face full of teeth.

"You have a sherry?" asked Lowell doubtfully, fully expecting the common look of confusion he had met at the request in his journey through the West.

"We do indeed," smiled the barman, flashing his

brilliant array of dentures. "Oloroso, Moscatel, or Manzanilla, all the best imports from Jerez in Spain. Name your preference."

"My word!" gasped Lowell. "You *do*, you actually have it?"

"Of course, sir. Our aim is to please."

"You hear that, Jack. Now you must try some, the Moscatel if you will, barman."

It was Lowell's deeply held wish to bring Coffin Jack into some kind of understanding of the finer things in life, an educational desire he had so far unsuccessfully fulfilled.

"You sure?" grunted Jack, looking with disdain at the thumbnail-sized glass of amber liquid.

"Sip it, Jack. Taste the mellowness and full flavor, let it linger and roll around inside your mouth. Give time to appreciate the sweetness and richness of the experience."

Tentatively, Coffin Jack duly sipped.

"*Pah!*" spat Jack, spewing his mouthful in a disgusted stream across the bar. "*Glah!* Give me whiskey right quick," he ordered the bartender, whose smile had started to slip. "Quick! I gotta get the taste of that stuff out my mouth."

"Oh, Jack," sighed Lowell. "I do declare, there is no hope for you."

Speedily, the barman was pouring whiskey into a shot glass, but Jack snatched the bottle from his hand and glugged down one third in an attempt to swill his mouth out.

"*Hah!*" he shouted, gratefully. "My God, Lowell! How can you drink that candy-assed crap?"

Lowell looked away in despair and settled back with one elbow on the bar, to sip with pleasure at his own glass.

"You got eats?" Jack grunted to the barman.

The fixed smile appeared again. "We do indeed. This week is vegetarian week, a new experiment by our imported chef. He is all the way from Europe, you know?"

"Do tell," said Lowell, rising to the bait.

"Oh, God!" groaned Jack.

"We have a delightful avocado dish, of asparagus leaves on a bed of chives, highlighted by roasted green beans and slivers of carrot in a hot beetroot sauce. Mouth-watering, if I do say so myself."

"Sounds delightful," gushed Lowell. "I do believe I have re-entered civilization again."

Jack frowned, his big fists bunching and fingers flexing. "Give me a steak," he rumbled. "If you ain't got it, show me the cow and I'll kill it myself."

Lowell chuckled patronizingly. "Jack, Jack, you are too much, you really are."

The barman foolishly took his side, with a winning smile he asked, "Your friend is somewhat straightforward in his tastes, I take it?"

"I fear so," said Lowell agreeably. "A large steak, well done with potatoes and gravy will fit the bill."

Jack's brow darkened, and he fixed his beady eye on the barman. "You're getting mighty near the edge, fancy boy, so just go get it," he growled. "Afore you do, tell me this, you got any wholesome entertainment 'sides that dumbass pounding the keys over there?"

The barman drew himself up and flicked his head to one side in a show of tiresome bother, "Upstairs," he said. "Third door, that will be Miss Eva Reddy. I believe she is open for entertainment at present."

"Good," rumbled Jack. "I have need."

"Must you, Jack?" pressed Lowell.

"Look, boy," said Jack. "Just 'cos you got a preference for dinky drinks and prairie-dog food, don't mean I got to suffer as well. Some of us have pressing matters of a more fundamental nature, you understand?"

Lowell, whose memory was fixed on the lost love of his heart, his dear Rita, so savagely murdered those months before, understood Jack's protest only too well. His only experience of carnal love before meeting Rita had been trapped in a platonic admiration of Miss Beatrice Hicks the editor of The Holy Roller, since then he had been held in a confusing emotional whirlwind and yet, since knowing Rita, the physical aspects of lustful passion had not been lost on him.

But such thoughts were interrupted as the swing doors of the saloon swung open and the imperious telegraph clerk pushing in followed by a burly sheriff and two deputies.

"*There they are!*" bawled the clerk, pointing a quivering finger accusingly. "Do your duty, Sheriff."

The sheriff, a bluff fellow in a yellow shirt and buckskin vest with a large silver star hanging in plain view, pushed forward.

"You the boys been threatening the clerk?" he asked, fronting the two at the bar with one hand on the butt of the high-holstered Schofield at his ample waist.

Jack lowered his head and Lowell noticed with tired dread the slight smile tightening his friend's cracked lips.

"Not really," grunted Jack. "It was more like 'advising'."

"Advising?" asked the lawman.

"Yep, give service or get served," added Jack.

The sheriff drew a deep breath. "Well, we don't have none of that behavior in Simpering Blessing, mister. I reckon you'd best hand over your firearms and step along to the jailhouse with me."

"Just like that, huh?" said Jack pushing himself up from the bar.

Lowell quickly stepped forward. "Sheriff, I beg you do not take umbrage. I believe there has been some sort of misunderstanding here."

"Certainly not," snapped the clerk spitefully, drawing himself up in a posture of justified affront. "I was bodily threatened by this fellow. A gun was held to my person and my life placed in jeopardy."

"That so?" asked the sheriff.

"Well," admitted Jack slowly, "you could say that. The punkass should be grateful I never took his nose off along with what little brain he has."

The two deputies carrying shotguns swiftly spread out behind the sheriff, one on either side.

"Damn you," grunted the sheriff, "I was having a quiet day up until now."

With that he went for his sidearm.

It was a fool move considering who they were

facing.

Coffin Jack's Colt was in his hand before the sheriff cleared leather and three shots rang out. They were so close together that the roar of gunfire sounded like one continuous blast.

There was a chaos of noise as the rest of the clientele in the saloon dived for cover and the deputies opened up and returned fire. The barman disappeared from sight with greased dexterity and Lowell stood bewildered as lead whistled around on either side of him. One of the nicely appointed mirrors was vaporized in a blast of double aught and some of the fine woodcarvings erupted in splinters that left the displayed nymphs legless and headless. Amidst the racketing din choking smoke from the black powder cartridges blew in pale clouds and flame spewed in every direction.

It was over in brief seconds.

As silence returned to the bar room the mist slowly cleared and Lowell stared wide-eyed at the party of lawmen. One of the groaning deputies clasped a bloody forearm, whilst his shivering companion winced in pain with one hand clutching his torn shoulder whilst the other still held an empty shotgun in trembling fingers.

The sheriff sat spread-legged and bewildered on the floor between them, the gun in his fist had its barrel expanded and torn open like peeled fruit, Jack's bullet having entered the open end and blown the barrel apart.

Jack was calmly shunting out empty brass and reloading from his ammunition belt.

"Reckon I'm getting soft," he admitted to Lowell. "Would have been a time…"

"You let them *live*!" gasped Lowell in shocked surprise.

"Yeah," sighed Jack. "You're having a bad influence on me."

"Why, that's most admirable, Jack. At last some symptom of altruism, it's wonderful."

"I doubt it," he looked at the trembling clerk, who was over by the door hovering nervously between fear and flight. "Now, you got any mail for us? Yes or no?"

"Here, here," gushed the clerk, hurriedly pushing a handful of mail into Lowell's hand. "It's all there, I promise. I made sure, everything from Miss Hicks and a telegram for your friend," he jabbered nervously.

"Right," said Jack. "Get out and take these fellows with you. I got a lunch coming and I don't want no more interruptions. We clear?"

The wounded deputies helped the stunned sheriff to his feet and stumbled out guided by the distraught clerk.

"The next sonofabitch gets in my face and I'm going to rip it off," Jack promised their disappearing backs before turning to the re-appeared barman. "Now I'm gonna get my pecker sorted and I want my dinner on the table pronto; is that too much to ask?"

# CHAPTER TWO

"What you got?" burped Jack, pushing his finished dinner plate away.

Lowell pulled down his gold-rimmed spectacles and looked at Jack over the top of them, he nudged the pile of opened envelopes and telegraph slips.

"Miss Beatrice is most upset, it seems."

"Do tell," said Jack in a bored tone as he picked at his tombstone teeth with a fingernail.

"Yes, she is concerned that I have not sent her any copy, in fact that I have not been in contact at all. The poor woman has sent request after request," he lifted some of the mail in example and let it flutter back down on the table. "I have been very remiss, I fear."

"Guess you've been otherwise engaged."

"True but it is no excuse. Miss Beatrice is a lady of some social standing and also my employer, and so being should be dealt with in a polite and considerate fashion."

"Lowell, I thought you'd gotten past all that?"

"All what?" asked Lowell with a bemused look.

"All that dilly-dallying over female foibles."

"A gentleman just does not behave like this, no matter the cause."

"Bet you never thought of that when you was rolling with Miss Rita," sneered Jack.

"Don't go there," warned Lowell. "That is an entirely different matter."

"That a fact?" huffed Jack. "Best thing you can do right now, is go upstairs and seek out Miss Eva Reddy, let her blow your pipes. Guarantee you'll see things straight after that."

"Oh, Jack," sighed Lowell in disgust. "Please."

"So what's that billet-doux of mine say?"

"Rather obscure I think," said Lowell, lifting the telegraph slip. "It says; "*Sinner, I shall come and seek your repentance*" and it's signed by one, *Reverend Ka Daver*. I trust you know the man?"

Jack pouted his lower lip. "Never heard of him."

"You don't know this minister?"

"No, sir. Never been one much for the church attendance."

"Perhaps it's a charity circular from a good man seeking offerings for a worthy cause then."

"Hrmph," grunted Jack indifferently.

"Well, Jack, if we see the man I'm sure a few dollars in kind offering would not go amiss."

Jack's attention had drifted up to the third door of the gallery above. "Got to go," he purred, pushing back his chair. "Another kind of offering I got in mind right now."

"Very well," sighed Lowell, "I shall attempt to

write a suitable reply for Miss Beatrice. I do hope she will forgive my tardiness in making contact."

"That's it, Lowell, you go play with your pen, and I'll go play with mine."

As Jack departed, Lowell sorted the pile of mail and amongst the jumble found a letter he had missed. It had been enclosed in one of Miss Beatrice's letters with a covering note and was a small but rather official looking envelope with the name "The Electric Telegraph and Post Company" printed in an elegant and staid script across one corner.

"*Dear Lowell,*" Beatrice had written in her attached note. "*Despite not hearing from you for some time and sorely concerned for your wellbeing, I pass on this letter that has been forwarded to me. I must presume you are somehow engaged in fruitful works of an uplifting nature and this has restricted your ability to remain in contact. We at the office miss your company terribly and look forward to some word from you or your speedy return at the earliest convenience.*"

Lowell understood the veiled message beneath the words. There had been nothing more than a polite understanding between the two of them but Lowell's early adoration of the young Miss Hicks had made it plain in the polite terms of the society they moved in that his interest was indeed amorous. She, for her part, had not been unaware and in the methods of the day had happily returned his signals of affection without any word being plainly spoken. Now it appeared Beatrice pined for him and could not understand his sudden silence.

It all caused Lowell some distress. He had fallen head over heels in love with Rita Bodey, the rancher John Carne's niece, and in doing so had swept all thoughts of Beatrice Hicks from his mind. Rita's subsequent murder had brought him to his lowest ebb and only the wretched thought of vengeance against the perpetrators had kept him going.

With all the repeated and feverish requests for contact from Beatrice left unanswered he now felt some misgivings of guilt overlaying his earlier more base desire for revenge.

Sadly, and by way of a momentary distraction, he broke open the envelope from the Telegraph Company.

"*Esteemed sirs, I write to you on behalf of our president, the Honorable J. J. Jameson, who humbly requests that he might have the pleasure of your company at a meeting to discuss lucrative business of a mutual interest. If you will call at our offices in Austin, Texas full arrangements will be made. Have no concern for accommodation or stabling, all will be handled by our staff.*

*I look forward to the pleasure of your company, I am, sirs, your humble servant, Ernest Leaf, Company Secretary.*"

Lowell pushed the letter to one side, too dismayed to give it much attention at the moment, and he took out pen, ink and paper from his portfolio and brought to mind again the fair Miss Beatrice as he attempted to console her concerns and write again in a mode he had almost forgotten since meeting Coffin Jack.

The sound of joyous female squawks of appreciation and the repetitive bumping noises coming from the rooms above brought a shake of the head and a sad smile to Lowell's lips as he poised his pen nib and dipped it into the inkpot ready to begin his missive.

He began three times before finally settling on a simple approach and with head down and engaged in his writing he mapped out his letter of resignation.

*"My dear Miss Hicks, pray forgive my delay in answering your letters for so long a time but here on the wild Frontier events do move at an incredibly hurried pace. I am at present in the company of an interesting character called, most bizarrely I know, Mister Coffin Jack and am involved in a series of unusual and sometimes mysterious adventures that have, I fear, drawn my attention away from the mission you have placed in my unworthy hands.*

*I must say that although your directive was to discover reports of uplifting events of some spiritual value, unfortunately I have found little to fulfill your optimistic hopes. The country is rough and rugged beyond description and the people themselves formed from a similar mold, yet despite these shortcomings I must say there is also something of a wild beauty that draws me to my surroundings.*

*However, it would be false of me to say that I have been closely concerned and fully engaged with the terms of my employment and the mission you have engaged me for. I am perhaps an unworthy soul for such high office and therefore find that I cannot in all honesty continue in my role as a member of your staff, under such circumstances and in all honor I can only offer my resignation for this sad failure. I therefore lay down my pen for the last time in the service of The Holly Roller.*

*I sincerely hope you will forgive me, my dear Miss Hicks.*

*Yours affectionately..."*

Lowell hesitated, then quickly scratched out the last few words and re-wrote his ending more formally.

*"Your obedient servant, Lowell Devereux."*

Lowell set down his pen and read through the manuscript a few times, but his mind was not on the words. His thoughts were with his dead Rita and the sad recognition that he would never see her again ran through him with almost tangible pain.

"I am glad to see you still have your pen in hand, Mister Devereux."

The female voice startled Lowell from his doldrums and he looked up to see a vision before him. She was a small woman, even in her neat lace-up boots she came to no higher than Lowell's chin. Her full and robust little figure was dressed in travelling clothes and the bright curls that shone like spun threads of pale gold around her features were hidden under a black veil and the wide brimmed hat that she wore.

In Lowell's confused frame of mind he thought for a moment that some apparition had suddenly appeared before him and he gaped in amazement. Then slowly, the figure raised her hands and lifted the veil.

"*Miss Beatrice!*" gasped Lowell.

"Yes indeed," said Beatrice sharply, the reprove obvious in her tone.

"But where have you come from?" asked Lowell, swiftly rising to his feet.

"From many miles," said Beatrice crossly. "I have travelled far across this infernal land to find you, Lowell."

"How on earth did you manage that?"

"Like a paper trail game, I followed my forwarded letters from pillar to post until I tracked you here. Where have you been, Lowell? What have you been doing? I was filled with dread when we did not hear from you. My dear Mister Devereux, I fretted so, considering you may have fallen foul of wild savages or that some other terrible occurrence had befallen you. I just had to know."

Lowell looked at her in blank surprise.

She was a pretty little thing, with softly rounded features and bright blue eyes. Her breasts were large, almost too large for such a small creature and her nipped-in waist filled out her hips nicely above the drop of her skirts. Her clothes were dusty from travel and she looked tired as she cocked her head to one side and furrowed her brow in a show of concern.

At a loss for words Lowell could only sigh, "My dear lady."

Beatrice looked down at the paper-strewn table. "You have been writing to me perhaps?"

Her hand reached for the letter that Lowell had just finished but Lowell quickly shuffled the papers together and stuffed them into his jacket pocket. "No, no," he said hurriedly. "Merely some notes, nothing more."

Beatrice drew a long breath. "Well, I have taken rooms in this unfortunate place and would like to change out of these travel stained clothes. I wonder if you will at least carry my luggage up to my room? The service here does not seem to include a baggage attendant."

"Of course," gushed Lowell, hurrying around the table between them, glad of any distraction from the shock of her sudden arrival. "Where is your room?"

Beatrice glanced up to the gallery. "The second door along, so the fellow at the bar said."

Mentally, Lowell sighed as he picked up Beatrice's carpetbag and led the way up the stairs to the room next to where Coffin Jack was still noisily engaged.

He showed her into a clean and simple room with drape hung windows, an iron framed double bed, a dressing table with mirror and washstand and a folding vanity screen.

"Well," she said, looking around. "It will have to do, I suppose."

"Not quite the Astor Hotel, I know," Lowell agreed, setting down the bag on the bed. "But really quite nice by most normal standards out here."

Beatrice bustled across the room and pulled the drapes over the windows. "We must talk, Lowell. I have to know what has been going on, after all not a word from you for some six months."

"I know, I do apologize," murmured Lowell, abashed and unsure of how to proceed.

"You know we had an unspoken understanding, my dear," continued Beatrice archly as she opened her bag. "I have come to think of you dearly, not just as an employee but more as a prospective fiancé given your earlier approaches and, in truth, such a prospect filled my heart to overflowing. To be so suddenly cut off wounded me most sorely and, I must admit, it threw me into some distress."

She did not look at him, her cheeks were flushed pink with embarrassment at the admission of affection and she distractedly threw clothes from the carpetbag onto the bed.

"It is complicated," muttered Lowell.

"I dare say," said Beatrice, pulling the long hatpin from her hair and sweeping off the wide brimmed hat. "There is an explanation I am sure, and I look forward to hearing it."

"Perhaps over dinner?" posited Lowell, anxious to escape and rally his thoughts.

"No, Lowell, we must talk now." Beatrice was determined and showing some of the boldness that had first attracted her to Lowell. "You will stand there. I shall go behind this screen and change and you may tell me exactly what has happened to you over the past months."

With that she swirled away, opened up the folding screen and disappeared behind it. Lowell stood across the room, awkwardly stepping from one foot to the other as he heard the discreet sound of buttons unsnapping and the rustle of clothing being removed. Above all these subtler sounds and in the momentary silence between them came the tireless knocking of Coffin Jack's bedhead against the wall.

"What on earth is that dreadful hammering noise?" complained Beatrice.

Lowell bit his lower lip. "I fear that is my associate, Mister Coffin Jack."

"Ah," said Beatrice. "He is the local mortician or a carpenter perhaps?"

"He is certainly nailing something down," admitted Lowell numbly.

"And how came you by knowledge of this man?"

"It is a very long story, Miss Beatrice, perhaps I can explain later."

"Lowell, I am not letting you out of my sight. You will stay here and understand that I have made my mind up. I have determined that you are to be the man for me. It is most forward of me I know, and I am sure my late departed father would most seriously disapprove but these are modern times and as a modern woman I must engage in forthright action rather than await due etiquette."

Lowell's heart sunk into his boots at the confession.

"Beatrice, I think…" he began and then his eyes widened as she stepped out from behind the screen.

Beatrice Hicks was completely nude; she wore nothing at all but a pair of dark stockings that reached up to her naked thighs.

"I believe most men like this sort of thing," she said with an apparent show of boldness and yet there was an underlying coyness in her apparently wanton attitude.

Lowell marveled at her tiny figure highlighted by a shaft of light passing around the edge of the drapes. She was physically curvaceous and her unmarked skin smooth and pale, she stood with one hand decorously covering her lower parts and the other pressed daintily between her large round breasts that were proudly tipped by delightful points of pink.

"We have waited too long, Lowell."

"Oh, dear," moaned Lowell, trying to avert his eyes but drawn inevitably to the lush figure before him.

"You will take me now as a husband and lover, I care not for what society may think," said Beatrice, stepping across the room and offering her hand to him. "We shall make love together. I fear I am a little inexperienced and at a loss so you shall have to lead the way."

She stood below him looking up and Lowell smelt the sweetness of her scent and looked into her eyes as they stared at him devotedly. "Do not deny me, dear Lowell. I have waited so long for this moment."

Her breath was hot on his cheek and she stood on tiptoe and kissed him fervently on the lips.

"You must know that I love you," she whispered.

The kiss was soft and moist and for a heady moment Lowell was lost in the tenderness of her touch. The enveloping press of her warm fulsome body aroused him, and he forgot all the shortcomings and dismay he had felt previously. His mind was in a whirl, since last he had seen Beatrice he had ridden with Coffin Jack and suffered Indian attack, been imprisoned, fought against overwhelming odds and killed men in the process. He was no longer the timid innocent she had known or still believed him to be.

He lifted her in his arms and carried her to the bed.

"Yes, Lowell," she breathed. "Oh, yes."

It was the work of minutes for Lowell to clear the bed and throw off his clothes, in desperation he fell on Beatrice and made rapid and almost savage love to her. And yet, even in his moment of climax, it was only Rita's face that he saw before him. It was her sobbing words that he heard and rather than the pillow of Beatrice's plump body beneath him it was Rita's lean frame he encountered. His energetic union was over too quickly and the aftermath full of the extreme anxiety he felt at being torn between the images of the two women.

He felt no joy on completion and with tears sliding down his cheek Lowell pulled himself away and sat, head in hands on the edge of the bed.

"Lowell," she whispered. "What's wrong? Was I too inept? I know I shall improve with time. Please, do not be distressed."

"No, no," said Lowell, shaking his head savagely. "It is not you, dear Beatrice. It is I. I am a faithless man and not worthy of you. I have done things, Beatrice, things that you would not believe. I have shot down and killed men and ridden this terrible land in the company of a hired assassin," he paused a moment before making the last full confession. "I have loved another and she is in my heart still."

Quickly, Lowell climbed to his feet and without daring to look at the silent woman left lying shocked on the bed, he hurriedly dressed and stumbled from the room just as a monstrous bellow erupted from the room next door and walls seemed to shake inwards as Coffin Jack also reached a satisfyingly high point of ecstasy.

# CHAPTER THREE

All that survived on the bare plain were a few stunted trees, their blasted limbs stripped of foliage and reaching upwards like withered hands seeking forgiveness. Everywhere was a hot dry land deprived of sustenance and giving no hope of shelter or succor except to those coldblooded creatures incapable of producing their own body heat. The raw earth ran dull red underfoot and the thick air hung low and spread a dense heat that quivered in the air and pressed oppressively on the figures standing alone in the vast space.

It was here that the meeting had been arranged.

"He comes," said Gravedigger.

Both Krone and Phantom Dog could not guess how he knew but they looked off in the direction the domed head of the dwarf nodded and saw the thin shivering shadow in the distance as it approached through the heat haze.

"You think he's up for this?" asked Krone.

"Why would he not be?" shrugged Gravedigger.

"I don't know, I guess these religious nuts have

agendas all their own."

"Better not let him hear you say that," advised Gravedigger.

"Why? He something kind of special, is he?"

"When the mood is on him," Gravedigger said in an offhand manner.

"Don't bother me none," grumped Krone.

"But then you are a fool," muttered Gravedigger.

"Hey!" growled Krone. "Watch your mouth."

Gravedigger cast him an evil look from his yellowish eyes and raised the sharpened shovel, gripping the shaft tightly, a low hiss escaped from his slit lips.

"Be still, Krone. Do not try my patience."

Krone raised a challenging eyebrow and looked down his nose at the peeling dwarf. He was about to say something antagonistic when Phantom Dog touched his arm and shook his head. Krone sniffed and looked away, his lips compressed in anger.

"Your Indian friend is wise," whispered Gravedigger.

They all turned as the tall figure of Ka Daver drew his pony to a standstill and sat in the saddle looking down at them.

He was tall and gaunt, a slender figure dressed entirely in black wearing a high-crowned hat with a wide round brim, the split-tailed white collar hanging to his chest was that of a preacher and the only thing that said otherwise about him were the twin long-barreled Colt pistols holstered at his waist outside the tailed frock coat. Dusty and grimed from travel, the coat and clothes were as moth-holed and frayed at hem and cuff as the figure that wore them.

The angular face was drawn in tight fractions, the skintight over the bones and showing every angle of a jutting jaw and hooked nose. Under the shade of the hat brim two cold eyes gleamed as they studied the waiting men.

"What is it you wish of me?" he asked.

"You know who I am?" said Gravedigger.

Ka Daver twitched; it may have been a slight laugh that hunched his shoulders.

"I know you, who could mistake that flaking skin; you look like a door of peeling paint, Gravedigger. Or indeed a whitened sepulcher that introduces the way to the afterlife. If you will repent your sins and kneel before me, I will lay hands on you and cure you of the ailment that rots your flesh."

Gravedigger was indifferent, he touched the unfortunately ravaged skin on his jaw and a rain of brittle fragments fell away. "I like the way I look," he said. "I have been this way since birth, it does not trouble me."

"But then you do not have to look at you," said Ka Daver.

"That's a fact," chuckled Krone in sly agreement.

Ka Daver leaned forward in the saddle, the leather creaking as he moved. "It is a mark of the soul," he said. "The outer body will bear the weight of your sins; it will carry the result of all the offenses committed. Our land is filled with those warped and distorted by their misdemeanors, sickened by their failure to kneel and bow down before the majesty of true righteousness."

His tone was that of a sermon offered from the pulpit and presented with all the confident assuredness of one who knows he is right in all things.

"Pride is also a sin, is it not?" observed Gravedigger.

"Do not test me," snarled Ka Daver. "I speak not from myself but only as a vessel. I cannot help being chosen; it was not of my making. You will hear me, or you will perish, that is my message."

His hands twitched on the reins and a slow movement was made towards the two pistols.

"We are not here for war," Gravedigger said quickly. "We come to discuss the loss of your brother."

"Yes, your message told me he is no more."

"That's right," chipped in Krone. "We was with him when he got it."

"My brother was a mighty man; this Coffin Jack must have been truly great to bring him down."

"He's a mean sonofabitch all right," agreed Krone.

"He shall be brought to a justified end," Ka Daver promised.

"We ask," said Gravedigger, "that you will join forces with us. We intend to continue with your brother's task that was so sorely interrupted. We wonder if we might leave this Coffin Jack to your attentions?"

"It is already underway. He is forewarned."

"Ah, I see," sighed Gravedigger. "Then we may attend to matters without fear of interruption?"

"Vengeance shall be mine," said Ka Daver. "But I would know more of your mission for I smell the touch of financial benefit in this."

Quickly, Krone shrugged dismissively. "Not so much, just a lousy rancher needs seeing off."

"Do not play with me," snarled Ka Daver, fixing Krone with a malevolent stare. "You will make fair offering for my part. I shall call on you for my portion, my collection plate shall be handed around and you will fill it from your bounty."

"Don't worry," supplied Gravedigger, planting his shovel in the ground and leaning over the handle. "You will receive fair part of the rewards."

"See that I do, dwarf, or the full suffering of penitence shall fall on your shoulders."

"We go now to the ranch to finish the affair."

"And shall I go to finish mine?" said Ka Daver, spinning his pony around and riding off without a backward glance.

"Something else, ain't he?" muttered Krone as the tall figure rode out of earshot. "Mighty high opinion of himself."

"He is useful only as distraction," growled Gravedigger, resentfully watching the disappearing shape as it wavered into nothing through the haze. "When we are done with our business we shall see about that particular prophet."

Ka Daver rode on thoughtfully, crossing the empty plain in an easy manner and letting the pony set the pace.

He was untouched by feelings of the intense heat; his thoughts were far away in a momentary grieving for his dead foster brother. They had grown up together and their differences in nature had not impacted on their mutual dislike of the overbearing minister that had raised them. But the zeal of the preacher, their foster father, had impressed itself on Ka and he had taken on board the religious cause, albeit a warped version whilst his brother had followed a more primitive and occult path.

It could not be any version of brotherly love that troubled Ka; it was more a sense of injustice that preyed on him. That the one he had grown up with and with whom he had shared the same bizarre extremities at the hands of their adoptive father, had vanished from existence and been cast to the four winds as if he had never existed.

Ka Daver decided it was time to pray for guidance.

Alone in the desert, he dismounted and knelt down beside his pony. Throwing his hat aside he held his hands wide in the Oran's prayer position and raised his eyes skywards to stare into the glare of the sun.

"I am bereft of a brother," he cried loudly. "Set apart and alone. It would do me good to see the scales set right and the balance leveled. Tell me the way."

He mumbled on, working his way through long Biblical tracts searching for answer, whilst keeping his gaze fixed upwards as the hot sun beat down on his head and its glare blinded his eyes.

A long bony finger tapped him on the shoulder.

Surprised, Ka Daver twisted around to see the cowled figure of Death standing over him.

The skeletal creature stood some fifteen feet high and towered above him, its giant bony frame was covered with a tattered black shroud that trembled and quivered despite the fact that there was not a breath of breeze to ruffle it. In one hand Death grasped a great long-bladed scythe and in the other a large hourglass sand clock set in a wooden frame. The soft grains in the clock silted down freely, glittering as they fell and the glass bowls that held the falling sand seemed to shimmer across the surface with a constantly changing iridescent gleam.

Ka's eyes ran up the giant figure until he reached the pale skull and empty eye sockets looking down at him from inside the hood.

"You have come for me?" he asked, annoyed with the faint tremor evident in his voice.

The skull-head clicked its teeth together in dismay.

"Not yet, pard."

"Then why are you here?"

"Because I'm tired," Death confessed.

Throwing back the cowl, he placed the large hourglass down behind him and sat on it with a heavy sigh. His bones squeaked and creaked in complaint as he bent his frame, there were no tendons or ligaments to hold them in place or to cushion the joints and the parts rubbed one against the other noisily.

"Here," he said once he had settled. Suddenly, he threw down the scythe with a hefty sounding thud onto the dusty ground between them. "Take the damned thing."

"Me? And why should I do that?"

Ka did not know if it was the immense size of Death that diminished him but he felt distinctly intimidated; it was not a condition he was used to and for the first time in his life he felt bemused and unsure.

"I have had enough," groaned Death. "Since the beginning of time I have serviced the funereal cause and it is too long, I wish to rest."

"But surely yours is an eternal task."

"Reaping souls can be a dad-blasted bore you do it long enough," complained the skeleton irritably.

"And now you offer *me* this commission?" Ka asked in amazement.

"You or anybody who's willing," yawned Death. "I just need a break."

"But I am a mere mortal, this cannot be."

"Don't you believe it, pal. Anybody can do this job, though I warn you the hours are not up to much. No days off or holidays, even He got a Sunday, me? I'm at it every goddamned minute of every goddamned day."

"Surely," Ka pressed, "yours is a holy task; you set the hour, the means, the method and place of passing. It is a truly awesome charge, the ultimate possession over life and death."

"You think so? You want to try?" Death rested his chin on one crooked hand, the bones of the fingers clicking impatiently against the arch of his cheek. "Go ahead, give it a go, I give you leave. Take up that scythe and go harvest a few souls, see how it feels. You like the job, it's yours."

Ka Daver was tempted; to fulfill such an impressive position filled him with a sense of suitability, of the true position he had known within himself that he should have fulfilled since childhood.

He licked his lips and rubbed his fingertips against his thumbs as the temptation rose within him and the scythe took on the role of a willing symbol of promised power. He reached out a tentative hand towards the long-bladed tool.

"Can't have no hate though," cautioned Death. "No love neither, got to be totally impersonal and objective. Not a flutter of compassion, just do them in whatever the state. Good, bad, indifferent, you don't make the judgment, just go do them, that's all you got to do."

Ka drew back his trembling fingers from the scythe nervously.

"See," said Death, "ain't so easy, is it?"

"You must have taken billions," Ka gasped in awe.

"Oh, yeah, more than you can ever imagine. Think on it, from the beginning of time I been farming this planet. Walking the earth from end to end just harvesting as I go. Damn me! If it ain't a tiresome task. You sweep here and that's another million or two on the glory road, you sweep there and another multitude heads homewards. If only it was a sight more interesting."

"Can't you make it so?"

"Oh, sure. You try at the beginning. You know, devising various means and getting all kinds of ingenious variety into it but it still pales after a few millennia. But you'll be new to it; you'll love it at the start. Think on it, there's all them natural disasters to foster, then you got plague, that's a particular favorite. Wars are good too. Sometimes there's a spot of competition around like you and your brother, lone stars at the murder game. Good for a little gleaning, but not really up to much on the grand scale. Take the job, this way you can get your belly full." He leaned forward convincingly. "Now just imagine that."

"It still sounds a tad mechanical," frowned Ka.

"But it is," pressed Death. "That's just it; I'm nothing but a damned meat grinder these days. It's all so modernized, used to be a time I had to balance each soul against a featherweight, real careful and exact you understand? Too heavy, it went that way and too light, the other. Think on that, it called for some intervention on my part, a little judgmental interplay. Now, I just turn the hourglass over and when time's up, well that's it."

"Let me think about it," frowned Ka.

Death shook his head and Ka thought he detected a smile creasing the jaw full of teeth.

"Sorry pal, time's up. You had your moment of choice and I got a pandemic in China to consider. Best keep it in mind though, death ain't all it's cracked up to be, now is it?"

The giant vision shimmered and began to flicker away, leaving only a vaporous outline of the space it had filled in Ka's sight.

Ka Daver slumped down, his head spinning as he blinked awake. He became aware and only then realized that he had been involved in no more than a heat-induced illusion. And yet, he wondered, had there been a message from on high brought to him by the vision. Did he perhaps need to change his view of things?

With the ponderous weight of this indecision preying on him he slowly mounted up and continued on his way.

# CHAPTER FOUR

"What you in such a goldarned hurry for?" Jack grumped.

Lowell turned in the saddle and poked a jibe at his companion. "You're certainly getting soft, Jack."

"*Me?*" growled Jack.

"Sure, just look at you. Can't get up in the morning, need to have your breakfast before we go. All that and an expanding waistline indicate a certain tendency towards a slowing of the wits."

Jack looked down at his waistband, patted his faintly pot-bellied gut and pouted. "You think so?"

"Was a time," criticized Lowell breezily, "when you were as slick as a sack full of sidewinders, now I'm not so sure."

Jack narrowed his one good eye and frowned.

"You're just pissed."

"Certainly not," snapped Lowell haughtily.

They had set out before sunup and Lowell had needed to drag Jack from the tender embraces of Miss Eva Reddy and virtually force him into his size twelve boots. Lowell had spent the night alone fretting over his unfortunate meeting with Beatrice. He had not returned to her room or dared to have any connection with her before they left and had determined that they be on their way at the earliest convenience. Even now, the sun was just cresting the eastern horizon and blasting into Jack's sleepy eye, a thing that did not endear him to the journalist's early start.

"Yes, y'are," insisted Jack. "Something happen last night, did it?"

Lowell remained adamantly silent with his back to Jack as he steered his mule onward.

"You get that letter done to your boss?" pressed Jack. "Was that what this is about?"

There was no answer from Lowell.

"Something's got under your blanket," mused Jack. "I told you; you should have had a go round with Miss Eva Reddy. Guarantee she's a game one, certainly gave as good as she got."

"So, I heard," came Lowell's muffled reply.

"Listening at the keyhole, was you? Well, I never had you down as no preevert, Lowell."

"I am most certainly not a pervert, Jack; the whole place could hear your caterwauling. It was disgraceful. I don't know how you do it, you somehow manage to reduce the most tender of moments into a debauch of physical and vocal pandemonium."

Jack jutted his jaw and twisted his ugly face into an angry frown; he was unsure of the exact meaning of Lowell's phraseology but chose to pick on the one word he understood. "'T'ain't *disgraceful*, it's natural, is all. Just 'cos you got such a tight ass you can't even get yourself laid proper, ain't no fault of mine, no need to take out your bitterness on me, you little pipsqueak."

"Who said I did not get "laid", as you so crudely put it?"

Jack lowered his brow ponderously and studied Lowell's straight and stiff back suspiciously. "You *did?*"

"Most assuredly," sniffed Lowell. "Miss Beatrice arrived in town last evening and we... Um... We had a moment of connubial bliss, you might say."

"*Oh, really?* Well, bless my soul! So what happened? Where is the poor gal? She too bowlegged to see us off after your ministrations?"

Lowell's shoulders slumped. "I cannot say," he sighed. "We parted at something of an impasse."

"What "pass"? We ain't been through any pass yet awhile."

"No, no, not a geological anomaly. I mean a kind of blockage; it's difficult to explain."

"What, you got a bowel problem, that it? Hot tar water, that's your solution, Lowell. Ream you out like a river in flood, I swear it."

Jack's clumsy attempts at reassurance were not the slightest sweetener to Lowell's distressed state. Lowell's literate nature often made communication difficult and with the shortcomings of Jack's more simplistic outlook the significance was quite often misunderstood. As a man who could barely read and write, it had been Jack's initial desire to use Lowell's more erudite capacities that had been the cause first drawing the two of them together.

"I cannot get dear Rita out of my mind," Lowell's voice cracked in confession. "She appears before my eyes, even during that most private of acts."

"Can't screw no dead woman," Jack grunted bluntly. "Leastways, unless you're sick in the head."

"She is forever with me," wailed Lowell, breaking down with his shoulders heaving in barely suppressed sobs. "I could not face poor Beatrice or fulfill her expectations with the beloved ghost always at my elbow. It seemed so unjust."

"Still," murmured Jack, in a vain attempt to cheer up his companion. "Least you got your rocks off, huh?"

"What shall I do?" moaned Lowell. "I have taken advantage of a dear lady. An upright and God-fearing woman who had no right to be so ill-used in such a fashion. I am the most despicable of human beings."

Jack raised his eyebrows in despair, "Well, at least you can tell me where we're going. Maybe I ain't had no bacon and eggs yet awhile but perhaps you can satisfy my appetite on that score."

Lowell sniffed back his tears and straightened his back. "There is word that those two mealy-mouthed swine, Krone and Phantom Dog are to be found in a township ahead and that is where we are bound."

"That so? And what is this place?"

"Why, look here!" exclaimed Lowell, pointing at a sagging road sign amidst the shadows of fast approaching evening, it stood tottering on a leaning pole alongside the trail. "The very place."

The sign read: "*Dead End, 5 mile on. Approach with caution.*"

********

Dead End was a sprawling township made rich by gold strikes in the overlooking hills that formed a steep barrier on three sides of the sloping ground that was home to the three hundred and sixty souls left remaining. The town's gloss had now tarnished somewhat as the lodes had diminished but there was still enough of the precious metal found to make the community viable. The jumble of shacks and false fronted wooden buildings had grown to no distinct plan or pattern but spread out more or less organically. The only static and stable rendezvous for the entire shamble of scattered structures was the Main Street that focused on the one major edifice that centered the town, The Impossible Result Saloon and Assay Office. A brick-built structure, the only one in the place, constructed by an early winner in the mines and duly designed with all kinds of extravagant and flamboyant architectural features. Gothic gargoyles spouted from the crenellated stonework that fronted the saloon and the conical and pointed tips of two tiled rooftops gave the place more the air of a medieval castle than a drinking hall.

Dead End had been a wild place originally but was now trying to settle into a more reserved and calmly established urban area. The amenities stretched to a bathhouse, a chapel, a police officer and even a resident judge.

There was no avoiding the saloon; it was the only place in town that was actively occupied, as the buggies and saddle ponies tied to the hitching rail outside indicated. Jack and Lowell duly pulled up and dismounted outside.

Without waiting, Jack bashed the swing doors in and loudly banged his way inside. He stood in the doorway and cast his eye in every direction across the crowded room before bellowing, "I'm dry as a post!" and stomping his way over to the bar. With a brusque sweep of his elbows, Jack cleared himself a space at the packed bar and leered his good eye across at the woman standing serving behind.

"Don't just stand there, gal," he growled. "Can't you recognize a man dying of thirst?"

The woman, who seemed vaguely familiar to Jack, eyed him disdainfully for a long moment. She was rake thin and somewhat imperious and wore a voluminous head of frizzy hair that shot from her head in an explosion of red that owed a lot to liberal soakings in vermilion dye.

"I know you?" she asked, obviously partially recognizing Jack just as he did her.

As Jack mused on the subject, Lowell arrived at his elbow.

"Why, bless my soul!" he exclaimed. "Isn't it Maybelline from Doomesville?"

"Don't know the woman," she said haughtily. "I am Miss Jane Margaret Fray and I run this establishment."

"But surely," pressed Lowell. "You remember, Jack. The saloon run by that black fellow, he used to keep Maybelline... I mean Miss Fray, bound to the bed with a ch..."

"What'll it be?" the woman interrupted swiftly

before Lowell could continue.

"Whiskey," grunted Jack, oblivious to the nature of the woman and only concerned with a cup of that which cheers.

"I suppose a glass of sherry wine is out of the question?" asked Lowell tentatively.

"What's that?" frowned the erstwhile Maybelline and now Miss Fray.

They had saved the then deranged woman from the clutches of a barman who kept her as a sex slave in his back room and it was Jack who had fought a machete-wielding Mexican to free her from the awful servitude.

"Then water will be fine," said Lowell. "But how have you been, Miss Fray? We were concerned for your wellbeing and found you gone from Doomesville on our return. It would appear that your circumstances have much improved since those days."

"I'm fine, just fine," she replied hurriedly. "Janson!" she called to one of the other sweating barmen, all of whom were hard pressed by the rush of clients. "See to these fellows, will you? I have matters to attend to."

With that she hurried off and Lowell watched her go with a quizzical glance. "Most strange," he muttered. "You see that, Jack? She barely had the time of day for us."

"Suits me," growled Jack. "I got my own little lady here," he said, clutching the whiskey bottle placed before him.

Lowell watched Miss Fray make her way through the crowd and weave a route to the rear of the saloon where a raised area housed the gaming tables.

"Well, last time we saw her she was barely able to string two words together she was so crazed."

"She certainly ain't no loon now," said Jack as he poured. "A mite stuck-up, you ask me. Skinny bitch even took time to look down her nose at me, the sassy whore."

"Really, Jack. That's no way to speak of a lady."

"Last time I seen that particular lady she was laid on her back on a bed with her legs spread wide enough for the noon train to make headway."

"You do remember then? It was one of Ska Venger crew you put paid to so she might go free."

"Was it?" slurped Jack, more interested in downing his glassful and quickly pouring another.

"Yes, and old Mister Carne's brother lit out with that Ariadne woman, you recall Jack? We wondered what became of them."

"Can't say I did. Let it ride, Lowell, it's all ancient history."

Lowell was standing up on tiptoe though, eager to see where Miss Fray was heading. "You miss the point, Jack. It may well be that she might have heard something of the whereabouts of Krone and the half breed."

"I doubt that, more likely she'd try and forget all about the Carne ranch and what went on there."

"Damn me!" snapped Lowell irritably, as he tried to hoist his body up to see over the heads of the crowded saloon. "Sometimes I do despair of you."

"Will you get down," growled Jack. "Jumping about like some kind of jack-in-the-box. I'm trying to drink here, you realize that?"

"*Oh, my!*" gasped Lowell suddenly and he quickly dropped down hiding himself in the folds of Jack's cloak. "You see who she's getting?"

Jack's upper lip trembled, and he glared at Lowell. "Get out of my coat," he snarled. "They going to think you're some kind of lady-man-fellow you carry on like that."

"He's coming over," whispered Lowell. "It's Carmody Carne."

The well-dressed and silver-haired, rather handsome man in his fifties who approached them, beamed welcome with a hand outstretched in greeting. "Well, well," he said. "I do not believe it. Coffin Jack and Lowell – was it Devereux? Yes indeed, it was. How are you, gentlemen? Been a while now, has it not?"

"Mister Carne," said Lowell, forced out from cover and taking the offered hand. "So pleased to see you."

Jack merely looked over his hunched shoulder and nodded briefly.

"But what brings you to our humble establishment?" asked Carmody.

"You *own* this place?" said Lowell in surprise.

"We do, Miss Fray and I. You have met the lady, of course."

"We did indeed," agreed Lowell. "And much changed since last we met."

"So she is. A veritable rebirth. Once out of that tiresome situation she has blossomed and show the most remarkable skills in organization; now

I do not believe I could ever manage this place without her help."

"And may I ask what became of Ariadne Bendix whom you carried off in rescue?"

"Oh, Ariadne is around here somewhere. She does not get out much nowadays, I fear. The wounds, you know? They left a mark."

"I dare say," said Lowell. "She was cut rather badly as I recall."

"Near to death, Mister Devereux. Quite at the door, in fact."

"Take something to put that one down," Jack muttered into his glass.

"What was that?" asked Carmody.

"Pay no heed," cut in Lowell. "Jack is somewhat short without his daily alcohol level. So, have you heard from your brother?"

"Dear old John, no, not a word. I presume all was made good after that gang of ne'er do wells were seen off."

"You heard about Rita, of course?"

"Ah," sighed Carmody, "I did. A most sad affair, I must say. My only niece cut down in her prime, awful, awful business."

"We are after the villains who committed the crime and wondered if you might have any word on them."

Carmody frowned and rubbed his chin. "Can't say that I have but surely the entire gang was terminated?"

"No, these two escaped."

"Ah! I see and you have been after them all this

time; it must be over six months now."

"Six months, three weeks and five days," Lowell supplied.

"You keep tally, Mister Devereux, but then you were quite fond of Rita, I think?"

"She was my heart," murmured Lowell gently, with a slight break in his voice.

"Too bad, too bad," Carmody sympathized. "Well, look, please treat this place as home, won't you? I'm sure we can find a room for you, although we are quite heavily pressed at the moment. Now I must rush off, I am the Assay Officer you see and it's a demanding task when all the miners are in to have their pokes weighed." He turned away, obviously eager to be off. "Near the end of the month, that is why we are so crowded. Please excuse me and so nice to see you again."

With a swirl of his well-cut coat tails he was lost in the crowd in an instant.

"There you have it," said Lowell turning back to Jack who had managed to make a serious dent in the bottle whilst they had been talking. "Now we know what became of them."

"And you're the better for knowing?" asked Jack.

"Well, no, not particularly but it is pleasant to discover what becomes of people and to see that they are well and on their feet, does it not?"

"That fellow is a mite too greasy for my liking; he never did explain why he never told his brother about the copper find."

Jack, you are far too suspicious, you really are."

"Then tell me, how did he manage to get ahold of

this joint? Answer me that."

"I could not say. A windfall perhaps, a win at the tables, who knows?"

"Exactly, nobody does."

A sudden hush fell over the whole room and the two turned to see what had caused the silence.

A ghostly looking female figure had entered through the swing doors. She was draped in finely embroidered white silk veils from head to foot and wore so many layers that she seemed to drift across the floor as if it was not legs that carried her but some mysterious cloud. The crowd parted readily before her and she wove a path directly towards the two and only stopped when she stood before Coffin Jack.

"Remember me?" she asked in a voice as hushed and inviting as a soft summer breeze.

"Hard to forget," grunted Jack, eyeing her cautiously.

"Isn't it Ariadne Bendix?" prompted Lowell, at once recognizing the melodic tones.

"Ah," she breathed. "You *do* remember me."

The voice held the same enchantment as ever and her slight breath puffed out the light veils when she spoke. They clung like gossamer about her and the web-like texture effectively hid her face from view. The face that Lowell remembered as so beautiful it filled men's hearts the instant it was seen.

"Dear Mrs. Bendix," said Lowell softly, "are you quite recovered from your ordeal?"

Almost regally, the figure offered a gloved hand

to Lowell, who gently lowered his lips over the offered fingers.

"Recovered? I doubt that can ever be safely said," she whispered.

Jack sniffed and glowered at her accusingly. "You got something of mine."

"I have? Why, Mister Jack, you must explain."

"You took it on our last parting. Something of mine, from in here," Jack punched a bunched fist into his chest. "I know you're a witch, woman, so don't play no games with me."

She tipped the veiled head coquettishly to one side and her lustrous voice purred from behind the cover of her veil.

"I did, didn't I?" there was a hint of humor in the tone. "And you want it back, do you?"

"I do."

"Then as all else, it has a cost."

It was hard for Lowell to understand what was going on but he did remember that Ariadne had begged for Jack to take her with him but he had refused and on their parting, the strange woman had held out her hand towards him and left Jack as if he had been struck in the side although she had never actually touched him.

"What's the price something like you can ask?" Jack's tone was brutal and it was all too obvious he despised the woman.

"I'll whisper in your ear," she teased.

"*Ariadne!* What are you doing?" It was Carmody who brushed through the crowd, a worried expression on his face.

"Just a word with old friends," Ariadne answered blithely.

"Perhaps you should rest, my dear," said Carmody. "It is not good for you to test your strength."

"Oh, I am quite strong enough for these two gentlemen, I assure you," there was a tinkle of laughter in her voice.

"Let's see what you're really made of," snarled Jack lunging forward, and then, with one grasping hand he bunched the veils covering Ariadne's face and wrenched them away.

She screamed piteously and there was a collective gasp of horror from those watching who automatically fell back.

The face was hideous, it had been torn and ripped, the flesh sewn back in jagged flaps that created a ridged jigsaw of the features. No hair grew on the bald head and one eye appeared higher set than the other, the nose was gone, and the lips were an open wound, a veined purplish cavity that wailed now in anguish.

"*You dog!*" she roared at Coffin Jack. "You unspeakable spineless bastard!"

"Ain't so pretty now are you, honey bun?" sneered Jack. "Don't have men falling at your feet no more, do you? Can't wind them around your finger and then toss them over when the money runs out, can you? She got you by the short hairs, has she?" he asked Carmody, who stood frozen in shock. "Don't let it happen," Jack went on. "She got the skills all right; the dark skills from the other side but don't pay it no heed. Let her go, man, she won't ever bring you no joy."

The crowd at the bar had backed away and stood in awe, a bordering circle of aghast staring faces, and as each eye drank in the terrible sight of the maimed features, Ariadne drew herself up and suffered the exposure with a sudden perverse show of pride.

"Then you will see it all," she growled at the watching men, the voice was deep and raw in her throat and came out more masculine than feminine. She began in a maniacal fashion to tear at the veils surrounding her. They ripped as she clawed at them, the frail material tearing in strips and the separated parts floating in the air as if it were a strange vapor that surrounded her composed of drifting slips of flagellated skin.

Her naked torso was soon exposed and the inhuman wounds she had suffered at the hands of Ska Venger's gang displayed a body shredded and slashed, the stitching and sewing of repair so inadequately handled to make her seem no more than a barely human composition of monstrous abnormalities. The ugliness was absolute it reached from her dissected breasts to her back, her stomach and her thighs, every surface marked by a map of horror. Once it had been a firm and luscious body, the skin so smooth and flowing that no man could resist it but now it was a devastated desert, so ruined that it was void of any hope of desire and affection.

"No, no," cried Carmody, at last coming out his stunned sleep. He rushed forward tearing off his jacket to cover her.

"*You!*" cried Ariadne, brushing him aside and

pointing a wavering finger at Coffin Jack. "You will suffer for this. Be sure of it, not now, not here but in days to come, I will make you pay, I swear it."

"Give back what you took, and it might save your pesky soul," Jack answered calmly.

"*He* comes," leered Ariadne. "I have called him and now he comes for you, Deathdealer."

Jack rubbed his hooked nose between finger and thumb and took a bland stance leaning back against the bar. "That a fact? But that don't help you none though, does it? They all seen you for what you is now."

Ariadne halted in her tirade to look around at the gathered crowd, all of them fixed to the spot and too shocked to look away. She hissed at them, the sound of a poised rattler about to strike and the crowd instinctively pulled away, crushing the ones at the back.

"Won't work no more, witch," said Jack. "Admit it, you ain't got it no more. Best give it up and be on your way."

Ariadne backed away towards the door, never taking her eyes from Coffin Jack, who watched her leave with his stony face unmoved by her predicament.

"Go on," he said. "Get your sorry ass out of here."

"I have it," she said pointedly, her glare fixed on Coffin Jack and as the swing doors parted behind her the voice faded as she left. "I have it still."

# CHAPTER FIVE

"Best you leave as well, I think," said Carmody.

"Good Lord!" breathed Lowell, relieved now that the terrible sight of Ariadne had departed. "What the devil happened to her?"

"There was little I could do," said Carmody. "I tried to get her some help, but she was near death. The doctor in Doomesville was quite useless; he did what he could but as you can see he was not up to the task."

"I remember that particular physician quite well," said Lowell sourly. "Indeed hopeless, as you say. But you have cared for Ariadne since?"

"Well, it was Miss Fray that really came into her own there. The two of them formed a bond of sorts and I believe that Ariadne helped Miss Fray recover her wits after a fashion. Ever since the two have been very close and are forever in each other's company. It is a blessing really. I think Ariadne would have gone quite mad left to her own devices."

"She's gone way past that," growled Jack.

"Believe me, she is not so bad, Mister Jack."

Jack studied him a long moment. "I don't know if you take it for kindness or you're just too plain dumb to see but you can take it as read that that one is hell on wheels and best left well alone."

"Well we must beg to differ on that particular point, now, really you must leave."

As he ushered them out, Lowell glanced around the room that had become a mumbling crowd of restless individuals who all stared after them with the stark memory of Ariadne's awful appearance imprinted on their retinas. He saw Miss Fray standing at the back, straight and tall and rising above the rest as she occupied the raised area at the rear of the saloon. Her eyes were fixed on them, a blank stare empty of significance yet Lowell did not like what he saw and recognized a deep and undying hatred buried there. The woman said nothing and made no movement only following their departure with that ominous vacant look.

"What a sight was poor Ariadne," said Lowell as the saloon door swung shut behind them.

"Ain't she a picture?" chuckled Jack. "Reckon that's the one thing old Ska managed to get right."

"Why such animosity, Jack? It was a dreadful fate to befall that stunningly beautiful woman, surely you can see that."

"What I see," rumbled Jack, "is what goes on inside that bitch, she got more scurrying in her dark heart than a hatful of spiders."

Lowell shook his head in despair; it was hard for him, even now, to escape the mysterious hold that

Ariadne had held over men. A powerful siren-like quality that irresistibly drew males to her like moths to a flame.

"And what was it that she has of yours?" he asked.

Jack looked glum. "A good part," he answered bluntly.

"*A good part*, how do you mean?"

Jack shook his head indicating he would say no more on the subject and began strolling off along the sidewalk.

The two of them had reached the corner step of the saloon when a figure stepped out from the alley alongside the building and blocked their path.

"Senors, it is I," said the man, respectfully removing his sombrero.

"*Tomas!*" cried Lowell. "What are you doing here?"

Tomas had been one of John Carne's vaqueros that had helped them during the fight with Ska Venger. Many of his Mexican compatriots had either died or been sorely wounded in the fray and it had been long months since the three had met.

"I have come with some news for you."

"I knew it was you," said Jack reprovingly. "Smelt you clear round the corner."

Tomas had an unfortunate hygiene problem that often-offended Jack. The Mexican thought little of personal cleanliness and cast a tainted aura of stale sweat and unwashed clothing around whenever he was close.

"What is it, Tomas?" pressed Lowell. "Are things not well at the Homely Crossing Spread?"

"Senor Carne is not so good as he was, I think he did not yet get over the death of the senorita," the Mexican explained. "The ranch is fine; we have made many improvements and now…" he stuck his chest forward and grinned proudly. "I am the new foreman, it is a great honor, no?"

"Well, it weren't no promotion for dint of your dress code, that's for sure," muttered Jack critically eyeing Tomas's worn out chaps and grubby frayed shirt.

"A very great honor," said Lowell commendably. "But tell us what is wrong."

"They have come again."

"Who? Who has come?"

"It is strange, and I am fearful to tell you. They are creatures of the night, I think. Many of my men have fear; they do not like to go out in the dark and those with the herd say that unholy things appear when they stand their watch. It is also said that the ones called Krone and the Indian have reappeared and that is why Senor Carne tells me to come to you. He is afraid they have conjured up something of evil again."

"Can you stand downwind of me?" butted in Jack, holding his nose high in the air. "I fear there's a skunk loose in the vicinity."

"You hear that, Jack?" snapped Lowell. "Krone and Phantom Dog, they are there over at Homely Crossing."

"I heard."

"So, do we go?"

"Sure, we'll go come morning."

"Can't we go now?"

"You heard him," grunted Jack, lifting the eyebrow over his good eye and Lowell saw the orange glow that burned inside. "*Creatures of the night!*" Jack intoned in a mocking, exaggeratedly spooky voice.

Lowell was cautious. "What? What do you think they are?"

"Hell if I know," shrugged Jack. "But best we come on them in daylight, don't you think?"

Although eager to get after the two hated men, Lowell had to accept that they would only move when Jack had decided and at no other time. Coffin Jack was a killing machine and Lowell was fully aware that his own capabilities in that area of expertise were limited so he followed in Jack's wake and allowed him to take the lead in matters of a tactical nature.

"So where do we stay tonight?" he asked.

"Well, we ain't welcome in the saloon no more, so I guess it's the stable yard for us. Might be the head wrangler there'll let us sleep in the hay loft."

"Please excuse me, senors," interjected Tomas. "I fear I can stay no longer, much as I would enjoy your company, but I must ride back now. Senor Carne will have need of me."

"There's a relief," breathed Jack. "A night with your balmy breezes is more than a body can stand."

"Gracias, Senor Jack," smiled Tomas, unoffended, as Jack's blunt comments often sailed over his head. "But I cannot leave Senor Carne alone, he has the difficulty with his legs these days and cannot get about so well."

"We understand perfectly," added Lowell. "Pray tell Mister Carne to have no fear, we shall be there as promptly as we can."

"Very well. Adios, senors, and *vaya con Dios.*"

Graciously, the Mexican replaced his sombrero and slipped away back into the shadows of the alleyway.

Jack sucked fresh air thankfully. "Lord! Don't know how that man lives with himself."

"We could have gone with him," said Lowell.

"Nope, the ponies need rest and so do we. Come on, let's get the horses on to the stables then maybe we'll get some supper."

They moved around to pick up their horses from the hitching rail but froze as a loud call echoed down the length of the street.

"*Coffin Jack!*" boomed the voice from the lengthening shadows at the end of Main Street.

"What now?" sighed Jack, tilting his head so his good eye could search the darkness.

"It is I, Preacher Ka Daver."

"Who?" muttered Jack.

"It's that one who sent you the telegraph," whispered Lowell. "You know, the one who wanted some kind of offering."

"No, sorry, fella!" bawled Jack into the shadows. "We ain't making any donations today."

"It is not your money I want, Coffin Jack. It is your soul," came the gloomy response.

"Join the queue, buddy. Been looking for that particular item myself for years."

"Stand forward and meet your Maker, Death-dealer."

Jack caught the warning drift and stared off into the darkness. "You gonna quit hiding and come out in the open?"

At his words, Ka Daver stepped forward into the dimming light and stood as an angular black shape, tall and menacing.

"Step up here," said Jack. "You got problems with me, mister? I don't reckon I know you."

"You knew my brother," said Ka, moving down the street towards Jack. "It was at your hand he met his end."

"And who might that be?"

"Ska Venger, my beloved kin cast now into everlasting darkness by your villainy."

"Oh, that ugly sucker. Well, gotta say there's a certain family likeness."

"Don't rile him," warned Lowell in a tense whisper. "He looks rather dangerous."

Jack's face was set tight and he muttered from the corner of his mouth.

"Step aside, Lowell. Let me handle this, just give me some room."

Lowell obediently backed away to the hitching rail and horses that were tied there behind them. Up on the boardwalk outside the saloon the curious customers who had heard the shouting were clattering out to take a look and Lowell quickly waved them back inside.

"You mock me, Deathdealer," Ka said, closing in on Jack. "That is your fashion, but I am above your petty insults. I am the right hand, the righteous one, born to bring justified salvation to this land."

"Hrmph," grunted Jack, folding back the coat flap from over his gun.

"Mine is the eye that sees, Coffin Jack. I am come to demand restitution; wickedness cannot go unpunished and it is demanded that a life is forfeit for a life."

They stood almost toe-to-toe and Jack's jutting jaw and glowing eye stared into the shadowed features of the preacher.

Jack shuffled his right foot back and slightly to one side. "You want to give me a heads-up on something?" he asked.

"Speak then, wha…"

Suddenly Jack swung his body back from the waist and then using his back leg to push off from he launched himself forward. His forehead connected with Ka's face with an almighty smack, a sound not unlike a washerwoman flapping wet clothes against a stone in the river. Ka was caught totally unprepared; his attention being fixed on Jack's fingers twitching over his Colt. He staggered back a few steps, his unfocussed eyes rolling in his head as he tried to figure out where the stunning hammer-blow had come from.

Jack was a brutal man when it came to a fight and he did not hesitate. With an almighty swing his right boot curved up and buried itself deep in Ka's crotch with a loud muffled thud that was plain to hear down the whole length of the street.

Ka bent at the waist in agony and slowly collapsed

into a fetal position, rolling around with both hands clutching his bruised testicles. Jack stepped over him and pressed his boot onto the preacher's neck, shoving his head down flat against the ground.

"Looks like failure runs in your family," he glowered, his good eye blazing the color of a burning coal. "You want to take me on, holy man? You'd better come at it with more than your miserable Sunday sermon spouting."

Ka was making indeterminate gurgling noises, his mouth opening and shutting like a fish out of water. "My – followers – will – finish – you," he gasped.

"I ain't never seen such a sorry excuse for a man of the church," said Jack, leaning over and resting one elbow on his knee as his boot pressed into Ka's throat. "You really think you can come at me just with all them fine words. Man, you ain't got a lick of sense."

From the corner of his blazing eye, Jack saw the movement. Ka was surreptitiously reaching down and drawing a long-bladed knife from his boot top. Jack moved in a flash and grasped the offending hand, twisting it hard until the knife fell free.

"You is just too persistent," intoned Jack, turning the arm even more until Ka squealed in pain. "Reckon we got to put you on hold."

With that Jack rotated the outstretched arm savagely in a spiral motion and Lowell standing behind winced as he plainly heard bones crackle and snap. Jack swung back and twisted the other way until a second crunch of destroyed bone followed. Ka howled and writhed where he was, pinned under Jack's foot.

"Time's up, Preacher man," said Jack, drawing his Colt. "You're going on ahead, might be we meet up some time over there in the unlikely event we end up in the same place."

The double click was audible as Jack levered back the hammer from half to full cock on the pistol. He pointed the gun at Ka's trapped head, "Say "Hi" to Saint Peter."

"*Jack!*" Lowell cried.

Jack sighed in irritation, thinking that Lowell was about to start in on one of his do-good-to-others speeches, "Not now, Lowell, I'm busy."

Lowell's interruption was followed by a loud crack as he fired off his Winchester, the sound bringing Jack's head up sharply.

Three dark riders were charging out of the shadowed road end. Men dressed all in black the same as Ka Daver, but across their chests were painted thick white crosses that glowed in the dimming light, with their long coat tails flapping they urged their ponies on. In contrast to the pale crosses, each man's face was painted totally black, the features indeterminate except for a ring of white that showed around their eyes.

Lowell's rifle bullet caught the forerunner, twisting his body sideways in the saddle and flipping him over onto the ground.

Jack stepped away from Ka and crouched down, fanning the Colt as he loosed off at one of the other runners. The thunder of the horse's hooves was loud as they charged towards them down Main Street, the racket deafening as both Lowell and Jack fired volleys simultaneously and the attackers answered.

Divots of dust flew up around Jack's feet and the brick wall of the saloon behind him clattered with missed shot.

Jack aimed a bead at one oncoming man, but his black-faced target hidden in the shadows made it hard to see if he had been successful. Then a spreading mist of red plumed out behind and the rider's hat flew off as he dropped forward limply over his pony's neck.

Of the three men initiating the charge, two had fallen, one to Lowell and the other to Jack. The remaining rider fell to Lowell's bullet as he shot the horse out from under the man. The pony faltered as if running into an invisible wall, then it dived down and impacted on the roadway, throwing the rider free.

An agile man, the attacker hit the ground, rolled over and came up on one knee, his pistol held ready in his hand.

Lowell was fumbling with a jammed breech, his hand frantically working the Winchester's lever. The fallen rider took aim leveling his gun along his extended arm.

Jack popped him from the side, delivering a .45 slug that knocked the man from his feet and dropped him stone dead in the dirt.

Swinging around, his Colt at the ready, Jack looked to find and finish Ka Daver. But the spot on the street where he had lain was empty – the preacher was gone. Even with a broken arm and busted balls, the missionary zealot had made his escape.

"*Hot damn!*" cursed Jack.

"Are they done?" Lowell called, at last managing the free the rifle of its block.

"They is, but I ain't. Where'd that bastard go?"

"Who are these people, Jack?"

"Beats me but there's no asking them now."

Lowell crossed over to one of the fallen men and turned the body over, as Jack calmly reloaded his Colt. Behind him noisy groups were tumbling out of the saloon and filling the street.

"I don't recognize him," Lowell called across. "He's covered in this wretched black paint though. I presume that Ka Daver has his own little crew of penitents following him around and these are some of them."

"Sure looks that way," Jack agreed, slipping the Colt back in the holster. "Say, Lowell, I'm getting mighty hungry. Time we got fed, don't you think?"

A short, bewhiskered and bald-headed, pot-bellied man dressed only in boots and a large bath towel around his middle burst out of the bath house down the street and, waving a six-gun in the air, strode towards them.

"What the hell's going on here?" he called. "Can't I get my ablutions done without some asshole kicking up a fuss?"

Striding up, he glanced at the fallen figures in the street then cast a suspicious eye at the gloomy figure of Jack standing over by the saloon alley.

"You the instigator of this mess? Who the devil are you?" he roared, waving the gun in Jack's direction.

"Taking in mind that you're a tubby little fellow with attitude, standing buck naked in the middle of Main Street and speaking right loud, I guess you got to be the law."

"Me? I'm Sheriff Barnes Wayfell, duly appointed police officer in this here town. You want to tell me what happened?"

Jack arched his eye and studied the tubby half-naked man. "Seems like you'd best get your pants on, fella, before that towel slips."

"Don't you tell me what to do!" shouted the sheriff angrily. He was obviously a man on a short fuse and his cheeks glowed red right past his mustache and up to the top of his bald head.

Some of the crowd watching on the saloon porch shouted out that it was the dark riders and their leader who had started it and the sheriff turned at their call, trying to question them and at the same time keep his eye on Jack and Lowell. It was a difficult pose to maintain and sure enough, the towel began to slip. With one hand full of six-gun and the other trying to maintain his dignity, the sheriff's face reddened even further in embarrassment rather than anger as his towel slid down to reveal the pink cheeks of his ample posterior.

"Mighty fine figure of a man," chuckled Jack. "You got any more on offer, Sheriff?"

"Goddamn it!" snarled Wayfell. "You wait right there, I gotta get my duds on then I'll be back."

He scurried off, trying to maintain an air of civic

poise as the crowd on the saloon veranda hollered rude catcalls and jibes after him.

"Come on," said Jack as Lowell sauntered over to join him. "Let's go find somewhere to eat; killing always gives me an appetite."

"The Grub Steak and Grill – A Penultimate Dining Experience," was not all it was cracked up to be going by the sign outside. It was small and hot, darkly ancient, and rich with the carbonized scent of well-done meat. At one end was a great bed of glowing charcoal set in an open brick fireplace with racks of ribs and great slices of steak tossed on a metal grill above.

The seating on the plain beaten earth floor was made up of not too stable hand-made, three-legged stools and tables that had a tendency to tilt over if not balanced on correctly. Great barrels of beer made up one side and the other, were two elderly women, sweating and clothed in grubby pinafores holding command of the counter. The ladies dashed from serving, to cooking and back to the counter to take payment in a tireless rotating fashion.

They were friendly enough given the somber appearance of one-eyed Coffin Jack and they welcomed the two without hint of criticism.

"Howdy gents, I'm Abigail Wayfell and this here is Winnie Tobego; welcome to the Grub Steak."

The woman who spoke was a stringy, dried and wrinkled no-nonsense kind of woman in her fifties and her companion, a small dark-haired diminutive creature with downcast eyes, who appeared to be a wisp of nothing.

"You boys take a place and we'll be with you directly."

"You related to that sheriff?" asked Jack.

"I am, for better or worse I wed old Barnes thirty-five years back. He had my best years, can't say I had the same."

The little one called Winnie sniggered at that and scurried off to check the grilling meat.

"We just had the pleasure," said Lowell politely.

"Is that right? A pleasure was it?" she asked dubiously.

"Indeed, it was, although the sheriff was a little discommoded at the moment."

"That so?" frowned Abigail. "What was the old fool's problem this time?"

"Seems like he didn't approve of his bathing ritual being interrupted," rumbled Jack.

"*Hell!* No wonder he was upset, that miracle only happens once a six-month."

Lowell wrinkled his nose at the unbelievable conditions that most folks appeared to live under on the Frontier. Jack said nothing but merely scratched his hooked nose and looked off vacantly into space.

"Passing through, are you?" asked Abigail.

"We are indeed," piped up Lowell. "On our way across to see Mister John Carne at the Homely Crossing Spread."

Abigail shook her head. "Poor old Mister Carne sure had a belly full recently. You see him, you tell him "hi" from me and tell him I'm sorry for his loss. That niece of his was a right fine young woman and didn't deserve to end that way."

"We shall, of course," said Lowell obligingly, although his face darkened at the reminder of Rita and all she had meant to him.

"So, name your pleasure, we got meat and we got meat. That comes in the regular form or there's chorizo sausage and bacon alongside biscuits and gravy, eggs and potatoes. All with the best pot of beer you'll find south of Abilene."

"Nothing green at all on the menu, I suppose?" asked Lowell tentatively.

Abigail barked a loud laugh. "Well, green stuff goes in one end of a cow so you could say those steaks are full of natural herbal richness, if that's your fancy."

"Give us two of the biggest darned steaks you got," Jack said decisively. "And the beer to go with it. I'm hungry, woman, so don't short change me on the meat front."

"You got it, stranger. I *do* like a man who knows what he wants."

They seated themselves on the tottering stools and waited for the meal to be prepared.

"You know, Jack," said Lowell, "something came to mind that I had forgotten about."

"Hrmph," grunted Jack, his nose stuck in a jug of beer.

"We had a letter. I had plain forgotten about it what with all my digressions with Beatrice."

Jack wiped foam from his face with the back of his hand. "Well, I guess you've seen the last of her."

"Perhaps," said Lowell doubtfully.

"You ain't thinking of going back there, are you?"

"I don't know," Lowell confessed. "I feel very bad about the whole affair."

"Aw, dammit, come on, Lowell. You both had your fun, don't sweat on it so."

Lowell fluttered his hand dismissively, not wanting to go into it and he reached inside his jacket for the letter. "Never mind about that, here, I shall read it to you?"

"Ain't gonna to put me off my dinner, is it?"

"Very well, the précised version then. It is from the telegraph company and apparently the right honorable J.J.Jameson is requesting our presence at the company's head office in Austin. His secretary who en-scribes this letter promises it will be most beneficial to both parties."

"I'll bet!" Jack sucked air through his teeth. "Jameson! That's the sucker who set up the whole thing with Ska Venger, ain't it? I got a bone to pick with him."

"So he is," Lowell agreed. "But why would he approach us, do you think?"

"He lost his point-runner, ain't he? Now Ska's gone to his reward he needs someone else to fill his boots and run old man Carne off his land."

"But surely, he must realize we are his opposition in the matter, he cannot be that foolish."

"He's a businessman, Lowell. The only thing he figures on is *money*, money profit and loss, that's what makes his world go round. He probably reckons if he can pay us enough then we'll do anything he asks."

"What a shallow fellow!"

"Those guys don't operate like you, Lowell. It's all just buy and sell to them. I should know I worked for enough of them."

"You *did?*"

"Deedy-do, at both ends of my gun," added Jack wryly.

Lowell shrugged. "Then I suppose I should write and decline his offer of meeting."

"No, don't you do that, we should check it out. We'll go see him after we've been over to the Carne place."

Just then Abigail arrived with two huge steaks and Lowell looked with awe at the forearm-length oval dinner plates stacked high with meat and potatoes.

"My God!" he gasped. "I'll be constipated for a week if I eat all this."

Jack had no such misgivings on that score and was already working hard with knife and fork.

# CHAPTER SIX

The view of The Homely Crossing Spread looked much as they remembered it from the hillside above. There had been some extensions to the corral and the mustangs milling about inside were a sad reminder to Lowell of his first meeting with Rita. He pictured her again sitting astride the rail and bawling out the vaqueros, and the pain in his heart started up again at the memory.

As they started down the hill a lone rider raced out from the ranch and rode up fast to join them.

"You are here!" cried Tomas, waving as he came.

"Oh, Lord!" sighed Jack mournfully. "There goes the fresh air."

"Come," said Tomas, drawing his pony up alongside in a rather unnecessary rearing turn. The vaquero was an excellent horseman and he liked to prove his skill at every opportunity. "Mister Carne is anxious to see you."

"You got back okay then?" asked Jack. "Didn't see no ghosties on the way?"

"No, nada, senor. All was quiet."

"Guess the atmosphere was not to their liking," observed Jack, pulling his pony upwind of the unfortunate Mexican.

They found John Carne in his large front room where nothing much had changed. The walls were still decorated with hunting trophies and the bookcases full of books. The only difference was the man himself, not a young man when they had last met, now he seemed to have aged at an alarming rate. He sat pale and slouched behind the desk in his office chair, the once straight back bowed, and the muscles of his face slack with pouched eyes holding a watery glaze more fitting for a man of ninety rather than in his fifties.

"Thanks for coming, boys," he breathed, the sound of his voice throaty and tired as if even the effort to speak was a little too much for him. "I didn't know who else to call."

"We're glad to be here," said Lowell brightly, hurrying forward and taking the old man's trembling hand in his. "How have you been?"

"As you see," said Carne, patting Lowell's hand affectionately, "can't seem to shake off this melancholic sickness, or whatever it is."

"Have you seen a doctor?"

"Ach!" snarled Carne dismissively. "Never had any call on the medical profession my entire life and don't intend to start now."

"Perhaps that's a little rash," chided Lowell, studying Carne with a worried frown.

"Coffin Jack," said Carne, looking away at the tall figure of Jack. "You're looking fit and well."

"Better than you," grunted Jack, never the subtle one.

"That's for sure. But I feel better for seeing you two and that's a fact. Let me get you boys a drink."

"That'd be the best medicine for any ailment," agreed Jack.

Carne struggled to get up from his chair and they could see he needed the use of a walking stick to help him rise.

"You stay there," fussed Lowell. "I'll get it for you."

"*Let him do it hisself!*" snapped Jack. "He ain't dead yet."

"My word, Jack. You can see poor Mister Carne is in difficulty; don't be so obtuse."

"*Obtuse!* Another one of them fancy words of yours, Lowell. I don't know what it means but you vex over that fella and he ain't going to last long, I promise you. He got to do things for himself, you know it, don't you, John Carne?"

"Maybe, maybe," sighed Carne. "There just don't seem much point any longer without Rita."

"Ah! Give me a break, will you?" barked Jack. "No point in sighing and weeping over the girl, she's gone and that's it. The world ain't ended."

"Stop it, Jack!" snapped Lowell. "Do you have absolutely no fellow feeling?"

Jack pouted his lower lip and thought about it. "Not much."

"Well a little consideration would not be amiss here. I believe Mister Carne has lost a great part of his life, as I have too and no doubt a well of sorrow has to be replaced."

"Well it ain't gonna happen by sitting on your duff. Now get up, John Carne. You was a man once and you can be it again."

"You're right, of course," sighed Carne, trying to pull himself erect. "This apathy I feel is overwhelming and I'm afraid I'm avoiding my duties. I should never have called you men here; it's my own problem after all."

Lowell tutted. "Don't be silly, Mister Carne. We're glad to help. Ignore Jack, it's just his way."

"No, your friend speaks the truth; we must go on despite the grieving. Now, those drinks," shakily Carne pulled himself free of his chair and lurched unsteadily over to the drinks cabinet.

Lowell anxiously moved to help but one look at Jack's glowing eye and negative shake of the head and he stopped himself.

"Your hand shaking good, old man?" asked Jack gruffly. "Well don't waste any of that precious stuff, you get it all in the glass, you hear?"

"Jack you are so brutal," hissed Lowell.

Carne chuckled, "Coffin Jack, you do a man good. Lord, I do believe you're better than a tonic. Here see, a glassful for you."

"The same for you," grunted Jack. "And take her down fast. None of that sipping, like Lowell here does."

Carne duly obeyed and after a swift swallow at last some color appeared in his cheeks.

"My, that's better, it surely is," he said with an air of relief.

"That's the way," said Jack approvingly. "Now spit

it out, what's the problem here?"

"Call in Tomas, he can explain."

"*No!*" snapped Jack. "You call him, he's your hired hand."

"Yes, yes," replied Carne weakly. "Of course." He made his way unsteadily over to the door and with one hand supporting himself on the doorframe he called out. "You there, Tomas? Get in here."

"I am here, senor Carne," said Tomas, instantly popping his head around the door, where he had obviously been waiting for the call.

"Come on," said Carne. "You tell these fellows what's been going on."

Tomas respectfully swept off his sombrero and standing over by the doorway began, "They have come here some days," he said. "The ones called Krone and the Indian, but they are come with a small man, how do you say? Que es muy pequeño, enano – a dwarf. He is always seen with a spade in his hand, a strange character, no? But my men say he has others with him, they only come in the night hours and carry the stink of death with them."

"They ain't the only ones," muttered Jack, sniffing the air emphatically.

"Have you ever heard of this dwarfish fellow, Jack?" asked Lowell.

"I reckon. Sounds like the one they call Gravedigger, cold little sucker that likes to inhabit burying grounds. It's told he can raise the dead or at least some version of them. Pesky little critter, mighty cunning so they say."

"Why do you suppose he's joined up with Krone

and Phantom Dog?"

Jack allowed his gaze to look out of the window. "My guess is they're onto the same tack as before. They want this here land and all that copper you got underneath."

"You *really* think he has some kind of dead people with him?" asked Lowell doubtfully.

Jack clicked his teeth and raised an eyebrow meaningfully but said nothing.

"They are frightening the men," said Tomas. "They are all too full of terror to go out on the night shifts and then when this happens the cattle are stolen away as they are not watched."

"It's true," added Carne. "The herd's been depleted by about thirty-percent since this scum arrived in the neighborhood."

"My men say they are like shadows, these people. They think it is devils that come and some of the vaqueros have disappeared. I do not know if they have run off in fear or perhaps something worse has happened to them."

"Your guys got the jitters over some night vapors?" asked Jack derisively. "What's the matter with y'all?"

"They are superstitious, senor Jack. Only simple religious men from my own country, to them it is a great danger to their souls."

"Well, hellfire! I guess we have to prove them wrong. What d'you say, Lowell?"

Lowell's voice dropped to a low, vengeful tone, "If it takes me to Krone and the half-breed, then I will go through anything to get even with those two."

"Then I reckon we got some nighthawking to do,"

growled Jack with a slow grin. "We'll see just how ghostly these nightriders really are."

The two started their patrol just after supper and by full dark they were moving through the brush on the slopes of a wide valley were the cattle browsed. The earth on the slope was bone dry and powdery and the brittle brush crackled underfoot as the ponies forged a way through.

"Best we split up," grunted Jack. "I'll head over to the south side you keep along here."

Lowell licked his lips. "Do you think there's anything in this ghostly appearance thing?"

Jack shrugged. "Where that midget Gravedigger is involved, anything is possible."

"I'd certainly prefer Krone and the Indian than any apparition, that's for sure. At least I know they will take a bullet and fall down from it."

"Just keep that Winchester in hand. I reckon if Gravedigger is calling up old bones, a regular slug will still have the same result."

"I really hope so."

"Adios and stay sharp," said Jack wheeling his dark pony Nameless around and riding off.

Lowell watched the trail of white dust that followed as Jack rode away down the long hillside. Beyond in the gloom he could make out the shadowy outlines of the cattle spread across the valley floor their forms black against the pale earth.

Sliding out his Winchester and laying it across his lap, Lowell urged his own pony on. He quartered the ground before him cautiously as he moved, paralleling the line of the hillside just below the rim. Jack had warned him about riding the skyline and how, even at night, his outline might be seen against the starry sky. And there were plenty of stars out tonight he noticed, the clear and dry air allowed a dazzling array across the sky and they scattered above in a luminous haze in every direction. The moon that hovered just below the horizon had not risen yet and the sky was still a deep blue background to the stellar display.

Inevitably, Lowell's mind slipped back to memories of Rita. It had not been far from here they had first made love on a hillside and he mellowed as he recalled the tryst. Two young people, inexperienced and naïve but finding such passion for each other it had stunned them. How it contrasted with his hasty fumbling with Beatrice. With that thought, all pleasant recall of Rita slipped from his mind and was overtaken by his guilty departure from Beatrice. He could have at least said goodbye, he reckoned. What an arrogant manner-less prig he had become and how he would never have behaved in this manner before coming out West and meeting Coffin Jack. But, he maintained, it was no use laying the blame for his own shortcomings at Jack's door. Jack was as he is, the Deathdealer, he made no bones about and continued his violent and murderous path without any thought of remorse. No, Lowell's problems were of his own making and to find that such a culpable figure lay within himself was a shock to a city boy raised amongst the bone china teacups of society and brought up to offer polite deference rather any act of aggression.

With his mind in this turmoil of self-flagellation Lowell continued to ride on with his lonely watch.

It was a shift in the star positions that caught his attention. At once they had been above the rim of the hill but now, they seemed to be scattered before him in the shadowy outline of the hillside in front. Lowell pulled his pony to a halt and searched the night, trying desperately to see what it was causing the firefly effect.

They were moving he realized, and they were neither fireflies nor stars.

With a start he picked out indistinct black shapes bounding and leaping down the hillside towards him. It was their eyes he had seen reflecting the pale starlight.

"*Hold up!*" he called, levering a shell under the hammer. "Hold up and stand, I say. Who are you and what do you do here?"

No answer came just the sound of the brush crackling and swishing as the running shapes neared. There was a panting chant though, low and repetitive but clear in the night air as they came.

"Stop or I shoot!" Lowell shouted in loud desperation, hearing the tremble in his own voice.

As he called out, the sound echoed off the hillside and came back to him as hollow as he felt in the pit of his stomach.

Just then the full moon rose through a few ragged clouds scattered on the horizon and the whole hillside was suddenly lit in a searchlight beam.

Lowell saw what faced him then.

Ragged creatures, black and shambling some of

them hopping and striding out stiffly as if on stilts. They began to offer a gargling sound as he came into their view in the moonlight and the whole hillside appeared to move as the scurrying shadow-figures centered hungrily on Lowell.

Lowell shouldered his rifle and fired, loosing off at one of the foremost figures in the wave. It exploded as if made of fired clay, the pieces spraying out in a boney eruption that collapsed in a scattered heap. Swinging left, Lowell picked another nearing target and fired again. The thing pivoted on the spot and jumped high off the ground. Jack fired once more, and the creature flew apart in a dusty cloud in midair.

There was a smell that forced its way into Lowell's nostrils, a damp, mildew stench, that spoke of places deep underground and of rot and decay. They were desiccated figures of corruption, Lowell realized as he looked at the advancing creatures, some with their white bones showing, others with ribbons of putrid flesh hanging in ragged strips from their withered frames. The moonlight gleamed on their clammy figures, what flesh remained was slick with grave moisture and as they came, they reached out towards him with slimy grasping fingers.

"By all that's great!" Lowell gasped, his eyes wide with horror. "There are hundreds of them."

Lowell turned his pony and digging in his heels he fled. He rode fast, glancing over his shoulder to see with a tremor of fear that the things were coming after him. Bounding, stumbling, hopping, and leaping they ran across the ground, some falling in their haste and rolling away down the hillside before picking themselves up and coming on again. They seemed to be driven by a blind urgency, some kind of wailing instinct to capture and, it came into Lowell's mind with horror; that they meant to regain a taste of life by consuming him.

With a shock, he felt the sudden bow wave of wind as Coffin Jack galloped past him going in the opposite direction. Jack bellowed out a loud roar, he held a pistol in one hand and his rifle in the other and rode Nameless using the grip of his thighs as guidance rather than the reins.

"Jack, there are too many," Lowell called after him.

But the only reply he heard was the crack of pistol and rifle and the same loud war cry as Jack crashed in amongst the army of creatures. He fired to left and right blasting apart the boney conscripts of Gravedigger's army, even Jack's pony Nameless took a part, snapping and tearing with its teeth. The dark stallion kicked up behind like a mule and bravely charged Jack in amongst the dead things that swirled like a cloud of bees around him.

Lowell could do little else. He turned his pony around and rode back full pelt into the melee. They swayed before his attack as Lowell forced his screaming pony to smash into the ranks surrounding Jack. Lowell fired until his rifle was empty then he used it as a club, smashing and cracking the brittle figures before him as if they were made of china.

Sharp fingers reached for him, raking at his legs, and tearing the cloth of his trousers and jacket. Lowell felt the sharp pains as they dug in with their long fingernails and he smashed down with the rifle stock, slamming the butt into half-human faces, and watching the decaying features split apart and collapse under his blows.

He heard Jack calling out above the grunting cackling din of the heaving mass.

"Gravedigger! Come on out, you stunted ass. Come face Coffin Jack, he has a bullet with your name on it."

There was a far-off jangle, the sound similar to that of a metal triangle being beaten to call the ranch hands to breakfast or to sound the alarm. The army of dead stilled and backed away; their growling figures full of spiteful resentment at being ordered away from their prey. They snarled and chattered collectively, the sounds making no sense other than those of bloodlust and anger. They moved back slowly, opening out their ring and leaving Lowell and Jack isolated in the center.

Jack wasted no time, quickly reloading both his rifle and six-gun. Lowell's eye roved with distaste over the retreating army and then he raised his gaze to the skyline above and saw the small hunched figure outlined there against the moon glow. Lowell noted the raised shovel the figure held as he beat against it with the distinctive ring that had called the invaders off.

"You want me, Coffin Jack?" Gravedigger called down to them.

Jack raised his eye from his reloading and studied the lone figure. "I want to mount your damned head on my wall, you little runt," Jack called back.

Gravedigger chuckled, his laughter rustling in

the now silent night. "I always liked you, Jack. Such a sense of humor."

"You call these beggars off, Gravedigger or I'm gonna ream your ass."

"Now, now, Jack. Don't take on so, this is merely a word of warning for you and your friend there. I have business here and I don't want you interfering, so clear the way and leave me to it and all will be well."

"Listen, you pokey midget," Jack roared back. "You really think a passel of bones you dug up is going to scare me off? I think not. See here, I hold responsibility for this place. You take on these folks, you take me on as well."

Gravedigger lowered his spade and rested both hands on the handle, his hunched shoulders bowed over his small frame. "So be it," the sigh was evident in his voice. "Then I fear I will have to bury you along with all the others. I'd hate to do it, why not move along, Jack? Why be so fractious? It is only some lonely ranch hands in the middle of nowhere; what can it matter to you?"

Jack raised his Colt, leveled his sight, and fired one off. Smart as the flash of gunfire, Gravedigger raised his shovel protectively and the bullet whanged against the metal blade and ricocheted out into the night.

"Tut-tut, Jack," said Gravedigger. "Did you really think it would be that easy?"

"You want me to say any particular words over you when I put you under, Gravedigger?"

Gravedigger roared a laugh. "Just say, "Here lies

the man who put Coffin Jack in the ground."

"You're pissing me off now," growled Jack, his eyes glowing with an angry orange light.

"Can't have that, can we," said Gravedigger smugly. "You go think on it some, Jack. You know what I say makes sense. Failing that, I guess I'll be seeing you around." With that he sunk his shovel-head sharply into the ground and as if in answer, the entire army surrounding them seemed to melt. The ragged figures dissolved and slipped back into heaps of dust that integrated themselves into the ground so completely that it was as if they had never been standing there.

When they looked up again Gravedigger was gone and the skyline clear.

"My God!" breathed Lowell. "That was unbelievable. Jack, an army of dead corpses brought to life, how on earth can that be?"

Jack sniffed and holstered his guns; he sat a moment resting his hands on the pommel. "You got that right, Lowell. How on earth, you ask, well the earth is the very thing."

"The *earth!*"

"Sure, grave dust. That's how Gravedigger carries them around, we find out where he keeps the dust and we blow those poor souls back to where they belong."

"Jack!" said Lowell in amazement. "How the devil do you know such things?"

Jack shrugged. "Misspent youth, I guess."

Lowell was rueful. "Well, I won't ask about that."

"Best not," Jack agreed dolefully.

# CHAPTER SEVEN

"It has to be in some sort of hallowed ground," Jack insisted, both knuckles resting on the territory map spread on Carne's desk.

"You are saying this creature keeps the dust of his victims collected in a cemetery?" asked Carne, his eyebrow raised in curious disbelief.

"That's what I'm saying," Jack agreed, head tilted so his good eye could search the map. "Gravedigger lives in graveyards, that's where he's been his whole life. He's been so close to the dead for so long even his flesh rots the same."

"How gruesome," observed Lowell.

"What you got around here in the way of burying grounds?" asked Jack, giving up on the map.

Carne nodded. "Well, there's only the one that I know of and that's in Doomesville, just outside of town."

"Ah, yes, I remember it," said Lowell. "You recall, Jack? The one with all the black birds around it."

Jack shook his head. "No, that's too obvious a

place. I reckon Gravedigger would find somewhere a lot more secretive for his precious cargo than that."

"There is one more," piped up Tomas. "But this is not hallowed ground that is blessed by the church."

"Don't matter just so long it's sanctified," Jack said quickly. "Where is it?"

"It will be the old Apache burying place up in the hills. Nobody goes there anymore. I think it is a little scary for many people."

"Sounds perfect," said Jack. "The dead ain't as fussy about religion as the living. Don't matter to them whether it's Christian, Hindu or Aboriginal, they all got the same six foot resting over them."

"They say this place is haunted," added Tomas gloomily.

Jack looked down his nose at the Mexican and was cynical, "Yeah, has to be don't it? Some old warrior shaman who was a giant of a man and could bowl over people with bolts of lightning, right?"

"No, senor, this one uses the wind and the rain."

"*Rain?*" grinned Lowell. "Here in this dustbowl country, I doubt it."

"That is what they say, senor."

"Well, we'll haul ass over there come daybreak and take a look," said Jack. "You'd better show us the way, Tomas."

"*Me*, senor? Oh, I pray you don't ask me that."

"Listen, you dummy," Jack glowered at him. "Any old dead shaman up there will run in terror he smells you coming anyway."

"It's alright, Tomas," Carne said quickly. "Just show them the way; you won't have to go in there.

Isn't that right, Jack?"

"Hrmph!" Jack grunted.

"You can leave it up to us, Tomas," Lowell added as way of reassurance. "There'll be no need for you to go all the way."

"Lordy," breathed Jack. "I don't know why you folks is so scared of the dead, it's the one sure thing you got coming anyway."

"It's not the coming, Jack," reproved Lowell. "It's the unknowing."

"What's to know? You get the call, you go."

"No, I mean it's what comes afterwards."

Jack shrugged dismissively, "Well, that's a whole new ball game and nobody knows about that, so why wonder?"

Lowell sighed, from experience he knew there was no point in entering into any profound philosophical or esoteric discussion of the obscurities of the afterlife with Jack. The Deathdealer saw only the most pragmatic and tangible attitudes as viable.

"Perhaps we should get some rest then," said Lowell, being as pragmatic as possible.

"You got that right," Jack agreed. "Ain't much time left though, it's an hour or so 'til sunup and I intend to be on the trail by then."

By the time they left, Jack was obviously feeling on top of the world and frisky at the prospect of a challenge whilst Lowell was somnolent and still dull with interrupted sleep. The vaquero, Tomas, was used to early rising and it made little difference to him, he only felt the nervous tension of the superstitious as they approached the high country and the entrance to the Apache burial ground.

Tomas pulled up his pony well short of the marked valley that he pointed out to the others, "It is up there, senor Jack. I will go no further."

Jack cocked an eyebrow. "Why you so a-feared of all this nonsense?"

"Listen to me, senor, I beg of you. I know these Indians, even the fierce Apache fear the dead. They think the departed ones return as ghosts and have resentment for the living. The dead hate that they cannot enjoy more of life and are jealous of those that can. Such is their concern that the Apache are quick with their departed; they put them under the earth as soon as possible and they give to them all their possessions into the grave. Then they burn the person's house and move away less the dead one comes back. It is not a thing to ignore, I think."

"And this place up here is watched over by some ghostly shaman, you say?" asked Lowell sleepily.

"That is so, senor. He is called Goan-nah-tah, one of great power whilst he was alive and now in death he has even more. So much he can control the weather, so the Apache say."

Lowell raised his eyes to the big clear blue sky above and the bright morning sunlight that streamed with golden blessing over the rocky cliffs and valleys around them.

"Well, my forecast is fine and dry. I can't see us getting wet this day."

"Come on, enough of this chiff-chaff," grunted Jack. "Let's go see if Gravedigger's found a home here."

Leaving Tomas behind they rode in single file up the narrow pathway that led to a v-shaped crack in the rock face rising above them. Alongside the trail, the rocks fell away in a steep incline to the desert floor far below and Lowell woke up quickly as he looked over the precipitous drop.

"If one fell, it really is quite a way down," he observed.

Jack grunted and kept his face fixed firmly in front but from the rigidity of his back Lowell could tell something was wrong.

"You don't like heights, Jack?" he asked.

"No, I don't like heights," snapped Jack in quick response.

"Jack you are quite something else, do you know that? I have never known an entirely more fearless person in my life before and yet you are timorous over such a thing. What is it, does it make you giddy, being up here?"

Secretly, it did Lowell's heart good to know that there was some element of Coffin Jack's character that could be considered near human as it made him less of an impassive and emotionless person in the journalist's eye.

Jack's reply was short and crudely to the point, "The only thing I get giddy about is a big legged, big assed woman with hungry eyes and great breasts. Now, shut up and ride."

They entered the narrow opening and the ponies' shoes clattered over stone, the sound echoing back at them repetitively as they moved between the enclosing walls of stone. The long narrow pathway eventually opened out into a wide flat area littered with piles of rocks marking each Indian internment. Above them on either side rose the numerous dark openings of caverns cut into the rock face, the doorways hung with colored ribbons, feathers, and charm dolls. There was a stillness in the air, not a breath of wind entered only the heat of the rising sun that simmered back from off the stone walls.

"Are we going to have to search in all of those?" asked Lowell, indicating the caverns. His voice boomed in the silence and rebounded eerily around the canyon.

"Well old Gravedigger ain't gonna make it easy, you can bank on it," observed Jack solemnly.

"The sooner we do, the quicker we leave, I guess," said Lowell, glancing around suspiciously and feeling a shiver run through him despite the heat.

The two dismounted and began their search, each scaling a separate side of the cliff face and independently taking a cavern of choice to explore. Lowell found them to be holes hollowed from the rock, not very deep and just large enough to hold the swathed remains of a dried-out corpse along with the individual's belongings and devoid of anything else but age.

He scurried from one to the other, finding at first the exploration simple enough. A quick look inside for anything suspicious and then on again. As they moved deeper into the canyon the older caves became larger and deeper and Lowell had to enter completely inside one of the larger caves to see if anything lay further back in the shadows.

The files of bodies entombed in the cavern were differently prepared and very ancient. There were eight of them, four on each side and they sat upright and cross-legged, the corpses trapped frozen in rigor with the wrappings about them rotted away to leave the desiccated remains visible. The dry air within the cave had kept the bodies intact and had mummified them. Bony faces with thin blackened skin stretched so tight over the faces that the teeth were bared, and the missing eyes, long since decayed, watched with only shriveled and blank sockets.

It felt uncomfortable to Lowell to move amongst such static, yet somehow lifelike, forms of death and there was an unnerving sensation that he was wrong to be in there with them. As if he were invading their privacy and that the long-departed bodies might still hold some offense at the intrusion into their centuries old sleep.

Then he found them.

Stacks of white ceramic jars clean and dust free shaped like large eggs and evidently recently stored in the back of the cave. There were heaps of them laid one on top of another. Small jars with skin lids kept in place by bands of twine.

Lowell stumbled back over the rough ground and past the ranks of seated ancients to the cave opening. He leaned out and looked for Jack on the canyon floor.

"You there, Jack?" he called out, the words bounding back at him hollowly. "I believe I have found them."

As he stared out, Lowell saw the floor below

suddenly tilt and then the whole canyon seemed to distort, sliding into a strange oblique perspective for a brief moment. Lowell blinked and rubbed his eyes, thinking that his tiredness had deceived him momentarily and then he was distracted as Jack appeared from one of the caves opposite.

"You got 'em?" called Jack.

"Up here, but did you feel that just now?"

"Feel what?" asked Jack making his way across.

"Some movement, a shift I think."

"No, not a thing. The sun getting to you?"

"I don't think so, perhaps I am a little tired though, that's probably it."

Jack heaved himself up into the cave mouth and glanced around at the mummified figures. "Look a mite worse for wear, don't they?"

"Presumably, they have been here for quite an extended period."

"Uhuh," Jack agreed. "Where is this dust then?"

"At the back of the cave, stored in jars, I believe."

They made their way to the rear and Jack nodded at sight of the heaped containers. "That's it, that's them."

"What do we do with them?"

"We got to empty them out," said Jack, bending forward and picking up one of the jars. As he did so, Lowell felt a distinct tremble in the rock beneath his feet.

"There!" he cried. "What is that?"

Jack sniffed indifferently his attention focused on the find. "Earth tremor maybe."

Lowell looked around fearfully. "Let's get this

done, can we? The sooner we are finished here the better I'll feel. Have to say, I don't much like this place."

Jack quirked a smile. "You're beginning to sound like that Mexican." He lifted the jar and slammed it down on the rock floor, splintering the clay and releasing a heap of dust. "'T'ain't nothing here but…"

It was the squeal of sound that interrupted Jack, almost as if a small child had wailed in anguish. The Deathdealer pouted, then picked up another jar and repeated the process. A long drawn out sobbing moan keened in the cavern.

"Is that you who's doing that?" asked Lowell.

"Hell no!" snarled Jack. "It's them poor beggars trapped in the jar, they're going on to their proper place and maybe they don't like it too much. Come on, give me a hand."

Obediently, Lowell picked up a jar and he felt the eggshell smoothness under his touch and also a slight vibration on the cold surface of the vessel. With a show of distaste, Lowell threw the jar at the cavern wall and smashed it. Quickly they began the demolition, breaking as many jars as they could, throwing them two-handed and constantly being deafened by the cries accompanying each act of destruction.

The grave dust piled high about their ankles as they worked but there were hundreds of the jars and although each one held no more than a handful of the powdery remains it soon built up.

Again, the ground shook underfoot and they both paused, looking around cautiously. A few rocks fell from higher up and pattered down at the cavern floor.

They stared at each other for a brief moment and then hurriedly returned to the task, wanting to finish as quickly as possible.

"Goddamn it!" complained Jack. "That little bastard sure brought a heck a lot of them with him."

Lowell began heaving some of the fallen rocks at the heap of jars, hoping to destroy more that way than by the throwing them individually. The smash of broken ceramic and the cries of the released filled the cavern until the air vibrated with noise, the sound pressing in against the eardrums and adding to the general air of unsettlement.

But then a strange howl began that overrode the racket inside the cavern.

"What the devil?" asked Lowell as a dry wind full of gritty dust snapped in and seared at his skin.

Jack glanced at the cave opening. "It's coming in from outside, must be a sandstorm."

The intensity of wind picked up and the dreadful howl grew louder as the wind whistled through the cavern doorway. Bitter sand particles lashed at the two as they continued to wreck the piled jars, it whipped at their clothing and came in savage gusts that sent them staggering.

"Maybe there is a shaman guarding this place after all," Lowell called over the wind. "You think so?"

"I couldn't give a hoot, just get this done," snarled Jack, stamping and kicking at the jars with renewed energy.

With a show of grim relief, Lowell picked up the

last intact jar and hurled it viciously at the wall.

"There, now can we get out of here?"

"You bet," Jack agreed, heading for the opening.

That's when the rain started.

It did not just fall; it dropped with a venom neither had experienced before, a great sheeting curtain that made the view outside completely opaque and invisible. They stood just inside the cave entrance and watched the rainfall drop with the vicious intensity of bullets. Jack attempted to step outside and staggered under a battering of raindrops, he was instantly soaked, and it was only Lowell's helping hand that brought him back safely under cover.

"Hot damn!" Jack cursed. "That ain't natural."

They moved back from the doorway, as the splashing and angled rain seemed to be trying to enter. They could hear the clatter of rocks falling down outside as the intensity of water ran in great gushing rivulets down the mountainside. A force of water equivalent to a river in flood deluged down into the narrow canyon and above the roaring the two could hear the splash and lap as the floor below the cave began to fill.

Lowell stared at the waterfall outside and it seemed for a moment that a distorted form appeared in the twists and turns of liquid. A face with heavy brows and a great hooked nose took shape, the head bound in a bandana that kept the tangled fall of hair back from the high cheekbones. The features were as mobile as the water, turning and reshaping amidst the great gushing fall. An opening below the nose in the appearance of a misshapen mouth gaped and worked as if trying to form words and yet no sound came above the continuous roar.

"Oh, my!" Lowell's voice quivered. "Look here. It would appear Goan-nah-tah is present after all."

Jack stared back belligerently at the face, he hunched his shoulders and stood large in the cave mouth, his good eye glowing.

"Look here, Indian," he bellowed. "Let's get to the chase. We ain't here to disturb your people, we're just here for the sick intruder who buried his own amongst yours."

The great head that virtually filled their vision outside the cave shimmered and twisted as if in an anguish of anger.

"Gravedigger ain't no Apache," Jack insisted. "What you protecting him for? We just favored you with a cleaning up in here. No need to take it out on us."

It was clear now that the overfull canyon had brought the water so high that it was beginning to lap at the lip of the cave. It overflowed the edge and Lowell looked down with trepidation as the water ran over his boot tops.

"We're going to have to get out of here, Jack. We'll drown we don't move soon."

"I guess that's this sucker's intention," said Jack, frowning at the watching face in the water.

"Yes, he doesn't appear to be paying any heed to your entreaties."

Jack shrugged. "Maybe I should be speaking in Apache."

"Oh, you think that might make a difference?"

"Well, if it don't understand English…"

"Go ahead, give it a try."

Jack turned angrily on Lowell, "What makes you think I speak Apache? The only communication I ever had with them savages is to shoot them."

Lowell raised his eyes despairingly the ceiling. "Well that's most helpful."

"We got to jump," said Jack decisively.

"*Jump!*"

"Yeah, look here. I reckon that water out there will have to be running through the canyon mouth. We get in the flow it will carry us free."

"And doubtless straight over that long drop at the valley entrance. Remember?"

"Ah, yes," Jack agreed rubbing his jaw thoughtfully. "I plumb forgot about that."

The water had risen to their knees and as Lowell watched, the frail mummified figures were lifted from their seats and began to bob about like ducks in a pond.

"Maybe we could catch hold of something on the way," he ventured, as one of particularly unpleasant leering corpses bumped up against him.

"It's a thought," agreed Jack. "Okay, grab a hold," he said, reaching out a hand.

They grasped wrists and stepped nervously through the swirling intake to the stand at the cave mouth.

Jack twisted his ugly face in anger as he stared back at the Indian shaman's features that seemed to be watching them with a kind of smug confidence from the sheeting run before them.

"And you can go to hell too," roared Jack as he and Lowell lunged forward.

The two leaped straight into the hanging face that shattered and broke apart before them as they fell into the battered and lashed waters beyond. Plunging in below the surface they pushed out into mid-stream. The force of water was intense, and both were tumbled and pulled in different directions, the rock walls veering dangerously alongside them. Dislodged stones and boulders splashed down from higher up and hit the water with volatile force raising great gushers as they smashed in with bomb-like violence. The sinking rocks sailing past the two as they were dragged underwater and on towards the narrow entrance to the canyon.

Lowell's lungs were bursting and within the underwater turbulence his grip was tugged away, and he lost contact with Jack as he was spun upwards towards the surface. Lowell's head popped above the surface and he gasped for air, but the falling rain still fell, and it hit his face with the impact of a battering ram making it difficult to breath. Orientation was impossible in the swirling waters and Lowell had to trust in the pull and drag as he was projected along in a rush heading towards the narrow opening of the canyon.

The waters picked up speed as they were forced into the channel and Lowell looked around in desperation for some projection he might catch hold of. But he was speeding too fast, the sides of the entrance valley running by in a blur as the surging flow dragged him on. He rode the breasting wave, a small figure lost in the turmoil and above the noise of the stream he could hear the approaching roar as the water burst from the valley entrance and fell in a giant waterfall to the plain far below.

There was no rain falling outside the boundaries of the canyon and Lowell could plainly see the disappearing edge of the waterfall approaching before him. A great curving vanishing point that dropped away, its edge streaming with a misty spray patterned by rainbows.

In desperation, Lowell twisted this way and that but there was no opportunity to fight against the tug of water that seemed determined to carry him as well as itself over into the oblivion of the drop.

He raised his hands in a desperate but pointless gesture of resistance and as he hit the boiling edge of the waterfall, he felt himself suddenly jerked upwards and away, the force of water carrying him out in a swinging curve. It felt as if his arms had been jerked out of their sockets and he looked up amidst the mists of spray and saw that the noose of a lariat was locked tightly around his two wrists.

He was swung to one side of the roaring flow and then he made out the figure of Tomas, standing spread-legged on a flat rock overhang as he pulled Lowell in towards him.

The Mexican was a wiry man much practiced with the lariat when riding as vaquero with the Carne cattle and he handled it well, swinging the dripping figure over towards the safe haven of the cliff face away from the falling water. Lowell slammed into the rocks and gratefully clung onto the hard face as he stared at the streaming gusher that poured away and vanished far below him.

With Tomas's help he clambered up to join him and slumped down, his chest heaving as the Mexican loosened the rope about his wrists.

"Thank you," Lowell panted. "Thank you, Tomas. I am most grateful."

"Di nada," grinned Tomas, looping his lariat into a coil.

"What of Jack? Have you seen him?"

Sadly, Tomas shook his head. "No, senor, I have not seen him pass by. But there is much water, it may be he has gone underneath."

Lowell remembered that they had both lost contact under the water and he swiftly climbed to his feet to stare at the tumbling stream of foam that shot out directly from the valley mouth. It was impossible to see anything amidst the boiling white gush and Lowell hung his head and feared the worst.

Then, as suddenly as it had come, the water began to slow. The forceful waterfall lessened and as the pressure dropped off and the canyon gradually emptied, soon only the remains slopped lazily down the rock face and glittered away in sparkling streams reflecting the sunlight.

It was then that Lowell started in surprise as he saw the sodden figure of Coffin Jack stepping carefully through the puddles and streams at the valley entrance below.

"Jack! Jack!" Lowell called, waving to the figure below. "Are you alright?"

Jack looked up ruefully at the figures standing on

the ledge above.

"I'm goddamned wet," he complained. "Ain't had a bath like that in a coon's age."

"You see, senor, I told you," said Tomas smugly. "The shaman, he control the weather. The wet and the wind."

"Well, sorry to say you missed out on the dip, Tomas," snorted Jack derisively. "Would have done your smelly hide a sight of good to take a little immersing."

Tomas turned to Lowell a question on his face. "Why does senor Jack always mention this thing of some bad smell. I can smell nothing."

Lowell shook his head and whispered confidentially, "Don't worry, ignore it, it's just his thing."

"What happened to the ponies?" Jack called up to them. "Is my Nameless okay?"

"Si senor," Tomas replied. "Both the horses left the valley when the storm started, they are safely below."

"Damned ponies got more sense than us humans," grumped Jack. "Come on, we're done here. Let's get back and dry off."

# CHAPTER EIGHT

The growing city of Austin sat between the two creeks named Shoal and Waller that both bordered the spreading town and snaked through the outlying buildings and down to the Colorado River that formed a natural southern boundary. It was easy for Jack and Lowell to find their way around as the place was divided into an elongated yet simple grid layout with roads marked off with tree names and Texian points of interest. The impressive Capitol Square surrounded by the apparatus of State sat on the major approach along the broad Congress Avenue, but the site of their interest was a building where the lesser Ash Street met Rio Grande Street.

The Jameson Building sat on a corner plot just south of the university and was a relatively quiet area away from the busy central section that surrounded the State offices. It was an impressive edifice that rose to three floors and one look at it intimidated Lowell.

"Looks like money, Jack," he observed, rubbing his chin, and adjusting his glasses thoughtfully.

"Hrmph," was Jack's only comment. He held a dislike for any urban area and was naturally restless at being in the bustling conurbation where buggies and freight wagons mixed freely with a hive of pedestrians that were all seemingly hell bent of some purposeful activity.

Jack's dress and demeanor held some interest for the passersby and as they maneuvered their ponies through the busy streets, heads turned, fingers pointed, and comments were whispered. Jack pointedly ignored the gawping city dwellers and when they pulled up outside the head offices of The Electric Telegraph and Post offices, he beckoned a small Negro street child over and flipped him a few cents to watch over their horses for them.

They made themselves known to a doorman who presented them to an agitated clerk, a man who obviously had much on his mind. Lowell showed him the letter they had received from Ernest Leaf, Jameson's personal secretary.

"Ah, indeed, you are to be expected in *his* office," the clerk whispered with a touch of awe. Sweat beaded his troubled brow and his distracted demeanor created a general air of uncertainty and distress that seemed to run through the ethic of the whole building. "Forgive me, yes. Rooms to be arranged and you have horses to be stabled? Yes, yes. I'll see to everything, now if you will follow me, gentlemen. I'll see if Mister Leaf is available."

"He'd better be," rumbled Jack. "I didn't come down here to wait on no office boy."

The clerk glanced up at the imposing figure of

Jack with his weathered cloak and single eye and quickly looked away.

"I'm sure everything will be fine," he mumbled nervously, scurrying off ahead and leading them through busy open-plan offices where numerous noisy clerks were hectically engaged at rows of desks and where papers were being passed from one to the other as if lives depended on the outcome.

"You really do have a lot going on here," Lowell observed.

"Indeed, indeed," gushed the clerk. "Much to do, much to do."

"Is this all in aid of The Electric Telegraph and Post Company?" Lowell asked.

"Oh, indeed no. Mister Jameson has many interests and a wide variety of investments. There are a wealth of businesses attended to here on the Chief's behalf."

"An entre-peenoor then?" observed Jack blandly, secretly pleased that it was without a doubt Lowell had expanded his vocabulary no end.

"Much more," stressed the clerk. "The Chief is a diverse and active man of business with affiliates across the entire country. Now, come, please hurry, we must not keep the great man waiting."

"That so?" said Jack darkly, his attitude being one unimpressed by such lordly distinctions.

Somewhat out of breath they entered a long marble-floored corridor and, heels clicking on the hard stone, they arrived before a set of imposing double doors that reached as high as the ceiling. After a breathless pause as the clerk apparently gathered his courage, he knocked timidly.

The doors opened a crack and in a hurried whisper the clerk announced the callers. At his words, the doors were flung wide to show a diminutive, balding man dressed in both a neat suit and an ascetic attitude.

"So pleased," he said in an obsequious tone, hurrying forward and holding his hand outstretched in greeting. "I am Ernest Leaf; it is I who sent the invitation. So agreeable you could come."

There was an air of subservience about him and he weaved in a strangely girlish way as he moved. A man who bore an attitude that was obviously of one with an intention to please.

Lowell took the proffered hand that was unpleasantly damp and softly limp to the touch.

"Lowell Devereux," he introduced.

"Yes, yes," said Leaf. "And this..." He glanced carefully up at Jack. "Must be the renowned Mister Coffin Jack, it is an honor, sir. I know Mister Jameson is most eager to meet you."

"Will that be all, Mister Leaf?" interrupted the clerk.

"Yes, of course, get along with you, I'm sure you have plenty to do," Leaf allowed a little show of bored petulance as he dismissed the clerk with a wave of fluttering fingers. "Now, come this way, sirs." He bade them enter the office through the double doors and offered an extravagant bow and a wide and simpering smile as he did so.

The room was large, with ceiling to floor windows, a wall of bookcases, a desk and dark wood furniture. It was a gloomy place with the stale scent of ageing papers, beeswax polish and unmoving dust.

"If you will wait one moment, gentlemen, I shall apprise Mister Jameson of your presence."

He had them sit on a small, stiff-backed, and hard-seated settee whilst he knocked on an adjoining office door and vanished from sight.

Lowell watched dust motes swirl and glide down through the beams of sunlight coming through the windows; his eye strayed across to the desk piled high with hefty ledgers and piles of official looking documents.

"You are not impressed?" he asked Jack.

"By what? Paper and dust. Don't mean diddly to me."

"But, Jack, this is obviously a momentous enterprise and Mister Jameson must be an imposing character to have created it all."

"Pisses in the same pot as the rest of us every morning, don't he?" grunted Jack offhandedly.

"Please, Jack," Lowell said nervously. "I hope you will moderate your language in his presence."

"Look here, Lowell. This is the same sonofabitch who set Ska Venger loose on us, you forgotten about that?"

"No, I have not forgotten but let us be open-minded; maybe he had no knowledge of just what kind of an evil creature Venger was," Lowell stressed. "I can't believe a businessman of this caliber would have even stooped to meet such a character."

Jack sucked his teeth and looked skywards. "You

got a lot to learn, boy."

The door opened and the bald head of Ernest Leaf poked out. "Will you come in, gentlemen? Mister Jameson will see you now."

Jameson was a corpulent, ruby faced creature with bold mutton-chop side-whiskers that billowed from his rosy cheeks with wiry abandon to join with an equally wild and volatile head of graying hair. He did not move from his place as they entered but sat behind a large desk in a high-backed chair and held all the presence of kingship as he eyed them speculatively.

"There, there," said Leaf, fussing about them as if he were a fish weaving in a bowl as he showed them to the two chairs set before the great man's imposing desk. "Pray be seated."

"You Jameson?" asked Jack, ignoring the waiting chair, and lunging forward with a jabbing finger.

"I am," boomed Jameson in forceful and proud reply, although he watched Jack's approach with some caution.

"You the one set Ska Venger loose on the Carne property?"

Jameson looked away for a moment, a brief glance to the single tall window situated to one side of the room. "An unfortunate affair," he allowed.

"Damn right," said Jack angrily. "A sight more than *unfortunate*, I'd say."

"It was not my understanding that the fellow would behave in such a way," said Jameson, his apologetic gaze returning to meet Jack's eye. "His brief was to make presentation to Mister Carne only.

To bring to his attention my desire to purchase or lease the property for mining purposes, I fear it got somewhat out of hand."

Jack chewed his lip a moment. "Lot of people died out there, Jameson, including Carne's niece."

Lowell noticed Leaf wincing visibly at Jack's forthright approach. The secretary's fluttering hands made some show of trying to restrain Jack but wisely, he realized he would be attempting to hold back a hurricane and held off.

"A sad loss," Jameson allowed. "Truly sad, I was most distressed to hear of it but be assured gentlemen it was not my intention that matters should end that way. I am, of course, prepared to make full restitution to Mister Carne for any inconvenience. For his niece, I fear there is little I can do now but offer sincere condolences."

His expression never changed, and the words came out sounding of grief but showing no demonstration of it.

"You think I don't see you as you is? I think you know the right words, Jameson, but you ain't got an ounce of intention in them," said Jack, looming forward threateningly over the desk. "If I could hang it on you for certain I'd nail your hide to that wall behind you right now."

"Jack, Jack," interposed Lowell, plucking at the Deathdealer's sleeve, as he knew full well how Jack could be when he was riled.

"Oh, dear," wailed Leaf. "Please, you cannot think for one moment that Mister Jameson intended harm in any way."

Jack shook off Lowell's restraining hand. "We clear, mister?" he asked, staring hard at Jameson.

The businessman shuffled in his chair a moment, stretching his neck awkwardly in his stiff collar, "I'm sure I fully deserve your disapproval and I do humbly beg apology. But that was not why I asked you here. It was my wish to request if you would set things right, to go yourselves and put my proposal before Mister Carne and do it in a kindly and considerate manner."

Jack sniffed and stepped back a pace, replying cynically, "That didn't take much to guess at."

"You shall of course be suitably rewarded whether the deal goes through or not. I had a figure of one thousand dollars in mind, I hope that will amend any friction existing between us and soothe your justifiable resentment. I can have Leaf draw the funds immediately."

Jack stared down his nose at the man. "I don't want your damned money."

Jameson turned quickly to Lowell. "Mister Devereux, I see you are an educated man. Can you understand that my intentions were only honorable and there was no desire for unsightly bloodshed or indeed any act of violence?"

Lowell stood uncertainly at Jack.s side, looking from one to the other before offering a deep sigh and dropping his shoulders. "Miss Bodey and I were promised in matrimony," he said softly. "Her passing was a very great loss to me and the vile killers who took her life will certainly meet a just end if I have anything to do with it."

"Of course, of course," Jameson agreed quickly. "And all of my resources are at your disposal to expedite such an outcome, I assure you."

"Then tell us where those two villains, Krone and Phantom Dog are right now," snapped Lowell, suddenly sharpening his attitude and a biting gleam entering his eye.

Jameson was bemused. "I... I fear I do not handle these affairs personally, perhaps..." he looked across at Leaf and raised questioning eyebrows.

Leaf shrugged. "I am not sure, sir, but the last I heard they had returned to Doomesville."

"You don't say," said Jack, turning and fixing his glaring eye on the secretary. "And how'd you know such a thing?"

"They contacted us asking for money, for payment..."

"Which we denied naturally," stepped in Jameson quickly.

Jack turned to Lowell; "There ain't nothing more for us here."

Lowell nodded in agreement.

As they made for the door, Jack turned to Jameson one last time. "I find out you're behind all this in the worst way and I'll come back here and squash you like a bug and that's a given."

Jameson said nothing in reply, but his red face grew deeper in color and he met Jack's gaze with narrowing eyes.

As the door slammed behind them, Jameson rotated in his chair to focus a withering stare on Leaf.

"So much for getting them on our side, you fool."

"Who could know, Chief?" whined Leaf pathetically. "I had hoped sufficient funds would override any lesser moral considerations. These kinds of men usually operate with only gold as a motive. It surprises me as much as you to see their attitudes in this matter."

"You're an idiot!" barked Jameson. "They are aggrieved; could you not see that revenge would be a sweeter reward for the likes of them."

He sat in his throne-like chair, mulling over the meeting and pulling irritably on the whiskers at his cheek as he did so.

"I cannot allow this to pass," he muttered angrily. "Nobody comes into my sanctum and threatens me to my face in such a manner."

"Indeed no, Chief. I concur, most definitely I do, you are too highly placed to allow it."

"Then we shall see just who this Coffin Jack thinks he is," Jameson spat. "Insulting me like that, squash me like a bug indeed. Get hold of the brother, Carmody Carne. It was all his idea in the beginning, let's see if he wants to play a more active part in this now."

As Jack and Lowell strode away down the corridor, their boots resounding on the marble floor, Jack turned to Lowell. "See, he weren't so special, was he?"

"It was his false commendments of pity and apology that were so blatantly untrue, that opened my eyes to the fellow's true character. The man wore dishonesty on his sleeve as plain as if it were written there."

"Told you so."

"You did indeed, Jack. I should have not been so quick to take things in a lighter tack."

"Well, we sure wasted our time here. It was about as I expected and I'm damned sure that beggar was behind it all."

"Did you mean what you said in there? I mean about squashing him."

Jack arched his eyebrow and his wild eye roved over to Lowell. "What do you think?"

"At least it was not all a wasted effort. We now know where Krone and the Indian are."

"Maybe, we'll see."

On their way out they were met by the sweating clerk at the doorway. "Gentlemen," he said. "I hope your meeting went well. I have arranged hotel rooms for you both and the ponies will be taken to the stables…"

"Shove it," said Jack, brusquely pushing past.

"A wasted effort, I fear," Lowell said apologetically. "We shall not be staying. And might I say in passing, I'm sure that a young man of your talents could find himself some better occupation than running around for Mister Jameson, who is obviously an overbearing ogre of the most odious sort."

"What? Oh! …" gasped the clerk.

"Yeah," said Jack, leering back and fixing a glaring eye on the clerk. "Get a life."

Their route back from Austin led them through a small township called Klaneptick Losers, a failed lumber mill town amongst hills populated by scattered loblolly pine. It was here that Jack decided, as the twilight was approaching fast and they did not want to stumble through dark forests, they should spend the night. They settled for the run-down hotel that had at one time catered for the mill workers, loggers and lumberjacks who had serviced the town in the past.

The place was run by a disgruntled old woman, named Faye Spout who cared little for custom but preferred the companionship of a large gin bottle, which she slipped rapidly out of sight at the sound of the hotel door opening. A small florid lady, with unkempt white hair and a stained sack-like dress that assured an observer that there were no undergarments to support the gigantic breasts and flaccid stomach underneath. Her beady-eyed face was pitted and as pale as milk, the skin apparently never seeing the sun. However, all this sagging softness was made up for by a tongue as sharp as any lumberjack's axe.

"Can I help you?" she asked suspiciously from behind the foyer counter, casting a rheumy eye in Jack's direction as he loomed towards her. It was a bare board kind of place, the foyer aged and dusty and smelling of something that might have been cooked at one time, but a long time had passed since. High up near the cobweb-populated ceiling hung an array of moth eaten and decomposing hunting trophies, their stuffed heads spilling sawdust from splits in the disintegrating skin.

"You the owner?" asked Jack.

"I am, Mrs. Spout. What you want?"

"Rooming House, ain't it? Then I guess I want a ride on a paddle steamer."

"We ain't got no river around here," Mrs. Spout came back just as smartly and with a venomous look.

"No, dear lady," Lowell interrupted. "Jack makes a little joke. You have rooms available?"

Mrs. Spout leant a beefy elbow on the counter and looked down her nose at Lowell for a moment, "Course I got rooms, hotel ain't it? You got all your faculties, young man?"

"Indeed, ma'am. We'd like rooms for the night."

"Well, take your pick," she said brusquely, her voice dropping to a confidential whisper. "We only got one other occupied by a couple; they's in the Honeymoon Suite."

Without a second glance at her, Jack swung his saddlebags over his shoulder, hoisted his rifle and made for the stairs.

"No women, no fighting, and no drinking in the rooms," snapped Mrs. Spout as Jack set his foot on the lower step. "You want feeding at breakfast?"

"What kind of fare do you offer?" asked Lowell.

"Same as always," sniffed Mrs. Spout indifferently. "Beans."

"Sounds delightful," said Lowell, following after Jack as he trudged on upwards.

The head of the stairs turned into a long, wide corridor with doors leading off from each side, and Jack, never being one to want to be too far from a ready exit tried the first on the right-hand side. He tilted his head to see better from his good eye as he gave the dark interior the once over. "This'll do me," he grunted.

"I'll be just across the hall," said Lowell.

Lowell sighed and shook his head in dismay as Jack slammed the door in his face, there was little charm in his associate. Try as he might, Lowell had failed to instill any modicum of the social graces into the Deathdealer. His partner was a man of mean disposition, small manners and often, total indifference to those around him. Why he bothered with Lowell, the young journalist had no idea. Their association had started out due to his accomplishment with the literate use of words, and somehow that had developed as one or the other of the pair saved each other's lives along the way. Somehow they had bonded and whilst Lowell still secretly kept a diary of their adventures, notes that he planned at some future stage to turn into a book, meanwhile they continued their drifting lifestyle with only the motivation that vengeance and lucky chance provided.

"And good night to you too," Lowell said as pushed open the door to the room opposite.

Lowell's jaw dropped.

The half-naked young woman that sat on the bed yelped and clutched a silk nightdress to her bare breast so clumsily that the material barely covered the expanse of her spreading bosom.

"I do beg your pardon," Lowell gasped.

"What can you mean by this, sir?" said the wide-eyed young woman in a strong Southern accent. She was a pert, pretty, young creature of about eighteen years with coiling auburn hair piled high and leaving a long, elegant neck clear to her bare shoulders. From what Lowell had glimpsed of her body he determined she was athletically slender and filled out in all the right places.

"A mistake, ma'am," said Lowell, averting his eyes. "The creature downstairs gave no indication which rooms were occupied."

"Well, I just don't know," said the girl, trying hurriedly to spread the silk inadequately across her ample breasts. "You'd best be gone before my husband returns. Mistake or not, he will not take too kindly to your presence here." She arched a warning eyebrow. "I should warn you he is a most intemperate man of volatile disposition."

"I do so sincerely apologize," said Lowell, bowing his head as he began to close the door.

"You are new here, sir?" the girl called.

"We are, ma'am. My friend and I are passing through."

"I am Louise Buchanan," she introduced coyly, with a touch of pride. "Mrs. Louise Buchanan, we have newly taken our vows."

"My felicitations, ma'am. I hope you will be most happy."

Lowell went to close the door again, but she interrupted him once more. "Sir," she said, "I see you are an educated man and as a stranger I would risk asking you a personal question."

"Please," said Lowell, slightly puzzled and yet intrigued.

"I am unused to the marital state you find me in, sir. I have never known the company of a man before this night, having being raised in a foundling convent and so I am unsure of how to progress with my husband. I wonder if I may ask you a pertinent question in regard of correct protocol?"

"Well," said Lowell, nervously hovering in the doorway, "I'm not sure if it is proper under the circumstances."

"I have no one else," she begged plaintively. "The nuns were so lacking in information. What is your name, by the way?"

"Again, I apologies, Mrs. Buchanan," Lowell bowed his head in deference. "Lowell Devereux, at your service."

"You do speak well, Mister Devereux. It does my heart good to hear again the tones of a gentleman. I have indeed been bereft of convivial conversation. Are you versed in the classics, I wonder?"

"Yes, I am, but ma'am, your question? I really do not think I should be here at your bedchamber door at this time, it is most improper."

"Oh, phooey! Mister Buchanan won't mind a bit. He is a rough old stick but a hive of fun when the fancy takes him," she wriggled her bottom on the bed and the nightdress slid to reveal the sheen of one long leg in the lamplight. "I need to know, Mister Devereux. Given the nature of expectations of a connubial sort, is it to be my duty as wife to supply willingness at any time. Mister Buchanan is most pressing in the early hours, tell me, is this normal?"

Lowell drew a deep breath and allowed his gaze to flow down the full length of her attractive body. He gulped as the stirrings of desire coiled up his spine.

"I should say that would not be found surprising,

ma'am. Given the splendor of your attributes."

"Oh, sir," she said, ducking her head in embarrassment. "You are truly most gallant."

"Not at all, and now, ma'am. I really must go. I give you good night."

With that he pulled the door closed before she could make any further calls on him.

Flushed and breathing heavily, Lowell moved down the corridor and took the next empty room along. He threw himself fully clothed on the bed and lay staring up at the ceiling. His heart beat fast and he could feel it booming uncomfortably in his chest. His mind was on Rita and the feel of her lips on his, of the softness of her body as it coiled about him. Louise Buchanan had been an unfortunate reminder of the joy he had discovered with the now lost love of Rita. As he stared up at the dark beams of the ceiling his thoughts were suddenly occupied again by memory of Beatrice who invaded his softer recall of Rita, the two becoming entwined and tangled in his mind.

He jumped as he heard a door slam shut.

There was a mumble of voices and Lowell determined that the walls were no more than thin planks and what he could hear was the Buchanans next door almost as clearly as if they were in the room with him. There was the thump of boots being dropped on the floor; the rustle of clothing removed and the creak of bedsprings then the low mumble of continued conversation.

Lowell tried to keep the sounds out of his head, but his natural curiosity was aroused and he could not deny himself overhearing.

Then it began. At first quietly but gathering momentum until a regular beat was maintained. The pounding of bedsprings and the steady sound of female gasping came clearly through the thin frame walls.

Lowell raised his eyes heavenwards as he pictured the young Mrs. Buchanan spread out on the double bed, her nightdress thrown aside and the body of an indistinct male probing her glorious figure with relish. In his mind's eye, whilst the regular sound of rising lust continued as Louise Buchanan's gasps grew louder, the sobs taking on the sighs and groans of a wilder pleasure, Lowell imagined that her partner was a monkey-like, dark and hairy figure of oafish quality and his heart sunk that one so fine should be subjected to so bestial an assault.

However, and he had to admit as he lay in the dark and listened, she certainly sounded as if she were enjoying it.

Things reached fever pitch, and Louise's cries cut the night as she begged and coerced even greater attention. Her humping partner grunted loudly and there was one single combined drawn out wail before all settled again to the restless scraping and winging of the bedsprings.

Silence followed, not even the low murmur of voices.

Lowell let out a long breath, not even realizing he had been holding it in. He knew then it would be a long night.

He awoke blurrily.

Some loud noise had awoken him.

"No!" he heard a female voice cry out. "Don't!"

There was the sound of a sharp smack and a painful wail.

"I beg of you, do not."

Again, the crack of a fist meeting flesh.

Lowell bounded up in bed. He was still fully dressed and realized he must have fallen eventually into a restless sleep.

The sounds were coming from the next room and were now compounded by the sobbing of a woman's tears.

A man's voice bellowed, "You damned slut! You will do as I tell you or I'll beat you to a pulp."

"No, please. Not that," came Louise's begging voice.

"You're my wife. I own you and you'll do all I say."

"But I cannot, please, William, do not ask that of me."

More beating followed, a thump and the sound of furniture falling and glass breaking.

"Get over here," came the husband's angry voice. "I'll give you the beating you deserve, you hear?"

"No, William, not the quirt! Do not whip me, I beg of you."

Lowell could stand no more, he pulled his pistol from the gun belt hanging beside his bed and, swinging the door wide, he dashed from the room. Anger twisting his face, Lowell raised his boot and kicked at the door to the adjoining room expecting it to fly open and for him to be able to confront whatever foul act was in progress.

The door was locked, and his kicking boot bounced back.

Silence followed the heavy thump of his boot.

Lowell tried again but it was a solid door and it did not budge.

"What's going on in there?" cried Lowell desperately. "If you've hurt that poor woman, I'll have your hide, you animal."

"Mind your affairs," a growled answer came from the other side of the door.

"Is that you, Mister Devereux?" Lowell heard Louise's trembling voice ask.

"It is, are you all right?"

"Please, Mister Devereux, do not trouble yourself."

"You know this dude?" asked the male occupant.

"He dropped by earlier, William. It was just conversation."

"You bitch!"

A smack was followed by a plaintive cry.

Lowell was desperate and trembling with uncertainty, he stared at the reluctant door and raised his pistol ready to shoot out the lock.

"What the devil's going on?" rumbled Jack's sleepy voice in his ear.

"He's hurting a woman in there," cried Lowell. "And this blasted door won't give way."

Jack frowned and ran tired fingers through his rumpled hair.

"Lord, is that all? Lowell it ain't none of our concern. You know how it damned well is, all married couples have their ups and downs, for Christ's sake forget it and go back to bed."

"He's got a horse whip, Jack!" Lowell said desperately.

"So have I," shrugged Jack. "What's to tell?"

"Jack," hissed Lowell in a low voice. "He intends her harm. We cannot allow this."

Jack ran his tongue over his tombstone teeth and looked at the closed door ruefully.

"*Hey, numb-nuts!*" he called. "You going to keep it down in there?"

"Mind your own business," came the snarling reply. "I have to come out there, I'll take your heads off, you stupid pair of dummies."

"That a fact?" said Jack, his eye beginning to glow malevolently. "And who might you be who's so scary?"

"I'm Wild Bill Buchanan, you might have heard of me. Don't tangle with me, I raise Cain and bring down perdition on all my foes."

"Oh, my," said Jack. "A regular hard man, huh?"

With that, Jack raised his foot and with one momentous blow cracked the door so hard it fell off its hinges and dropped into the room inside.

# CHAPTER NINE

As Jack filled the doorway, the man inside lunged forward.

He was neither ape-like nor hairy, as Lowell had imagined but a smallish man, slight and quite fine-featured and in fact handsome in a fair-haired boyish way.

Bill Buchanan, or Wild Bill as he preferred, did the foolish thing of waving a large bladed Bowie knife in warning at Jack instead of thrusting it straight in.

"Get the hell out of my room," he snarled.

Coffin Jack dipped his head down as if looking at an errant schoolboy.

"Best put it away, sonny," he said.

In answer, Wild Bill slashed at the air between them two times. "Get out!" he snarled in reply.

Looking over Jack's shoulder, Lowell could see Louise crouched on the floor. Her nightdress was ripped down at the shoulder and he could see bruises marking her upper arm and a red mark glowing on her cheek.

"I have to get that off you, I'll shove it in your ear," Jack promised the knifeman.

"Take that!" barked Wild Bill, lunging forward.

This time he meant business and went straight for Jack's midsection.

Nimbly, Jack sidestepped and caught Bill's wrist in his large hand, the two struggled as Bill tried to free himself from Jack's hold. In desperation he swung out and kicked Jack hard on the shin. Jack frowned in annoyance.

"Goddamn!" he growled. "You sure are a pesky little snide, ain't you?"

With that, Jack landed a hammer blow on Bill's face that sent him flying across the room. He slid over the bare boards on his behind and ended up slamming his back against a chest of drawers, where he sat stunned.

"Mrs. Buchanan, are you alright?" asked Lowell, hurrying over to the woman and helping her to her feet.

"A little in disarray," she managed, leaning on Lowell's arm with her head resting against his shoulder.

Even with everything going on, Lowell noted the pleasant scent of her subtle perfume and felt the silken touch of her hair against his cheek. He could not help but notice the warm pressure of her nubile body pressing up against him and for a moment his mind was frozen, and everything stood still.

"Get your hands off her!" shouted Wild Bill, from where he crouched. Shaking his head to clear it, he was quickly on his feet and with the glinting blade of the sharp pointed knife held out in front he dashed across the room aiming for Lowell.

Jack stepped in again and in an almost bored fashion held out a blocking arm as solid as a fence post and Wild Bill, running at full tilt was bowled off his feet. He cartwheeled over and crashed into an occasional table and lay on his back amidst the splintered remains.

"You just stay there," warned Jack.

"Come on," Lowell said to Louise. "Let's get you out of here."

"But where? Where can we go?" she asked plaintively.

"I'll take you to my room, we can sort out your affairs later."

"He wanted me to perform obscene acts," she whispered. "I could not, Mister Devereux. I could not do it, but he would force me to do so he promised."

"The lowly beast!" growled Lowell. "Do not worry, we shall protect you."

Jack listened to all this and snuffed his disapproval, but he knew Lowell was a sucker for any female in distress and kept quiet even though the whole business was increasingly tiresome to him.

"Can I go back to bed now?" he asked.

"Of course, Jack. Thank you so much."

There was a scream from behind them and the sound of running feet as the enraged Wild Bill, who was obviously a man undeniably stupid and knowing no better, charged across the room. Jack leaned back, clamped the knife hand by the wrist in both of his. Stuck his foot out so that Wild Bill's boot was trapped at the ankle and swirled the held hand up so that it curved around and in one continuous blow, the bright blade was buried deep in Bill's ear.

Wild Bill howled and Jack, with a face set in stone, gritted his teeth and increased the pressure until the long blade disappeared completely from view. Bill jerked a couple of times at the end of the stuck steel, his mouth opened wide in a silent scream and then his whole body went limp.

"I warned him," Jack justified to Lowell. "I said I'd do it."

He let go his grip and the body of Wild Bill tumbled in a heap to the floor.

Louise let loose a sob of distress and freeing herself from Lowell's arms she rushed over to kneel at her fallen husband's side.

"Oh, my dear boy," she cried. "What have they done to you? You have killed my husband."

She cradled Bill's bloody head in her hands and looked at Lowell desperately.

"A little extreme, don't you think, Jack?" said Lowell frowning disapprovingly at his partner.

"I told him," Jack stressed apologetically. "Didn't I? You heard me, he had fair warning."

"But they were just married."

"Lowell! He was trying to kill us."

"I know, I know. But you always overreact in such a zealous and violent manner, now this poor child is left a widow woman."

"Better that than having fourteen inches of steel stuck in your heart, wouldn't you say?" growled Jack.

Lowell was patient. "Jack, Jack, there are ways of doing these things. Far better to disarm him and let the law take control."

"Is that right?" spat Jack. "Well, where were you when it came to all this disarming?"

They were interrupted by the figure of Mrs. Spout appearing at the doorway. She was dressed in a long and grubby chenille dressing gown and her wild hair was tied in bunches of paper ribbons. There was no doubt she was half drunk as her sharp voice was edged with a slur.

"What in God's name is going on in here? I told you *no fighting*."

She looked down at the fallen figure of Wild Bill and the pool of blood slowly spreading over the floor. "Oh shit! Who's going to clear that up, 'cos it ain't gonna be me?"

"Well, damn him and the rest of you too," growled Jack irritably. "I'm going back to bed."

"Don't worry, Mrs. Spout, we'll take care of everything," promised Lowell.

"You'd better," she snapped back. "And it'll cost you for damages."

"Indeed, indeed, not to worry," pressed Lowell, taking Louise's arm and leading her away from the body and out into the hallway.

"My poor William," she breathed in a stunned tone. "He was so young."

Jack cast an assessing eye at her as she passed by him. "Why the hell you marry that lowlife?" he asked.

"It was a whirlwind romance," she said vaguely. "I

could not deny him, he led me straight to the altar."

"Be back in the church real soon now, I reckon," Jack confided quietly to Mrs. Spout with a nod towards Bill's remains. "Mind you if I was as pretty as that little chickadee I wouldn't have gone within a yard of that asshole. Makes you wonder, don't it?"

"There's no accounting for undying love and things of the heart," said Mrs. Spout, with a faraway and whimsical look of romance in her eyes whilst trying to hold herself primly even though she wavered drunkenly on the spot.

"Guess you'd know all about that, huh, ma'am?"

Mrs. Spout glowered at him and turned on her heel, almost fell and then recovered and wove her way unsteadily down the hall heading for the stairs.

"Mind you don't fall, ma'am," Jack called after her with a show of false concern. "Couldn't do with another accident in here."

"You shut your trap," she slurred over her shoulder.

"Hrmph!" rumbled Jack, heading for his room.


Lowell ushered Louise into his room and fluttered around making sure she was comfortable. He laid her on the bed and covered her with a blanket.

"There my dear, are you comfortable?" he asked.

"So kind," she whispered. "My head is pounding. I fear he struck me an awful blow. Do you have a glass of water?"

"Of course, of course," he hurried to fetch a glass. "You must rest, would some kind of sedative work."

"You are too kind, Mister Devereux. Anything to ease this infernal head."

"Pray call me Lowell, dear lady," he paused a moment. "He beat you about the body too," Lowell glared angrily at the marks so visible on her arm and jaw.

"Yes," she said, touching her swollen cheek carefully. "When in a rage there was no stopping him."

"Well, he will trouble you no longer."

Louise's shoulders heaved, and she began to cry.

"I shall go right now and find an apothecary. I'll beat his door down if I have to; he will have something to calm you I'm sure."

"Don't trouble yourself, Lowell. You've done so much already."

Lowell, who was mightily upset to see the woman so distressed, anxiously made for the door.

"No, no, it is no problem I will do it right away. Please wait here, I'll be back as quick as I can."

When he had left, Louise threw herself back on the bed and studied her painful bruised arm with a look of annoyance.

The door opened suddenly, and she looked up in surprise.

Coffin Jack filled the doorway.

"Why, what can you mean, sir? Coming in here unannounced."

Jack's ugly faced creased into what might be considered a smile and he made his way over to the bed collecting a chair on the way. He set the chair down next to the bed and straddled it, his arms resting on the straight back.

"You and me going to have a talk, little lady."

"I beg of you, not now. I am most disturbed by all

that has gone on."

"You can cut the Southern Belle routine, sister. I know who you are."

"What!" she gasped. "What do you mean?"

"Yes, indeedy. I seen you when you danced tables over in the Solstice Mine diggings. Remember that? You really think you could hide your light under a bushel that well, you're too easy on the eye to be forgotten."

Louise glared at him and allowed a long sigh to escape her lovely lips. She knew it was no longer any use and that her disguise was discovered.

"What do you want?" she asked, her voice altering and the Southern accent sliding away.

"You got Lowell hooked; he's a simple fella, nice enough but not too bright on the uptake. So first off, you lay off him, you understand? Next, I want to know who set you and that fool lying next door up on this."

Louise drew herself up in the bed and folded her arms across her chest. Her demeanor immediately shifting from that of lost and vulnerable Southern lady to a more hard-bitten sort and one of a lower order into the bargain.

"You got it all, ain't you?" she spat, frowning deeply at the Deathdealer. "What were you doing at the Solstice Mine anyway?"

Jack released a long sigh. "Killing someone, of course. That's what I do, now spit it out before I start in on you."

"Two fellas, they got a hold over me. Forced me to take this on, there weren't supposed to be any killing involved."

"Who were they and what's the hold?"

"Couple of guys, gunman called Krone and some half breed Indian."

"Phantom Dog?"

"That's him, creepy guy who don't say much. They got my little brother Dooby, the kid's only twelve years old. They promised to cut him up like sausage if I didn't oblige with this bit of playacting."

"And the dead guy in there?"

"Oh, some other dummy they hired. Afraid he got into the role too well and overshot his part as antsy husband. Sucker really enjoyed the hitting part," she said, ruefully rubbing her bruised arm. "Look what he done to me."

"What did you expect? They let loose some no-account back-shooter like Bill Buchanan; he's going to enjoy every moment of it. Wild Bill!" Jack spat derisively. "I got cats wilder than him back home, he weren't no more than a fly-by-night baby killer."

"Well, he wasn't listening to anybody, that's for sure. Didn't do a thing he was told to do."

"He ain't listening no more now either and it ain't just wax filling his ear."

"They're coming for you," Louise confessed. "The plan was for me and Wild Bill to distract you both by having a family ruckus. Krone's hired a passel of men, they'll be out there waiting to come in."

Suddenly, Jack sat up straight.

"*Lowell!*" he barked. "Where'd he go?"

"To find a chemist, said something about getting some medicine for my vapors."

"Goddamn! They'll have him by now."

There was a clumsy clatter of noise in the hall outside the door.

"Better be ready," said Louise nervously pulling the bedclothes up. "I reckon they be here right now."

"Get some clothes on," ordered Jack, getting up and setting the chair back under the door handle. "Use Lowell's, he's small enough to fit you."

"What you going to do? I ain't got no part in this, I don't aim on getting caught in any crossfire."

She was ferreting through Lowell's saddlebags searching for clothes and tugging out a shirt and some work pants.

"Lady, you're already a part," said Jack, spinning the chamber and checking the load on his Colt. "We're going out the window and you're tagging along with me."

"Are you crazy! It's a goddamned fifteen foot drop out there."

"Well, I reckon you'll bounce real good, now get moving; you ain't got much time."

Louise was tugging on the pants when the handle turned, and the door was tested. Jack leveled his pistol.

"You fellas ready to die?" he bawled.

There was a chuckle from outside. "Why don't you just open up and come quietly? There's too many of us out here to argue with."

Jack moved over to a spot alongside the door and pressed the muzzle of the Colt hard up against the thin wall.

"You there, mister?" he asked quietly.

"Yeah," came the reply.

"You listening close? I got something to tell you."

"Yeah, what is it?"

"Your mother sends her best."

"Mom? What you know about my mom?"

"Well, son, it's been a long time and we need to tell you we're both concerned about you."

"Pa? Is that you, Pa?"

"There's the little ones too," said Jack, figuring out the man's height by the sound of his voice. "I got a heartfelt message to pass on."

"What's that?"

"Put your ear close and I'll whisper."

"Okay, what is it?"

Jack pulled the trigger.

The bang blew a hole straight through the wall and the head of the listening man on the other side. There was a cry and the sounds of hurried movements in the corridor.

"Goddamn! Tom's pa just went and killed him!" came a cry of disbelief.

"That weren't his pa, you damned fool!" shouted one of the others. "That was Coffin Jack."

"Lie flat!" Jack ordered Louise, dropping prone as he said it. A flurry of shots followed his words and Louise immediately took his lead and dived down to the floor. The wall and door imploded as lead poured through, the panicked shooting from the corridor outside blasted great chunks of planking and wood splinters in an explosive cloud. Gun smoke and flaring muzzle flash filled the room and the roar of gunfire was deafening.

The opposite wall of the room took all the flying bullets and the window frame burst apart and shot out into the street in a cloud of broken glass, a mirror and water jug erupted into pieces and shot whanged off the edge of the iron bedstead.

Jack waited until the fusillade was finished and the gunmen outside started to reload. Then he rose to his feet.

"Out the window!" he ordered, taking a stance opposite the door.

Wide-eyed, Louise looked at all the destruction and without a word made her way to the empty window frame.

Jack stood full on and began panning shots at the silhouettes moving in the corridor. He could see them clearly through the destroyed wall and door and as he picked his shots, figures bucked and dived away shouting in anger and pain.

With a quick glance over his shoulder at Louise, Jack quickly shed his empty brass and reloaded fast. She was hanging on by her fingertips obviously too frightened to let go and drop down.

Jack moved over and grabbed one of her wrists in his fist, with his gun hand aimed under his armpit at the door behind, he leaned out and lowered Louise down until she had only a few feet to fall. Then he let go.

Jack fired off another few rounds in retaliation as shots from the corridor began to pepper the room again and then he vaulted out through the window.

# CHAPTER TEN

The four men who grabbed Lowell treated him with rough efficiency.

Lowell hardly had time to gasp, "What?" as the four moved out from a darkened alleyway and swept Lowell off his feet. One of them had his hand firmly clamped over Lowell's mouth before he could holler for help and they lifted him from the ground and carried him bodily over to a set of waiting horses.

Swiftly gagged and bound hand and foot, Lowell was thrown across the back of one of the ponies and they left, riding at speed.

Bouncing and bucking, Lowell struggled to stay aboard as he twisted his wrists in an attempt to free himself. It was impossible though, fighting with the moving pony and the tight bonds left him exhausted and he settled to concentrate on staying across the horse's back.

He wondered who these grimly silent men were; they said little and maintained a steady pace into the night.

It was only as dawn was breaking that they slowed down, and Lowell looked about to see the black outline of a township closing around them. He recognized the place. It was Doomesville the town not more than a few miles from The Homely Crossing Spread where they had first arrived before their fight with Ska Venger.

Nothing had changed in the intervening months; it was still a bleak little town with few of the occupants ever seen on the streets. In fact, the cemetery outside of town seemed to have more life going for it than the rest of the place.

They came to The Abandon Hope; the one saloon in the town and Lowell was dragged unceremoniously from the horse.

"You did well, boy," praised one of the men, a rangy looking fellow with a scarred cheek and unshaven chin. "Keeping abreast that pony without falling off. Must be a regular horseman to do that."

Lowell mumbled something from behind his gag and the man unloosened it. "Guess we don't need that anymore, no one here going to pay you any heed you call out anyway. Come on, somebody here wants to see you."

With that they unfastened Lowell's leg bindings and, leaving his hands tied, led him up the porch step and into the saloon.

"Where you boys been?" asked Casper Lee Krone from the bar, where he was cupping a half empty bottle and glass. "They get the other one?"

"No idea, Boss," said the scar faced fellow. "We took this'un and lit out fast."

"It's the other one's the problem. This one's just small fry."

"Well, I guess we just got to wait on them," said the scarred man, whose name was Jake Boosun.

Lowell glared at Krone; he could see the half-breed Indian sitting silent and unmoving further back in the shadows at the far end of the saloon.

"*You murderous scum!*" he burst out.

"Oh," said Krone blandly. "You know me so well. Lowell Devereux, ain't it?"

"I have promised to kill you, Krone."

"Is that so? And why might that be?"

"It was you and that other swine up there that murdered Rita Bodey."

"Do tell, was that her name?" said Krone, turning away and sipping his drink. "Couldn't rightly leave her there, could we? Not after you and that other asshole done for Ska and his woman. I mean, fair's fair, ain't it?"

Lowell fumed. "You will pay, I swear it."

"She was a pretty one; I'll give you that. But how do you reckon you'll last long enough to claim your precious payback."

"As long as I have breath I'll come for you."

"I'd do you in right now, you and your big mouth," said Krone, fixing Lowell with a hard look. "But we need you a spell. We get hold of your buddy Coffin Jack, then we'll see you both out together."

"Why you waiting on the other one?" asked Boosun.

Krone looked at the man, "You ain't never heard tell of Coffin Jack? Where you been all your life?

Coffin Jack's a killing machine, don't underestimate him. He gets away from the others then we'll need this one as bait. Leastways that's what I'm told by Gravedigger."

"Where is this Gravedigger fella?" asked Boosun.

"I am here," said a dark voice as the door to the room at the end of the saloon opened and the small figure of Gravedigger stepped out.

Boosun took one look at the chalk-faced dwarf and wrinkled his lip as the smell of corruption entered the room with the tiny man but he made no comment. The atmosphere shifted with Grave-digger's entrance, an air of still menace followed the small figure and it brought a hush to the watching men.

"We have things to do," said Gravedigger. "You men, go over to The Homely Crossing Spread and fetch John Carne here. Let there be no argument, anybody stands in your way cut them down. I want him here when they bring in Coffin Jack."

Krone looked at Boosun and the others. "You heard him, go get the rancher."

As they trooped out, Krone turned to Gravedigger. "What you done with that old fart who run this place? What was his name? Ebenezer Bucket, had more mouth than the Colorado River."

Gravedigger lifted the shovel he held and placed it carefully on the bar top, Krone noted the sharp edge was stained wet with a broad splash of deep red.

"He was rather tiresome, wasn't he?" Gravedigger allowed. His head was bowed down and hidden in shadow and by the dim light from the few oil lamps alight, Krone noted the gentle shift of flakes of white skin falling from the lowered head.

"Guess you'll be wanting to see this Coffin Jack real bad now," Krone chided. "After him losing you your army of them dead things."

Gravedigger raised his silvered head of hair, the eyes glittering dull yellow under the shadowed eyebrows. "Oh, be assured, he will pay for that."

"Seems that Indian shaman of yours wasn't no help either, don't it?"

There was bravado in Krone's words, a certain smug confidence now that the Gravedigger had been seen to be bested and the gunman believed that the dwarf had been brought down a peg.

Gravedigger's weathered claw of a hand reached out for the shaft of the shovel resting on the bar, "Do not test me further, Krone," he warned.

"Well, just saying, you was playing hot shit with all your corpse army and this dead medicine man and it didn't amount to nothing, did it? Makes a body wonder that's all. You know? Is you all you're cracked up to be."

"Why don't you try and find out?" snarled Gravedigger, his small body dropping easily into a defensive pose.

Krone placed the bottle and glass down and glanced over Gravedigger's shoulder at the silent Phantom Dog who was rising slowly to his feet.

"Maybe we should do just that," said Krone quietly, his hand dropping to the gun at his side.

"Stupid!" spat Gravedigger. "So stupid!"

"Maybe so," muttered Krone, his eye on the closing Phantom Dog behind as the half-breed, moving as quiet as a cloud, drew the broad bladed butcher knife from his belt. "But you know how it goes, little man. If you can't cut it, you get cut."

"You forget," said Gravedigger, grasping his shovel tightly. "I live with the dead; I hear their whispers in the night. Nothing escapes me."

With that and seemingly fired by an explosive force, Gravedigger sprung straight up, leaving the ground as if a spring had been released and rotating in mid-air with the slashing blade of the shovel flying out in a savage arc.

Krone's jaw dropped, his fingers barely touching the grip of his pistol as he watched the dwarf reach twice his height in the air and deliver a blow that separated Phantom Dog's head from his shoulders in one neat slice. The half-breed barely had time to change expression, not that he had many to run through before his grim features hit the floor with a bouncing thud. The headless figure of the man, wavered on the spot for a moment, the legs quivering uncontrollably before it tumbled forward a great gush of blood escaping from the ruined neck.

Lowell stepped back quickly from the ghastly spreading flow and followed Krone's gaze with the same amount of awe as Gravedigger landed lightly on his feet again. He crouched; the bloody shovel held before him, the glowing yellow eyes fixed on the gunman.

"Now," he said softly. "You have a further query?"

Krone's fingers left the vicinity of his firearm rapidly, "Oh, my," he gasped breathlessly. "Oh, my, indeed."

"Very foolish, Krone," said Gravedigger. "Very foolish indeed. Believe me you are nowhere near the challenge Coffin Jack offers; do not even consider yourself on a par. I can take you out like that," he snapped the shovelhead down sharply so that the ax-blade edge embedded itself in the side of the bar. "Just like that."

Krone raised his hands in surrender. "Now don't take on so, Gravedigger. You sure are the greatest, I wouldn't think of arguing on that score. It was just a question, I don't know what got into the Indian, he must have gone crazy there for a moment. Lost his head as it were."

He did not mean it quite like it came out, but Gravedigger took it as an amusement and chuckled patiently, a few crumbs of flaking white skin falling from his creased cheeks as he did so.

"Well, you can get this trash out of here and clean the place up," said Gravedigger, indicating the still twitching remains. "And you," he said to Lowell, "take a seat if you will."

Nervously, Lowell shuffled over to one of the saloon's set of tables and chairs and did as he was told. As Krone distastefully heaved the half-breed's remains out through the saloon door Gravedigger crossed over to stand before the journalist.

"You are a writer of sorts, I believe?" he said, studying Lowell closely.

"That is my profession."

"You are employed by a religious newssheet of some kind?"

"Nominally, although there has been some difference between me and the owner."

"Indeed? Not surprising given the company you keep. Coffin Jack is a dark soul to travel this country with."

Lowell swallowed. "Perhaps but there are aspects of the man I must say I find engaging."

"Oh, yes. I would be most interested to hear those." Gravedigger leaned forward curiously, and Lowell felt the penetrative effect of the yellow eyes boring into him, he could smell the grave dirt smell of the creature. An intrusive, heavily dank scent aged and full of the rot of worms and decay.

There was a crash as the door flew open and Krone and a party of men tumbled in.

"They didn't get him!" Krone barked. "These dumb assholes let him slip through their fingers, him and that bitch we hired got away."

The three surviving members of the raid stood looking disconsolate and nervous.

Gravedigger stood silent a moment. "No matter," he said finally. "He will come to us, have no fear of that. If anything, he will come for this one," he jerked his head in Lowell's direction and a flurry of flaked skin left his features in a small cloud. "That is why I wanted him taken. He was our backup for failure. Coffin Jack will come for him."

The sound of approaching hoof beats sounded outside.

"Who's that?" asked Krone spinning around, his hand going fast for his gun. "He here already?"

"They are back with the rancher, that is all," said Gravedigger. "Getting to be quite a party, isn't it?"

Coffin Jack and Louise moved quietly through the graveyard at the edge of town. She looked up with some trepidation at the barren trees surrounding the perimeter and the solemn rows of black crow birds that occupied the bare branches.

As they made their way between the grave markers, Louise felt the earth begin to shudder underfoot. It trembled and rippled as if a minor quake was in progress disturbing the surface.

"What's that?" she asked in a concerned whisper.

"It's them," said Jack, his attention fixed on the small town of Doomesville, visible beyond the trees in the coming dawn light.

"*Them?* Who's them?"

"Those down there," said Jack irritably, not wanting his attention taken from the view.

"You mean these in the graves?"

"Who else you see around here?"

Louise stared down at the ground and tested it gingerly with her foot.

"Well, why they doing that?"

"'Cos I'm here."

She looked at him curiously. "What you got to do with them?"

Jack shrugged. "It happens. Forget about it, they start up with the complaining whenever I'm around."

"*Dead people complain?*" she said, staring at him in disbelief.

"Well, I guess I put so many of them under there they got good cause."

"Holy mackerel!" breathed Louise, wondering

just who this big, raggedy-assed one-eyed man was as she followed him, stepping as daintily as she could on the heaving soil.

"Now listen to me," said Jack, taking her arm and pulling her over close to the boundary fence. "They'll be waiting for us. They'll be holding Lowell captive knowing I'll come get him. So I need you to do something for me, okay?"

The birds in the trees above ruffled their feathers and fluttered noiselessly, their black beaked heads rotating and watching the couple carefully with beady eyes.

"Well, I don't know. What do you want me to do?"

"I need a diversion so I can get in close."

"Like what?"

"You can get to the other side of town; they won't be expecting a woman. So any lookouts they got will reckon you're just an early riser out to get wood for your breakfast fire. So you mosey over there and start something off, something to distract them."

She spread her hands in query. "What sort of distraction you talking about?"

Jack's eye glowed a flicker of orange in annoyance. "Use your damned initiative, stampede some ponies or something. If it's noisy all the better."

"What are you going to do?"

"I'll make my way around; I'll have to take out their sentries before I go in. Look there, you can see a few of them around the saloon. That's where they'll be holding Lowell and that's where I'll find Gravedigger and that dickhead Krone."

"I ain't too sure about this, mister," Louise said

nervously.

"You seen what Lowell was like," Jack said leaning in close to her. "He didn't treat you with nothing but kindness and respect, did he?"

"Yeah, but that was when he thought I was some kind of Southern lady."

"It don't matter. You can tell the sort of respectful man he is, you got to help him out now."

"Shoot!" sighed Louise, looking across at the gap of open ground between the graveyard and the town. Her face took on a determined look. "I sure hope that sucker appreciates this."

With that she ducked her head between the bars of the fence and wormed through, starting off striding across the open ground heading for the town.

Jack nodded his head in satisfaction and watched her go before he too slid off at an opposite angle and headed for the outer town buildings. As he ducked down and covered ground at a crouch, he pulled out his Colt and held it down alongside his leg.

The first sentry he came across was on the outer fringes keeping track of the approach road. The man was leaning against a shed wall, chewing on a stick of wood, and staring indolently out at the horizon.

When Jack popped up in front of him, the sentry dreamily mistook him for one of the other gang members in the pre-dawn light.

"My time up?" he asked, thinking his watch was over.

"Sure is," agreed Jack, banging the butt of the pistol down hard on the forehead. He must have had a thin skull as the broken bone folded under the impact of the terrific blow and the fellow sagged into Jack's arms without a murmur.

"You just stay there and keep good watch," said Jack, resting the man up against the wall in a sitting position. "Don't go away now."

Then he was gone, circling around to come up on the rear of the saloon.


As he was hustled inside, John Carne looked from one to the other of the occupants of the saloon, his eye settling of the bound figure of Lowell.

"What's going on here?" he asked. "These fellows come fetch me from my bed at this hour. What you men want, and what's Lowell Devereux doing here all tied up?"

"You know who we is and what we want," said Krone from where he stood leaning against the bar.

"You!" spat Carne. "You're the one murdered my niece."

"Never mind that," said Gravedigger sharply.

Carne looked down at the small figure, his lip curling as he took in the deformed shape. "And who might you be?"

"They call me Gravedigger," the dwarf answered, settling his shovel, and resting on the handle. "We are here to discuss the sale of your property, or let us say more properly, the handing over of title and deeds."

Carne huffed a laugh. "You some kind of circus freak, are you?"

"Most definitely not," answered Gravedigger.

There were three other men in the saloon besides

Krone and Gravedigger, and Carne's eye carefully swiftly swept over them turning at last to Lowell. "Are you alright, Lowell?" he asked.

"Things might be better, Mister Carne."

"And Coffin Jack?"

"Mister Jack will be with us shortly, I'm sure," cut in Gravedigger. "Now, please, pay careful attention to what I about to say."

"I got nothing to say to you," said Carne, turning on his heel and heading for the door. "Don't worry, Lowell, I'll be back with my men and we'll see these rascals off."

"I think not," chuckled Gravedigger and he gave a nod to the men. Two of them lunged forward and grasped Carne by the arms whilst the third delivered a heavy punch to the pit of his stomach. Carne gasped and folded over.

"Don't do that!" shouted Lowell. "Leave him alone."

"You are an elderly man, Mister Carne," said Gravedigger ambling forward, his shovel held ready. "I don't believe you can take too much of this kind of punishment with your advanced years. What I want from you is the signing over of the deeds to your land. A simple signature and this will all be over."

He nodded again and Krone barked a laugh as one of the thuggish nightriders delivered a hard crack to Carne's jaw, swinging the ranchers head around and leaving a smudge of blood trickling from his lips.

"I faced all kind of foe in my time to build that place," Carne growled quietly, spitting blood from his mouth. "Wolves, snakes, Comanche Indians,

378 | TONY MASERO

rustling scum, even Union raiders one time. You really think I'm going to hand it over to a midget like you, just like that?"

"Tut-tut," sighed Gravedigger standing before Carne and resting the sharp point of his shovel on the rancher's boot toe. "Such bravado does you proud, sir. But I think you will shortly change your tune."

With that he jerked forward and leaned heavily on the shovel, forcing it down and through the leather of the boot and the toes underneath.

"*Don't!*" screamed Lowell as Carne let loose a roar of agony.

A welter of blood flowed from the torn boot and Carne wailed out in a long cry of pain.

"We have another foot I see," said Gravedigger. "Shall we move on?"

"Yeah, go on, do it," urged Krone, his eyes gleaming spitefully.

Gravedigger swung the shovelhead across and rested it on Carne's other boot.

"Now, what do you say, Mister Carne? You going to toe the line?"

Jack took the second man from behind.

He had been crouched up in a hayloft with a rifle held ready across his knee when Jack came on him, entering the darkened barn and climbing the ladder quietly.

The lookout was a small, bowlegged fellow. A cowhand by his dress and probably favored for the high spot by his expertise as a long shot with the rifle.

The floor creaked under Jack's weight and the man spun around at the sound. Having the advantage of height, Jack kicked him hard under the chin before wresting the rifle from his grasp. He lifted the stunned fellow up one-handed and swung him like a rag doll against the frame of the hayloft's opening, flattening his face against the woodwork with a solid sounding *clunk*.

Considering he had to move on quickly, Jack thought he would expedite matters by tossing the limp form out through the opening and dealing with him more permanently when he climbed down.

The guard grunted as he hit the ground twenty foot below in a puff of dust and Jack scaled down the ladder, carrying the rifle with him.

The fellow was groggily rolling on the ground when Jack came up on him.

"How many he got on watch?" Jack asked.

"Wh… wha…" blurred the lookout.

"I said, how many you fellows out here keeping watch?"

"You broke my damned arm," complained the guard dazedly, half-sitting and favoring his dangling limb.

"I'll break your damned head you don't give me answer directly," growled Jack, his demon eye lighting up the pre-dawn in a flare of red.

"I dunno," said the man wearily. "Four, five, I ain't sure."

"Two down and a few more to go then," said Jack, swinging the rifle around and bringing the stock hard against the side of the man's head. The thwack sent the fellow's head spinning, and he slumped over in an unconscious heap. "Thought I'd bust your head anyway," muttered Jack, moving off into the shadows.

Louise could feel her heart beating fast as she scurried through the darkened streets.

The skyline was beginning to lighten, and the cold crystalline air was sharp in her nostrils. All Louise could feel though was the sweat on her brow as she hurried on. So far no one had challenged her, in fact she had not seen another living soul and it was with some relief that she spotted a storage yard with a stacked pile of rectangular tins, the red coloring indicating that they contained coal oil.

She climbed through the surrounding corral fence and made her way over to the stack. Unscrewing the lid of one she ducked her head and sniffed. It was coal oil, the highly inflammable mix used in lamps. Perfect.

"What you doing about so early, missy?"

Louise gasped and froze as a figure moved out of the shadowy barn door.

"Oh, Lord! You frightened me, sir," said Louise, going into homely and terrified housewife mode.

"Beg pardon, ma'am. Just seem you're out and about real early."

He stepped forward and Louise saw the scarred face of Jake Boosun staring at her.

"Just need some lamp oil," she explained innocently. "We're out of it and my husband needs his breakfast made ready."

"Sure," said Jake easily, eyeing her up and down as he did so. "You live around here?"

"Sure do," she said brightly. "Right across there," she fluttered a hand in vague direction.

Jake liked what he saw and was tempted to keep the girl's company for a while; he casually leaned against the stack of tins. "Must be hard for someone like you, living in this deadbeat place."

"Well, it's certainly not very cheery," she said, her fingers straying to the open tin's handle. "But one does what one can."

"You have any socials around here? I always was one for a regular hay-riding shindig."

"Not so you'd notice," said Louise, ducking her head in a show of coy shyness.

"That's a real shame, I do love a good time."

"What you doing here, if I may ask, mister?"

"Oh, we're just passing through."

"Well, real nice to meet you," said Louise, taking a firm hold on the coal oil tin.

"Aw," said Boosun, taking hold of her wrist. "Don't rush off; we're just getting to know each other. Look here, let's try a step or two right now."

Louise cocked her head to one side. "I think you might be a rapscallion of a fellow, you ain't up to no good, are you?"

Boosun chuckled. "Be glad to let you find out."

"Well, I don't know," said Louise, looking over her shoulder in the direction of her supposed dwelling. "If my husband finds out…"

"No fear of that," grinned Boosun. "Come on along inside the barn, we can try a two-step inside there out of sight."

"You reckon," said Louise, smiling winningly.

"Sure do, come on I'll show you dance steps you never seen before."

Still carrying the can and playing a part, Louise followed him a little wistfully inside, through the open doors of the barn.

"My, but it is dark in here," she said. "I can't see my hand in front of my face. They got a lantern you can light?"

"I expect," said Boosun, the eagerness to please plain in his voice as he felt in his vest pocket searching for matches. "Over by the door maybe."

There was the clatter of a glass flume being raised and Boosun grinned with success as he struck a Lucifer down the doorframe.

"There you go," he said and turned to face Louise, his scarred face gleaming in the light from the match.

It was the moment she had been waiting for.

She flung the open end of the can in his direction and a jet of liquid splashed out and over the flaring match. There was an instant explosive bloom of light that enveloped the gunman, and Boosum screamed in rage and surprise. The flames shot up and enveloped his twisting body in an instant and he staggered around blindly, a pillar of light inside the barn waving his arms as he frantically tried to douse the flames. Louise headed for the door leaving a trail of coal oil spilling from the can. As she left, she flung it over at the pile of remaining cans and fled as fast as her legs would carry her.

Behind her the blazing figure of Boosun pirouetted into a final paroxysm of desperate twirling before the fire sucked the air from his lungs and he collapsed in a flaming bundle to the ground. The splashed remains of Louise's spilt trail instantly took up the fire and it ran in a tight curving line straight to the heap of waiting cans, in a second the pile was alight.

Desperately, glancing over her shoulder as she ran, Louise turned the corner of an outbuilding and ran straight into a tall dark figure whose body felt as hard as a brick wall. Louise bounced off the figure and fell flat on her back onto the ground.

"Thou art a creature of lust and fornication," said the dark outline, bending over her. "I smell it on you. Your parts are awash with sin and those chaste lips cannot hide the corruption within."

Louise noticed he had only one hand, the other, the left one being lost at the wrist where a great bunch of dirty bandages covered the stump.

"Who are you?" she asked in a trembling voice.

The man adjusted his preacher's collar and hoisted the gun belt holstering two Colts fixed high about the middle of his frock coat.

"I am the Reverend Ka Daver," he replied. "And I am here to save you."

# CHAPTER ELEVEN

The dull boom of an explosion brought all heads around in the saloon.

"What the hell was that?" asked Krone.

"He's here," rasped Gravedigger, with a touch of satisfaction.

"Who? Coffin Jack?"

"Yes, indeed. You two," he ordered the men holding Carne, "go see what is happening. You can leave Mister Carne; he will not be going anywhere."

The two hurried to the door, letting go of Carne as they went. The elderly rancher stumbled and almost fell, catching himself against the bar.

"Goddamn you!" he snarled, favoring his damaged foot.

Gravedigger chuckled wheezily, "Be walking with a limp now, old man. You going to sign off on that property before it gets to be a wheelchair you need permanently?" With that he raised the shovel threateningly.

"Goddamn you to hell."

"Fetch Mister Carne paper and pen, Krone. I do believe he just abdicated his position and has decided to see sense."

"What about out there?" asked Krone looking nervously towards the door.

"Don't worry about that, it is merely a diversion. That will be resolved presently. The present matter is more pressing, paper and pen for Mister Carne."

The two men standing at the swing doors could see a great glow growing in the sky over towards the far side of town.

"Looks like they got a fire started," one said over his shoulder.

"That sure woke the town up," said the other as people stumbled from their houses and began hurrying towards the scene. "Look at 'em go. 'Bout time something woke this godforsaken hole up."

"Be on your guard," warned Gravedigger. "Coffin Jack is near."

"How are you bearing up, John?" Lowell asked the rancher softly.

Carne gritted his teeth against the pain. "Won't be so hot on the dance floor no more, I reckon."

He looked down at the sliced toe of his boot and the pool of blood that seeped out and followed his footsteps.

Lowell had been working on his tied hands whilst the distraction had been going on, but he was bound tightly and could make no headway with the knotted twine.

"You really are a foul little creature, aren't you?" he growled at Gravedigger.

The dwarf rested on his shovel and cocked his domed head to one side, studying Lowell with his yellowish eyes.

"And your purpose is almost served, Mister Devereux. I should enjoy your last few moments as best you can."

"Here! I got it," said Krone, hurrying back with an inkpot and dip pen.

"Set it on the table," ordered Gravedigger. "Mister Carne, would you care to take a seat?"

With a nod of his head, Gravedigger indicated the table before Lowell's chair and as Carne hopped over, Krone set down a sheet of paper and the inkpot and pen.

Shuffling awkwardly, Carne seated himself and with a deep sigh took up the pen.

"What do you want me to say?"

Gravedigger sniffed and looked upwards as he mused on the content, "Just say that you freely surrender and hand over full land rights and title of The Homely Crossing Spread and all appurtenances to the bearer forthwith."

Without looking up, Carne began to scribble on the page. Outside could distantly be heard the sound of screams and cries as the townsfolk battled the flames. Then the steady repetitive sound of explosions came as more cans of oil blew up and sent streamers of liquid fire arcing high into the sky.

"They set up a bucket chain," called one of the men out on the porch excitedly. "Jesus! That's one hell of a blaze going up."

"Never mind them!" snapped Gravedigger. "Keep

lookout for the Deathdealer."

"Somebody coming," warned the other man.

Gravedigger scurried over to the doorway and peered out. He saw a tall dark outline silhouetted against the billowing fire's clouds behind as they rose highlighted by the glare of breaking dawn light. The figure was pushing a slender female form in front of him and coming steadily towards them.

"Is it *him*?" breathed Gravedigger, squinting against the coming light. "No, no! It's not, it's that fool Ka Daver and who's that woman he has with him?"

Gravedigger started forward and took a step down from the saloon porch. "Ka Daver!" he called. "What are you doing here?"

"I am come with the remission of sins in mind," intoned Ka Daver, roughly pushing Louise before him.

"What happened to your hand?" asked Gravedigger.

"Shorn off," explained the oncoming Ka. "Broken beyond repair and if any limb offend thee it is best cut away."

"Rather radical, don't you think?"

Meanwhile, Krone who had one eye on Carne as he kept writing and the other curiously on the saloon door, called out, "Hey! What's going on out there?"

"You're never going to know," came the soft voice behind him.

The three in the saloon spun around and saw the broad shape of Coffin Jack coming in from the back room and standing in the center of the room. His tattered cloaked coat hung draped around him and he eyed Krone solemnly, his head bent forward so that the good eye glittered like a burning coal in the deep shadow cast by his hat brim.

"Jack!" breathed Lowell, thankfully.

Without thinking and in an instinctive panic, Krone went for his pistol; he was fast, but Coffin Jack was way faster. He ripped off two fanned shots even before the gunman had cleared leather.

Krone bucked back where he stood, he kept his feet and with a snarl of surprised anger tottered a step or two away.

"You damned well shot me," he complained, looking down bemused at the leaking holes in his shirtfront.

"I saved the best 'til last," said Jack, grimly raising his pistol and aiming carefully.

"Wait," wheedled Krone, squeezing his midriff with the blood running between his fingers. "I got some pain here."

"Best put paid to that then," said Jack, pulling the trigger and blowing a major hole in Casper Lee Krone's forehead. The skull collapsed like a china bowl under the impact of the .45 slug and sent a great gush of gray matter shooting out the rear.

The gunman went spinning backwards, his boot heels working on the board floor as he tumbled towards and then out through the swing doors.

The two gang members still standing on the porch turned in surprise as Krone shot through the doors and landed in a bloody heap in the dust of the street. The gunshots from the saloon being muffled and unheard amidst the many explosions from across town.

"*He's inside!*" screamed Gravedigger. "Get him."

The men bolted into action.

The first through met the barring arm of Coffin Jack who stood waiting beside the doorway. His swinging forearm met the coming man under the chin and chopped the wind from his throat. His following companion came in hard on the heels of the first. He carried a short-barreled shotgun and Jack caught the barrel in both his hands and dragged the man inwards. The fellow promptly tumbled over the fallen man in front and Jack swept the shotgun from out his grip.

The two guards lay in a tangled heap on the floor and Jack stepped in and over them. He raised the shotgun and brought it down heavily on the first man, jarring his head and dropping him prone. The second struggled both to rise and go for his sidearm at the same time. He rolled away but Jack was after him, swinging the shotgun as he came.

The man was up on one knee as Jack whirled the shotgun down. With an almighty crack he dislocated the fellow's jaw and as the dazed repercussions sunk in, Jack finished the job with another well-placed blow between the eyes.

"You fellows okay?" he asked turning to the others.

"John's wounded and can't walk and I'm still hogtied," explained Lowell.

"Mister Carne," ordered Jack, heading for the door, "see to Lowell. I've got other fish to fry. That little runt Gravedigger is still around."

"I'll do it," promised Carne, struggling to his feet.

"Be careful, Jack," warned Lowell. "I heard them say Ka Daver is out there as well."

As Jack stepped out onto the porch, he briefly saw a small shape scurrying away from the corner of his eye. But it was Ka Daver that took up his main interest.

The preacher stood before him in the street holding Louise tightly in front as a shield. The flames behind were spreading as other of the town's wooden buildings swiftly caught alight. It was before a sea of fire that Ka Daver stood outlined and he looked like a creature from hell.

"Now, Deathdealer, is the time," Ka Daver boomed it out so loudly it seemed to rattle the windows of the saloon behind.

"You hiding behind a woman's skirts, you danged pansy," answered Jack, standing tall on the porch shotgun in hand.

"I'm sorry, Jack," said Louise with a sad shrug.

"She means something to you?" asked Ka. "She is no more than a fallen woman, a whore whose fleshly impediments keep her from salvation."

"She got more religion in her hot body than you got in your entire dick brain, you ass."

Jack was moving gingerly sideways along the porch, still holding the shotgun alongside his right leg, and aiming to come up above the body of Krone lying below him on the street.

"I have the right, Coffin Jack," roared Ka. "You slew my kin and shall repent and die, for I have seen Death and by his word shall become him."

"You damned blowhard," spat Jack. Suddenly, he dived forward from the porch, landing on his belly in the dust before the body of Krone, the shotgun leveled in front. "Get out the way, Louise!" he bellowed.

As Louise pulled herself from Ka Daver's grip, the big preacher let her go and went for his pistol. His gun was out and firing in an instant, the bullets plucking at the covering corpse before him as Jack cocked and fired the shotgun.

Both barrel loads took Ka Daver just under the right knee and blew a cloud of bloody flesh and bone away from under him. Ka Daver tumbled over wailing loudly as the prop of his leg left the vicinity and he lost his balance.

Jack climbed to his feet tossing aside the empty shotgun as he did so. He looked down at Ka Daver who was sitting up now and anxiously clutching the stump of his shredded leg in both hands.

"Why am I forsaken?" the preacher bawled pitifully. "Am I not righteous enough?"

"Guess not. The wages of sin and all that," shrugged Jack, turning his back and walking over to the saloon.

"You would leave a wounded man so?" begged Ka Daver. "Where is your pity? You are Satan's spawn, I shall bleed to death like this."

"That's the plan," muttered Jack over his shoulder.

Louise rushed over to join him; she clutched his arm as they stepped inside.

"Guess I owe you one," she said as he pushed the doors open.

Jack arched a seductive eyebrow. "Or maybe two."

**********

In the city of Austin, Ernest Leaf was opening a welcoming door for Carmody Carne and Jane Fray.

"This way, if you will, Mister Carne. Please hurry, Mister Jameson wants to see you most urgently." He nodded in a faintly curious way at Jane Fray, wondering just what this emaciated creature with such a burst of lurid red hair could possibly have to do with a discerning gentleman like Carmody Carne.

Jane for her part ignored the secretary. She had risen from the destitution of spirit after her enforced imprisonment and now strived to acclimatize herself to her new life with a show of indifference and pride. A life where she was free of the constant sexual demands her enslavement had laid on her, and now she sought, using her own natural cunning and perceptiveness, to make her mark.

She had been driven quite mad at the time, she knew it, but now and with Carmody and Ariadne's help she had managed to readjust her thinking and found herself to be a capable creature and quite up to the tasks that her newfound freedom allowed. But in the depths of her heart, where the vestiges of her craziness still dwelt, she held an almost irrational devotion and gratitude to the two of them and would do all she could to protect and prosper any plan they might contrive.

The loyalty she felt extended to a secret infatuation for Carmody, an admiration from a distance that she dared not express for fear of any rejection. Yet it was evident to others in the way her attention often strayed to him, in the same way a faithful dog might follow its master.

Carmody for his part felt nothing of the kind in response, he saw only a woman that had come from a situation so desperate that she was able to care for Ariadne and not be disturbed by her grotesque appearance. This had helped him considerably and enabled them to buy and run The Impossible Result Saloon with success, a success that had indeed netted them good returns and ultimately denied the name of the place.

"Good day to you, sir," said Jameson with a beaming show of bonhomie as he rose from his desk with his hand extended in greeting.

"Good day," answered Carmody, inclining his head politely and taking the offered hand. "May I present Miss Jane Margaret Fray, presently acting as our business administrator. I hope you will allow her presence during our meeting as I trust her implicitly and value her acumen in all things."

Jameson studied the thin woman intently, his small eyes taking in every aspect of her appearance. He considered that she had the look of an overly made-up street girl about her, with her dyed hair and scrawny figure, but if Carmody fancied the likes of such a creature that was his business.

"Of course," he said, offering Jane an unctuous smile. "Please, will you sit?"

Leaf held chairs ready for them stationed before Jameson's desk and the two took their places.

"Some refreshment perhaps?" offered Jameson.

"Most kind," said Carmody. "But we have come

some distance and must return soonest to attend to matters there. So, if we might proceed?"

"I must thank you for making the journey," Jameson said amenably. "I would have come to you, but I also have many pressing matters and my diary is full to overflowing, is that not so, Leaf?"

The secretary rubbed his hands together obsequiously and gave a weak affirmative grin.

"So, Mister Carne," Jameson went on. "It is concerning your original plan that I have asked you here. When you first came to me with the notion of your brother's tract supplying the copper we so desperately need, I had hoped the matter would be settled rapidly. But, as you are perhaps aware, the intervention of various parties has created delay. I need that copper wire, Carmody, if I may be so bold as to call you so? I need it desperately. The spread of our telegraph network is growing rapidly and if we are to make any headway against the opposition, I must have the material means to accomplish that expansion."

Carmody nodded understanding. "It seems my brother is most unwilling to part with the land. Lord knows why, as far as he knows it is a worthless piece of dirt populated only by cactus and beef. And as it is solely in his name, I have no power to do anything about it. Our father allowed it so, seeing me as a wastrel and drifter, to which there was some truth at the time of his passing, and in all honesty I must allow this sad appraisal as, I fear, I enjoyed life more than labor. He bequeathed full title to John, seeing him as the one who would continue arduously with the ranch that he had spent his whole life creating. So that is how things remain, I fear you are stuck solely with my brother on this."

"I understand that you have tried to reason with him to no avail. And I have attempted to encourage him also; unfortunately, the gentlemen chosen to carry my message did so with irrational ardor in an extreme manner. Leaf here hired them, perhaps not the best of choices," he frowned accusingly at his secretary who had, in fact, had little to do with the hiring of Ska Venger but he accepted the blame with a bowed back. Leaf was a servile and weak creature only too willing to please and being without any sense of self-worth such accusations of censure constantly fell on him. "Now, I hear, that the remainder of those individuals have taken it into their heads to go it alone and cause even greater resistance from John Carne. It is all most unseemly, Carmody. A simple business transaction gone wildly astray."

Carmody crossed one leg over the other with slow precision. "And I am here for what reason?" he asked calmly.

"I wonder if you would be prepared to take it upon yourself to see the matter to a successful conclusion. If you will and it proves to be a success, we would be prepared to offer most agreeable and substantial rewards."

"What exact rewards are we talking about here?" piped up Jane shrewdly.

Jameson looked at her sharply, his eyes glittering for a moment until he hooded his anger at the interruption. "Why, a place on the board of the company, no less. This will come with bonuses and stock options that will bring annual returns of an excessive amount, I assure you. More than that, I will offer a... let us say, a consultation fee, of five thousand dollars for your assistance."

Carmody turned his head to look at Jane. "Sounds most agreeable, don't you think?"

Jane answered with a single sharp nod of the head in confirmation.

Carmody turned back to face Jameson. "As you are aware my brother is an intractable man. Since the loss of his much-loved niece he has become even more firmly entrenched in his attitude. And now, with more irritation pestering him I cannot say how he will respond. It may take... How shall I put it? Extreme measures to ensure he parts with the property."

Jameson leaned across his desk and fixed a hard stare on the man opposite.

"And you are not bothered by such measures?"

"I see no problem," Carmody answered easily. "We have had little to do with each other. I have spent my time travelling and experiencing the wider world whilst he has lived on that dusty desert his whole life. We have gone our own ways since childhood and there is a great gap of separation between us. Suffice to say, he is to me, little more than a stranger and on a personal note I quite honestly find his intractable behavior quite irritating."

"Very good," smiled Jameson. "Then, I trust you will put your best foot forward and achieve a satisfactory result at the soonest possible moment."

"We'll want this in writing," snapped Jane.

"*In writing?* My word," Jameson glanced across at his secretary. "Well, I suppose it can be arranged, don't you think so, Leaf? Why not? The proviso being of course that success is achieved, and the land is signed over to us."

"I can draw up a contractual agreement immediately, Mister Jameson," Leaf said.

"Yes, see to it then."

"And an advance," added Jane.

Jameson gritted his teeth and offered a fixed smile. "Well, well, you definitely have a tenacious business associate here, Carmody."

"Miss Jane is most able," Carmody agreed amiably.

"I want no delay," Jameson snapped, his voice now harsher and more direct. "No excuses or facile reasons for failure; either you do this or I shall take the matter in hand personally and if that is necessary then I can assure you..." he turned to fix a steely glare on Jane, "that there shall be no emolument of any kind. I hope we are clear on that."

"I think we are done here," said Carmody rising smoothly to his feet. "We understand each other perfectly, Jameson. Have no fear, it shall be attended to."

He offered his hand across the desk and Jameson took it and they shook.

"Miss Fray," said Jameson in parting and she nodded her bush of vermilion hair once in reply. At the door as she passed Leaf, Jane said quietly, "I'll want those contract papers soonest."

Leaf wilted under her intense stare. "It shall be done, ma'am."

Once outside on the street, Carmody paused a moment and turned to Jane.

"What do you think, my dear?"

"There's money to be made here," she said quickly, "if you've no quibbles about dealing with your brother."

"You trust this fellow?" he asked, glancing up at the building towering above them on the busy street.

"Trust him? Pah!" she spat. "I wouldn't trust him to walk ten paces. No, but what you must do, is to get the land signed over to you personally. Then you hold the power to take it to whomsoever you please; as a result, Jameson can only deal with you for whatever amount you desire. Either that or you have option to go to the competition."

"There is only one way to achieve ownership, I fear. John knows my indifference to cows and the land he holds so precious and he would never dream of handing it over willingly."

"How so then?"

"Why, on my brother's demise, as I shall then inherit. It is a legal certainty; he has no other heirs now that his niece Rita is gone."

"A final solution then? You have no qualms, Carmody?"

"None, poor John is being recalcitrant and foolish in this, there is no reason for me to behave in the same manner."

"Shall we return and let Ariadne know the news?"

"In time, my dear. In time, but first I must make a call. To visit with an acquaintance, I came across on my travels in Mexico."

Jane cocked her head curiously. "Do I know this person?"

Carmody smiled thinly and shook his head. "Certainly not and I doubt you would enjoy the experience."

"Why is that?"

"He is a man of many strange and dark ways and he lives in an isolation barely this side of normal existence."

Jane frowned. "Sounds an odd one. How is he known?"

"By one name only. They call him Reeper."

"We are going now?"

"We need to time our journey perfectly for we must arrive at nightfall, for only then in the darkness of night are we able to meet up with Mister Reeper."

# CHAPTER TWELVE

The flat of Gravedigger's shovel caught Jack on the back of the head as he entered the Abandon Hope Saloon. It was delivered with a force of such venomous hatred that the blow knocked Jack clean out of his senses and he fell full-length face down on the floor.

Louise gasped in shock and leapt back as Gravedigger loomed out of the shadows behind the door.

"Come in, girl," he leered at her. "Do not hesitate."

She looked around and saw that Lowell and John Carne were gagged and under the gun of the last of Gravedigger's remaining men. Lowell showed her apologetic eyes and shook his head sorrowfully.

Gravedigger quickly caught hold of Louise's wrist and she felt the distasteful touch of his scaly flesh close over her skin.

"So young," said Gravedigger, looking her up and down as he dragged her inside.

He only came up to her waist and in the gloom of the saloon it was as if a small and ghastly-distorted child were pulling her along.

Gravedigger stepped lightly around the fallen Jack. "Now we are all here," he said with satisfaction. "And all matters shall soon be settled. Sit over there next to your friends." He pushed her lightly in the direction of the others and knelt to peer down at the fallen figure of Jack. Checking that Jack was unconscious, Gravedigger swiftly relieved him of his gun belt and then leaned close to Jack's ear.

"One blow, Deathdealer. That will be all it will take; one simple chop of my trusty shovel and your head will be parted from your body and I will take personal pleasure of laying you in the ground. Separated though," he chuckled, enjoying his moment of victory. "The head in one place, the body in another. Will you be able to find your way around the Other Side then, I wonder?"

Rising from his bent knee, a malevolent smile on his face as he tossed the gun belt aside, Gravedigger lifted the shovel and placed the speared end of the blade against the back of Coffin Jack's neck.

Lowell wrestled feverishly with his bonds and made noises of complaint from behind his gag.

"You have some comment, Mister Devereux?" asked Gravedigger, looking up. "Take their gags off," he ordered the gunman, a scrawny looking unshaven individual with a cast in one eye.

"You sure, Boss?"

"Why not? I need a word with Mister Carne anyway, we have business to settle; isn't that so?"

"I have not signed it yet," said Carne as the gag was pulled from his face.

"Very well, untie him. Get it done quickly, Mister Carne, time is pressing."

He stepped over and squatted down on Jack's back in the manner of medieval gargoyle affixed to the wall of an ancient building. A small grotesque taking his perverse pleasure by ridiculing his fallen enemy.

"Quite comfortable," he said, shuffling his crouched position. "Coffin Jack has a broad back; it would do well to have him carry me so. I could be as a potentate from the East being borne aloft by a great beast of burden, don't you think it would look fine?"

His rusty laugh sounded hollow in the silent room and it was only the distant sound of the inferno across town that could be heard apart from his grim chuckle.

"Your arrogance does not fit your stature, sir," said Lowell, at last free of his gag.

"And what would you know of me, Mister Devereux?" said Gravedigger angrily. "Size isn't everything, you know?"

"It helps," Louise muttered drily.

"Be quiet, whore!" snapped Gravedigger. His anger had caused him to puff up and the rain of pale dried skin dropping from his face was like a small snowstorm.

"Looks like you're falling apart there, mister," observed Louise.

"Be still or I'll have you all gagged again." He crawled to one side, hopping from Jack's back with the slow lethargy of a toad. "Have you done yet,

Mister Carne?"

"It's done," said Carne, finishing with a flourish.

"And how is your foot now?"

"I think I lost the toes, you little skunk."

"Heh, heh!" grinned Gravedigger, lifting his shovel and advancing on the rancher. "There's so much more to lose yet. Your niece, your land, your toes and now maybe your life."

Jack still lay were he had fallen, totally stunned he had not moved since Gravedigger's mighty blow and Lowell cast worried eyes in Deathdealer's direction but he made no sign of stirring.

"Is he dead, do you think?" he asked Louise in a whisper.

She shrugged unknowingly; her eyes fixed on the terrible dwarf as he crossed the room towards the seated figure of Carne.

"*Ola, senors!*" came the cry from the doorway and the swing doors swung open to reveal the figure of a Mexican swirling off his sombrero and giving a cheerful smile all around. "I am here."

The scrawny gunman and Gravedigger both spun around. "Who are you? What do you want?" asked the dwarf.

"Oh, please excuse me. I thought you might like to know your friend outside is wounded. The leg is badly damaged and needs some medical attention."

"It's Tomas," breathed Lowell quietly to Louise. "Quick, can you loosen my bonds whilst they are distracted?"

"Who the hell is Tomas?" she answered, scrabbling with her fingers at the knot.

"Should I bring him inside?" Tomas continued, acting the part of simple campesino. "Perhaps one of you might help me?"

"I don't give a good goddamn about that fool Ka Daver," snarled Gravedigger. "He can rot in hell for all I care. Now, get out of here."

"Oh, I am sorry to interrupt," said Tomas, holding his hat before him in a polite manner. "I have meant no offense."

"Get out," growled Gravedigger. "Before I cut you in half."

Jack's broad hand snaked out and encircled Gravedigger's ankle. In one motion he lifted and flipped the dwarf over onto his back. As Gravedigger landed with a thump on the boards, Jack reared up to his full height.

"Thanks, Tomas," he said. "You're like a ripe breath of smelling salts, brought me to my senses right well."

Lowell's hands fell loose from the ropes and without pausing he leapt from his seat and tackled the gunman, who was in the process of taking aim at Jack. The two of them flew across the room as Lowell barreled into the lightweight frame of the gunman; they slammed up against the bar and began an untidy wrestle as Lowell sought to grab the gun from the fellow's hand.

Gravedigger was backing away from Jack on his elbows and heels and Jack stepped forward and brought down his boot on the Gravedigger's foot, pinning him fast.

"Not so fast, you ugly little punk," growled Jack.

"We got a score to settle."

Gravedigger's yellow eyes opened wide in fury and hate, and he swung his shovel wildly causing Jack to step back to avoid the blow. In an instant, Gravedigger had bounded to his feet and crouched ready to deliver another swinging strike.

"Come and get it, Deathdealer. We'll see who's the best at dealing out death here."

He whirled the shovel dexterously in a fast spinning display that made the silver of the sharp edge flash in a continuous sheen as it whistled through the air.

"You really think that's going to stop me?" growled Jack, hopping from side to side as the blade edge whipped past.

"Come on then," taunted Gravedigger. "I'll chop you up like sliced beef."

He had backed up to the seated figure of Carne, who was still at the table, pen in hand and with the signed promissory note of title deed before him. Carne looked down disdainfully at the hunched figure crouched before him and busily engaged in his demonstration of skill with the bladed shovel. Carne lifted the inkpot and upended it over the silver haired, white-faced dwarf.

The dark ink dropped in a gush over Gravedigger's head and dripped down over his pale forehead and streamed into his eyes.

"Pah!" he spat as it ran into his mouth and he blinked ferociously as the sudden splash of liquid filled his eye sockets.

In that moment he lost sight of Jack completely

as he struggled to clear his vision. Coffin Jack held no such hesitation. He stepped forward boldly and clutched at the shaft of the shovel, the two of them struggling as Jack tried to wrench it from the blinded Gravedigger's desperate grip.

Finally, Jack tired of the fight and lifted the small figure bodily from the floor. Jack raised him high above his head towards the ceiling, then, as if using a hammer, he slammed Gravedigger back down on the boards. The dwarf gulped and fell away with a vibrating shudder and Jack stepped in.

Jack's good eye glowed with a deep resonating fire of red. His dander was up, and he needed payback for the lump he could feel on the back his head.

"Enjoy the ride, Gravedigger," he snarled.

Raising the shovel, he brought it down in a savage swoop. The tip entered the soft pit of Gravedigger's stomach and Jack forced it down until the head almost disappeared from view. Gravedigger glugged piteously and a fountain of blood spurted from between his gasping lips.

"One more?" Jack asked solicitously, lifting the bloodied head out with an unpleasant sucking sound.

Louise screamed in horror and Carne turned his head away as Gravedigger's guts spilled out wetly from his split stomach and ran in coiling purple tubes like irate snakes across the floor. Vile liquid pumped and spread in a dense pool below the body, filling the air with a rank and noxious smell.

"No? No more?" Jack asked the quivering figure beneath him. "You had enough?"

"He's done for," observed Carne through gritted teeth.

"I sure hope so," said Jack, tossing the shovel aside.

He turned to see Lowell still struggling with the gunman and rolling about with both of his hands fixed like glue to the gunman's wrist and trying to shake his six-gun free.

"Oh, Lowell," frowned Jack, moving over towards them. "You ain't never going to get it right, are you?"

Just then, the gunman, twisting like an eel, spun inside Lowell's grip and rolling away, let loose a shot from the gun as he moved. Lowell flew backwards with a scream of pain and clutched at his side.

Jack lurched forward but the gunman was ready, he rolled over fast where he lay and turned the gun on Jack. His roving eye squinting as he took aim along the barrel.

There was the blast of a shot being fired and the gunman's cast-eye rolled in his head as his body was thrown aside as if he had been hit with an invisible club. He slumped over sideways, his head banging against the bar as the pistol fell from his dead fingers.

Jack looked over his shoulder at the figure of Tomas in the doorway, his sombrero still clutched before him. Slowly, Tomas lifted the hat away to reveal the smoking gun in his hand. He shrugged ambiguously and said nothing.

Jack allowed a smile. "Nice work, Mex. You sure shoot better than you smell."

Louise was kneeling beside the wounded Lowell, cradling him in her arms and Tomas crossed over quickly to Carne. With a glance at the ruined foot, Tomas said, "We must find you a doctor this minute, senor."

"Good to see you, Tomas, bless you for coming," smiled Carne. "We'd better take care of Lowell as well."

"It's not bad," piped up Louise with a thankful expression. "Just a graze."

"It certainly does not feel like just a graze," complained Lowell bitterly as his eyes rolled upwards and his head lolled back, and he fainted away.

Jack looked at them all with a wry twist of his lips as he noted he was forgotten, and they were intent on each other. It was a common factor in Coffin Jack's life that he should be sidelined once his work was done and he was well used to it. He moved away from them as Ka Daver came into his mind. He paused at the door, looking out into the street but there was no one there. The place where Ka Daver had lain was empty, a pool of drying blood and his dismembered leg and boot were still there but of the man himself there was no sign. Only the light from the shivering flames and racing shadows of the burning town filled the space.

*********

It was more than eight months later before Lowell felt fully recovered from his wound. Despite Louise's early diagnosis it had, in fact, proved to be somewhat worse than a graze and Lowell had the long scar to prove it. He had stayed with John Carne at The Homely Crossing Spread and Louise had also stayed on there to nurse him. Perhaps his recovery had been extended beyond necessity thanks to her attentions for an affectionate bond had grown between them, despite her earlier deceit to protect her young brother.

John Carne had lost all the toes on his right foot and now needed a crutch and a rag-stuffed boot to get around but with Tomas's help he still managed to run the ranch and had recovered well.

None of them had seen Coffin Jack; he had just disappeared without a word on the day of Gravedigger's death. Whilst they had all been concerned with their wounds and each other, Jack had slipped away, recovered his pony Nameless and gone off, nobody knew where.

Lowell guessed he had returned to his cabin and the feral cats up in the Four-Points mountain range, but he had been too engaged with Louise to take time out and make the journey himself. He had found life quite amenable and comfortable at the ranch and John Carne had also taken to Louise in a manner that suggested she was filling the hole left in his heart by his niece Rita's demise. Perhaps it was so for both men.

On the day the knock came, Lowell was sitting in Carne's large living room, a book from the library on his lap. Louise was out visiting the town of Doomesville as it slowly recovered and was being rebuilt after the destructive fire she herself had started but refrained, quite wisely, from telling anyone.

Carne and Tomas were also away, busily engaged with the vaqueros in the day-to-day running of the ranch and nobody was due back until suppertime.

Lowell was relaxed, his mind pleasantly engrossed in the content of the book. As he heard the rap he rose lazily from his seat and made his way over to the front door, rather petulantly annoyed that his reading should be interrupted.

"Can I help you?" he asked.

A veiled woman in black stood there with a small bundle in her arms. She said nothing.

"Everybody's away, I'm afraid," said Lowell. "Is there something I can help with?"

Slowly the woman lifted the veil covering her face. Lowell started back. "*Beatrice!* My God! What are you doing here?"

She cocked her head to one side and looked at him quite coolly for a long moment, then she proffered the small bundle towards him. "I thought you might like to meet your daughter."

Lowell's eyes widened as he looked down at the sleeping infant. Round-faced, glowing with health and with the fine golden hair of her mother, the child was a picture of angelic peace.

"*Mine?*" was all he could manage to say.

"Yes, it appears our one night together was all it took."

Lowell's mind raced and with some shame he remembered their rushed night of passion and his early leaving without a word.

"I… I am so sorry," he gasped. "I don't know what to say."

"Her name is Henrietta," said Beatrice. "Isn't she wonderful?"

It would not sink in and Lowell was frozen on the spot his mind dazzled by the outcome. He was a father! This was *his* child and the woman who he had used so terribly was the mother. It was hopeless, at once filled with joy at the presence of the small bundle and at the same time filled with guilt over the way he had mistreated Beatrice, Lowell felt numbed and helpless.

"Perhaps you would like to come in," he managed to say.

"No, I won't," she said in a firm voice. "I only came by to let you know about the baby. I won't take up any more of your time or expect more from you, Lowell. We shall, of course, terminate our working arrangement. I hardly think it proper that a newsssheet of our nature could accept an illegitimate birth by the owner anyway, do you? No, I shall sell the paper and devote my time to bringing up Henrietta."

"But, Beatrice, I feel so bad about this," pleaded Lowell. "I had no idea, I promise. You cannot go away. I will not permit it. I must care for you and the child that is my duty. If only I had known, if you had told me. Why did you say nothing?"

"Hardly seemed right under the circumstances, now did it, Lowell? You had your way and then you left. I understand, that is how the modern man behaves, it is to be expected. Your confessed love for another made it quite plain. So, do not concern yourself, we shall manage quite well. I have money set by and with the paper sold there will be fully enough to raise and educate Henrietta."

"Dear heavens! Beatrice, you have it all worked out. But this is such a shock to me, please allow me time to adjust."

"Take all the time you want, Lowell. I'm afraid it's

a matter that no longer concerns me."

With that she turned on her heel and strode off towards the hired buggy and driver that was waiting for her.

Lowell solemnly watched them drive off and he stood there in a daze until they had completely disappeared from sight.

He had lost the bright love of Rita and in doing so had also lost his promised Beatrice. Now there was Louise to contemplate. But he had a daughter, Henrietta, to consider as well. It seemed to Lowell in that sad moment that he was beset by a contrived plot by unknown forces intent on wearing his heart thin.

What should he do? He wondered.

What on earth should he do?

# A LOOK AT: STAGELINE: THE COMPLETE SERIES

This is the story of Whip Roundel, driver of the Hostrum and Hayes stagecoach, as it leaves its depot and heads out into this troubled land with only a single guard on top and a precious cargo of five passengers inside. Whip is a haunted Reins-man, handy with a whip and backed by a history full of anomalies, now he faces the challenge of a desperate journey that will bring back bad memories.

Cosum Beech, the lone shotgun guard, has been riding shotgun and conductor with Whip for the past two years. Life hasn't always been simple for Cosum and it's about to get more complicated.

There may be a Civil War going on back east but far from the front down in Arizona and New Mexico Territory the stage still runs on time, wending its way through a rough country without law and order and beset by the threat of rapacious bandits and Indians left free to run wild. Even whilst the region is contested by military elements of both North and South, with so many away fighting the war it remains ripe pickings and a killing ground for those predators waiting on the sidelines.

Stageline: The Complete Series includes: The Whip, Riding Guard, Bold Deceiver, Arrowpoint, Dead On Time.

*AVAILABLE NOW ON KINDLE*

# ABOUT THE AUTHOR

Tony Masero grew up in a deprived and grey post-war London where the only relief from bomb craters and food rationing were colorful Western books and movies. The pictures on the screen displayed wide sunlit spaces, glorious forests, breathtaking mountain ranges and most importantly adventure and a great sense of freedom. His love of that early thrill has subsequently inspired many of his own books. Living far from the Wild West and any kind of armed culture he made up for it by practicing longbow archery in the forests of southern England.

At the age of three Tony Masero's father, a renowned woodcarver, placed a pencil in his hand, an act that resulted in a later career as a Designer and then Illustrator. Working in the international advertising and publishing world Tony Masero produced a great deal of art for book covers and through the research involved in their creation is where his interest in writing began.

Research is important in his own books and many of his tales are based around some historical incident or characters that truly existed. From there the imagination takes flight and for a person with a visual frame of mind his books are often imbued with a natural pictorial quality and full of human characteristics that are true to us whatever our origins.